TOUCHING
THE CLOUDS

Books by Bonnie Leon

SYDNEY COVE SERIES
To Love Anew
Longings of the Heart
Enduring Love

THE QUEENSLAND CHRONICLES
The Heart of Thornton Creek
For the Love of the Land
When the Storm Breaks

ALASKAN SKIES
Touching the Clouds

TOUCHING THE CLOUDS

A NOVEL

BONNIE LEON

Revell

a division of Baker Publishing Group
Grand Rapids, Michigan

© 2010 by Bonnie Leon

Published by Revell
a division of Baker Publishing Group
P.O. Box 6287, Grand Rapids, MI 49516-6287
www.revellbooks.com

Printed in the United States of America

Library of Congress Cataloging-in-Publication Data
Leon, Bonnie.
    Touching the clouds : a novel / Bonnie Leon.
        p.   cm. — (Alaskan skies ; bk. 1)
    ISBN 978-0-8007-3359-9 (pbk.)
    1. Women air pilots—Fiction. 2. Bush pilots—Fiction. 3. Alaska—Fiction.
    I. Title.
PS3562.E533T68 2010
813′.54—dc22   2010008206

Scripture used in this book, whether quoted or paraphrased by the characters, is taken
from the HOLY BIBLE, NEW INTERNATIONAL VERSION®. NIV®. Copyright
© 1973, 1978, 1984 by International Bible Society. Used by permission of Zondervan.
All rights reserved.

Published in association with the literary agency of Janet Kobobel Grant, Books &
Such, 4788 Carissa Ave., Santa Rosa, California 95405.

10 11 12 13 14 15 16   7 6 5 4 3 2 1

To Silver Hanrahan,
my online friend
and aviation expert.
You are missed.

— 1 —

Kate Evans pushed open the screen door and stepped onto the broad front porch of her parents' farmhouse. This was supposed to be her wedding day. Instead, her lace, floor-length gown hung in her closet.

Shifting her pack over one shoulder, she moved to the railing. Closing her eyes, she savored the feel of a cool breeze on her skin and breathed in the subtle fragrance of sun-heated grass. Richard's image stormed against her peace. She could see his blond curls spilling onto his brow, his wounded eyes. He'd always been steady, but her announcement had staggered him. She wanted to love him enough to stay, but the turmoil she'd been feeling had escalated until she felt she had no choice—she just couldn't go through with it.

She gripped the porch railing, anxiety sweeping over her like a summer squall. Had she made a terrible mistake? It was one thing to postpone the wedding and quite another to call it off altogether.

They'd been friends since childhood and were comfortable with each other. But did that mean they belonged together? If she stayed, she'd be forced to give up her longtime dream and would have to settle for a commonplace life. She'd end up resenting Richard, and she couldn't bear the thought.

Shaking off her doubts, she turned her gaze to her mother's flower gardens. The well-tended yard was bordered by patches of rich soil embracing velvety pansies and roses that hummed their splendor. In contrast, a flower bed on one side was congested with brightly colored dahlias that shouted at the sun. Beyond were the apple orchards. The flowers were off the trees now, which were loaded with small green apples.

Kate folded her arms across her chest. She couldn't have picked a worse time to set out on a venture. It was 1935 and much of the country was in the midst of a crushing drought, and despite President Roosevelt's New Deal, the economy was in shambles.

She heard the screen door creak open and turned to see her mother step onto the porch. "Hi, Mom," she said as cheerily as she could manage.

Joan Evans lifted a picnic basket. "Here's some food to take along." She managed a smile.

Kate took the basket. "Thanks."

Joan picked fading leaves off a hanging basket of red lobelia, then turned kind eyes on her daughter. "We spent a lot of summer evenings on this porch." She pressed her fingertips to her lips. "I remember you and Alison, sleeping out here and gabbing until all hours."

Kate took a deep breath and let it out slowly, trying to release the rising ache in her chest. "Those were good days." Memories, like a slide show, flitted across her mind until she purposely pushed them aside.

"Kate, you explained why you're going, but I know there's more."

"I told you, I want to do something with my life."

"You don't think being a wife and raising a family is doing something?"

"It is, but it's not right for me, not now. I have to . . ." There was no way to describe how she felt—as if her heart would shatter if she didn't get away. She had to do something that mattered, something better than just being what people expected, a farm girl who got married and had babies. And better than the girl who larked about with planes.

Joan settled into a wicker chair.

Kate knew what was coming, and she didn't want to discuss any of it. She sat on the edge of a chair and set her pack on the ground. She held the basket in her lap. Clasping her hands around it, she pulled it against her stomach, hanging onto it as if it were an anchor.

Joan began gently. "I know a day doesn't go by that you don't remember and feel the burden of . . . of Alison's death." She studied the dead leaves she cradled in her hands, then looked at her daughter. "It was a long time ago. It's over. You can't get that day back. You have to go on with your life."

Kate pursed her lips. She'd decided not to speak, but no matter how she tried to hold back the words, they spilled out anyway. "You don't know what it's like—every day knowing she's dead and that it's my fault. If I hadn't been so full of myself, so careless, Alison would still be alive. She'd be married and have babies and her mom and dad would still be happy—and they wouldn't hate me."

"Not living your life won't bring her back, it won't make anything better."

"I'm trying to live my life. But I can't do it here. Every time I go into town I'm afraid I'll see her mother or father . . . or her brother or—"

"Kate, you can't let the past rule the present."

"That's just it. As long as I stay here, everything *is* about the past. I need to start over in a place where I can prove my-self, a place where I'm free to live without shadows of that horrible day dogging me." She shook her head, squeezing back tears. "After the accident, I was too afraid to even go up in a plane. I thought I'd never fly again, but Dad helped me and I did. I'm a good pilot because of him. Now, well . . . I'm twenty-five years old, and I've got to do something with that ability while I still have time. And I want you to be proud of me."

"We are. You know that."

Kate chewed on her lower lip. "Okay, but I've got to be proud of me too."

"Alaska's a dangerous place, especially for pilots."

The front door opened and Kate's father stepped out. "So, Katie, you ready?"

She grabbed her pack and stood. "All set."

Bill Evans slung an arm around his daughter's shoulders. "Well, let's go then."

Kate strode toward her bright red Bellanca Pacemaker, which sat on the airstrip behind the house. Nerves made her stom-ach jump. She studied the name painted on the side of the fuselage—Fearless Kate. Was she fearless or just pretending?

She set her belongings in the back of the plane, then walked around the craft, examining it to make sure it was flight ready. There were no signs of dents or fuel leaks, exposed or hang-ing wires, and the tires were in good shape.

She moved to the plane's door. "She's ready to fly."

Her father squinted against the early morning sunlight. "I checked the fuel—it's fine. And I put extra cans of gasoline in the back in case you need some." A breeze caught at his salt-and-pepper hair sticking out from under his hat. "Oil's good too."

"Thanks, Dad."

He moved to his only child and gently grasped her arms. "I'm going to miss my flying partner. We've been a team for a long while."

"I'll miss you too." Kate blinked hard, holding back tears. "I still remember the first time we went up. I was so scared I was shaking. But that was the day I knew I had to fly."

He smiled, the creases at the corners of his eyes deepening. "You got everything you need?"

"I think so. Mom made me enough food to last a week. And I've got my tools, extra blankets, and water . . . just in case."

Kate dared a glance at her mother. Joan's lips were drawn tight and her chin jutted up slightly.

"It's time to go. I've got a lot of miles to cover." Kate moved to her mother. "I'll write. I promise."

Joan's brown eyes pooled with tears. She brushed the moisture away. "I packed your grandmother's Bible in the basket. She'd want you to have it."

Kate's throat tightened. She could still see her grandmother's weathered hands lying on the pages of her Bible as she read.

The sound of an approaching vehicle carried from the road. Dirt billowed around it in a dusty squall. Kate's stomach clenched. Richard. She'd hoped he wouldn't show up, and yet she'd have been disappointed if he hadn't.

His Ford pickup ground to a stop, and the sturdily built man stepped out. His expression determined, he walked toward Kate. "We gotta talk."

"We've said everything there is to say." Kate folded her arms over her chest, hoping to match his resolve.

"Not everything." He grabbed her elbow and pulled her several paces away from her parents.

Kate wished there was some way, any way, to avoid what was coming. What could she say? There was nothing that would make this easier. Why couldn't he understand?

Out of earshot of her parents, Richard stopped. Facing Kate, he held her hands in his. She liked the feel of his strong, calloused grip. Her determination wavered.

"Why are you doing this? Today, we were supposed to start our life together."

"I explained—" She disengaged her hands.

"No you didn't. A week ago, one week before our wedding, you came to me and said you had to move to Alaska, that you had to fly and that you couldn't live an ordinary life. *And* that you *couldn't* explain why." He shoved fingers through his hair. "I don't get it, Kate. This is beyond even you." His tone was angry.

"I know. I'm sorry. But . . . I have to go. If I get married, I'll never have a chance at my dream."

"Your dream of being a bush pilot?" He shook his head. "That's not a dream, it's a death wish . . . and it won't bring Alison back or prove—"

Kate pressed her hands over her ears. "Stop it! I know it won't bring her back." She dropped her hands. "I just want to fly."

"You can fly, here."

"It's not the same." Kate squared off with Richard. His blue eyes were lit with pain and anger. "I don't want to hurt you. Please believe me."

"Then why aren't you walking down the aisle with me today?"

Kate didn't have an answer. It was true, she didn't fully understand why she had to go. "I'm sorry." She turned and walked toward the plane.

"Kate!"

She kept walking.

"If you go, that's it. You'll never see me again."

She forced herself to keep moving. She loved Richard, but he wasn't enough.

"I mean it, Kate."

Ignoring him, Kate hugged her stricken mother. "I've got to go, Mom. I love you."

The truck door slammed and the engine of Richard's pickup growled. The tires spit dirt and rocks as he tore out.

Kate pressed a fist to her mouth as she watched the truck disappear. Why couldn't he be enough? Turning to her parents, she said, "Tell him I'm truly sorry."

Bill circled an arm around Kate's shoulders. "We'll tell him."

She leaned against her father. He'd always understood her.

The wind sighed, lifting dust and fallen leaves into the air. A longing for peace swelled inside Kate. If only she could settle for an ordinary life. "I better go."

Joan caught Kate in her arms and studied her daughter with adoring eyes. She brushed a strand of auburn hair from Kate's forehead. "I remember when I first laid eyes on you. Oh my goodness, you squalled, outraged at having been born. And you've fought my attempts to gentle you ever since." She glanced at Bill. "You've the same spirit as your father." She swiped away tears. "I haven't given up on your settling down and having a family one day."

Kate looked at her booted toes, then at her mother. "One day."

"Richard will be here when you get back. He'll wait . . . if you're not gone too long."

Kate took a deep breath, the weight of her decision heavy in her chest. "You think so?"

Joan nodded. "He loves you."

Her father rested a hand on her shoulder. "I'm proud of you . . . for not settling. You're a good pilot, don't ever forget that. Alaska will be better off because of you."

"I hope you're right." Worry pricked Kate's confidence. She rotated her shoulders back, trying to relax tight muscles, then looked to the sky where downy white clouds drifted. "It's a good day to fly." Her gaze moved to the grass runway bordered by apple orchards. "I'll miss having fresh apples— heard they're hard to come by in Alaska."

"We'll box some up and send them," her father said.

"I'll hold you to that." As Kate walked to the plane, panic swept over her, and she felt like that little girl again, taking her first flight and scared out of her wits.

"I'll crank her for you." Bill moved to the side of the Bellanca, engaged the hand lever in the flywheel, and started cranking.

Kate climbed into the plane, pulled the door closed and latched it, then moved to the front of the craft and settled into her seat. When the flywheel was singing along pretty well, she pulled on her helmet and called out the window. "All set?"

Bill stepped back. "It's ready to go."

Kate pulled the ignition and the engine came to life. Bill handed the crank to her through the window, and she stowed it.

With the engine's roar in her ears, she checked the oil pressure and temperature gauges—they were normal. Gas level was good. While the engine warmed, she double-checked her gear, then logged her time of departure.

With one more look at her temperature gauge, she waved out the window and then pulled it closed. The windsock that sailed from a pole alongside the airfield kicked from west to east.

Her adrenaline pumping, she moved to the east end of the grass runway, turned the plane into the wind, and revved the engine. The cockpit smelled of fuel and oil.

Her mother lifted a hand, but didn't wave. Her father flagged his hat at her. With a hand on the stick and her feet resting on the rudder pedals, Kate moved the craft forward. Increasing speed, the plane rolled down the airstrip while Kate's heart battered against her ribs. She'd done this a thousand times, but it had never mattered so much. Then a picture of Alison flashed into her mind. *This is for you.*

With one final glance at her parents, who stood with their arms linked, she increased power. She felt the plane lighten as its wheels left the ground and then the momentary sense of weightlessness as she lifted into the air.

The farm and its orchards fell away. Kate soared over the trees and looked down at the familiar patchwork of the family ranch. Large oaks hugged the old farmhouse, and chickens hunted for bugs in the yard. Apple trees stretched out in long green rows.

The sun's glare flashed across the windshield, blinding her for a moment, and then she could see the endless blue sky. Kate felt joy working its way up from her toes, displacing her fears. She couldn't keep from smiling.

She soared over soft brown hills that reached toward green forests and white-capped mountains. She made one more pass over the farm, then turned the plane in a wide arc. As she approached the landing field, she dropped down until she was just above the trees.

Buzzing the field, she dipped the wings of the plane back and forth in a salute of farewell, her joy mixing with a touch of regret at the sight of her mother leaning against her father. Bill and Joan waved, and Kate headed toward the white craggy peaks of the Cascades.

— 2 —

Dry grasses and scrub trees passed beneath Kate's plane. Beyond stood the mountains that served as a barrier between eastern and western Washington. They were no small obstacle. Kate had crossed them before and knew lethal downdrafts and dangerous side winds waited for unsuspecting pilots. Her eyes fixed themselves on Mount Rainier in the distance. Even from this distance she could feel its strength. Her thoughts moved to what lay ahead—first Vancouver, then on to Southeast Alaska, and finally Anchorage.

Winds were calm as she approached the Cascades. Below, the dark waters of Rimrock Lake huddled between pine forests. Kate's stomach tightened. Horrifying images bombarded her. She could still feel the icy waters. When her plane had hit, the lake had sucked down the craft as if hungry for lives. That was seven years ago, but it felt like yesterday.

I'm sorry, Alison.

Accusations from the past swirled at Kate. *Why did you go to the lake? It was foggy. You knew better.*

Self-loathing swelled inside her. She'd convinced Alison to take a jaunt in her father's plane that day. When they left home, the skies had been clear, but when they reached the lake, fog clung to the hillsides and sprawled across the waters.

She should have turned back, but she didn't. And then . . . it was too late.

I'm sorry. I'm so sorry. She swiped away tears, relieved to see the lake fade into the collage of trees.

Kate barely crested the mountains when her eyes latched onto Mount Rainier. It stood amidst the rugged Cascade Range like a gleaming white jewel. As always, its power was startling.

As she negotiated the pass, she soaked in the splendor of forests, roiling rivers, and fields of white. Today, the mountains were merciful, sparing her from treacherous currents. The crossing was calm and heartening.

Leaving the Cascades behind, she approached Seattle. Lakes, looking like dollops of blue, speckled the landscape. Silver ribbons of water divided rich farmlands huddled in the broad valley that lay south of the city.

Kate's attention turned to the blue waters of Puget Sound and the metropolis of Seattle with its stacked hillsides and long piers that reached into the bay.

Her eyes followed a scar that slashed across a section along the waterfront. Tin roofs, black stovepipes, piles of trash, and clotheslines marred the beauty. Images of those swept out of their homes by drought, dust storms, and poverty had been plastered across newspapers for months. Shantytowns, better known as Hoovervilles, sprang up across the country. Kate gladly left behind Seattle's mecca for the homeless and headed for Vancouver.

After a decent night's sleep, Kate felt refreshed and ready for the next leg of her trip. She walked across the airstrip, Vancouver drizzle wetting her hair and clothes. She glanced at a gray sky and craved the previous day's sunshine.

An airport employee waited for her at the plane. He smiled and extended a hand. "Morning. I'm Donald Brown."

"Kate Evans." She made sure her grip was strong, feeling a need to convince him that she was sturdy. Women pilots were often under extra scrutiny.

"Got your plane gassed up and did a general check to make sure she's ready to fly."

"Thanks," Kate said. "I appreciate the help."

"Heard you're heading north. Did you get a report on the weather?"

"I did, from a pilot who flew in from Port Alice last night. He said it was raining pretty good and that the winds were stiff—kept him on his toes."

Donald grinned. "They measure rain by the foot up there."

"That's what I've heard," Kate said, but even poor weather conditions couldn't suppress her enthusiasm.

"Weather along the coast can get bad real fast, even in July. So be cautious."

Kate buttoned her jacket and pulled on her leather helmet. "I'll be careful, but I figure my Bellanca can handle most anything."

Donald glanced at the Pacemaker. "Good solid plane, all right. Still better set her down if it gets rough."

Kate nodded, but she wasn't thinking caution, she was thinking adventure.

Wiping moisture from his face, he said, "I'll crank her for you."

"Thank you." She moved to the plane.

"Not many women, or men for that matter, willing to fly the Alaskan Territory."

Kate pulled open the door and chucked in her bag. "I don't understand how pilots can stay away." She flashed him a smile before climbing inside. She grabbed the crank from the cockpit and handed it to Donald. "I appreciate your help and your concern."

With a nod, he moved to the side of the plane.

Kate closed the door, climbed up front, and dropped into her seat. After logging in her time of departure, she adjusted her helmet. Donald gave her the thumbs-up and she started the engine. He handed the lever to her through the window.

"Good luck," he called.

"Thanks. I'll need it," Kate hollered and then closed the window. After one final check of the gauges, she moved away from the hangar and taxied to the end of the airstrip. There was no wind. She'd have to power up a bit to ensure a safe takeoff. *Now the real flying begins.*

Kate moved down the runway, the churning in her stomach starting up again. She glanced at her grandmother's Bible, lying on the passenger seat, and remembered that her parents were praying for her. She wasn't alone.

After five days of remarkable, wonderful, and unpredictable travel, Anchorage was finally within reach. The thrum of excitement and hope buzzed through Kate.

And then, Alison's smothered laughter and the anguished faces of her dead friend's parents ambushed Kate. For a moment, she felt dizzy and disoriented. Her gaze wandered over the endless wilderness. *What was I thinking? I'm not ready for this.* She felt small and afraid.

An unexpected blast of wind thrust her plane upward. She gripped the stick and fought for control. *Pay attention!* Currents, created by mountain ranges, tossed Kate's plane about as she worked her way through the lower elevations. She put her mind on the business at hand, trusting in the Bellanca's sturdiness despite her shaken emotions.

Below lay the spectacular beauty of the Alaskan wilderness—white peaks, gray and black rock formations, ice fields, and steep valleys. The mountains gave way to rounded knolls and sparse foothills. The winds subsided and Kate relaxed. Small patches of white stood out against the green backdrop. It took a few moments for Kate to realize the white splotches were sheep grazing on the short grasses on the hillsides. Juniper and alder forests hugged mountains that seemed to flow toward the sea, and frothing waterfalls looked like slashes of white against dark cliffs. As she continued north, ponds and bogs replaced grasslands and forests.

And then it was there—Anchorage. The community huddled along a huge slate-gray bay.

"I made it!" Kate whooped.

Euphoric, she headed toward the settlement. It was small, but looked like a real town.

Kate soon found the airport. She banked the plane and circled the field, which consisted of two dirt runways, a wind sock that flapped frantically, one small building, and what looked like a night beacon.

She lined up with the north runway and headed down, anticipating the moment that her wheels touched the ground. A crosswind caught her plane and tossed her sideways. Kate gripped the stick and with a careful touch to the pedals maneuvered the craft back into position. She cheered when the wheels connected with the earth.

The plane bounced twice before rolling smoothly to the end of the strip. Turning her Bellanca toward the building, she stopped in a small grassy area off the runway. Letting out a big breath, she pulled off her flying helmet and closed her eyes. "I'm here. I'm really here."

Kate grabbed her handbag, took out a brush, and pulled it through her hair, then dug out a compact and put on fresh lipstick. *No use looking like I just climbed out of bed*, she thought, rubbing her lips together. She tossed the compact and lipstick into the bag and headed toward the back of the plane.

She knew her parents were probably waiting to hear from her. *I'll call them the moment I'm settled.* Richard bombarded her thoughts and a pang of sadness caught her unawares. She managed to dismiss him . . . for the moment.

She climbed out of the plane and looked about, hoping to find someone working. There was no one. Calculating in her mind how much money she had, Kate headed for the building. *I hope they need a pilot.*

When she reached what she figured was the office, she stopped at the door to gather her thoughts. She'd rehearsed what to say a hundred times, but at the moment she couldn't get hold of one reasonable thought. She reached for the door-knob and turned it. With as much self-assurance as she could muster, she stepped inside.

All was quiet. The small room had only one window. A cast-iron stove squatted in a corner, and a scarred wooden desk with a matching chair sat alongside the far wall. Spare parts and tools were piled on workbenches. There was the sharp smell of diesel, making Kate feel more at home. It reminded her of her father's shop on the farm.

Still holding onto the doorknob, she leaned into the room. "Hello. Is anyone here?"

A moment later, a stocky man wearing a heavy plaid shirt and blue jeans stepped into a doorway that led to a back room. He wiped his hands on a rag. "Afternoon. What can I do for you?" His cheek bulged with what Kate guessed must be tobacco.

"Hello. Are you the manager?"

"Suppose I am. Mostly I just try to keep planes in the air." He shoved the cloth into a back pocket.

Kate moved the rest of the way indoors and closed the door.

She wiped moist palms on her pant legs, then extended her right hand. "I'm Kate Evans."

The man had a solid grip. "Glad to meet you. George Parker."

Kate managed to smile. "I just flew in from Washington State."

George's eyebrows peaked. "That's quite a trip."

"It is. I flew up the coast. I don't know that I've seen so much green in all my life."

George nodded. "It's a pretty flight, all right." His eyes darted to the window. "You on your own?"

"Uh-huh."

A moment of awkwardness fixed itself between them. Kate dredged up her courage. "I'm looking for work . . . as a pilot." Before George could respond she continued, "I grew up flying planes. My dad taught me. I'm a good pilot and—"

He held up a hand, palm out. "I have to stop you there, miss. Sorry, but I don't need a pilot. Not right now anyways. Even if I did, couldn't afford one."

"I'd work on a job-by-job basis—you get paid, then I get paid."

He studied her and shook his head. "Nah. Just don't need anyone. Things are slow. Wish I could help." He shoved his hands into his front pockets. "I'm glad to have you here, though. We can always use more plucky ladies."

"And how would you know if I'm plucky or not?" Kate tried to keep her tone light, hoping to disguise her disappointment.

"Figure if you flew here on your own, thinking you'd pilot the Alaskan Territory, you've got to have spirit, or you're just plain stupid." He grinned and then spit tobacco juice into an empty coffee can parked alongside the desk.

Kate liked the notion of being spirited. In a newspaper story

22

she'd read, one of her heroines of the skies, Marvel Crosson, had once been referred to as plucky. "Well, I wouldn't describe myself as stupid." She stepped back toward the door. Realizing she had no notion of where to go, she stopped. "Can you give me the name of a hotel where I might stay?"

George rubbed the whiskers on his cheek. "There aren't many places around here. But we've got a fine hotel down on Third. Real nice place."

"How do I get there?"

"It's not far. Just follow the road toward the bay, and when you hit Third, take a left. You'll run right into it."

"Doesn't sound too complicated." Kate grabbed the doorknob. "Do I need to sign in my plane?"

"Yep. And you better tie it off too. Never know when the wind's going to kick up." George grabbed a dog-eared ledger from a table and handed it to her.

Kate filled in the information and headed for her Bellanca.

Her bag slung over one shoulder, Kate stood on the side of the road and stared at the hotel. It was nice, too nice. She glanced up and down the street, hoping for something more affordable. Nothing.

Figuring she might as well find out how much it cost, she pushed open the door and stepped onto a thick carpet. Not a good sign for someone needing to be thrifty. She felt underdressed and out of her element, but she straightened her spine and walked toward a counter. She'd probably be heading out the door in another minute.

A clerk was checking in another customer. His hair was slicked down with grooming oil. So was an overly tidy mustache, which seemed to dance above his lip when he talked. He called for a bellman. "Show Mr. Dalton to room 202."

"Certainly," a pudgy young man said, taking the key and

dropping it into his uniform pocket. He picked up two suitcases. "Right this way, sir."

The clerk turned to Kate and gave her a critical inspection.

She was suddenly aware of her unorthodox clothing—slacks, a flight jacket, and her knapsack.

He made no effort to disguise his disapproval. "Can I help you?"

Self-conscious, she touched her disheveled hair. "I was . . . just wondering about your rooms."

"What would you like to know?"

"Can you tell me how much the cost is for one night?"

The corner of his upper lip lifted slightly. "I'm sure more than you can afford."

Indignation replaced Kate's discomfort. "Cost is not an issue. I was merely curious. I'll take a room." Setting her mouth, she met his eyes with a hard stare.

He lifted an eyebrow. "Certainly." Moving to a guest register lying open on the counter, he picked up a pen. "Your name?"

"Kate . . . Katharine Evans."

"Address."

"I . . . don't have one yet. I just arrived in town."

"What was your address before you arrived in our fair city?" His tone was patronizing.

"Three fifty-seven Reservoir Road, Yakima, Washington."

The clerk recorded the information and then turned the ledger toward Kate. "Sign, please."

Her anger had fired off so much adrenaline, Kate had to fight to keep her hand steady. She managed to sign her name, knowing it was foolish to stay in such an expensive establishment. She ought to walk out.

"It's five dollars a night . . . in advance."

Shock reverberated through Kate. *Five dollars! That's pure robbery!* Doing her best to look unconcerned, she took a coin purse from her bag, dug out the exact amount, and set it on the counter.

"You can have room 210." The clerk handed her a key. "It's on the second floor."

"Thank you." Kate headed toward the stairs, chiding herself. Once again, she'd let her pride get the better of her. She found her room, pushed in the key, and opened the door. Standing in the corridor, she stared inside. The same plush carpet that sprawled throughout the hotel extended into the room. There was a full-sized bed and a bureau. Brocade curtains framed a window where afternoon sunlight slanted in.

The bellman she'd seen in the lobby approached her. He walked as if he were attempting not to wrinkle his perfectly pressed uniform. "Can I be of service?" The chin strap of his cap cut into a double chin.

"No. I'm fine, thank you." All Kate wanted was rest.

The bellman remained. "How long are you staying in town?"

"I don't know yet. I hope a long while."

"Well then, welcome."

"Thank you." Kate soaked in his kindness. It felt good. "Do you know where I might find a job?"

"What kind of work?"

"Anything."

"Heard the general store needs someone."

"They sell quality goods and pay on time."

It wasn't flying, but it was a job. She needed something to hold her over until she found a position at an airfield. "Where is it?"

"About a block from here." He walked into the room and moved to the window, then pointed up the street. "See, right there."

Feeling hope stir, Kate looked in the direction he pointed. "I'll go right away. Thank you."

He smiled. "Anything I can do, you let me know. My name's Bill."

"I'm Kate."

He headed toward the door and then stopped. "By the way, don't worry about Howard."

"Howard?"

"The front desk clerk. I overheard the way he talked to you. He's got his nose so high in the air that when it rains he nearly drowns." He chuckled. "He's new and won't last long."

Kate smiled. "I hope not."

After Bill left, Kate explored her room and was ecstatic to find a clawfoot tub. A hot soak was just what she needed.

She dug her only dress out of her bag, tried to smooth the crumpled linen, then hung it in the bathroom. She turned on the bathtub faucets, hoping the steam would take out some of the wrinkles.

After stripping off her travel clothes, she lowered herself into the hot water, rested her head against the end of the tub, and closed her eyes. Weary muscles relaxed, and sleepiness enveloped Kate in a warm, steamy cocoon. Forcing her eyes open, she picked up a bar of perfumed soap and lathered her body. She washed her hair and rinsed it under the faucet, then climbed out and towel dried.

Kate stood in front of a mirror and studied her reflection. The crumpled dress hung from her tall slender frame. "I look awful," she said and pulled on a sweater, hoping it would disguise some of the wrinkles. She ran a brush through short bobbed hair, applied fresh lipstick, and then dabbed a drop of perfume on the inside of each wrist. With one more glance in the mirror, she headed for the door. Rumpled or not, she had to go. She needed a job.

A bell hanging from the mercantile door jangled as Kate stepped inside. A balding man, wearing spectacles, stood behind a counter. He squinted as he wrote in a ledger. When she approached, he straightened and looked at her, lifting the glasses.

"Afternoon. What can I do for you?"

"I've just arrived in town and was told you might be hiring." Kate smiled and hoped he didn't notice the condition of her dress.

"Could be." He looked at her with interest. "Ever work in a store?"

"No. But I'm sure I can learn. And I'm strong—I grew up on a farm."

"You look strong, all right . . . for a woman. I need someone who can lift fifty-pound sacks. You think you can do that?"

"Absolutely."

"Where you from?"

"Yakima."

"Washington?"

"Yes. My parents own an apple farm."

"Long way from home. What brings you here?"

Kate wasn't sure how to answer. If she told him she was hoping to find a job flying, he might not hire her, but she didn't want to lie. Reluctantly, she said, "I fly . . . I'm hoping to work as a bush pilot."

The man smiled sympathetically. "Then I guess you do need a job."

Kate wasn't sure what to think of that, but it didn't sound good.

"I need a clerk. The gal who used to work for me took off with her boyfriend, without a word to me or my wife." He rested a hand on the ledger and looked straight at Kate. "Can you be here at eight o'clock tomorrow morning?"

"I sure can. Earlier, if you need me to."

"No. Eight is early enough." He smiled. "Guess I better get your name. The missus will want to know."

"Kate Evans."

He wrote down the name, then looked at her. "I'm Albert Towns."

"It's a pleasure to meet you."

"You have a place to stay?"

"I'm at the Anchorage Hotel."

"That's a pretty classy place. Can't pay you wages to cover that."

"I'm hoping to find something less expensive."

Albert scrubbed his clean-shaven cheek. "We have a room in the back of the store. It's not much, but it'll keep you warm and dry. There's a little kitchen with a sink and a small bathroom. Sofa's not bad for sleeping. And my wife just painted it."

"That sounds just right."

"You want to have a look?"

"I'm sure it's fine." *And right now I don't have any other options.* She extended a hand. "See you tomorrow?"

He shook her hand. "Tomorrow."

Kate strode toward the door. *A job and a place to stay! I've got to call Mom and Dad.*

She hurried her steps, hoping the hotel had a phone and wondering how much it would cost to call home.

— 3 —

Paul Anderson walked along an Anchorage street, taking in the sights and sounds of the community. He lived a mostly solitary life on Bear Creek and rarely came to town, so even something as ordinary as an automobile seemed noteworthy.

He slowed his pace and decided to browse the storefront windows. He stopped at one with a display of jewelry, which included fine watches. Taking out his pocket watch, he studied the gold timepiece, then flipped open the front. It was just after nine o'clock. He closed the watch and then turned it over, running his thumb across the letters *G. A.* engraved on the back. Gerald Anderson had been a good man. Paul could still see his father's large hands as they snapped open the watch. He'd always been a stickler about being on time.

A breeze kicked up, swirling dirt into the air. Paul slid the watch back into his pocket and continued down the street. A pair of boots in a store window caught his eye. It would be nice to replace his old ones. He glanced down at the toes of his Harvesters and decided they'd do for another year. Summer was nearly over, and he'd soon be switching to fur-lined winter boots anyway.

He noticed a man and young boy standing in front of the next window display. The boy was looking at something, his nose nearly pressed against the glass. The man leaned over and rested an arm across the child's back. Paul figured they were father and son and felt an ache in his throat. His son would have been about the same age.

Heaviness of spirit settled over Paul as his mind carried him to the what-ifs of his life—if Susan had lived . . . if his son had survived . . . if his home were still in San Francisco. He caught sight of his reflection in the store window. His usual serious expression had deepened into one of misery. Straightening, he lifted his hat to brush thick brown hair off his forehead and looked up the street.

Two children barreled past him. One of the youngsters bumped into Paul, knocking off his cap. He stopped. "Sorry, mister."

"Not a problem." Paul reached down and picked up the cap and handed it to the boy.

He planted it on his head, nodded at Paul, and then took off after his friend. Taking in a long, regretful breath, Paul watched them go and wished life had turned out differently.

He headed toward the general store. Might as well complete his shopping and get on home.

The bell announced his arrival as he stepped through the door. He liked the mercantile; it felt homey and always smelled of grains and spices. He removed his hat and scanned the room, searching for Albert or Helen. He looked forward to seeing them. Aside from Patrick, who lived on the property next to his, they were the closest thing to friends he had in Alaska.

Albert Towns set a bag of grain against a wall and straightened. "Howdy." He moved to Paul and grasped his hand, shaking it vigorously. "Good to see you. Where've you been keeping yourself?"

"Out at the creek." Paul clapped Albert on the back. "Time to stock up for winter."

"Summer came and went so fast I barely even got a look at it. Wish winter would hold off for a while."

"It's only the third week of August. We've still got some summer left."

"Hope you're right." Albert moved to a counter and, taking a pencil from behind his ear, wrote in a ledger. He glanced up. "So, you going to be in town long?"

"Have to leave today."

Albert straightened. "Too bad. I know Helen would like to see you."

"Wish I had the time. Tell her hello for me."

"Sure will." Albert pushed the pencil back over his ear. "So, what can I get for you?"

"I need flour, sugar, rolled oats, beans, and rice."

"How much you figure?"

"A hundred pounds of flour ought to see me through."

"I've got plenty." Albert headed toward the back of the store.

Paul followed. "I need fifty pounds of beans and rice, and twenty-five pounds of sugar."

Albert stopped and peered at Paul. "Fifty pounds of rice?"

"Something wrong with that?"

"No. Just never eat much of it."

"It's great in fish pie. And the fishing was good this summer so I'll be making a lot of it."

"I'll have to give it a try."

"Come out to my place sometime and I'll make it for you."

31

"Just might take you up on that. That is, if I can get away. Helen keeps me tethered pretty close to home these days." His eyes sparkled with humor. He stopped at a row of barrels. "We'll get you set up."

After Paul and Albert hauled sacks of staples to the register, Albert set a bag of sugar on the counter and asked, "You need traps?"

"I figured I'd get them at Susitna. Not enough room this trip." Paul pulled a list out of his front pocket. "I do need a few other things. Some shells for my shotgun."

"How many?"

"Four boxes ought to do it."

Albert picked up a wooden crate from the floor and set it on the counter. He placed the sugar inside, then grabbed the shotgun shells from a shelf behind the register, and added them to the box. "How are things out there on the crick?"

"Not bad. Had a good growing season. Haven't seen much of Patrick recently. He's putting a new roof on his place. I offered to give him a hand, but he said his boys and Lily are all the help he needs."

"Lily's always been up to most any kind of chore. And his sons are getting pretty grown up, I expect."

"I doubt the two younger ones are of much help, but Douglas is a hard worker."

"Tell Patrick hello for me." Albert rested his hand on the bag of sugar. "You need bullets?"

"Cast my own."

"You're becoming more of a sourdough every year." He shook his head. "I couldn't live so far from town. Too lonely out there."

"It's peaceful." *And private,* he thought. Paul didn't much like the world.

Albert glanced at the clock on the wall near the front door.

"Hope you don't mind, but I'll have Kate finish up your order. Helen's under the weather and I promised to make her some lunch. It's nearly one o'clock—she's probably grousing about my being late." He chuckled.

"Nothing serious I hope."

"No. Just one of her headaches. Doesn't get them often, but when she does, they lay her low."

"Have her steep ginger root in water and drink it. And she should stay in a darkened room."

"You know about doctoring?"

"My grandmother used to suffer from headaches and she swore by ginger tea."

"I'll take some with me. Can't hurt to try it." Albert glanced about. "Now, where'd Kate get to?"

Paul spotted a tall, slender woman standing on a stepladder near the end of a row of kitchenware. "That her?" He nodded toward the woman.

With a glance down the aisle, Albert said, "Yep. Hey, Kate. Can you come up front for a minute?"

Taking long, easy strides, she walked to the register. Paul liked the way she moved, as if she were comfortable with herself. When she looked at him, vibrant amber eyes took him by surprise. He offered what he hoped was a casual smile.

She nodded and turned to Albert. "Do you need something?"

"I promised Helen I'd make her lunch. Can you take care of the rest of Mr. Anderson's order?"

"Sure." She flashed Paul a friendly smile and her warm eyes locked with his.

"Paul, this is Kate Evans. She moved up from Yakima, Washington, several weeks ago and has been working with me in the store. "

"Nice to meet you." Paul thought he smelled perfume—

Evening in Paris. His heart constricted. That had been Susan's favorite fragrance.

"Good to meet you," Kate said.

Albert moved to a vegetable bin. "Do we have ginger?"

"I don't think so. Would you like me to order some?"

"Yeah. See how soon we can get it in." He grabbed his hat and coat from a peg on the wall behind the register. "Don't know what I'd do without you." He looked at Paul. "She does a better job of running this store than I do." Pressing the hat onto his head, he said, "Too bad she doesn't plan to stay."

"I'll probably be here a good long while," she said.

"Good." He winked. "Make sure Paul gets everything he needs. He lives way out on Bear Creek, wouldn't want him forgetting anything."

"I'll make sure." Kate turned to Paul. "Bear Creek . . . hmm, I think I've heard that name more than once since I started working here."

Paul grinned. "There are a few of them around. The Bear Creek I live on is a tributary off the Susitna River."

Kate nodded as if she knew all about the Susitna. Paul doubted she did.

Albert shrugged into his coat. "I'll be back in about an hour." He headed for the door.

"Say hello for me," Kate said. "I wish there was something I could do to help."

"Not to worry. She'll be right as rain in a day or so." He stepped out and closed the door behind him, the bell jangling.

Kate placed her hands on the counter and settled her gaze on Paul. "So, what can I do for you?"

Paul tried to ignore Kate's long-limbed good looks. He stared at his list. "Just have a few things left. I was hoping you had some heavy cotton, something I could use for a work shirt."

"We've got a lot of different fabrics." She moved toward a shelf with bolts of cloth. "Do you have a color preference?"

"Brown. Probably two and a quarter yards will do." He reached for a bolt of dark brown fabric and rubbed it between his fingers. "This seems about right."

Kate lifted it off the shelf.

"And maybe some blue too. And plaid wool."

Handing the material to Paul, Kate lifted the other bolts from the shelf. "Does your wife have buttons and thread?"

Paul hesitated and then glanced at her as he answered, "I'm not married." He thought he might have glimpsed a glimmer of interest in her eyes before he looked away. "I do need buttons and thread, though."

She raised an eyebrow. "You do your own sewing?"

"Is there something amusing about that?"

"No. Of course not. It's just that I never knew a man who could sew."

Paul liked her forthrightness. He allowed himself to smile. "Living in the bush means doing for yourself."

She moved down the aisle. "The buttons and thread are here."

"Thanks. I think I remember where everything is." He was drawn to Kate . . . and he didn't want to be drawn to any woman. He held the bolt of cloth against his chest, using it as a barrier between himself and her.

"I'll take care of this, then," she said, lifting the fabric out of his hands and adding it to her stack.

She walked to the register and set the cloth on the counter while Paul made his choices. He glanced up and found her watching him. She quickly returned to measuring and cutting

35

the cloth, while he wrestled with ambivalent thoughts—in spite of himself, he wanted to know more about her.

When he set the thread and buttons on the counter, she asked, "Anything else?"

"One . . . more thing." He headed down another aisle and returned a few moments later with two pairs of long underwear. As nonchalantly as possible, he added them to the rest of the supplies. He could feel heat in his cheeks and hoped Kate didn't notice.

"So, you live on Bear Creek, huh?"

"Yep."

"Does the Susitna River flow into Cook Inlet?"

"It does. It's on the north side of the inlet. Once you reach the mouth of the Susitna, you go up a ways and Bear Creek empties into the river. I live near the mouth of the creek."

"That's a long way from nowhere."

"I like it that way." Paul manipulated the conversation around to Kate. "How about you? You have family in town?"

"No. They live in Washington."

"Albert said you're looking for a different job?"

"Looking, but not finding. I'm a pilot." She set the underwear in with the other supplies.

"Never met a woman pilot."

Kate studied him. "Does that bother you, me being a pilot?"

Her tone held a challenge, and Paul figured she had a chip on her shoulder, probably for good reason. "No. It's just fine. A woman ought to be able to fly as well as a man." He offered a lopsided grin. "But it is kind of ironic that you were surprised that I sew . . . since you live what most would consider to be unconventionally."

Kate folded the fabric. "I was just surprised, is all." She laid the cloth in the box.

"You been flying long?"

"Since I was little. My dad had a plane." She blew her bangs off her forehead.

The gesture was appealing. Paul turned his attention to his supplies.

"Before I left home, I heard there were lots of jobs for pilots up here. There were stories about the adventures waiting here in Alaska. I've been looking, but there doesn't seem to be any need at all, at least not for a woman."

"I met a fella last night who just started up an airfield. Maybe he could use someone."

"Where? At Merrill Field?"

"No. It's a new outfit—small—down by Lake Spenard."

Kate's eyes lit with interest. "Who do I talk to?"

"Sidney Schaefer. Young fella, but he's got big dreams and seems to have a lot of drive." Paul doubted Kate had a chance at a job and wondered if he should have kept his mouth shut. No use getting her hopes up.

"I'll check with him. Thanks." Kate placed the thread and buttons in the box.

Paul couldn't hold back a caution. "Dangerous line of work, flying."

"Yes, but so are a lot of other jobs. And I never feel happier than when I'm in the air. I love it up there." Her expression turned blissful. "The world looks different, more beautiful."

"Been a passenger a few times. It's been a while, but I remember enjoying it. So I guess I know what you mean."

"Maybe I'll take you up some day." Color flushed Kate's cheeks and she glanced down one of the aisles. "Do you need anything else? Fruits or vegetables, spices?"

Paul placed his hat on his head. "I've got plenty of vegetables. The garden outdid itself this year. And I'm set for spices. Could use some coffee, though."

Kate moved to a nearby shelf. "How much do you need?"

"Four cans should be enough."

She took two cans down and handed them to Paul, then grabbed two more and headed back to the register. "Anything else?"

"This ought to see me through the winter."

Kate tallied his order. "That'll be thirty-two dollars and twenty-one cents. Would you like it on your tab or will you be paying cash?"

"Cash." He pulled a wallet from his back pocket, fished out several bills, then reached into his front pocket for the change and counted it out.

Kate studied the pile of goods. "Do you need help?"

"No. I usually haul it all down to the docks in a wheelbarrow."

"Mr. Towns keeps one out back."

"Yeah. I've used it before." Paul moved toward the back of the store. He hesitated, figuring he ought to say something else. "Thanks. It was nice meeting you."

"You're welcome. And it was nice meeting you too." Kate smiled.

Feeling ill at ease, Paul mumbled, "Guess I'll see you in the spring."

By the time Paul had the supplies packed in the boat, his shirt was wet with sweat. He was thirsty. After returning the wheelbarrow to its place, he grabbed a soda off the store shelf.

Kate was busy reorganizing canned goods and Albert had taken up his place behind the counter. Paul found himself wishing Albert hadn't returned.

"This is a nickel, right?"

"That's right."

He handed Albert a coin. "How's Helen feeling?"

"Still kind of rough." He pulled open a drawer, fished out a bottle opener, and handed it to Paul. "Wish I had some ginger for her."

"My mother used to swear by it."

Albert's brow creased. "I thought you said it was your grandmother."

"Oh . . . right." Paul searched for a proper response. "She did, but my mother suffered from time to time too. It was a family thing." He removed the cap from his soda and took a quick drink, then handed the bottle opener back. "Well, that does it for this year."

"Take care of yourself. Maybe we'll have another mild winter like the last one."

"I'm not counting on it. Besides, hard winters mean better pelts."

"You're right, there. Say hello to the Warrens for me. And tell Patrick to hurry up and finish that roof of his." He smiled, his blue eyes alive with mischief. "I've been practicing my chess game for the next time he comes to town."

Paul smiled and gave him a nod. "Will do."

The bell jangled and Albert stepped away to help another customer. Paul turned away from the counter and browsed a few of the shelves for any last-minute items while he finished up his soda. His thoughts wandered to Kate, and he glanced at her, wishing he could spend more time with her. The idea surprised him. It had been a long while since he'd wanted to spend time with any woman—not since Susan. He reached for his resolve, reminding himself that he'd never care about someone that deeply again.

Kate stepped to the end of the grocery aisle, acting as if she wanted to say something. She offered him a small wave. "See ya."

Paul gave her a wave, stepped back to the counter to leave the empty soda bottle, and walked toward the door.

Before he could step outside, Kate stopped him. "How about I take you up in my plane next time you come to town?" Her face looked flushed, and she hurried on. "You said it's been a while and you enjoyed it. So how about a free ride?"

Paul smiled. Was she was interested in him? Or maybe she was just trying to make a new friend. He decided it wouldn't hurt. "Sounds good. We'll do that." His eyes rested on hers for just a moment, and her blush deepened. "I'll see you in the spring."

Paul turned his dory northwest and headed out over the inlet. The bow cut easily through calm waters, but the boat's small engine labored under the weight of the supplies.

Clouds hugged the foothills of Mount Susitna. Paul studied the mountain known as "The Sleeping Lady." If he used his imagination, he could see the silhouette of a woman reclining on her back, staring at the sky, her hair flowing down around her shoulders.

A picture of Susan lying in the shade of an oak came at him from the past like a hurtling spear to impale his heart. The day had been hot and she'd decided to rest. He'd fished while she lay on the grass, gazing up through the leaves of the tree.

God, how could you have allowed it? I trusted you. Then a voice in his head rebuked him. *And she trusted you.*

— 4 —

Sunlight burned brightly against Paul's eyelids. Hoping to linger in sleep a little longer, he rested an arm over his eyes. It was no use. He was awake. In frustration, he rolled over and looked at the clock on the bureau—8:15. A list of chores rattled through his mind.

Paul sat up and dropped his legs over the side of the bed. When his feet touched the floor, spikes of cold jolted him. He'd been so tired the previous night, he'd fallen into bed without starting a fire.

He rested his arms on his thighs and stared at the floor. He remembered the woman he'd met at the mercantile. *What was her name? Oh yeah, Kate.* For a few moments he allowed himself to mull over the memory of the Alaskan newcomer. Then he forced all thoughts of her from his mind. He'd decided—no women, not ever.

Blowing out a breath, he pushed his fingers through tousled hair, grabbed his pants and pulled them on, then fumbled his way into the kitchen. He lifted off the lid of the firebox, crumpled paper, and shoved it inside. After adding kindling, he lit the newsprint. Soon a small fire danced and popped.

He added a couple larger pieces of wood and slid the firebox lid back in place.

After filling a coffeepot with water from a hand pump in the sink, he tossed coffee grounds into the basket, and then set the aluminum percolator on the cooktop. With the pungent aroma of coffee in his nostrils, he moved to the sink and splashed his face with cold water. Shivering, he towel dried.

Now fully awake, he fed chunks of alder and birch into the fire, enjoying the sound and smell of burning wood. Barking dogs announced a visitor. He glanced out the window just as Lily Warren stepped onto the porch. It was early for a visit. He wondered what she wanted. Paul draped the towel over the back of a chair and went to the door.

The seventeen-year-old girl looked at him with her usual quiet smile. Although her father was white, she looked more like her native mother. "Morning," she said.

"Good day, Lily."

She glanced at her feet, then turned warm brown eyes on Paul and held out a basket. "Mama thought you might like some fresh sourdough biscuits, since you just got back last night. She baked them fresh this morning."

Paul took the basket. "Your mom must have started baking early."

"You know Mama, she's up before the birds."

Paul knew all about Sassa. And she was more interested in his marrying her daughter than in filling his stomach. "Tell her thank you for me." Paul wasn't sure just what to do. He didn't want to give Lily the idea that he took her mother's ambition of making him a son-in-law seriously. Still, it seemed rude to leave Lily standing on the porch. "Would you like some coffee? I have a fresh pot brewing."

"Yes. I'd like that." Lily stepped inside.

Paul closed the door. He wished Sassa would stop trying to match up Lily and him. He was too old for her—fifteen years were too many to overcome.

Lily's eyes lingered on Paul's bare chest. He glanced down, realizing he didn't have a shirt on. "Uh. Just a minute. I'll be right back." He hurried to the bedroom, grabbed the shirt he'd flung over the back of a chair the previous evening, and pulled it on, then pushed his feet into slippers. Still doing up the buttons on the shirt, he returned to the front room. He could feel heat in his cheeks. "Sorry."

"Oh, I don't mind." Lily smiled sweetly.

"It's not proper for you . . ." Paul fumbled around for the right thing to say. "Well, it's just not right." He tried to smile, but it felt more like a grimace. "It was kind of your mother to send over the biscuits."

"She figured you might like something fresh for breakfast, especially since you got in so late."

"How did she know what time I got back?"

"Saw your light."

Paul was glad for neighbors, but sometimes the few acres of land that separated the Warrens' homestead and his weren't enough. Setting the basket on the table, he said, "These'll hit the spot. Would you like one?"

"No thanks. Already had a couple." Lily sat at the rough-hewn table.

"Coffee will be a few more minutes."

"That's all right." A dark plait of hair had fallen over Lily's shoulder. She tossed it back. "What was Anchorage like?"

"Busy—a lot of people in town. Figure folks are getting set up for winter."

Lily propped her elbows on the table, clasped her hands, and rested her chin on them. "Mama and Daddy are going in next week. Wish I could go along. I have to stay and take care of my brothers."

Paul checked the coffee. It still wasn't ready. He wished it would hurry. He glanced at Lily. She looked like she was sulking. "Something wrong?"

"It's just that I never get to go anywhere. I want to see something besides this crick."

"I thought you liked living here."

"I do, but . . ." She shook her head slowly from side to side. "Sometimes I feel trapped. There's a whole world I've never seen. I wonder what the outside is like."

"It's not so great. Believe me."

She studied him, then said, "You never said why you left California."

A pulse of trepidation surged through Paul. No one had ever directly asked him why he'd left San Francisco. People in the bush seemed to understand that if someone wanted to share their past, they would. "I had my reasons." He glanced out the window. "Cold this morning. Wonder if winter's going to move in early."

"Maybe. The trees are already turning."

"You think we're in for a rough season?" He checked the coffee again.

"Hard to tell. But the critters are getting ready."

The coffee was boiling. Paul grabbed two cups off a shelf and filled them, setting one in front of Lily.

"Thanks," she said.

The aroma of coffee filled the room. "You like yours black?"

"I like milk, if you have it. Daddy's the one who says he doesn't believe in muddying up his coffee. Figures it's a waste of good milk."

"Sounds like Patrick." Paul took a can of milk down from

44

a shelf. Using the sharp end of a bottle opener, he punched two holes in it, then set the can on the table along with a spoon.

Lily poured a little into her cup and stirred it in, then took a drink. "Good." She gazed at Paul, her brown eyes inviting.

Her look unsettled him. Did she have feelings for him? "So, did your dad get the roof finished?" He leaned a hip against the counter, holding his cup in both hands.

"Nearly." Lily sipped her coffee. "But we lost some of the new shingles in a storm that blew through a couple of days ago. Barely got them up, and now they've got to be put back."

"I'd be more than happy to give him a hand."

"I think Daddy wants the boys to learn some responsibility. He won't even let me help."

"Okay. But I'm here if he changes his mind." Paul glanced outside. "Must have been a bad storm. I noticed a lot of trees down on the trail."

"It was bad. The wind came up all of a sudden. Thought it might blow us off the homestead." She set her mug on the table. "I don't really mind. I like storms. Makes life more interesting."

Paul cradled his cup in the palm of one hand. "While your parents are gone . . . if you need anything, just let me know."

"I'll be fine, but thanks." Lily straightened. "'Course, we saw a couple of wolves two nights ago. They were pretty close to the house."

"Wolves?"

"I've never seen them around our place before. Daddy figures they must be hungry—hasn't seen much game this summer."

"You have trash out?"

"No. We're real careful about that." Lily shrugged. "'Course we got the compost pile. Sometimes that'll draw in animals."

"I'll keep an eye out." Paul took a drink of coffee, then looked at it. "Took this off the stove too soon." With a shake of his head, he added, "Can't rush coffee."

"It's fine." Lily leaned back in her chair. "Mama thinks it's a bad omen."

"What is?"

"The wolves. She says them coming in so close isn't right." She tapped the edge of her cup with her index finger. "She's scared."

"Your mom? I didn't think she was scared of anything."

"She's not . . . not usually. But wolves spook her. Did she tell you that when she was little, a pack killed a girl in her village?"

"No."

Lily drank the last of her coffee and then stood. "Since seeing the wolves, she won't even go to the outhouse without a rifle."

"I didn't think wolves bothered people much."

"Never can tell what a wild animal will do." She glanced at his rifle leaning against the wall near the door. "Probably ought to keep your gun with you and watch out for your dogs."

"I will. But I doubt we have much to worry about. They're likely a long ways from here." Paul finished his coffee, then moved to the stove to refill it. "You want more?" he asked, hoping she'd say no.

"I gotta get back." Lily picked up her cup and set it in the sink before heading for the door. When she stepped outside, the dogs whined. "Sure do like your dogs. They're beautiful."

"Yeah, they're fine animals."

"If Nita ever has a litter, I know Daddy'll want one of the pups."

"I'm hoping to have some come spring." Paul moved onto the porch and closed the door behind him. Whining turned into barking. "They need a run."

Lily walked down the steps. "See ya," she said and headed for the trail that connected the two properties.

Paul remained on the porch and watched her go. Patrick and Sassa were good neighbors. He was thankful for them. They were helpful and weren't much for meddling. The only real point of contention was Sassa's idea of him and Lily getting married. He'd tried to be straight with her, but she wouldn't listen.

Lily's a pretty little thing, but even if she were old enough, there'll never be another woman for me. The sorrow he usually managed to keep tapped down swelled in his chest. Fighting memories, he stepped back inside the house.

The dogs whined and barked when Paul walked toward the run where they spent most of their time. The largest of the three, a big male, powered toward him and planted his feet on Paul's chest.

"Hey there, Buck, how you doing?" Paul buried his fingers in the animal's thick ruff and kneaded his coat. He'd named him after the character in Jack London's *Call of the Wild*. He moved to Nita, the female. She pressed in and nipped at Paul's hands. She was the most intelligent of the three, so he usually ran her at the front of the lead when they were out with the sled. He patted her head. Jackpot, the quieter and smallest dog, held back, his tail thumping the ground. Paul stroked his glossy black fur. Although more reserved, he was also the most determined of the bunch. He'd won him in a game of cards, hence the name Jackpot.

He unhooked Jackpot's lead first. "Did you guys miss me?" More panting and tail wagging was his answer.

Once free the dogs romped, bounding on and over one another. Paul headed for the trail, picking up a stick and sending it flying. All three dogs tore after it. Jackpot was the first to grab it. Although smaller, he was faster than the other two. Buck pounced on him, trying to wrestle away the prize. Jackpot held tight and trotted back to Paul with his offering. Paul took the stick and threw it again. While the dogs chased, he moved down the trail, accompanied by the occasional trill of a bird.

The air smelled like fall—sharp and clean with the scent of fermenting berries. He breathed deeply, nature lifting his spirits. Alder and birch leaves were turning color, showing up as bright flecks of yellow amid the greenery. Soon the forest would be ablaze with yellows, golds, and reds.

He stepped over a small birch lying across the path as the dogs bounded ahead of him and disappeared into the thick foliage. His attention went to the downed trees. There were several small birch and alder blocking the trail. They'd make good firewood.

Paul scanned the forest, wondering where the dogs had gone. Putting his fingers to his lips, he whistled, splintering the quiet. A few moments later the sounds of something crashing through the brush moved toward him. All of a sudden the dogs broke free of the underbrush, tongues hanging and carefree expressions in their eyes. They lumbered toward Paul, their tails beating the air.

He knelt and greeted his wilderness comrades. Buck nearly knocked him over.

"Okay. Okay. That's enough," Paul said with a laugh. "Time to head back to the house. I've got work to do."

He walked toward the cabin, the canines by his side. Paul

tied them, gave each a piece of salmon and some fresh water, then went to the shed to retrieve a handsaw and an axe. He'd limb and cut up the trees that were down on the trail, then load them onto a cart and come back for the dogs.

The first downed tree was very near the house. He cut away limbs and threw them into a stack for burning later. The tree hadn't broken completely away from the trunk, so he cut it free with an axe. Using a crosscut saw, he divided it into manageable chunks that he stacked on the cart.

After he'd taken care of two other trees, he sat on a stump to rest. He wiped sweat from his face, then chugged water from a canteen. He studied the area. It was a nice spot. A breeze cut through the forest, rustling the leaves and bending tall grasses. Brilliant pink patches of fireweed swayed. On a day like this it almost felt like home.

Although not as bad as they'd been in the early summer, mosquitoes still pestered him. He slapped one of the annoying insects dining on his forearm, then flicked off its remains.

Don't recall feasting bugs in San Francisco. His mind carried him back to his home. He remembered cool summer days with fog-laden mornings, and sunlight gleaming off the bay. He missed it. But there was nothing for him there, nothing but reminders of all that he'd lost and the shrieking blare of guilt.

He took another drink. He'd add one more tree to the cart, then go back to the house and get Buck and Jackpot. The two of them should be able to pull the load easily enough. He replaced the lid on the canteen and looped it over the cart handle.

A branch cracked in the underbrush. Paul studied the dense woodland, but didn't see anything. Breathing easy, he listened.

Something was out there—he could feel it. Cautiously he moved to the tree where he'd left his rifle. He picked it up, cocked it, and waited.

And then there was something . . . a shadow that moved in the deep green. A grizzly? This time of year, the huge carnivores were scavenging the last of the berries and any grubs they could find before denning up.

Several minutes passed, and when Paul heard nothing else, he decided whatever it was had moved on. He rested the gun against a tree and walked to a downed birch and set to work, hacking off limbs with his axe. Then, from the corner of his eye he caught movement.

He straightened just as a wolf darted into the shadows. His heart rate picked up and he grabbed his rifle. The large canine came out of hiding. Its golden eyes stared, challenging him. This wasn't normal behavior.

Paul kept his gaze fixed on the animal. Its lips curled back and it showed its teeth. A snarl came from deep in its throat. Paul held his gun ready. The wolf took a step toward him. To his left he heard the snap of a branch. Another wolf appeared. Like the first, it stared at Paul. And then there were three . . . four . . .

Tension ignited the air. Paul barely breathed. Palms sweaty, he gripped his rifle. This was bad. How could he hold off a whole pack?

The predators paced back and forth. Paul took a step up the trail, then another. They kept their distance. Maintaining eye contact with the wild animals, Paul moved toward the cabin, one determined step at a time. They followed.

Although wolves were not known for their aggression toward humans, Paul's mind raged with stories of attacks. He'd never been overly concerned about the predators, but now had to fight to quiet his racing imagination.

Before he could see the cabin, he heard the fierce barking of his dogs. They knew the wolves were here.

The first one who'd shown himself moved closer. *He's most likely the alpha*. Paul counted them again—one, two, three, four, five . . . six. Were there more? They kept pacing and darting in and out of the underbrush, tongues lolling, yellow eyes staring.

He raised his rifle and fired one shot into the air. They backed off, but only momentarily. Paul kept moving. They were all around him. He took longer steps and fought panic that told him to run.

The cabin was close now. He could see his dogs lunging on their leads. A large wolf sprang at Paul. He lowered the rifle and shot. A blast and a yelp splintered the air. The animal fell. Another charged from the opposite direction. Paul fired again. This time he missed and the wolf seized his upper arm, tearing cloth and flesh. Pain flashed through Paul's bicep.

He pushed his rifle against the animal's gut and pulled the trigger. The wolf dropped to the ground, lifeless. The others kept their distance. Paul finally made the porch steps where he stood with his back to the cabin. His dogs strained against their leads, snarling and barking viciously. If the pack came at them, they'd have no chance while tethered, but Paul dared not release them. *I should have closed them in the shed*, he thought, angry with himself for taking the sighting of the wolves too lightly.

For several minutes the wolves remained at the edge of the clearing around the cabin, remaining mostly hidden in the foliage. One moved forward, and Paul dropped him. The rest of the pack dissolved into the forest. He calculated how many shots he'd taken—five. He had only one shell left in the chamber.

Keeping his eyes on the woods, he backed up the cabin steps, opened the door, and grabbed extra bullets from a shelf just inside. Hands shaking, he plugged them into the magazine, then returned to his post on the porch where he remained, waiting and watching. His dogs quieted. The wolves did not reappear.

A sound came from the side of the house. Paul turned, training his gun at the noise. It was Patrick.

His friend raised his hands, a rifle in one of them. "Whoa, neighbor. It's just me."

Taking a deep breath, Paul lowered his weapon. "Sorry." All of a sudden his legs felt weak as the adrenaline wore off. He sat on the porch step.

Patrick's eyes went to the wolf lying in the yard and to Paul's bleeding arm. "Looks like you had some trouble here. You all right?"

"Yeah. They came at me." Paul wiped sweat from his brow. "One got ahold of me, but it's nothing I can't take care of." He shook his head, thinking about what could have happened.

"I heard the shots. That's why I came running." The long-limbed man cautiously moved to the dead animal. With his rifle aimed at it, he nudged him with the end of the barrel. "He's pretty lean." His eyes moved to the forest. "How many of them were there?"

"I saw six and killed three. There's two, dead, on the trail."

Patrick turned his eyes to the forest. "They'll likely be back. We better set out traps."

"Good idea."

Patrick moved to Paul. "You want Sassa to take a look at that bite?"

"No. I'm fine." He ripped the already torn shirtsleeve and tied it off to staunch the bleeding.

"Might as well make use of the pelts." Patrick headed toward the trail.

Paul followed, ignoring the burning in his arm. It would need cleaning and stitching, but that would have to wait while he and Patrick skinned the animals.

After stretching the last hide, Patrick said, "Sassa's got supper waiting for me. You want to join us?"

"Not tonight." Using his good arm, he gave Patrick a friendly clap on the back. "Thanks for your help."

"You'd do the same for me." He headed toward the trail, his rifle resting on his shoulder. "Take care of that arm."

"I will."

Paul set his rifle against the porch steps and moved to the dogs. One by one he released them and led them into the cabin. Tonight, they'd sleep indoors.

— 5 —

Kate glanced at the clock. It was nearly noon—time to leave. She'd been wanting to get to the airport ever since Paul Anderson had mentioned it. But with Helen out sick for three days, there'd been no time. Today was the day.

She handed Mrs. Sullivan her change and a bag containing thread and buttons. "Have a nice day."

The kindhearted woman tucked the money into a coin purse. "You too, dear." She snapped the purse shut, and instead of leaving, she smiled at Kate. "Did I tell you my son is coming to visit?"

"Next week, right?" Kate managed to conceal her impatience.

"Yes. I can scarcely wait. It's been nearly two years since he was home." She hobbled toward the door, then stopped and turned to look at Kate. "It's a terrible time for my rheumatism to act up."

"Maybe it'll be better by the time he arrives," Kate said, wishing she'd hurry on her way. Guilt flashed through her mind. Mrs. Sullivan was a caring woman who deserved her full attention.

"I dare to hope." Mrs. Sullivan shuffled out of the store.

"Have a good day," Kate called after her. She looked at the clock again and wondered if Helen Towns could spare her.

Dusting rag in hand, Helen walked toward the register. "Poor Mrs. Sullivan, she suffers so."

"She's very nice." Kate glanced out the front window. "I talked to Mr. Towns about taking time off today. I won't be gone long."

"Oh yes, that's right. He told me." She looked around the store. "I'm certain we can manage with *all* the business we have at the moment." She smiled, her blue eyes crinkling at the corners.

"Thank you." Butterflies took flight in Kate's stomach. Today might be the day.

Albert joined the women. He circled an arm around his wife's small waist and tugged her in next to him. Turning his attention to Kate, he said, "We'll be praying for you."

"Thank you."

Helen rested a hand on Kate's arm. "You'll do fine. Mr. Schaefer can't help but like you."

"Not everyone is as nice as you two." Kate clasped her hands in front of her, trying to wring out some of her tension. "I just hope he needs a pilot. And if he does, that he'll hire a woman."

Figuring it would be better to face Mr. Schaefer in flight attire, Kate hurried to her room and changed into slacks and a tuck-in shirt. She sat down, pulled on boots, and laced them. After running a brush through her hair, she picked up her perfume and was about to dab some on, when she thought better of it. She skipped the lipstick as well, thinking natural was best.

Pulling on her leather jacket, she headed toward the front

of the store, trying to maintain an air of calm. She smiled at Helen, who was working at the front register.

"Good luck," Albert called, then returned to stocking a shelf with canned goods.

Kate stepped outside. She'd decided to fly to the airstrip, so she headed toward Merrill Field. Nerves made her muscles tight, and every few steps she'd shake her arms, trying to loosen the tension. It didn't help. She stopped and took a deep breath, closing her eyes. *Lord, I need your help. Convince Mr. Schaefer to give me a chance.*

When Kate reached the airfield, she found George, the manager of Merrill Field, with his head inside an engine compartment.

He looked up. "Hi. Haven't seen you for a few days."

"I've been putting in a lot of hours at the store." Leaning against the fuselage, she said, "I heard the airfield at Lake Spenard might need a pilot."

"Yeah? I'm not surprised. Understand Sidney's doing pretty well over there." He pulled a rag out of his back pocket and wiped his hands. "He seems like a good man. Hope he has something for you."

"I figured I'd take my plane."

"Good idea. It's a fine aircraft. Wish I had a spot for you."

"Me too." Kate didn't know what else to say. She'd have preferred working for George. Momentary silence swelled until it became uncomfortable. "Well, I better get going."

"I'll crank your plane for you."

"Nah. You're busy. I can do it."

"Okay." He picked up a wrench. "Let me know how it goes."

"I will." Kate walked to her plane. For a moment, her desire to hurry nearly convinced her to skip the inspection, but she forced herself to take the time—better safe than sorry. Everything seemed fine, so she climbed in, pulled on her helmet, and then checked the gauges and oil. All was in good order.

After priming the engine, she climbed out and moved to the side of the plane. Using the hand crank, she turned the flywheel until the sound became shrill. "That ought to do it," she said, hurrying inside and pulling the starter. When the engine lit off, it sounded rough. Kate made an adjustment to the mixture and it evened out.

She turned the plane toward the runway and rolled over bumpy ground until she was lined up on the field. Her nerves still spiking, she studied the windsock—it fluttered west to east. Skies were clear. If only today was *the* day . . .

The Bellanca ran smoothly as Kate taxied to the end of the runway and took to the air. As always, exhilaration lifted her right along with the plane. For a few moments her body relaxed, then she tightened her hold on the stick. A lot was at stake. She'd been in Anchorage more than a month and this was the first solid lead she'd had. This might be her chance.

Kate was in the air only a few minutes when she spotted the airfield. *Smart of him to set up alongside a lake. He can use pontoon planes during the summer.* Memories of the dark waters of Rimrock Lake hurtled through Kate's mind. She'd managed to get back into the air, but had never attempted a pontoon landing since the accident. *I'll do it when the time comes*, she told herself, only half believing her own resolve.

She made her approach and settled easily on the dirt runway. What looked like a shed sat at one end of the field. She taxied toward it. A small slender man, wearing a broad-brimmed cowboy hat, stood at the doorway.

By the time Kate turned off the engine, he'd walked to the plane. He wasn't the type to stand out in a crowd, except for the way he was dressed. Along with his hat, he wore blue jeans and western-style boots. Kate figured he couldn't be more than thirty and wondered if he was the owner or one of the pilots.

She removed her helmet and climbed out of the plane.

"Afternoon," the man said. "That's a fine bird you've got."

"Thank you. She's been good to me."

He walked around the craft, studying it. "Interesting name you've got for her—Fearless Kate." He grinned. "Let me guess—you're Kate."

"I am." Feeling the heat of embarrassment, Kate glanced at the side of the plane where she'd painted *Fearless Kate* in black letters. "I was a bit exuberant when I first got her."

"No harm in that." He folded his arms over his chest and looked at her squarely. "I'm Sidney Schaefer. What can I do for you?"

"I was told you might need a pilot."

"Maybe. You know one?" Mischief lit his eyes.

Kate swallowed hard and got hold of her nerve. "I'm a good pilot."

His expression turned serious. "I'm sure you are. But I need experience and someone who's strong—strong enough to load gear for hunters and stow bagged trophies, someone who doesn't mind a bit of blood or puke, who can handle an aircraft in any kind of weather."

"I can do all that." Kate spotted a feed sack leaning against the shed. She walked straight to it and picked it up. It smelled and felt like potatoes. She carried the sack back to Sidney and set it at his feet.

He grinned and rubbed his clean-shaven chin. "Not bad. That's nearly seventy-five pounds."

"I've been working all my life. I'm strong and I know how to work hard."

"That's well and good, but it doesn't make you an ace pilot. What kind of experience do you have?"

58

"Been flying since I was a kid. My father taught me."

"What's his name?"

"Bill Evans."

"Never heard of him."

Feeling as if Sidney had made a dig at her father, Kate said, "He flies in Washington, and there's no better pilot."

"So, you're new to Anchorage?"

"I've been here about a month." Doubt assailed Kate. Would he even consider a woman pilot?

"What makes you think you can fly in this country?"

She searched for a satisfactory answer. "I have more hours in a cockpit than most. I've flown in good and bad weather—rain, snow, wind. And I've crossed the Cascades several times. Those mountains will give any pilot a run for their money." His expression told her he wasn't satisfied. "I flew here, on my own, from Washington."

"Alaska can throw more trouble at a pilot than they can think up. You know how to land in snow and ice?"

"We had plenty of that in Yakima."

"Do you have experience with pontoon landings?"

The dark waters of Rimrock Lake flashed through Kate's mind. She met Sidney's eyes. "Not a problem."

He studied her, then with a shake of his head, he said, "I don't think so. I'm sure you're a fine pilot, but . . ." His look was pained. "You're a woman. And this is rough country."

"Let me prove myself." Kate tried to sound like she wasn't desperate.

"If something goes wrong, I become the bad guy, the one who let a lady pilot join my crew. I'd like to help you out, but—"

"Fly with me," Kate blurted. "Test me. I'll take you anywhere you want. I'll show you what I can do."

Using the underside of his thumb, Sidney lifted the brim of

his hat, then squared his jaw as he studied her plane. "Fearless Kate, huh . . . All right—you show me."

———————

Nerves knotted the muscles up and down Kate's back, then moved down her arms and into her hands. She fought for calm, and hoped Sidney didn't notice. She increased power and rolled toward the end of the runway. *Do your stuff, Katie,* she could hear her father say, and felt bolstered.

The ground rolled by faster and faster. The end of the strip came at her, and she pulled back on the stick and felt the plane lift. Free of earth, the ground fell away below and she soared over Lake Spenard.

"How many hours you log in a plane?" Sidney hollered over the sound of the engine.

Kate didn't know how to answer. She'd flown nearly every day of her life. "What do you mean exactly?"

"How many hours you spend flying this bird?"

"I bought it in 1933, but like I said, I've been flying since I was a child."

"What kind of plane you have before this one?"

"I . . . I had another Bellanca." She waited for the question that would end her chances at this job.

"What happened to it?"

She compressed her lips and tried to think of a lie, but couldn't. "It crashed into a lake."

"All by itself?" Sidney's tone teased.

"No. I was flying it." Kate hurried to explain, "I was young and a friend and I—"

"Don't get in a sweat. You're not a real pilot if you've never had a crack up. And you must have done something right—you're still here."

Kate wet her lips and didn't say anything more. She was alive—Alison wasn't.

"You ever use your plane for work?"

"I used to haul equipment and fruit and vegetables."

"What about passengers?"

"Friends."

"Any strangers? You get along with people?"

"Most of them." Kate relaxed, figuring she'd survived the issue about the accident.

"How do you think you'll do when you have a snarly hunter who figures you should have shown up a day earlier than you did, or a sick kid who needed medical help two days ago and it's a full day's flight to the hospital?"

"I've never done anything like that, but I'm levelheaded. I'm sure I'd manage."

"You gotta do better than manage." He didn't wait for a reply, but charged ahead. "Ever have to keep a schedule?"

Kate thought the question absurd. "Almost everything in life has a schedule."

He gave her a lopsided grin. "You're a smart aleck, aren't you?"

"Maybe." She smiled inwardly, feeling as if she'd connected with the man she hoped would be her new boss.

Kate flew over Anchorage, then banked the plane as she circled the small town. She glanced at Sidney. "I won't let you down, not ever."

"Yes, you will. Every pilot lets people down, and it'll be more than once."

His words trounced Kate. She'd let Alison down, plus her father and Alison's family. She'd let them all down. She blinked back tears. Now was not the time. "I mean, if I say I'm going to do something, I will, and if I'm supposed to be somewhere, I'll be there—on time."

"You think so?" He smirked and leaned back in his chair. "Okay. I want you to head toward those mountains, the Chugach. Let's see how you handle a little turbulence."

Kate turned toward the mountains. At the sight of the formidable peaks, her heart pumped hard with anticipation and fear. The Chugach were daunting.

When the white peaks looked big in the window, Sidney pointed toward a gorge that ran between two jagged ridges. "Fly right through that canyon." He folded his arms over his chest, as if daring her to handle the unpredictable.

Kate kept her eyes on the mountains, but her mind puzzled over Sidney. Would he purposely put them in danger? Or did he trust her experience?

Although Kate was careful to stay on the upwind side of the canyon, the plane shivered and rattled. It dropped into an air pocket and was then tossed upward. As Kate met the challenge, she gained confidence. She knew how to deal with turbulent conditions.

She made her way up the gorge and the pitching increased. Her plane bounced as if it were a kite being tossed in a brisk wind. The walls of the mountains closed in. She waited for Sidney's instructions, knowing that if she didn't head back soon, there wouldn't be enough room to make the turn.

"All right, I want you to go back the way we came and then cruise over Cook Inlet."

Kate obeyed, happily. Sidney certainly couldn't doubt her abilities now. However, as she approached the inlet, she tightened her grip on the stick. Clouds had moved in, creating a low ceiling. She couldn't fly above the gray stacks—she'd have to maneuver beneath them.

Approaching the layer of black and gray, she calculated the distance between sea and sky. She was fine; there was plenty of space . . . or just enough. She ducked beneath the cloud bank, so low she could see birds fishing in the choppy waters below.

"Good, now follow the coast along the peninsula."

Kate relaxed a little and held a course that followed the shore. Some beaches were sandy, others rocky. All were littered with driftwood and other debris, some were barely visible beneath a confusion of logs and sea life.

"Have you ever made a beach landing?"

"Once, on my way up the coast from Washington. It was a little dicey, but I got down all right."

"You see that piece of sand down there?" He pointed at a stretch of shoreline.

"The one with the rock outcropping?"

"Yep, that's the one. Can you put us down on it?"

"I think so. I'll have to check it out."

Kate pushed the stick forward and decreased altitude. The beach looked unstable. There were rivulets of water running into the bay—which most likely meant mud or soft sand. She circled the proposed landing site, flying low enough to note obstacles. "It should be all right, maybe a little soft."

She looked at Sidney. "Are you familiar with this beach?"

"Yeah. It's not too bad, but you're right, the sand can get mushy. When you come in, keep the nose up a little, other- wise you're liable to plant it in the dirt."

Feeling both delight and apprehension, Kate made one more flyover, then set up for her run. She figured it would be best to descend on the end of the beach with the rocks. That way she could take off toward them and into the wind.

Keeping a gentle touch on the stick, she gradually de- scended. The earth rushed past her below the plane; she continued to decelerate and then felt the wheels touch down. Wet sand pulled at them. She remembered what Sidney had said and made sure to keep the nose up, then eased back on the throttle and rolled to a smooth stop.

"Not bad," Sidney said.

Feeling gratified at his compliment, Kate sat back and dropped her shoulders, easing the tension in her muscles.

"Now, do you have a plan for getting us home?" He grinned.

Kate knew better than to take off without making an inspection of the beach, but didn't want Sidney to think she was insecure or inexperienced. She decided caution was the best choice and said as boldly as she could manage, "I want to walk the beach first, to plan the best strategy for takeoff." She watched for irritation or disappointment on his face. There was none.

"Good idea."

Feeling almost lighthearted, Kate climbed out of the plane and headed up the beach. Sidney left the cockpit but stayed with the aircraft, leaning against it while he smoked a cigarette. Kate was thankful for time alone to relax and to gather her thoughts.

An onshore breeze carried the sharp odor of the sea and the calls of seabirds. Gulls hopped across wet sands, then complained at Kate's intrusion as they opened their wings and lifted into the air.

The direction of the wind would make for an easier takeoff, but the sand was soggy. Walking back and forth across the shore, she looked for the firmest areas. When she found a strip that felt solid, she walked its length, grabbing clumps of kelp, tossing them into the surf and rolling pieces of driftwood clear. Some she used to mark the runway.

She studied what lay beyond the rock outcropping. The trees were bent and not too tall. She looked the other direction. It was the same. If she made a mistake, there'd be no place to put down.

Kate walked back to the plane, pacing off the distance. Finally, she did a quick check of the area where she'd have to turn around and decided there shouldn't be any problem with the wheels getting bogged down.

"You ready?" Sidney asked, flicking away the last of his cigarette.

"All set." Feeling surprisingly calm, she climbed into the Bellanca and settled into her seat.

Sidney cranked the plane and the engine lit right off. He hurried around and climbed in beside her. "Let's get this bird in the air."

Turning the craft around so she was facing the make-shift runway, Kate held her breath, hoping she hadn't made any miscalculations. She studied the line of takeoff, double checked the wind and reference points, and then eased in the throttle, moving the plane forward. *Not too fast. You don't want to end up with the prop stuck.*

She picked up speed. The rock outcroppings rushed at them. She'd have to lift off soon. One wheel left the ground and her speed increased, then the other wheel followed . . . and she was airborne. The rocks and the trees were close. She gently pulled back on the stick and cleared the obstacles, then soared over the surf, leaving the dark waves behind.

"You know the way home?" Sidney asked.

"I do." Kate felt jubilant. He'd have to hire her.

When Sidney said nothing while she followed the coastline toward Anchorage, though, her confidence waned. She put down without difficulty and rolled toward the end of the run-way. Afraid to even look at Sidney, she turned off the engine.

He removed his flight cap and held out his hand. "You got a job with me, if you want it." He smiled broadly.

"I do." Kate shook his hand, barely managing to hold back a whoop of joy.

"It's only part-time. I need a pilot for a mail run. Think you can do that?"

"Absolutely." It wasn't everything she wanted, but it was a beginning.

"Mike Conlin's been filling in on that run. He'll take you out. Be here Monday morning, eight o'clock sharp."

"I'll be here."

Sidney studied her. "Prove yourself and I'll let you fly passengers."

"I will."

He climbed out of the plane and, before closing the door, said, "Don't disappoint me."

— 6 —

Kate's mind sprinted through questions, the same ones that had kept her awake most of the night. What would she come across today? How long a route did she have? Where was it located? What kind of weather would she face? What would Mike be like?

She slapped together a bologna sandwich, wrapped it in waxed paper, and shoved it into a bag, then added an apple and put her lunch in her pack. *At least I won't be on my own.* She felt only slightly reassured by the thought, because after today she *would* be on her own.

Standing in front of her bureau mirror, she studied her reflection. Her face was flushed and her hazel eyes seemed brighter than usual. She'd always wanted blue eyes. Pulling a brush through her hair, she could still hear her mother's reassuring tone. *"God knew exactly what he was doing when he created you. You're perfect."*

Kate felt a pang of homesickness and wished she had time to reread her mother's most recent letter. She'd talked about her father's last fishing trip and the upcoming apple harvest. Kate loved this season. It was a busy time on the farm. Often friends stopped by to help with apple picking and cider making. It always felt celebratory.

She leaned closer to the mirror and applied lipstick. Last year, she and Richard had stayed late to clean up and then drank so much cider they'd almost made themselves sick. In the letter, her mother mentioned that he'd stopped in for a visit. He was praying she'd return. *I'm not going back*, she told herself, but an ache twisted in her gut.

Forcing her mind back to the present, Kate put on a spritz of Evening in Paris, then tucked in her shirt for the umpteenth time. Standing with her spine straight, she told her image, "Guess I'm ready as I'll ever be."

She pulled on her leather flight jacket, draped her pack over one shoulder, and headed for the door. When she stepped into the store, she nearly collided with Helen Towns.

The older woman clutched her hands to her chest. "Oh! You gave me a start."

"I'm sorry." Kate grasped Helen's upper arms to steady her. "I'm a little keyed up and hurrying."

"That's understandable." Helen smiled. "The first day on a job is always the toughest." She gave Kate a quick hug. "You'll do fine."

"I hope so." Kate glanced toward the door. "I better go. I don't want to be late."

"Just one moment. I have something for you." Helen hurried to the storeroom and took a small container down from a shelf. "I baked these for you last night." She held out a canister.

Kate peeked inside. The sweet fragrance of cinnamon drifted from the tin. "Cookies. Thank you."

"Oatmeal raisin. It's my mother's recipe."

"They smell delicious." Kate pushed the lid closed. "I love oatmeal cookies."

Helen pressed her palms together. "Well, you better get moving."

Kate hurried through the store. Albert stood at the front door, a duster in hand.

"Your big day. After this, you'll be a full-fledged pilot."

"I'm only working part-time."

"That's enough." He smiled. "You'll still be able to work for us on your days off." He opened the door. "See you tomorrow."

Kate took long strides, swinging her arms freely at her sides. She could barely contain her excitement. The airfield was closer than Merrill Field, which on most days would be a good thing, but this morning she'd have liked more time to work out her nervousness.

It was a perfect morning, cool and clear. The air smelled clean, and fresh snow glistened on the mountains, foretelling of approaching winter. The sourdoughs who came into the store predicted it would arrive early. She wondered what an Alaskan winter would be like. All she knew were the stories she'd heard. It sounded exciting, but she wondered how bad the weather had to be to ground flights. And what if a storm came up and caught her off guard? *Stop worrying. You've flown in snow before. You'll know what to do when the time comes.*

As a child, she'd read books that talked of ice houses and Eskimos. She smiled at her childish naïveté. Of course none of it was true anymore. Anchorage was like other towns, except that a lot of the men who came in from the bush reminded her of grizzly bears. Most sported beards, chewed tobacco, and held with coarse language that they cleaned up only mildly in the presence of women. Most smelled like they could use a bath.

The man from Bear Creek, Paul—he didn't seem like the rest. He was more refined and he'd smelled of soap, not sweat. She wondered how he'd come to live in Alaska. *Next time I see him, I'll ask.* Even as she considered their next meeting, she knew better than to ask about his background. It wasn't done. Early on, she'd learned not to ask questions. Some Alaskans had left the states to lose themselves and didn't want their pasts dug up.

Since arriving in the territory, she'd met a number of re-markable people. Kate figured the ones who moved to Alaska were likely adventure seekers, which made them different right from the start. And the ones who stayed had to be the hardiest of all. She was determined to be one of those.

The airfield came into sight and her stomach did a little flip. She stopped and pushed down her nerves. *I can do this.*

When Kate stepped into the shop, Sidney stood beside a bench laden with tools and airplane parts. He straightened and glanced at the clock. "You're early." He smiled, which made his boyish face look even younger.

"Better than being late."

"Got that right." He wiped his hands on a rag. "Work never ends. You know anything about plane engines?"

"Just enough to get me back in the air when I'm stuck on the ground, at least most of the time."

The door opened and a thickset man with short black hair stepped into the room. He flung the door shut with a bang. Full lips clamped themselves around a cigar. In spite of the stogie, the man managed to scowl.

I hope he's not Mike.

"Hey, Jack, I'd like you to meet our new pilot, Kate Evans. She's going to take the inlet run."

"Heard you'd hired a dame." The cigar bounced as he talked.

Wearing a frown, Sidney said, "Kate, this is Jack Rydell, one of my pilots."

"Your best pilot." Jack pressed his backside against the workbench, crossed his legs at the ankles, and folded his arms over his chest. "Been flying Alaska for eight years, and I'm the best aviator you'll find in the territory."

Sidney shook his head. "And the most modest."

"Pleasure to meet you," Kate said, extending a hand, thankful the ill-mannered man wasn't Mike.

Jack grasped it halfheartedly, then turned to Sidney. "Thought I had a trip this morning."

"You do."

"Where're my riders?"

"Simmer down. They called in and they're running late. They'll get here."

"I don't have time to laze around while a bunch of trigger-happy hunters try to get their . . ." He looked at Kate, then continued, "Get their stuff together. It's just a scouting trip." He moved toward the door. "Guess I'll give my plane a once-over while I wait." He walked out of the building, slamming the door behind him.

Sidney shook his head. "Sometimes I wonder why I keep him around."

"Why do you?" Kate asked without thinking, then wondered if she was being too forward. After all, this was her first day.

He looked at Kate with resignation. "He's a good pilot."

The door opened again and Kate prepared for another onslaught from Jack. Instead, it was a young man who looked as if he'd never seen a stressful day in his life. He stepped into the doorway. Fingers tucked into his pants pockets, he leaned his slender frame against the doorjamb. A quiet smile rested on his lips as his pale blue eyes sized up Kate. "So, you're my student?" He lifted off his cap, revealing unruly brown hair.

Kate felt her skin prickle. She wasn't sure what she'd expected, but he wasn't it—he was much too good looking. Propelling herself forward, she held out a hand. "I'm Kate Evans."

"Mike Conlin." He snapped a piece of gum he was chewing and winked, but his grip was firm. "Nice to meet you." He turned his attention to Sidney. "So, how much mail we got today?"

"Plenty. Be glad for good weather."

"Better get to it, then." Mike stuffed his cap in his back pocket.

"Already packed it for you," Sidney said.

"Thanks." Mike looked at Kate. "So, you ready?"

"I am." Kate tried to sound confident, but felt anything but. So much was riding on her doing a good job. If she botched this, there'd be no other chances.

Hauling two canvas bags, Mike led the way to the airfield. Kate followed, a box tucked under one arm and a heavy sack draped over her shoulder. She wondered just how big a route she'd be covering. There was a lot of mail.

"So, yours is the Bellanca?"

"Uh-huh."

Mike headed for it and Kate followed, her stomach doing a dance.

Mike stopped beside the craft and set the bags on the ground. He stood back and studied the name on the side. "Fearless Kate?"

Embarrassed, Kate silently vowed that at the first opportunity she'd paint over the name. "That's what I call her." She added her mail to the pile beside the Pacemaker.

"Good name."

"I'm going to change it, just haven't gotten around to it yet."

"Why? Aren't you fearless? Isn't that why you're here?" He winked and then opened the rear door.

Kate hated being made fun of. "I was young when I first got the plane."

Mike didn't respond, but hefted in the mail and arranged it carefully. "When you've got a lot of weight, make sure you distribute it evenly so your tail end isn't too heavy. Otherwise you'll have a heck of a time coming out of a stall."

Kate knew that, but didn't say anything.

"I'll crank her."

Mike moved to the side of the plane while Kate climbed into the pilot's seat.

Once in the air, Mike took out a map and pointed to the area they'd be flying through. "We'll head down the peninsula and then cut across the inlet and back to Anchorage. We've got mail drops all the way—small towns, villages, homesteads."

Kate tried to relax, but her muscles felt like they were bunched up. She took a couple of slow, deep breaths.

Mike settled back in his seat. "I'll be glad to get this route off my hands."

"Why? Is there something wrong with it?"

"No. It's just that I make more money working for myself. I split the take with Sidney."

"Why do you split with him?"

"He maintains the airport and helps bring in business. He's got to make a living too."

"Sure. Of course." Kate hoped it wasn't too long before she could make trips of her own. She wondered how much this mail run paid. She'd been so excited to have the job she hadn't even thought to ask.

They flew along the Kenai Peninsula, making several stops, many of them on beaches. Some were soft and sandy, others rocky. There were a few grass airstrips, which Kate was more familiar with, but each stop required careful piloting. Mike was helpful but gave instruction only when needed. Kate appreciated that.

As the morning progressed, she felt more competent but also understood that flying in Alaska meant nothing was ordinary. She was getting a glimpse at how naïve she'd been when she thought she could easily step into piloting in the territory. A mail run had sounded simple. It wasn't. She was grateful Sidney hadn't cut her loose. Delivering mail would be a good jumping-off place, providing much-needed experience.

They stopped at places like Nikiski, Seldovia, and Ninil-chik. Although a bit overwhelmed by the unusual names and nonstop itinerary, Kate didn't feel fatigued. The challenges and new discoveries kept up her interest. And Mike's company wasn't bad either. She liked the laid-back pilot.

At first, Kate was nervous about how she'd be accepted, but she had nothing to worry about. Most people didn't seem at all put off by a woman pilot, and only a handful were even curious.

In Homer, Mike announced it was time for a break. They sat on a large sun-bleached log and shared lunch. A breeze touched Kate's skin and ruffled her short hair. The sun felt almost warm. Some tide pools glistened like glass and others housed sea creatures whose bubbles gave away hiding places.

Kate took in a deep breath, savoring the ocean's sharp fragrance. "I like it here." She unwrapped a sandwich and took a bite.

"The beach has a way of getting the knots out, all right."

Kate couldn't imagine that Mike had any knots. "How long have you been a pilot?"

"Long enough to know better than to fly planes in Alaska." He grinned.

"Do you really mean that?"

"I do." He took two bites out of a peanut butter sandwich. His cheek bulging, he said, "No one should fly in this territory. It's killing work. You'd be smart to turn around and go back where you came from."

Kate stared at her sandwich, her throat tightening. "Why me?" she asked, thinking it must have to do with her being female.

He blew out a breath. "It's not just you. We should all go home." His expression turned somber. "I'm serious, Kate. It's no place for a woman."

Irritation flared and Kate shot back, "Why not a woman?"

Mike shook his head. "I don't mean just women. Anyone in their right mind ought to go home."

She'd known flying here was dangerous, but she hadn't expected to hear such a negative viewpoint from an Alaskan pilot. She folded the remainder of her sandwich in the waxed paper and put it in her pack. Taking out the tin of cookies, she opened it and halfheartedly offered one to Mike. "Mrs. Towns made these."

"Heard she's a good cook." He accepted the cookie.

"She is." Kate selected one and took a bite, barely tasting the mix of spices and raisins. Confused and frustrated, she wanted to ask Mike more about why he felt the way he did about flying in Alaska, but decided it wouldn't be prudent, not on her first day. She chewed and tried to think of something else to talk about. Finally she said, "I can't believe how many people live in the bush. How do they find these remote places?"

"The natives have always been here. Others came looking for gold clear back in the last century and then stayed. And there are some who are still searching for it." He grinned. "Most just want a solitary life and like the idea of living off the land." He squinted as he studied a seagull hopping along the beach. "Some are hiding . . . from something or someone."

"That sounds ominous."

"Not really. There's all kinds of things people want to leave behind." Mike popped the last of his cookie in his mouth. "These remind me of my mother's. She was a great cook." His voice had taken on a wistful tenor.

"Where did you live before moving here?" Kate set the open tin between them on the log.

"Chicago. When my mother died, I figured it was time to make the move."

"What about your father?"

His eyes hardened. "Haven't seen him since he walked out on us. I was ten."

"Oh. I'm sorry."

Mike waved off her regret. "He wasn't any good, anyway."

"How did you end up here?"

He gazed at the ocean. "A friend taught me to fly when I was still in school. He came up several years ago and convinced me it was a good move. So here I am."

"Why do you stay?"

"You ask a lot of questions."

"I figure I ought to know something about my teacher." She grinned.

"I stay because I can't leave. Winter nearly runs me out every year, though." Bracing his hands against the log, he leaned back. "Something about this place . . . almost feels like a part of me." He took another cookie. "And I like the people. You can count on them."

"I've seen that. And I like it too. 'Course I haven't been through a winter yet."

Mike rested his quiet blue eyes on Kate, unsettling her. "How'd you end up here?" he asked.

"I love to fly and I heard there were jobs for pilots. There's not a lot of work in the Yakima area right now. Well, not much anywhere right now."

"That's it? You're here out of practicality?" He shook his head. "It'll take more than that to keep you here."

"It's not all about being practical." Kate brushed cookie crumbs off her shirt. "I want to challenge myself, to try something I've never done—"

"Ah, so it's adventure." He chuckled. "You're like the rest of us then."

Kate felt a prickle of annoyance. "I want more than an adventure. I want to prove I'm a good pilot."

"You don't know?" Mike raised his eyebrows, then shrugged. "I guess we all feel like that sometimes. But you won't prove anything, except that you don't have control over this territory. It controls you."

K ate made a wide turn, setting up for takeoff. With the
engine roaring, she hollered, "Where to now?"

"Kalgin Island."

She felt the plane lug down and drag. She throttled up,
but the craft pulled hard to the right. *Oh brother, I'm stuck.*
Knowing that the tail might come up and stand the plane on
the prop if she used too much power, Kate shut down.

Mike asked, "You got a shovel?"

"Yeah. In back."

He moved to the rear of the plane and found the shovel.
"Give me a few minutes." He disappeared out the door.

Kate followed and found him digging around the right
wheel. The beach was sodden.

"It's pretty soupy."

Embarrassed, Kate simply said, "I'll get something for sup-
port." She combed the beach for small pieces of driftwood
while her mind berated her carelessness. She pressed the wood
into the soggy ground in front of the tire.

"That ought to do it." Mike stood and brushed sand from
his hands. "Let's set her free. You give her power and I'll
push."

Kate wiped her hands on her pants, climbed inside, and dropped into the pilot's seat. Mike cranked the plane, and when the engine lit off, he moved to the wing strut. While he pushed, Kate powered up, and finally the plane rolled forward. Mike scrambled in and took the seat beside Kate. "All set."

Humiliation heating her insides, Kate headed the plane down the beach and into the air. "I should have been watching for that."

"It happens. Just be thankful it wasn't something worse. You could have lost your plane." Mike's smile disappeared. "Pilots lose more than planes all the time. In fact, they die pretty regularly."

Kate glanced at him. His expression was grim.

"All kinds of things can bring a man down." He snugged on his helmet. "That friend I told you about, the one who taught me how to fly—he took a run to Nome a couple years back and disappeared. Never was found."

He fixed his eyes on Kate. "I understand your love of flying. Believe me, I understand. But don't get careless, not for a minute. I'd hate to lose a good pilot. Especially one I like."

Feeling a flush of pleasure, Kate turned her eyes to the sky.

She flew to Kalgin Island and then on to Tyonek, a native village on the inlet. Mike continued with his instructions. He also told her what kind of conditions she could expect once winter set in. He painted a grim picture, but Kate figured she'd face that trouble when it arrived. Better to keep her mind on the job.

Late in the day, they headed up the Susitna River. Kate landed on a sandbar lying in the center of the waterway. She had a drop at Bear Creek, a tributary that flowed into the Susitna.

A boat headed toward them. A man rowed and a native

woman sat on the back bench with a youngster beside her. Two older boys knelt in the bow. When they reached the bar, the boys leaped out and pulled the boat onto the shore. The man unfolded his long-limbed frame and stood. "Hey, Mike," he called, a broad smile plastered on his angular face.

"Patrick. Good to see you."

Patrick helped the woman out of the boat, then headed toward them. "It's a fine day," he said, squinting into the sun.

"It is at that." Mike nodded toward Kate. "Like you to meet your new mail carrier—Kate Evans. Kate this is Patrick and Sassa Warren and their boys."

Curiosity on their faces, the children lined up beside their parents. Mike placed a hand on the smallest boy's head. "This is Douglas." He moved to the next child. "Ethan. And the tall one here is Robert."

"Hello," Kate said. "Nice to meet you."

The boys stared. Douglas asked, "Are you a girl?"

"I am."

Patrick put a hand on the boy's shoulder. "You'll have to excuse his bad manners."

"That's all right. He's probably never seen a woman wearing this kind of getup." Kate knelt in front of Douglas. "I'm dressed like this because of my job. It'd be hard to pack mail in and out of a plane wearing a dress."

His cheeks flushed, but he nodded understanding.

Sassa stepped forward and smiled. "I'm glad to meet you."

"It's good to meet you." Kate straightened and looked about. "It's beautiful here."

"We like it," Patrick said. "We have a homestead just up the crick."

While the boys bounded off toward the far end of the island, Mike reached into the back of the plane and came out with two envelopes and a package.

Sassa reached for the parcel. "It's about time." She held it out in front of her. "Books from the Sears catalog. The boys need them for their studies."

"I'll bet they'll be thrilled about that," Mike quipped as he took another box out of the bag. "This is for Klaus." He looked up the creek. "Haven't seen him for a while."

"Rheumatism's getting him down. I'll see that he gets it," Patrick said.

Mike handed the box to Patrick. "I've got a couple of letters for Paul too." He turned his gaze to a boat moving toward the bar. "Looks like he's coming out."

Kate watched a dory move through the calm waters of the creek and into the river. There was something familiar about the man in the boat. And then she realized he'd been in the store. He was the one who'd told her about the job at the airport—the one who lived on Bear Creek. She hadn't put them together.

The boat grated on the rocks as it came ashore. Mike and Patrick hurried to haul the dory out of the water. Paul jumped into the shallows to help. "Figured I'd come out and say hello." He glanced at Kate.

"Good to see you." Mike gave him a friendly slap on the back.

"You have mail for me?"

"I do." Mike held out two envelopes. "I was just about to have Patrick deliver them."

Paul glanced at the letters and quickly stuffed them into his shirt pocket.

Sassa reached into the front of her apron, took out an envelope, and handed it to Mike. "For my sister."

He gave it to Kate. "This goes to Homer."

He turned back to Paul. "By the way, this is your new mail carrier, Kate Evans."

Paul smiled. "Good to see you again." His voice was deep and steady. "So, you got the job."

"Thanks to you."

"You know each other?" Mike asked.

"We met at the store. He told me about Sidney and the airfield." Kate looked at the handsome man and wondered what lay behind his somber brown eyes.

"I'm glad it worked out for you," he said.

"Me too." Kate suddenly felt self-conscious and fumbled for something to say. "Thanks for the tip."

"You're welcome."

His gaze stirred something in Kate. She could feel a flush heat her cheeks. "We better be on our way." She took a step backward toward the plane and nearly tripped.

Mike caught her arm. "Easy there."

Blushing, Kate gave the small group a wave and headed for the plane.

Paul watched as the Bellanca lifted off and headed upriver. An unexpected sense of isolation enveloped him.

"That's a pretty young lady," Patrick said. "Wonder why she's piloting?"

"Figure she likes to fly," Sassa said. "And when did you start noticing the ladies?"

"Since I was about thirteen." Patrick laughed. "She's just the right age for you, Paul."

"No. She's not right for him," Sassa said. "He needs someone more sensible, with her feet planted on the ground, not flying off to who knows where."

Paul stifled a groan. He wasn't up to Sassa's shenanigans about him and Lily.

82

"You need a nice girl who'll settle down and have babies."
Sassa smiled.

It took great effort, but Paul managed to keep his mouth
shut.

"Lily would be just the girl for you. She's young and
strong—"

"Sassa, I've told you, I'm not looking for a wife. I'm happy
just as I am."

She folded her arms over her chest and fixed her dark brown
eyes on him. "A man needs a woman."

"I don't need anyone." Paul didn't want to sound unkind
so he added, "Lily's a nice girl. And one day she'll be some
young man's wife."

"Why not yours?"

"She wouldn't be interested in an old man like me."

"You're not old. Couldn't be more than . . ." She studied him, then raised her eyebrows and said, "You're young
enough."

"I'm thirty-two, way too old for Lily."

"Of course you're not." A breeze blew dark hair into Sassa's eyes, but she seemed not to notice. "You need a girl who
can care for your needs."

"Sassa," Patrick said sharply.

"She's a good cook and she'll clean your house 'til it shines.
She knows how to fish and hunt and keep a garden—"

Patrick put a finger to his wife's lips. "Enough."

Sassa pouted. "Paul, you think about it." Her eyes held
his for a moment, then she turned and called the boys who
had found their way to the tip of the sandbar. "Time to go."
They tossed the last of their stones into the water and then
charged toward the boat. Sassa climbed in. "Paul, would you
like to have dinner with us? Lily's cooking."

Sassa's persistence was beyond belief, but Paul managed

a cheerful reply. "Thank you, but not tonight. I'm making a trip to Susitna Station first thing tomorrow."

"Why you going to Susitna?" Patrick asked.

"Hope to trade turnips and potatoes for traps. I'm running an extra line this winter."

"Been thinking of doing that myself. Seems the critters are putting on some heavy fur."

"Hope that means extra fine pelts this year." Paul headed for his boat. "Have a good day."

He pushed the dory into the water and climbed in. Sitting on the middle bench, he set his oars in the water and rowed toward the dock below his cabin. His mind turned to the letters in his pocket.

Paul set the mail on a small table beside an arm chair. Although anxious for word from home, he brewed coffee, took off his boots, and pushed his feet into moccasins before settling into his chair with a cup of coffee and a plate of cookies. He wanted to savor the touch from home.

Resting his feet on a wooden footstool, he crossed them at the ankle, then picked up an envelope and slid a finger under the seal. As he unfolded the letter, he immediately recognized his brother, Robert's, tidy script. Memories rushed at him. They'd had such good times . . . once.

Robert sounded happy. All was well. The financial slide seemed to be improving. In fact, he had hopes of making a trip north the following summer and wondered if Paul would object to the company.

Paul let the idea roll through his mind. He missed Robert. Growing up, the two had been close. They'd hunted and fished together. Paul envisioned the summer salmon run and knew it would thrill Robert.

He considered what it would be like to have his brother and family here on his homestead. Pleasure sifted through him. The company of those he loved and the sound of children would be heartening. Then reality pressed down. Their presence would also bring the darkness. He wasn't ready for that, not yet.

Returning to the letter, he read, "It would be even better if you came home. We miss you. The kids ask about you all the time. Four years has not erased Rebecca and John's memories of their favorite uncle. They're always asking, 'When is Uncle Paul coming home?'"

Wonder what they look like. Paul envisioned the twins. When he'd left, they resembled their father and one another, but their personalities couldn't be more different. Rebecca was all girl, and John was the type of kid who pushed the limits.

He and Robert used to joke about whether he'd live to grow up. Now Paul couldn't imagine joking about such a tragic possibility.

He turned his eyes back to the letter.

"If you won't move home, at least consider a visit. You can stay with me and Mary. We have plenty of room."

Paul allowed himself the treat of considering the idea. The family had often gathered at Robert's place, which provided spectacular views of the San Francisco Bay. The children played and the adults talked—about work and life—while feasting on the delicacies created by the Anderson women.

It had been the best of times. Paul shut off the thoughts. No good would come from dwelling on the past.

"We love you. Stay safe this winter in your wilderness refuge." It was signed simply, Robert.

Carefully folding the letter, Paul slid it back into its envelope. With a deep sigh, he wondered if his brother was right. Maybe he should return. The thought of family drew him homeward.

This is home now. It's a good place with good people. He set the letter aside and picked up the other one.

He opened the envelope from his friend and former colleague, Walter Henley. His letter was chatty and upbeat. He shared the latest news from San Francisco, the gossip about the elites, and updates from the hospital. And, thankfully, he made no plea for Paul's return.

The following morning it was still dark when Paul loaded sacks of turnips and potatoes into his boat. When he shoved off, dim light promised a new day and revealed damp brush and fog suspended above the quiet waters of the creek. When the back of the boat cleared the shallows, Paul pulled the starter rope of his Johnson outboard, and when it kicked in, he steered toward the river.

Early morning was his favorite time of day. It felt almost mystical—the whisper of night lingering to join dawn mists. He could feel the dew on his face and breathed in the scent of ripe highbush cranberries. The grasses along the river were chest high and drooped with moisture. The hum of his engine was the only sound except for an occasional mournful call of a loon. The world slept.

He pressed his back against the inside of the stern and kept his hand lightly on the tiller. Unexpectedly thoughts of Kate bombarded him. He wished he could share this magical world with her. He was certain she'd love it. Shaking her from his thoughts, he turned his attention to the river.

At Susitna Station, Paul steered the dory toward a small dock. All was quiet in the isolated hamlet, except for a barking dog. Two men leaned against one of several log cabins that stood in a row at the edge of the river.

When his boat gently bumped the dock, Paul looped a rope over a post and tied it off. He'd made good time and hopefully would be home by midday.

At the end of the dock, he trudged up steps leading to a wooden sidewalk and headed for the general store. Moving past the two men he'd seen from the river, he nodded and kept walking.

Charlie Agnak sat in front of the mercantile, his chair leaning against the building and his feet propped on a fat stump. The native man smiled, his eyes becoming slits and his face crinkling into hundreds of lines that reminded Paul of a map.

He stood, his short frame barely reaching Paul's shoulders. "Good to see you. Was beginning to wonder if you'd come before the snows."

"How's business?" Paul asked.

Charlie shrugged. "Okay, I guess."

"I was hoping to do some trading."

"What you got?"

"Potatoes and turnips."

"People round here always want vegetables, especially when winter's coming." He hobbled inside the store on bowed legs.

Paul followed.

Charlie moved to a barrel stove. He opened the door, then picked up two chunks of wood from a bin and shoved them into the fire. "Cold today."

Paul scanned the small store and spotted the legholds hanging on a far wall. He crossed the room to have a look. "I need a dozen new traps. What you want for them?"

"Well now, that depends." He grinned and rubbed his chin. "How much you got to trade?"

"I've got about a hundred pounds of potatoes and I'd say fifty pounds of turnips."

"You have more at home?"

"Yeah and some carrots too."

Charlie joined Paul. "These are nice traps, the best—lightweight, and they got a good, strong grip."

"I can add fifty pounds of carrots," Paul offered, knowing that Charlie never made a deal without dickering.

Charlie pushed his fingers through black hair lying flat against his forehead, then with a smile extended his hand. "You got a deal." He took six traps down and limped to a register.

Paul grabbed six more and carried them to the front of the store. "I'll take the traps out and bring in my half of the trade."

"Good." Charlie leaned over a ledger and wrote in it.

Paul hauled in the first of the potatoes. "Where do you want these?"

Charlie nodded toward the north wall. "Set 'em over there." He stuck his pencil over his ear.

Paul deposited the sack against the wall, then returned to the boat for the rest of the vegetables.

"Doubt they'll stay in the root cellar long," Charlie said. "Already got people asking about spuds." He sat in a chair near the stove. "How're things on the crick?"

"No complaints. Had a run-in with some wolves, though."

"Wolves?" Using his pencil, Charlie scratched his scalp.

"Yeah. A pack came after me. Managed to shoot three of them and the others took off."

"They been back?"

"They came nosing around. But Patrick and I had traps set out. We got two of them."

"Don't hear much about wolves going after people." Charlie stared at the sacks of vegetables, then looked at Paul. "Fellas around here are saying we're in for a bad winter."

"Yeah. First week of September and there's already snow on Mount Susitna."

Charlie nodded. "You figure on being back before Christmas?"

"By Thanksgiving. I'll bring the carrots then."

"Good." Charlie folded his arms over his chest. "Have a sit and a cup of coffee."

Paul knew all about Charlie's coffee. It was black as mud and tasted worse. "I'd sure like to, but I've got to head home. There's work waiting for me." He hefted the remaining traps and walked to the door. "See you in a few weeks."

"Watch out for those wolves." Charlie propped his feet on the wood box next to the stove, looking like he was settling in for the day. "Say hello to Patrick and Klaus for me. Haven't seen neither of them in a while."

"Patrick'll be by, but I don't know about Klaus. His rheumatism's bothering him. I'll give him a hello from you, though." Paul opened the door and headed for his boat. He chucked the traps into the hull and then shoved off, heading back the way he'd come.

Darkness settled over the cabin as Paul set to work repairing a fur hat. Wood snapped and popped in the stove, and the aroma of burning spruce and alder pervaded the room. A lantern flickered, providing just enough light for him to see.

He bent over the hat, pushing a large needle with heavy twine into a torn ear flap. He pulled it through the other side and tugged it snug. If his ear was exposed to the cold, he could lose it to frostbite.

He squinted, trying to keep the stitches tight and even. His coarse hands caught on the fur. He stopped and set the cap in his lap. Turning his palms up, he studied them. They were chapped and calloused. A flash of memory reminded him of the work they'd once done and how they'd looked.

A *lot has changed*, he thought, feeling the familiar squeeze of pain in his chest. *Stay busy. Don't think.* But no matter how he tried, he couldn't keep the memories at bay and couldn't stop wishing things had stayed as they were.

— 8 —

Kate grabbed her gear and stepped out of the plane. A frigid wind cut through her as she made her way across the field to the workshed. Pilots Jack Rydell and Kenny Hicks stood outside the door, huddled in fur-lined coats. As usual, Jack had a cigar clenched between his teeth. Just the idea of the cigar stink that clung to the man made Kate's stomach turn. She wished there was some way to avoid him, but Sidney insisted all pilots check in after runs.

Keeping her head down against the strengthening gale, Kate wondered what she had done to get Jack's dander up. Only thing she could figure was her gender. He didn't like female pilots. He'd made that clear. *He probably sits up nights thinking of ways to get under my skin.*

She glanced at Kenny. He wasn't as bad as Jack, but he still needled her regularly. She didn't know where he got off ridiculing anyone—he was, at best, a mediocre pilot.

Not willing to let either of them know their teasing and disrespect unsettled her, she relaxed her shoulders and forced a smile. "What're you guys doing out here? It's freezing."

"Waiting on passengers." Wind grabbed at Kenny's hood and pulled it away from his face. Dark curls whipped wildly about his head. He pulled the hood back on. "How 'bout you? Done with the mail run?" He used a disparaging tone.

Not about to take the bait, Kate said amiably, "Yeah. It was a good day." She glanced at the gray sky. "Looks like we're in for it now, though."

"Yeah, storm's coming in." Jack moved his cigar from one side of his mouth to the other. "Won't keep me on the ground. Got a group heading for Nome."

Arrogant half-wit. Always has to be one up on everyone. "Might be wise to wait for the weather to clear."

"A little wind doesn't scare me."

Kate eyed him, wondering whether she cared enough to spar with him, then thought of the passengers he'd be transporting. "Your riders might feel differently." Kate couldn't keep the crankiness out of her voice. "You could be forced down."

Wearing a smirk, Jack said, "Don't worry about me." He turned his gaze to Kate's plane. "You worry about yourself and that albatross you fly."

Kate felt instant indignation. He could say what he wanted about her, but her plane was first-rate. "A pilot can hardly do better than a Bellanca Pacemaker. It'll handle just about anything."

"You try a Stinson and you'll never go back to that crate." He lifted his lip in a sneer. "A Stinson'll get you where you want to go a lot faster and without all the shuddering of that workhorse of yours."

"Better a workhorse that can go the distance than a thoroughbred that can't make a second lap." Before Jack could say anything more, Kate opened the shop door and stepped inside, slamming the door behind her. Fuming, she muttered, "What's wrong with that man."

Sidney looked up from where he sat, feet propped on the desktop. "What are you mumbling about?"

"Jack. He infuriates me."

Sidney grinned. "You're not the only one."

"Yeah, but I'm the only woman. He gives me twice as much grief as everyone else." She glanced at the door. "And he takes too many risks."

"You don't?"

Caught off guard, Kate said more quietly, "Not unless I have to." She knew she'd been pushing hard, but it wasn't easy being the only female pilot on the crew. There was always pressure to prove she could keep up.

"Don't let Jack get under your skin. It just feeds his oversized ego."

"Easier said than done." Pulling off her gloves, Kate moved to the ledger hanging on the wall, marked off her name, and filled in the time of arrival, then crossed to the stove and held her palms out to the heat.

"Glad to see you're back," Sidney said. "How are things on the peninsula?"

"Not too bad, but it'll probably be wicked by tonight." The heat made her cheeks burn, so she turned her back to the stove. She glanced at the window. "Isn't it early in the season for this kind of weather?"

"Yeah, but I'm not sure there's a normal for Alaska. It'll probably move through, though, and things will warm up again."

A gust of wind bashed the door. "You going to let Jack fly passengers up to Nome in this?"

"Already tried to reason with him." He sipped coffee from a tin cup. "He's his own boss, nothing I can do. And the people flying with him should be able to think for themselves." Sidney shook his head. "Jack'll catch it one day. He's got bush pilot's syndrome bad. A close shave'll usually cure most pilots, but not Jack. Only makes him feel more invincible."

"Is Mike out?" Kate asked, feeling a prickle of fear.

"He's in Talkeetna. Figure he'll stay put until the weather clears. He's mostly levelheaded." Sidney finished off his coffee, then walked to the stove and refilled his cup.

Kate watched the black liquid dribble into the tin. "Don't know how you drink that stuff. It's got more bite than a mama bear."

Sidney kept his eyes on Kate and took an extra-large slurp. "Ahh, good and strong, just the way I like it. You need to adapt your taste buds." He grinned, then with his voice laden with concern, said, "Frank's still out."

"Where is he?"

"Fairbanks. The storm's coming down from the north. Figured he'd put in a call by now. Haven't heard anything yet."

"Frank'll be okay. He's the most sensible one of us all." Kate grabbed a piece of peppermint candy from a dish that Sidney kept on his desk. Using her tongue, she pushed it into her cheek. "So, when do I get to take out something other than mail? I'm ready."

"You think a month of flying makes you ready?"

"I've been in a plane most of my life."

"Not up here you haven't." He set his cup on the desk. "I know you're antsy to take on more, but caution's your best bet."

"How long did Mike have to wait before he was given real runs? Or Jack?"

Sidney shifted his gaze away from Kate. "That's different."

"How is it different?"

"Well, they're—"

"Men?"

Sidney clenched his jaw.

"It's not fair. And you know it. I can fly with the best of

them." Kate's frustration drove her to push harder. "I understand the treatment from guys like Kenny and Jack, but I figured I'd get better from you."

Annoyance flickered in Sidney's eyes, and Kate knew she'd gone too far. If she wanted to keep her job, she'd best retreat. She stomped to the door, opened it, then stopped and turned to look at Sidney. "I'm sorry. I know you're just watching out for me."

Sidney gave a nod, but said nothing. Kate stepped outside and into the rising gale.

A gust of wind and spattering of snow blew in with Kate when she walked into the store. Warm, spiced air welcomed her.

Helen smiled from behind the counter. "I was wondering when you'd get in. I've been praying for you."

"I'm glad to be here instead of out there," Kate said, pushing back her hood. "It's really blowing." A corner of her mind went to Jack. She hoped he'd be sensible and cancel his flight.

"Mail came for you today." Helen pulled open a drawer.

"Who from?" Kate stripped off her gloves.

Helen fished out two envelopes. Looking at them she said, "One from your parents. And this says Richard Benning." She lifted her eyebrows. "And who is Richard?"

Kate stared at the envelope. "Richard?" She could see his handsome face and sky blue eyes. She hadn't allowed herself to think about him. "He's just a friend." Trying to act nonchalant, she took the letters.

Wind blasted the front windows. Helen reached for her coat. "I was just getting ready to head home. If I don't go now, I'm liable to spend the night here." She pulled on her coat, buttoned it, and snugged her fur-lined hood around her face. "Will you be all right?"

"Don't worry about me. I've got plenty of firewood. I'll just snuggle down and read a book."

"Okay, dear. I'll see you tomorrow, then."

Once in her room, Kate set the mail on the table, then stoked the fire. After putting water on to boil, she sat and unlaced her boots. She slid them off and pushed her feet into slippers, then picked up her mail and moved to the sofa. With her feet tucked under her, she pulled a blanket around her shoulders.

For a long moment, she stared at the envelope with Richard's bold handwriting. Was he still angry? She slid a finger under the seal, lifted out the letter, and opened it.

"*Dear Kate,*" he began. She took a deep breath. That didn't sound angry. "*Since you left, I've done nothing but think about you. I know you don't believe there's a chance for us and maybe there isn't, but I want to try. Love is strong enough to heal all wounds. If you can give me any hope, I'll wait for you.*"

Kate stopped reading and pressed the letter to her chest. What did she feel for Richard? An ache like that of homesickness pressed down on her. Had she been too impulsive? Piloting in Alaska was harder than she'd imagined. And yet, she felt as if she belonged here.

Her eyes returned to the letter. "*I'm trying to understand your reason for going. I want you to be happy, but please consider coming home. In the meantime be careful. I dread receiving word that something terrible has happened to you. I don't think I could bear that.*

I've been busy. Got hired on at a new government project and there'll be lots of work, as long as the winter isn't too hard. I'll be saving up money, maybe enough for a trip north. If you come down, even for a visit, maybe we can go fishing, and you can take me flying."

Kate's heart squeezed, remembering warm summer days spent at their favorite fishing spots.

"*I'm waiting. Please write back soon. All my love, Richard.*"

Melancholy settled over Kate. She missed him.

She folded the letter and returned it to the envelope. Could she return? Should she? Kate couldn't imagine giving up her new life. The possibility of Richard moving to Alaska flashed through her mind and hope flickered. Was it possible? Maybe she should ask him?

That night the gale charged down from the north. Temperatures plummeted, and winds howled, lashing Kate's bedroom window with icy pellets. The small stove in her apartment barely staved off the cold. Several times during the night she climbed from beneath her blankets to feed the fire. Each time her mind went to Richard and the possibility of his moving north. She couldn't imagine him leaving his home or his family. Everything that mattered to him was in Washington. It wouldn't be fair to ask him.

She bundled deeper beneath the covers, but still cold raised gooseflesh on her skin. Clearly, she'd need more blankets before winter truly set in. With the wind wailing outdoors, she lay in the darkness, her unsettled mind rolling around questions and doubts.

When the first light of day pushed back the darkness, Kate peered at the clock. It was nearly eight. Feeling as if she hadn't slept, she climbed from beneath her blankets and moved to the window. Ice had crystallized on the interior glass and she could barely see the frigid outside world. She hoped Mike and Frank were safe. She even felt concern for Jack. As infuriating as he was, Kate didn't want him hurt and hoped he'd stayed put.

She returned to her bed, the warmest place in the room, and briefly fell back to sleep. She woke to a hush. The wind had stopped. She scraped away enough ice from the window to see outside. The alley had been transformed into a sparkling white world. There was only an inch or two of snow, but like a frozen cape, it clung to everything.

She heard the door to the store open and wondered who had come in so early. No one usually showed up until 10:00 on Saturdays. A few moments later, a knock sounded at her door.

"Just a minute," she said, pulling a quilt around her.

She opened the door to Albert, who was bundled in an oversized parka, his face barely visible in the midst of a heavy fur fringe. His expression was serious.

"Is something wrong?" Kate asked.

"Got a call from Sidney."

Kate's stomach tightened.

"Says he needs you at the airfield."

"Did he say why?"

"Nope. Just that he wants you there quick."

"Okay."

Kate started to close the door, but Albert caught it. "You be careful. It's not a good day to be out. The wind's quieted down, but it's frozen out there and the snow could start coming down again." Albert gripped the door. "Don't do anything foolish."

"I'll be careful."

With a nod, he walked back into the store and called over his shoulder, "I'll give you a ride to the airfield."

Kate closed the door, and as she dressed, she prayed—for Mike and Frank and for Kenny and Jack too. She grabbed her gear and hurried out of the room. When she stepped outside, the cold hit her hard, sucking oxygen from her lungs. With her hood pulled over her face, she put her head down, stuck gloved hands in her pockets, and tramped toward Albert's Model A sedan.

Sliding onto the front seat, she said, "Time I got my own car."

"I'll keep an eye out for one." Albert pulled away from the curb. He gripped the steering wheel and peered through a space he'd cleared on the windshield.

When they reached the airstrip, the only planes on the field were Kenny's Stinson and Kate's Bellanca, which had already been started.

"I'll wait," Albert said.

Kate hurried toward the office, hoping Sidney didn't have bad news.

When she stepped inside he was bent over a map on his desk. He looked up. "Good. You're here."

"Is something wrong? Are the fellas okay?"

"Yeah, they're all right. But I got a call about some hikers at McKinley Park. They set out early yesterday, before the storm hit. They were supposed to be on a one-day hike, but no one's heard from them. They weren't set up for bad weather." He shook his head. "Tourists." Settling serious eyes on Kate, he said, "I need a pilot to have a look-see. You up to it?"

Kate felt a pulse of excitement. "I'm ready, but what about Kenny?"

"I'd rather you went. They got hit pretty good by snow up that way and the weather's still bad." He leaned back in his chair. "You don't have to go. I can call him."

"No. I'll do it," Kate said, ignoring the alarms going off in her head. This was her chance. And obviously Sidney thought she was up to the challenge.

Sidney grinned. "Didn't think you'd turn down the opportunity. I've got your plane ready. Even got the skis on for you." His brow furrowed. "You can land with skis, right?"

"Sure. No problem. Tell me where I need to go."

Armed with survival gear, a map, and hopes of finding the lost hikers, Kate flew over McKinley Park. Light snow swirled at her, pelting the windshield. Gusting winds bombarded the plane.

She caught sight of the camp at McKinley Park Station where the hikers had been staying. It wasn't much, just a cabin and a few tents, now barely visible among the trees piled with fresh snow.

Kate gazed out at the rugged countryside and figured the tourists couldn't have traveled too far from camp. She turned in the direction they'd reportedly headed and scanned the terrain. Anchorage had gotten very little snow, but it had dumped here.

The mountains were hidden behind low-lying clouds, but Kate knew they were there and she dare not fly too close. The fresh snowfall made changes in altitude hard to distinguish. Dwarfed spruce were piled with what looked like white pillows, and bare-limbed aspen reminded her of frozen white skeletons.

There'd be no footprints to follow, unless the hikers were moving, which she hoped they weren't. Of course prints left by predators might lead her to them. Word had gotten around about what had happened to Paul, and she thought about wolves being enticed by easy prey. A tremor of revulsion rippled through her.

Kate flew back and forth over the countryside, following a grid laid out in her mind. When she didn't find anything, she widened the search, careful to keep watch on her gauges. Even if she located the hikers, she'd need enough fuel to take off and get home again.

Her nerves prickled with tension as time ticked by and there was still no sign of the park visitors. How could she face Sidney if she didn't find them? How could she face herself?

The snow had stopped and the wind had quieted, which gave Kate hope. With her fuel measuring low, she dove down over a broad valley with a frozen stream winding through it. *Maybe they decided to follow the creek.*

Scanning the white mantle, she watched for anything unusual as she moved up the basin. *Lord, show me where they are.*

The sun cut through thinning clouds, turning the landscape brilliantly white. Everything glistened, reminding Kate how cold it was down there. She wondered how anyone exposed to the storm could have survived.

Her fuel dwindling, Kate knew she'd have to head back soon. She pushed on. They might be alive. She couldn't let them down.

She saw a flash of red. Was it blood? Wolves had likely made a kill. She told herself it was probably a moose.

Turning the plane toward the splotch of crimson, Kate pushed the stick forward and headed down, just above the trees. As she approached the place with the scarlet stain, she steeled herself against what she'd find.

And then she saw it.

"It's a jacket!" Kate laughed. "A plaid jacket!"

A shadow appeared from beneath a white mound. An arm waved. Someone was signaling her! "They're alive!" Kate could barely believe her good luck.

She tipped the wings to acknowledge that she'd seen them, then made a broad turn and searched for a place to put down. Everything looked the same—white. Kate knew dangers lurked beneath the snow—snags, rocks, hollows. Her skin bristled with alarm.

She spotted an open section of ground. There didn't seem

to be any trees or other obstacles so she made a pass over it. Things looked good. She took one more run by the area and then lined up for a landing.

Three people tromped through the snow, waving their arms and looking up at her. Kate gripped the stick and rested her feet on the pedals. She'd have to finesse this one. Realizing she'd been holding her breath, she let it out and then breathed in slowly. She moved downward, squinting against the brightness of sun reflecting off snow.

A white world rushed at her and then disappeared beneath the plane. She felt the touch of skis and held the Bellanca steady, nose up slightly. And then she was down, rushing toward a limb she hadn't seen from the air, sticking up out of the crude runway. Kate held tight, hoping it would give instead of gouge. She passed over it without difficulty, slowed the plane, and stopped.

With a rush of relief, she pressed her forehead against the control panel. She didn't know whether to cry or to cheer. She heard shouts from outside and saw the three lost hikers hurrying toward her, floundering through deep snow. Elation swept through Kate and she climbed to the back of the plane and pushed open the door.

She'd barely stepped out when the grateful hikers rushed her, swamping her with hugs, pats on the back, handshakes, and words of gratitude. Kate laughed and then giving them a closer look, asked, "You all right?"

"We are now," the smaller of the three said, his chapped lips spreading into a grin.

"It was a humdinger of a storm. I was afraid I wouldn't find you."

"It was Mark who saved us. He knew what to do." The small man turned to one of the others who sported a heavy beard. "He showed us how to build a snow cave. We climbed in and kept each other warm." Extending his hand, he said, "I'm Tom Sheffield. And it's a pleasure to meet you."

Mark moved forward and grabbed hold of her hand, shaking it hard. "Figured we were done for."

The last of the three nodded at Kate. "Steve Jones. Thanks, ma'am. We were watching the skies, but didn't see nothin' all morning."

"I'm the best they had today." She grinned, feeling a sense of euphoria at having proven herself capable.

Tom rested a hand on her arm. "How 'bout that—saved by a woman." He laughed. "Wait 'til I tell my wife. She'll be saying she told me so and rubbing it in the rest of my days. But that's okay by me."

"We better get you home," Kate said, stepping toward the plane.

While her passengers piled in, she gave the craft a quick check to make sure everything was intact. Satisfied all was well, she climbed in.

After a perfect takeoff, she soared over the trees and headed toward home. She'd never felt such exultation. This was her first real Alaska rescue, a dream come true. Her mind flashed to Alison and she wished she could tell her about the day. They'd always shared everything. *She would have been proud of me.*

And Richard . . . well, Kate knew now that she couldn't return to Yakima. And he wanted a traditional wife, whether it was in the states or in Alaska. That wasn't her. Kate's life had changed forever. She was meant to be a bush pilot and an Alaskan.

K ate looked out the window of her plane. Her passengers were late. Hunters from the states, big-money types from New York, had scheduled a flight into the Talkeetna Mountains for a sheep hunt. All Kate had to do was drop them off and return to pick them up in a week.

She hadn't flown since rescuing the hikers. Compared to that, this was easy duty. Still, her nerves hummed along the surface of her skin at the thought of her first booked riders. She gazed at the sky where wisps of clouds looked like filigree against a pale blue background. Fear of failure niggled its way into her good mood. What if something went wrong? What if she botched things? As guilt from the past reached for her, she turned her attention to a map Mike had given her, along with instructions for the best spot to put down.

Kate studied the flight plan. She trusted Mike and figured there shouldn't be any difficulties. Folding the map so she could read it more easily, she set it on the passenger seat, then picked up her grandmother's Bible and opened it to Jeremiah 29. The leather was well worn and the pages yellowed.

She found the eleventh verse. It was underlined. " '*For I*

know the plans I have for you,' declares the LORD, 'plans to prosper you and not to harm you, plans to give you hope and a future. Then you will call upon me and come and pray to me, and I will listen to you.'"

Kate soaked in the promise and closed her eyes. *Watch over me, Lord. Help me do this right.*

Her prayer was interrupted by the sound of a pickup. It stopped in front of the office. Kate set her Bible back on the seat. *Must be my guys.* She climbed out of the plane and walked toward the building.

By the time she reached the shop, the men were already inside. She stopped at the door, sucked in a deep breath, and let it out slowly. "This'll be a breeze," she told herself and then stepped into the office.

Three men, dressed for the outdoors, stood in a half circle around Sidney's desk. When Kate shut the door, they turned and stared at her. They didn't look happy. Kate's stomach did a flip.

"Hey, Kate." Sidney pushed to his feet. "I was just telling these gentlemen about you."

Hand extended, she stepped toward the man closest to her.

Ignoring the gesture, he turned to Sidney. "I paid good money. And I didn't sign on for a woman pilot. You get one of your guys down here. Now."

Kate awkwardly withdrew her hand and tucked it inside her coat pocket. Anger heated up inside.

Sidney stayed calm. He raised his eyebrows slightly and smiled. Kate had seen him do this before when he needed to cool down a hot situation. "She's all we got today, fellas. If you want to fly, it's her or no one."

All three men sized up Kate. Finally the one who'd demanded that someone else be called said, "All right. But I'll never buy a ride from you again." He compressed his lips, crumpling his mustache into what resembled a crawling caterpillar.

Ignoring his comment, Sidney said, "We'll get you loaded up, but first I'd like to introduce you to your pilot." He moved to Kate's side and put an arm around her shoulders. "This is Kate Evans, one of my best."

Kate felt a jolt of surprise, but figured Sidney was just trying to make her look good. She wouldn't let him down.

He nodded at the man who'd spoken. "This is Carl Brown." Carl barely looked at Kate. "And his brothers Ralph and Norman."

Ralph, the shortest and roundest of the three, almost smiled before following Carl and Norman out the door. "Our gear's in the truck," Carl said, then glanced at Kate and asked, "Your plane the red one?"

"That's it," Kate said nonchalantly. Inside she fumed, but she wasn't about to give these guys the satisfaction of knowing they'd gotten under her skin. Besides, starting a war before getting in the air was ill-advised.

Carl led the way to the Bellanca, leaving Kate to get the provisions.

"I'll give you a hand," Sidney said, glowering at the hunters' backs.

The men watched passively while Sidney and Kate worked. Carl leaned against the craft, smoking a cigarette. He talked about the trophy he'd be bringing back.

With the last bag in hand, Kate walked toward the plane, trying to convince herself that once they were in the air things would improve. They'd see she was a competent pilot and behave appropriately. She imagined their surprise at her skill and the apology that would follow.

Ralph approached her. "So, how long a flight is it?"

"Not far. I'll drop you outside of Palmer, along the Matanuska River." The odor of liquor hung in the air.

He looked at the plane. "Ever have any trouble?"

"No, never." Kate hefted the bag into the back, thinking about Rimrock Lake. It didn't count—she'd been barely more than a kid then.

With everything loaded, Sidney said, "You're set." He eyed Carl. "Better watch out for bears. The sound of a rifle will bring them in."

"How do you mean?" Ralph asked, his eyes widening slightly.

Sidney smiled. Kate knew he was playing with them. "A downed animal is an easy meal, and the bears know what it means when a rifle is fired off."

"Really?"

Carl smacked his brother between the shoulder blades. "He's pulling your leg. Bears are hibernating now."

"That's partly true. Some of the females are denned up, but those big males are still roaming around." He set a hard stare on Carl. "If you get a sheep, you'd better bag it good and hang it in a tree. And camp away from the game." He headed for the office, wearing a smirk.

Kate smiled while she cranked the plane. The men piled in and found their seats. She boarded, closed the door, and made her way to the front, careful not to let her legs touch her passengers. Wearing slacks among this group made her feel exposed. After tucking the hand crank in its place, she dropped into her seat and started the engine. It whined and then caught, rumbling.

"It's freezing in here," Carl griped.

"When the engine warms up, we'll warm up," Kate hollered back, checking the gauges. Everything looked good. She turned and called over her shoulder, "Stay in your seats while we're in the air. It can get bumpy."

"Where ya think we're gonna walk to?" Norman asked, with a snicker.

Kate ignored the jibe.

Ralph leaned toward Kate. "Is there supposed to be foul weather?"

"No. But you never know what to expect when you're in the air." Kate glanced at the pudgy man. He looked nervous. She grinned and revved the engine.

While the Bellanca rolled down the runway and lifted off, the men were quiet. Kate turned northeast and headed toward the Talkeetna Mountains. "If you look out your windows you can see Cook Inlet," she called over the thrum of the engine.

"Hey, look there," Norman shouted. "A ship's coming into the harbor."

"You never seen a boat before?" Carl taunted.

Kate ignored her passengers and focused on flying. Once on course, she picked up the map and looked it over. It wouldn't be too difficult to find her way. She'd follow the Matanuska River until she reached the glacier and then she'd look for the landmarks Sidney had noted.

Unexpectedly, a sharp wind punched the plane in the side. The Bellanca shuddered and dipped.

"What's wrong?" Carl hollered.

"Just a little turbulence. Gets up under the wings and makes her vibrate. It's normal." Kate glanced back, unable to conceal a smile when she saw that Carl's complexion had turned pallid.

Kate flew north over forests of spruce, birch, and alder, now mostly bare. A broad valley emerged and the forests fell away. Trees stood in clusters amidst a patchwork of farmlands, and green earth could be seen where the snow had melted. The Talkeetna Mountains angled up from the valley floor.

They weren't as impressive as the Chugach, but they were still stunning.

"Looks like farms down there," Ralph said.

"Yeah. They're colonists from the Midwest."

"Read about that," Carl said. "It'll never work. The government's got things fouled up."

"Nothing worthwhile is easy," Kate said, barely able to keep her voice congenial. "The valley's got good farmland and the colonists are hard workers. They grow some fearsome vegetables. Biggest cabbages produced anywhere."

"Cabbages. Who needs cabbages?" Carl pulled a cigar out of his pocket and went to light it.

"No smoking." Kate gripped the stick more tightly and waited.

Without a word he returned the cigar to his pocket, and Kate blew out a relieved breath. She didn't want to spar with him.

The valley sprawled beneath the plane. It was beautiful. Kate wondered if her parents might consider moving to the valley. She'd have to ask them.

"Why'd they come up here?" Norman asked.

"Who?"

"The colonists," he said, his voice dripping with disdain.

"The drought decimated their farms, so the government moved two hundred families here to give them a new start. The plan is that they'll produce food for Alaskans." Kate was thankful she'd been listening when Albert told her about the colonists. It made her sound knowledgeable about the territory.

She followed the broad river, which was banded by several small tributaries. Gray water fed by the Matanuska Glacier cut through dirtied snow.

Leaving the valley behind, she used the river as a guide. The Talkeetna Mountains pressed in from the north and the Chugach from the south. Green spruce stuck up above woodlands of alder and birch. The river wound through the dense forests, sometimes narrowing and growing deep and then expanding and drifting into small streams.

"How far we got?" Norman asked. "I gotta use the john."

"Nearly there. If you can't wait, I keep a can stowed under the backseat." Kate felt a flush heat her cheeks. She kept her eyes forward.

"I can wait."

When Kate caught her first glimpse of the glacier, relief swept through her. She was nearly there. Now all she needed was to find the landing site.

The glacier looked like a giant frozen river winding out of the Chugach Mountains. She'd never seen anything like it.

"What's that?" Ralph asked.

"The Matanuska Glacier."

She flew closer to get a better look. The river of ice didn't meander. It was an undulating frozen flow, cutting its way through the mountains. Blue and white ribbons pushed up, forming jagged peaks that fell into small chasms. The amazing sight took Kate's breath away.

Reluctantly she swung back to her original course. She finally saw Sheep Rock with its distinctive dark jagged peaks jutting up from the forested landscape. She searched for the landing site.

"You said it wasn't far. I gotta go."

"It's right down there." Kate nodded toward a sandbar. She'd made it. Decreasing the power and holding slight back pressure on the elevator, she descended and made a pass over the landing strip. It was made up of small rocks and looked fairly level. There were remnants of snow from the rogue storm that had pushed through, but it looked good for landing. Kate's confidence grew. The Bellanca ought to do fine. She made a wide sweep and set up for the approach.

The plane touched down with little difficulty, bouncing only once when the wheels touched the crude runway. Kate rolled to a stop. Norman pushed open the door and hurried to a nearby bush to relieve himself.

While the hunters had a look around, Kate unloaded the supplies. She piled their provisions far enough away from the plane so they wouldn't be an obstacle when she took off.

"I'll be back in a week," she called. No response. "Be ready when I get here."

Carl gave her a half wave.

"Fine," Kate groused and returned to the plane. Revolted by the men, she watched them cross the sandbar and hoped their kind weren't what she could expect for passengers. Carl pointed at something on the ridge and made gestures Kate guessed had something to do with hunting strategies. She started the engine, thinking the hunters ought to be setting up camp. It would be dark soon. Deciding their problems weren't hers to worry about, she left them and headed back to Anchorage.

The week passed quickly. When it was time to return to the Matanuska to pick up the New York hunters, Kate set off with trepidation. She didn't like the Brown brothers, and she'd be glad to have the trip behind her. Climbing into the plane, she told herself that if she was going to be a bush pilot, she couldn't be picky about who flew with her. She'd have to toughen up.

Fresh snow had fallen during the night, leaving a layer of white on the trees and ground. Kate headed up the Matanuska and soon spotted tracks leading away from the river toward the mountains. She was ahead of schedule so decided to have a look at what had left the markings. They most likely belonged to wolves.

The prints wound through the forest and into a gorge. Although Kate knew better than to wander off her designated flight plan, interest drove her. *I'll follow just a little way. A quick look is all I need.*

She stayed low, making it easier to see the trail. Several times it disappeared beneath foliage but would soon reemerge. Finally, Kate was rewarded by the sight of a wolf pack. It had downed something.

The snow was bloodied and they were feasting on a fresh kill. Seemingly unaware of the plane, they ripped flesh from a moose that still steamed in the cold morning air. She circled back and flew over again, this time lower. Some of the wolves stared at the sky and cowered, but weren't intimidated enough to give up their prize. She looped around and returned for another look. The pack ate, this time barely aware of the plane overhead.

Kate turned back toward the river, thrilled at having witnessed wildlife in their natural, though base, state. Her thoughts remained with the wolves until she realized she'd lost her bearings. Everything looked the same. Alarm stood the hair on her arms on end. Then in the distance she spotted a familiar mountain ridge and blew out a relieved breath.

Life could change in a moment. She should have known better. Just like the day she'd killed Alison, she was being careless and larking about. Kate clenched her teeth. *When will I learn?*

It was late morning by the time she reached the landing site. She hoped her riders were ready to leave. When she flew over the sandbar, they were waiting with their gear piled beside them.

She put down without mishap. Two sets of magnificent

spiraling horns sat on the ground near the men. *So they got their rams.* Kate's eyes went to a canvas bag hanging from a nearby tree. She smiled. They'd been listening when Sidney warned them about bears.

Ralph and Norman moved to the tree while Kate climbed out of the plane and headed toward Carl, who stood beside the trophies. He walked toward her, clutching a half-empty liquor bottle in one hand. His gait was unsteady. Kate groaned. He was drunk.

"Where were you?" he demanded. "We expected you early. You said you'd be early." His words seemed to slam together.

"It's early enough." Kate wasn't about to tell him about her sightseeing trip. She watched as Norman lowered the meat from the tree, then turned her gaze to the pile of gear and back to Carl. "You ready?"

"Been ready." He took a drink from the bottle.

Kate moved to the supplies. "How about some help?" She didn't even try to keep the irritation out of her voice.

"What do you think I pay you for?" Carl smirked.

Kate ignored him. Ralph and Norman hauled the bagged meat toward the plane. "Put it behind the seats. Make sure to distribute it evenly. If the weight's not balanced, the plane won't maneuver properly. And we can't have too much weight all in the back."

Ralph hefted the game into the plane, then helped Kate with the gear.

Carl and Norman lugged the horns. They were still bloody.

"Looks like you had a good hunt," Kate said.

"We did." Norman grinned. "You should have seen—"

"Dry up," Carl ordered. "Let's go."

Kate shot him a look of annoyance. "Can you bag those horns? They'll stink when they warm up."

"Yeah, we got a bag," Ralph said, searching through a pack.

Kate double-checked the load, moving some forward so they wouldn't be too heavy in the tail, then she stood at the open door. "Time to head out."

After they got in, she climbed down and, pressing a foot against one of the tires, used the hand crank on the flywheel. When the whine reached the right pitch, she removed the crank, climbed into the plane, and closed the door. The compartment stank of booze.

"No drinking in my plane." She moved toward the cockpit. Carl slapped her bottom as she passed. Kate stopped and glared at him. "Don't *ever* do that again."

His mouth turned up in a lopsided grin. "I'll do as I like."

"I'll put you off the plane."

"You think so?" He tried to stand, but there wasn't room to fit his full height. "You gonna make me?"

They stared at each other. Kate wasn't a small woman, but she knew he had the upper hand. There was no way she could force him to do something he didn't want to do. She felt powerless.

"Cut it out," Ralph said. "I want to get home. I've had enough of the great outdoors." He pulled on Carl's arm and dragged him down to his seat.

Kate remained where she was for a few moments. That way it looked like she'd won the argument. She still had her teeth clenched when she took her place up front and pulled the starter. There was no response. She held back a moan and gave it another try. Still no luck. *I can't be stuck here with these baboons.* She turned it again, but it still didn't respond.

"You got a problem with this crate?" Carl tried to stand but fell back into his seat.

Kate didn't answer. Instead she climbed out and cranked

the flywheel again, then tried the starter one more time, and the engine turned over, roaring to life. Relief whooshed out of Kate's lungs in a big breath. She revved the engine, then readied for takeoff. When the plane lifted into the air, she turned toward Anchorage, thinking she couldn't get there soon enough.

Even though Kate had said no drinking, Carl continued. His talk became more belligerent with each swallow. He kept moving from one seat to another.

"Sit down! And stay put!" Kate hollered.

He ignored her and crawled toward the back.

"Hey, leave that alone," Ralph shouted just as a loud pop and a rush of air reverberated through the cabin.

He'd opened the door! Icy air blasted through the compartment. The sound was so loud it nearly drowned out the engine noise.

"The door's open!" Ralph shrieked.

Carl grabbed for it. Kate's stomach tightened. He wasn't steady enough. He'd fall out. "Carl, sit down! The wind will keep it closed!" Hoping to get him away from the door, Kate banked the plane and he stumbled backward. Carl clambered to his seat.

"Stay put!" she yelled. The door banged from bursts of air.

"What do we do?" Norman asked, his voice quaking.

"Everyone stays away from the door and we fly home. We'll be okay. Just stay in your seats." Kate had never flown with a door ajar, but she'd heard it wouldn't hurt the plane's lift or maneuverability.

"It's cold. Isn't there something we can do?" Norman whined.

"No. There isn't." Kate gripped the stick, unable to believe what had happened. She glanced back at Carl. The color had drained from his face.

"I'm not feeling so good," he said.

"If you upchuck on my plane, you'll clean up after yourself." Kate was furious. "There's a bag under the seat . . . or you can use the can."

Carl found the bag just in time. Looking limp, he slouched in his seat. He might have passed out. Kate hoped so.

Terror written on their faces, Ralph and Norman eyed the door. It continued to thump.

When Kate reached the airfield, she couldn't remember ever feeling more relief. She put the plane down without difficulty and was already thinking about what she'd tell Sidney.

Her mind shouted at her, drowning out reasonable thought. *I failed. I couldn't control my passengers. I'll never be able to do this. Thinking I could be a bush pilot was a cockamamie idea.*

Kate wrestled with the mental insurrection. *It was just one unruly customer. It could happen to anyone.*

She tried to focus on what she'd done right. *I managed to get us back on the ground safely.* Feeling slightly better, she decided that after this, she'd set rules from the get-go and she'd carry a pistol.

She turned and faced her clients. "I want you out! Get your stuff and get out of my plane!"

Ralph and Norman managed to haul Carl to the truck and then did as Kate had told them. As they gathered their belongings, they looked more humiliated than angry.

Kate wondered how she'd keep the events of the trip to herself. The guys would have a heyday with it. She looked around the field. Thankfully, Mike's plane was the only one on the ground. *He won't say anything.* But Kate wondered about Sidney. This was too good a story to keep to himself. In spite of her frustration, Kate laughed to herself and walked toward the office.

— 10 —

Kate leaned over the Plymouth Coupe and scraped ice off the windshield. She didn't want to go to work. She knew Jack and Kenny would be waiting for her. They'd already razzed her about the nearly disastrous hunting excursion, and she was certain Jack wasn't done with his taunting.

Even Sidney had made a few digs, although he didn't neglect to congratulate her on bringing the flight in safely. Mike stood up for her, applauding her levelheadedness. She liked Mike and warmed at the memory of his chivalry.

With the engine running, she walked around to the back and cleared the rear window. Mike had made her a sweet deal on the car, and Kate was grateful for a comfortable ride to work.

It was a short trip to the airfield. When Kate spotted Jack's plane, she figured she was in for it. Stepping out of the coupe, she tried to think of a snappy comeback, but her mind was blank. She could never get ahold of a good answer when she needed it. Later she'd think of something that would put him in his place, but by then it didn't matter. She wished he'd go to work for another outfit so she wouldn't have to deal with his horrible moods and cutting remarks.

Kate stepped into the shop, and warm air blasted her. It felt good. Looking around, she was surprised Sidney was the only one there. She relaxed a little.

He smiled and pushed away from his desk. "You're just the person I'm looking for."

"Me?"

"Yeah. Jack's down with a bug."

"Oh, too bad," Kate said, unable to keep sarcasm out of her voice.

"Yeah, well, I was hoping you could take a run for him."

"He'll hate that."

"Yep. He will." Sidney grinned.

Acquiring one of Jack's assignments felt a little like retribution. "What do you have?"

"There's a guy with business in Kotzebue. He's picking up reindeer antlers."

"Kotzebue?" Kate had never flown that far north. The idea triggered excitement as well as anxiety. "Glad to help Jack out anytime," she said with a smile.

"I'll get you a map." Sidney moved to a wooden cabinet standing against the wall behind the desk. He fingered through files, then pulled out a chart and pushed the drawer closed. "It's a long flight." He opened the map and spread it out on his desk. "You might have to make adjustments for weather, and the wind can get bad. You never know when a storm's brewing out in the Bering Sea."

Using a pencil he'd tucked behind his ear, he marked a route as he talked. "Your best bet is to head up Cook Inlet to the Skwentna River, then duck in through Rainy Pass. You can follow the Kuskokwim River to McGrath. If you need to, you can rest there. After that, head for Unalakleet." He circled the village on the map. "It's a good place to fuel up and stay over. You can make Kotzebue the next day."

Kate studied the map. Kotzebue was way north. "Will there be enough daylight? Nights are getting longer and more so up north."

"Shouldn't be a problem. October's not bad, even up there. Just no lollygagging. At first light get into the air and set down before dark." He returned to the map and made additional notations. "If it takes you longer, I've marked places you can stay."

Kate nodded, charting Sidney's instructions in her mind. "I'll take extra fuel . . . just in case."

"Good idea." Sidney folded the map and handed it to her.

"What about my mail run?"

"I'll get one of the other fellas to do it. Frank ought to be back tomorrow."

"Okay. So when do I leave?"

"Right now."

"Oh." Unsteadiness rolled over Kate. She wasn't prepared. "I'll need to make a trip back to my place to get some gear."

"No problem. I'll tell Mr. Brinks to be here in thirty minutes?"

"Okay." Kate headed for the door, making a mental list of the things she'd need.

"The plane will be ready when you get back," Sidney said.

At her place, Kate stuffed clothing into a pack, then grabbed a couple of apples, a loaf of bread and peanut butter, a tin of crackers, and two cans of sardines. Mentally, she went over the survival gear she kept stowed in the plane. It ought to be adequate.

She slung the pack over her shoulder and headed into the store. Albert was stocking a shelf of canned goods. "I'll be gone four or five days. Hope this doesn't put you in a bind."

"We'll be fine." Albert set a can of carrots on the shelf. "Where'd you say you're going?"

"Kotzebue."

He looked at her from beneath raised eyebrows. "Long trip. Likely winter's already set in up there. Isolated country."

"It'll be a first for me, but Sidney wouldn't ask if he didn't think I was ready." The idea swelled inside Kate—she was proving herself to the best in Alaska. "See you in a few days," she said, taking a step toward the door. She stopped and impulsively planted a kiss on Albert's cheek. "Don't worry about me."

He smiled kindly. "You'll be in my prayers."

With the engine warming, Kate stowed her provisions. When Mr. Brinks arrived, Sidney walked the tall, thin man across the field.

"Kate, I'd like you to meet James Brinks."

"Good morning," Kate said.

Removing one of his heavy gloves, he grasped her outstretched hand. "I appreciate you taking me on such short notice. Need to get this done before winter sets in."

"Not a problem. Glad to do it."

Sidney passed the man's bag to Kate. "Have a good flight."

"Thanks." Kate set the satchel in the back of the plane and turned to Mr. Brinks. "Climb in and we'll be on our way. You can sit up front with me if you like."

He moved forward and folded himself into the front passenger seat. His long legs barely fit. "It'll be nice to see where we're going. Better view from up here."

Kate latched the door, then moved to the cockpit and settled into her place up front. After a final check of the instruments, she referred to the map once more. Her hands shook slightly. Maybe Sidney believed in her, but she still had qualms. *Relax. It's just another flight.*

"Have you made this run before?" Mr. Brinks asked.

Kate was tempted to lie. Instead she looked straight at him and said, "No. This is my first time. But I've been doing a lot of flying for Sidney. I'm very experienced. We'll be fine."

"Oh, I'm not worried." He leaned back and folded his arms over his chest. "Just curious is all."

"The weather's good." *At least it is here*, Kate thought, hoping a storm wasn't building in the Bering Sea. The last reports had been fine, but in Alaska you could never count on the weather. "Do you have any other questions?"

"No. I've made this trip before. Though I must say your company is an improvement over Jack's." He grinned and a deep dimple appeared in his right cheek. "You can call me James."

"Okay, James, you ready?"

"I am." He settled deeper into his seat, which pushed his legs almost up against his flat stomach.

Her nervousness abating a little, Kate felt excitement build. Kotzebue was part of the "real" Alaska she'd been dying to see.

While she taxied toward the runway, her mind wandered to her mail run and then to Paul. She'd miss seeing him this week. She didn't understand why, but thoughts of him popped into her mind at will. He was intriguing. *And not bad looking either.* She forced her mind back to her present task.

Once in the air, Kate's instincts took over and her butterflies disappeared. Taking one more look at the map, she headed up Cook Inlet. With a glance at James, she shouted over the engine, "Sidney said you were buying reindeer antlers?"

"Uh huh."

"What do you do with them?"

"I buy pieces of antlers and ship them to a buyer in China."

"What does he do with them?"

James gave her a discomfited look, then said, "Well . . . they're used to . . . they're supposed to increase . . . sexual urges."

"Oh." Kate felt the heat of embarrassment creep up her neck and into her face. She kept her eyes forward and didn't say anything more.

———

As Sidney had suggested, she followed the Skwentna River and then made her way through a pass and over a succession of mountains. The weather held, but the mountain ranges created their own winds. The Bellanca shuddered as it was tossed and pitched by unseen currents. James seemed unperturbed.

All in all, the day passed pleasantly. Fall sunshine warmed the interior of the plane and cast golden hues over the landscape.

Alaska's diversity thrilled Kate. In just a few hours she'd flown over the steel gray waters of Cook Inlet and had cast a shadow over a montage of forests. Some were deep green, while others looked like tapestries of yellow and orange, the last of the fall leaves still clinging to trees. Silver rivers served as highways, and mountains, some broad and buried in snow, reached into the heavens while others rolled like waves across broad expanses of burnished tundra. The solitude was staggering.

An occasional gold mining camp or homesteader's cabin emerged from the wilderness. Kate wondered what it would be like to winter in a tiny cabin, cut off from the world. She decided she'd rather not know.

With mountain ranges ahead and behind, Kate tried to rein in worrisome thoughts of what could happen if the plane went down. She'd be like the proverbial needle in a haystack. She glanced at James. His arms were folded over his chest and his mouth was slack in sleep. He wasn't worried; why should she be?

Still, when the Eskimo village of Unalakleet came into view, she felt a rush of relief. In the growing gloom of dusk, it huddled on the shore of the Bering Sea like a beacon of hope in a wasteland.

James sat up and ran his fingers through his hair. Gazing down at the village, he said, "Good, I need to get out and walk. I'm beginning to feel like a pretzel."

"We're just in time. Sun's setting." A pale yellow ball rested on the edge of the sea. The sky glowed gold, pink, and plum. The ocean was a deep purple.

"Amazing—God's handprint," James said.

Kate could only nod agreement, unable to speak past the lump in her throat, overwhelmed by the power and presence of God's spectacular display.

Once the plane was on the ground, there was still a good deal of work to be done before Kate could find a place to lay her head for the night. "It's awfully cold," she told James. "I'd better drain the oil."

"I'll tie her down for you."

Kate grabbed a bucket and tapped the oil. She'd reheat it in the morning before taking off. James helped her drape a tarp over the engine and secure it, and the weary travelers headed toward the settlement, hoping for a hot meal and warm beds.

By morning, the weather had deteriorated. Clouds hung low over the sea, their underbellies distended just above the bay. A sharp wind whipped water into whitecaps and sifted frozen ground into icy clouds that whispered over the snow.

With freezing air blasting from the west, Kate used a firepot to warm the engine, then heated the oil and poured it into the pan. Fighting the winds, she and James set off, heading north along Norton Sound toward Kotzebue.

She studied the frozen, empty landscape. Back home, in Washington, there were windfall apples, just-ripened pumpkins, and dew shimmering in the mornings. "Winter comes early here," she said.

"It does."

Clouds swirled and winds buffeted the craft. Kate dropped to a lower altitude.

"You think we're in for a storm?" James asked.

"Don't think so. Hope not." Just then the village of Candle appeared, tiny and alone. "We're not far from Kotzebue now."

"Look at that," James said, gazing out the window at the frozen ground.

Kate looked but didn't see anything until a white shadow distinguished itself from the frozen tundra. "Is that a bear?"

"Yep. Polar bear."

Kate had never seen one before. Hoping for a better look, she made a wide turn, dropped closer to the ground, and flew over the animal. The bear kept moving, its broad paws seeming to skim over the snow.

"He's waiting for the sea to freeze up so he can get back to his hunting grounds."

"He's huge."

"Yeah, and dangerous. You don't want to face off with one."

The bear stopped, stood on his back legs, and peered at them, then dropped to the ground and loped off, heading for the shoreline.

"A friend of mine, in Kotzebue, said he had one track him. Nearly caught him by surprise." James shook his head. "Tom was just fast enough. Now he's got a bearskin hanging on his wall."

After one last look at the animal, Kate pulled back on the stick and left it behind. "I'd hate to have one sneak up on me."

The wilderness on one side and the Bering Sea on the other, Kotzebue seemed to sit on the edge of the world. Smoke, barely visible against a white backdrop, trailed into the sky from tin pipes protruding from rooftops.

Kate set down on a small airstrip at the edge of town. James helped put the plane to bed.

"See you at 10:00 tomorrow," he said. He pulled his hood nearly closed around his face and tramped toward the village.

Kate headed for a shack standing on one side of the runway. Smoke rose from a flue in the roof and drifted around the cabin, dressing it in a diaphanous vapor that faded in the arctic air. She'd been told someone would meet her there.

When Kate stepped inside, she was surprised to find that the cabin looked lived in. A small native woman with a round face and dark eyes sat in a chair beside a barrel stove.

"Oh, I'm sorry," Kate said, stepping back. "I thought—"

"No. No. You come in." The woman smiled and motioned for Kate to step forward.

Kate moved inside and closed the door. "Is this the airfield office?"

"Yes. My husband, he helps here, but he's at the store. So I am waiting for you."

A baby slept in a sling draped across the woman's chest. With a mewling sound, it yawned and stretched out chubby arms, its hands clenched. The woman lifted the nearly naked infant and held it up in front of her. "You hungry?"

Kate didn't know if she was talking to the baby or to her.

The woman turned her almond-shaped eyes on Kate. "You hungry?"

"Oh. Yes. A little."

"Good. Then you come to my house. I'll feed you. You can sleep there too."

Kate had assumed she'd stay at a roadhouse. "I don't want to impose."

The woman smiled. "No trouble for me. You come to dinner." She tucked the baby back into its pack, then turned her attention to Kate. "I'm Nena Turchik. This is Mary." She gave the baby a pat.

"Kate Evans. I'm glad to meet you."

Nena crossed to the door and stepped outside. "Come on," she said and hurried toward town. Although she wore a heavy coat over a mid-calf dress and mukluks, she moved swiftly.

Kate followed, each step crunching through a thin layer of snow. The air felt frigid and burned her cheeks and lungs.

Nena walked down a snow-covered street, then stopped in front of a small store. "This is it." She stepped inside and held the door open.

Kate moved into what looked like a mercantile and was instantly enveloped in warmth and an unusual mix of odors—oats, apples, and the distinctive smell of whale oil. A man who was nearly as short as Nena stood at a counter, sorting through a stack of papers. To his right there was a living area with a sofa and two cushioned chairs. Beyond that was a small kitchen with a rough-hewn table and chairs.

He looked at Nena, then Kate, his brown eyes smiling from beneath the ridge of a knit hat. "Good. You're here. Sidney said you were coming."

"He told you? How?"

The man chuckled. "You don't know about Mukluk radio?"

"Oh, yes. I do." Kate had listened to the radio station. Its broadcasts could be heard all across the territory, even in the remotest regions. The people of Alaska depended on it.

"Mukluk radio makes sure everybody knows the news." He stepped from behind the counter. "I'm Joe. It's good that you're here."

"Thank you."

Handing the baby to Joe, Nena picked up a small boy as he toddled out of a back room. She pressed a kiss to his cheek. "Hello, my little Nick." He put his pudgy arms around her neck.

Another boy emerged. "Mama, can we get candy now?"

"After dinner, Peter." Nena turned to Kate. "It's Halloween. You want to come with us when we go treating?"

"I'd forgotten about Halloween. Yes, I'd like to go," Kate said, although she would have preferred staying indoors where it was warm. However, she knew how important first impressions were and didn't want to alienate the Turchiks.

Kate joined the Eskimo family for a meal of fish pie and was surprised that she enjoyed every bite. "This is very good. Thank you."

"I'm glad you like it."

"I thought we might . . . well, I've read a lot of books and . . . I kind of expected something like whale blubber or—"

"You like some?" Nena stood.

Kate was taken aback. "Oh no. I just thought that—"

"I have some. But most people from the outside don't like it."

"Well, I've never tasted it, but . . ." Kate didn't know what to say. She didn't want to offend her new friends.

Joe laughed. "You don't have to eat our traditional foods. Outsiders are not used to it. We understand."

Kate nodded in relief.

Nena picked up the dish of fish pie. "You want more?"

"No, thank you. I've already eaten too much. I'm full up to here." Kate held her hand at chest level.

After the table had been cleared and the dishes done, Nena bundled up the two older children. Peter wore a cowboy hat under his hood and Nick wore a bird-like mask over his face. "We will go out for Halloween now." She smiled, her eyes becoming half moons. "There will be candy and fruit. And lots of fun." She moved toward the door.

Cold air nipped at Kate's cheeks when she stepped outside. Her eyes watered and she pulled her hood mostly closed around her face. Nena held a lantern aloft and walked behind the children, who scampered ahead. The cold seemed to have no effect on Nena or the boys.

The dark streets were alive with children dressed in costumes and fur-lined coats, and parents following their excited youngsters. Kate saw more than one child wearing a witch's hat, and one little boy sported an eye patch. All the children wore smiles, their dark eyes sparkling in the lantern light.

The festive mood was infectious, and soon Kate forgot about the cold and found herself having fun right along with the children. Each time they went to a house they were rewarded with gifts of hard candy or dried fruit. Nena kindly introduced Kate to everyone they encountered.

The children headed down an alley, and Nena fell into step beside Kate. "Do you like Anchorage? Is it very big?"

"I do like it, but it's a town like any other. Bigger than Kotzebue, though."

"Is there a Sears store?"

"You've never been to Anchorage?"

"No."

"They don't have a Sears store, but there are other department stores."

"What are they like?"

"Some are like your place. And there are shoe stores—"

"They sell only shoes?"

"Yes." Kate smiled, charmed by Nena's naïveté. "And there are jewelry and clothing stores too."

"Maybe one day I can go to Anchorage," Nena said wistfully.

"I can take you."

Nena shrugged. "I don't fly."

"Why not?"

"Birds fly, not people." She pursed her lips and glanced at the dark sky. Nena held her lantern higher and peered down the alley. It cast shadows across the snow and onto the houses.

Kate remembered the bear she'd seen earlier. "Do bears come into town?"

"Sometimes."

A prickle of fear moved up Kate's spine. She gazed down the dark street, praying a bear hadn't found its way into Kotzebue on this night. As she and Nena followed Peter and Nick, she couldn't keep from looking into the shadows.

After visiting every house in town, Kate and the Turchiks returned home. The boys dumped out their bags of goodies on the table and sorted through to find their favorite treats. Each was allowed two pieces of candy before hustling off to bed.

"Good night," Joe said, taking the baby and following the older youngsters into the back of the house.

Nena and Kate made up a bed on the floor. "I wish I had something better for you," Nena said.

"This is just fine." Kate climbed beneath heavy blankets, feeling warm and content. It had been a good day.

"I'm glad you came," Nena said. "You are a brave lady."

Kate pushed up on one elbow. "I hope I can come back soon."

"Me too. Goodnight." Nena stepped out of the room and closed the door.

Kate rested her head on the pillow and stared at the ceiling. Here in the midst of a frozen wasteland, she felt content. Her eyes grew heavy. *I belong here, in Alaska.* She snuggled deeper beneath her blankets, thinking life was nearly perfect. Then a picture of Richard came to mind. She needed to write to him and tell him that she would never return to Washington or an ordinary life.

After washing the last of the morning's dishes, Paul stood at the window and gazed out. The snow had stopped, leaving a hushed world of white. *I'd better get to the wood.*

Paul made a simple lunch of peanut butter and honey sandwiches and a slab of ginger bread. He put the lunch and a canteen of water in a pack, pulled on a coat, and with the pack over one shoulder stepped onto the porch. Cold air greeted him. He liked the frosty touch on his face and the sharp, clean feel of chilled oxygen in his lungs. The temperature gauge read twenty-eight degrees.

Fresh snow was piled on rooftops, hung heavily on evergreen boughs, and buried shrubs. The strident cry of a raven cut through the silent world. On mornings like this Paul felt confident he'd made the right decision to move to Alaska. He filled his lungs with the revitalizing air.

The dogs stared at him, alert and tails thumping. "Morning," he called, pulling on his hood and tramping down the steps, the crystalline blanket of snow squeaking beneath his boots.

He trudged through knee-high snow to the dogs and gave

each a pat and a kind word. They pressed against him. Nita whined and sniffed at his gloves.

Paul knelt in front of her and held her face in his hands. "Glad you're back to your usual self, girl. Figure you'll be having a family in a few months." He buried his fingers in her ruff and wondered what the pups would look like. Her tongue washed his face and he chuckled, pushing her back.

Buck barked until Paul gave him equal time. When he went to leave, the dog nipped at his sleeve.

"None of that." Paul scrubbed Buck's thick coat and considered letting the dogs run, but decided against it. The days were short and he had too much work to do to allow time for searching out adventurous canines. "I'll need you tomorrow when I haul in the wood."

He grabbed a shovel and a buck saw from the shed and set off down a barely defined trail. He geared himself up for a long day. If he wanted the timber ready for hauling before dark, he'd have to work steadily.

Thanksgiving was only two weeks out, and soon real winter would set in. The long season stared back at him like an endless dark tunnel of days. From the very first he'd fought the devils of the holidays. He couldn't stave off memories.

In the Anderson household, Thanksgiving and Christmas had always been big events. The house would fill with people, and the aroma of roasting meat and freshly baked breads and pies wafted through the home. There were games, boisterous conversations, and laughter. He could still hear the fun.

He remembered a time when he'd stood alone on the barren flatlands of the Mojave Desert with the hot wind sighing all around him. That's how he felt now—utterly alone.

He tried to shake off the melancholy and focus on the snow-laden tree boughs, brilliantly white against a flat gray sky. This was a beautiful place, and he had the company of his dogs and good neighbors. *I'm not alone.*

He trudged on. The trees he'd felled weren't far. They'd be buried now, so he'd have to dig them out before he could limb them. After that, he'd cut the timber into rounds and haul it back to the house to be split.

A set of tracks crossed the trail and disappeared into the forest. Paul stopped to study them. *Marten. A good-sized one.* He moved on and soon came across another set, only these were left by a fox.

Paul had planned to wait a few weeks before setting out traps, but now seemed a good time. Deciding the wood could wait one more day, he headed back to the cabin for the sled.

He cleared it of snow, set his pack on the cargo bed, then hurried to the shed. While his mind sifted through all that needed to be done, he set the shovel and saw in one corner, then hefted several leghold traps down from the wall. Adrenaline pumping with anticipation, he packed them to the sled.

After retrieving bait from the cache, he tromped back to the dogs. They whined and barked, begging to go along. Paul studied them. They could all use a good run, but he only needed one. Buck was the biggest and strongest.

"You're it," Paul said, scratching him behind the ears. The dog leaned against him, his tail beating the air. Paul unhooked his leash and Buck bounded free, leaping around and rubbing his broad side against his master's legs. The other two dogs whined. "Next time," he said. "I promise."

He secured Buck in the harness, then grabbed hold of the traces and stepped onto the footboard. "Okay, boy, let's go."

Buck lunged forward and set off down the trail.

While in harness, Buck forgot play—he worked. Never straying or sniffing at bushes or trees, he kept moving. Paul jogged behind part of the time. The sound of the blades skimming over the snow and the cold air splashing his face energized him.

At the place where the marten tracks led into the woods, Paul called, "Gee," and Buck veered to the right and cut a trail through the forest. Not far off the main track, Paul stopped at a patch of bushes. It would be a good place to set out a trap. Buck sat quietly and watched.

Paul lifted out his tool bag, grabbed a leghold, and then retrieved a chunk of salmon. He smoothed out an area hidden beneath the bushes and pounded a trap post into the ground. Using limbs and sticks, he constructed a box of sorts and set the bait at the narrowest point in the back. He pulled the jaws of the leghold apart, holding them with one hand while he flipped the tongue over the edge of one jaw and slipped it into a notch under the pan. Gently he released the pressure so as not to spring it, then placed the trap toward the back of the box. Last, he brushed snow over it to conceal it.

He stood, arched his back slightly, then stretched from side to side to relax tight muscles. "That's it. Let's go." He climbed onto the sled and Buck moved forward.

After setting out several legholds, Paul's growling stomach told him it was time to eat. He stopped, then grabbed a chunk of dried salmon for Buck and tossed it to him. The dog pounced on his meal. Paul sat on a partially exposed tree that had been downed. Taking out his canteen, he unscrewed the lid and took a long drink. Buck had already finished off his fish so Paul poured water into a pan for him.

The hush of piled snow enveloped the forest, making Paul feel like an intruder. He took another drink, found a sandwich, and settled down to eating. His eyes roamed the frozen forest. Mounds of white concealed brush and stumps. Large trees had deep swirling wells at their bases, and frost encased birch and alder limbs.

The world looked bright and unsoiled, but Paul knew it was a deception. The world wasn't pure. Reality stripped away his pleasure. If only things were the way God had intended them to be. Paul tried to imagine the world Adam and Eve had known—life without sorrow or conflict. It was too unfamiliar a vision to capture, and Paul was left with the reality of his tainted existence.

He finished off his sandwich, but left the rest of his lunch. It was time to get the last of the traps set. He'd circle back to the place he'd started.

Heading toward the main trail, Paul glanced at the darkening sky. He'd have to hurry. Annoyed, he thought, *There aren't enough daylight hours for a man to get his work done.*

It would only get worse—between now and December 21 the days would grow shorter. He liked Alaska but he wasn't an "Alaskan." Temperatures below zero aggravated him and the darkness sapped his spirit. After the winter solstice, he counted the additional minutes gained each day, anticipating the short summer nights.

Paul used ptarmigan wing sections for the last two leg-holds, hanging them from a branch above traps, hoping for larger prey such as fox. With any luck, the animal would jump for the bait and step on the trap. Even Buck was tantalized by the smell of bird. He sniffed the air and stared at the dangling wing.

Paul moved back to the sled and patted the dog's broad head. "You don't want any part of that."

When he approached the first trap he'd set, Paul noticed a raven hopping up and down in the snow. *He must have gone after the bait and gotten snagged.*

Paul wasn't especially fond of ravens, but he couldn't let the bird suffer, especially one that had been injured because of a trap he'd set. He edged toward the panicked raven. It flapped its wings wildly and pulled against the line.

"Watch it. You'll only make things worse," Paul said, his voice calm. The bird fought harder.

Buck growled and woofed, lunging against his harness.

"No! Buck! Sit!"

Although trembling with excitement, the dog obeyed. His eyes remained on the raven.

Paul took hold of the line that held the trap, then gently lifted the raven toward him. The bird continued to beat the air with his wings until Paul got him close enough to put his gloved hand over his head. The frightened creature still fought, ruffling his wings against Paul's hands. Finally, he quieted, giving in to the inevitable.

The bird's chest rose and fell rapidly, but he didn't fight. Paul figured he'd probably die. Holding the bird securely, he opened the trap and released its leg. "Sorry. But I guess that's what you get for being a scavenger." He held the raven against his chest. He was sure its leg was broken. If he let him go free, he'd certainly die. "I'll see what I can do for you." Keeping a firm grasp on the bird, he tucked him under his arm.

Once at the cabin, Paul kept the raven restrained in a sack while he devised a small cage from a wooden box. He affixed twigs across the top, creating a grill that let in fresh air and light and allowed Paul to observe and feed the bird without disturbing him.

When he'd finished, he took the raven out of the sack and wrapped a piece of cloth around its head, tying it so its eyes would remain covered while he attempted to repair the broken leg. Using a handkerchief, he secured the creature to a wooden plank, examined its leg, and decided he could splint it.

Paul immobilized the broken limb with a stick and bandages, then placed the bird in the cage and removed the cloth that covered its eyes. He put water and bread crumbs in and watched for a few minutes. *So now I'm a veterinarian.*

"If you live, you can keep me company," he told the bird. The raven trembled, but its breathing was less rapid. Paul covered the cage with a towel and set it in the middle of the table. *I read somewhere ravens can be taught to speak. Maybe I can teach this one.*

The following afternoon, Paul had just put soup on when someone knocked at the door. He opened it, surprised to find Lily standing on the porch.

She smiled sweetly. "Mama told me to tell you the mail plane's due. She wanted to know if you had anything that needed to go out. I can take it for you."

"No. Nothing today." Paul rarely had mail to send. Sassa knew that.

Lily remained on the porch, hands clasped behind her back. Paul wasn't sure what to do. He didn't want to invite her in. The raven let out a squawk, putting an end to the question of whether or not Lily would stay.

"What's that?" she asked, glancing inside.

"A raven. He got caught in one of my traps yesterday, broke his leg. I brought him home and fixed him up."

"Can I see him?"

"Sure."

Lily stepped inside and crossed to the table. Uncertain whether or not to leave the door open, Paul finally decided it was foolish to let in cold air and closed it. He lifted the towel off the cage.

She gazed at the bird. He stared back, his head cocked to one side. "He's big," Lily said.

"Yeah, looks like he's been eating well. I thought he'd be dead by now, but he made it through the night."

Lily pressed a finger against the slots of the cage. The bird pecked at it, but when he discovered it wasn't something to eat, he went back to staring. "He's beautiful." She looked more closely at the bandaged leg. "How did you know what to do?"

"Uh . . . my grandpa splinted a bird once, when I was a boy. I helped him."

"Really?" She looked at the raven a moment longer, then said, "Well, I better go. The plane'll be in soon." She headed for the door.

"I'll go with you." Paul grabbed his coat and hat. "Kate might have something for me." He doubted it, but he wouldn't mind seeing Kate.

He followed Lily out and down the trail that led to a dock.

Lily climbed into the dory and sat in the bow. Her brown eyes wandered over the scenery, then found Paul. She didn't speak. He wondered if she agreed with her mother—that the two of them would be a good match. He hoped not. Even though he didn't want to marry Lily, he cared about her and hated to see her hurt.

He untied the boat, then sat and grabbed hold of the oars. His reasonable voice told him, *She's good-hearted and pretty. And she knows all there is to know about living out here. She'd make a good wife.* Even as he considered the idea, he couldn't reconcile to it. Lily was too young, more girl than woman.

He dipped the oars into a stream of water wedged in by ice. "Won't be long before the creek is frozen up solid."

The sound of a plane carried from the Susitna River. In his mind, Paul could see Kate, tall and strong and determined. She was definitely not a girl.

He steered the boat through the narrow channel of unfrozen water and watched Kate's plane set down on the sandbar in the midst of the Susitna. He was surprised at how eager he was to see her.

When Paul reached the landing site, Lily climbed out of the dory and held it while he leaped to the shore. Together they beached the boat and set off toward the plane.

"Afternoon," he called as Kate stepped out of the Bellanca.

"Hi." She smiled. "How are you?"

Before Paul could respond, Lily said, "Good. You?"

"Can't complain. I've been busy." She reached inside the plane. "There's mail for you and your brothers." Kate handed her three boxes.

"Mama didn't say anything about a surprise. I wonder what it is." Lily's eyes shone as she stared at the packages.

"You know your mother," said Paul. "She's always thinking about you and your brothers."

Lily held the parcels against her chest and walked back to the boat. She climbed inside and sat down, tearing into one of the packages.

Kate looked at Paul and shrugged, her arms lifted at her sides. "Nothing else today."

"That's all right. Didn't expect anything."

An awkward silence settled between the two.

Finally Kate asked, "So, do you have plans for Thanksgiving?"

"No. Well, maybe. The Warrens will probably invite me to dinner. Me and Klaus—you know, the old fella up the creek."

Kate nodded.

"I was thinking I might take a berry pie," Paul said.

"Pie is one of my favorite desserts. My mother makes the best apple pie you've ever tasted." Kate rested her hands on her hips. "I didn't take after her. I'm not handy around the kitchen."

"That's all right. Not everyone can fly a plane." He smiled, feeling lighthearted.

"That's true." Kate glanced upriver. "Well . . . I better get going." She didn't move. Instead she asked, "Would you like to join the Towns's and Mike and me for Thanksgiving?"

"You mean in Anchorage?"

"Uh-huh. That's where we live." Kate grinned.

"That's a long way to go for dinner."

"Not when you're flying. I come out on Wednesdays. You can stay over in town, have dinner with us, and I'll bring you back the day after."

Paul didn't know what to say. The idea was tempting, but he wrestled with conflicting emotions. Thanksgiving with Kate was appealing, maybe too much so. When he looked into her warm hazel eyes, he knew he didn't dare. "I think the Warrens are expecting me. I don't want to let them down."

"Oh. Okay."

Paul thought he detected a hint of disappointment.

Kate edged toward the plane. "There's more mail to deliver. See you in a week."

"See ya."

Kate climbed into the Pacemaker and Paul closed the door behind her, then stepped back, watching while she taxied to the end of the landing strip. He'd been too eager to see her. He cared, more than he wanted to. Forcing himself not to watch her take off, he walked to the boat, pushed away from the shore, and clambered in.

"Kate's awfully nice. I like her," Lily said.

"Yeah." Paul heard the Bellanca make its run and couldn't stop himself from looking. Once she was in the air, he put the oars in the water and headed toward the cabin. Dragging his mind away from Kate, he asked, "So, what did you get in the mail?"

"Books." She held up two. "*Jane Eyre*. And *Little Women*. Have you read them?"

"Can't say that I have." He glanced at the disappearing plane and wished he'd accepted Kate's invitation. It was too late now. What would it have hurt? It was just dinner.

— 12 —

Kate hefted the last canvas bag of Christmas packages into her plane. Although she figured being a pilot would offer challenges and surprises, she'd never imagined herself playing the role of Santa. She liked the idea.

The image of Santa in a plane instead of a sleigh made her smile and brought a Christmas carol to mind. She sang, "Dashing o'er the snow . . . in my bright red cargo plane, o'er the fields I . . . fly, laughing all the way. Bells on bobtail ring, making spirits bright, what fun it is to ride and sing in my . . . Pacemaker tonight. O Jingle bells, Jingle bells, Jingle all the way. Oh what fun it is to fly in a . . . J6 series bird."

She chuckled. "Ethel Merman I'm not." Kate continued humming the tune while making sure packages were arranged so the weight was distributed evenly.

She'd be stopping at several villages en route to Kotzebue. December offered little daylight, so the run would take about four days there and another four back. The trip was treacherous. The vast tundra and miles of mountains and ice were a natural barrier between civilization and the small towns and villages strewn across the wilderness. Weather conditions were at best frigid and clear—at their worst, lethal. Still, Kate's holiday cheer overrode her apprehension.

Christmas was a mere three weeks off. She didn't know what she'd be doing for the holiday, yet the merriment of the season made her mood light. This would be the first Christmas she'd celebrate away from home and the first her parents had spent without her. She wondered what they'd planned. A pang of homesickness cut into her pleasure. And an image of Richard. Last Christmas they'd been talking about their life together. On Christmas Eve, he'd kissed her beneath the mistletoe in his parents' front room and then asked her to marry him. She'd thought he was everything she wanted. But things change.

Guilt niggled at her. She still hadn't written to him and promised herself she would as soon as she returned from this trip. It had seemed kinder not to, but she knew better. It wasn't right to let him think there was any hope.

Paul intruded on her thoughts. She didn't want to think about him. He wasn't her type—too serious. Still, she couldn't shut out the image of his broad shoulders, the set of his strong chin, and the warmth in his eyes. And the idea of him spending Christmas alone on the creek sent a twinge of sadness through her. *The Warrens will certainly include him. He won't be alone.*

Kate started the engine, and while it warmed up, she checked the craft for ice. The temperatures had been frigid, but the air was dry so that would help. Using a flashlight, she walked around the Bellanca, checking the fuselage and wings, the tail section, and any place where ice might accumulate and weigh down the plane. She'd have to be vigilant to watch for any accumulation—even frost could change the shape of the wings and disturb airflow.

The shop door opened and someone stepped out. A flash-light cast a beam across the snow. It was Mike. "Morning," he said.

"Hi," Kate said, glad they'd bumped into each other. She was curious about him and wished they had time to get to know one another better.

"So, you're making a run to Kotzebue."

"I've got Christmas deliveries."

"Playing Santa, huh?"

Kate grinned, her mind returning to her little song. She was glad he hadn't heard.

Mike leaned against the fuselage, his eyes lingering on hers. "What you doing for Christmas?"

Kate took in a quick breath. Did she see interest in his gaze? Doing her best to act nonchalant, she said, "I don't know. Sidney's heading to Seward so the field will be shut down for a few days."

"Forced vacation for us." Mike stepped back and looked over Kate's plane, then let his gaze rest on her. "You didn't answer my question."

"What question?"

"Christmas?"

"Oh. Well, I don't know yet." *It might be fun to spend the holiday with Mike,* Kate thought. Did she want more than friendship? They had a lot in common and he was fun.

"Maybe we could spend it together." His gaze held Kate's.

"That sounds nice," she said. "I'm not sure if Albert and Helen are expecting me."

"We can work something out." He smiled.

"Okay."

Mike folded his arms over his chest and his expression turned serious. "You won't have a lot of daylight this trip, and it'll get worse as you head north."

"I've got it figured out. I can fly in twilight and after dark if I have to. We've got a full moon."

Mike wasn't smiling. "Be careful."

Kate felt irritation stir. She was tired of men, even Mike, fretting about her simply because she was a woman. "I don't need you protecting me."

"Someone has to." He grinned. "You don't need to prove yourself all the time. We all know you're a good pilot."

"I am good. But you're wrong about proving myself. I can never let up. I'm always under extra scrutiny, because I'm a woman. If I succeed, no one notices, but if I fail, it's because I'm female."

"I don't think anyone is scrutinizing you, Kate, except maybe Jack. And you can't take him seriously."

She tugged on the sides of her flight cap and moved to the door. "I appreciate your concern, honestly."

"No matter who's flying this bird, it's a tough run this time of year."

She glanced at the parcels stowed inside. "Someone has to deliver these packages. Otherwise a lot of kids won't have Christmas."

"Let me tag along."

Kate toyed with the idea of having Mike for company. "You have trips of your own." She glanced at the shop. "And the guys'll have a heyday if you ride with me as my protector. I can already hear Jack. He'd razz me to my grave." She shook her head. "No thanks."

Mike took a step closer. "You can't let someone like Jack get under your skin and affect your decisions." He closed the distance between them. "That pilot out of Ketchikan that disappeared last week, they still haven't found him."

Mike stood less than an arm's length away. Kate put a foot on the steps, not sure how she felt about him being that close.

145

"I know. I heard. We all gamble. It's part of the job. And last time I checked you were risking your neck more than me."

"I do what I have to. You do *more* than you have to." He rested a hand on her shoulder. "Let me come along. Why do you care what anyone thinks?"

"I care, that's all."

"Okay." He squeezed her shoulder. "I'll be thinking about you."

Kate felt her heart quicken. "Thanks. I'll be thinking about you too," she said, and she meant it. She glanced at the sky, which was turning pink. "I better go." She stepped into the plane. "See you next week."

He moved back. "Maybe when you get back, we can go out or something."

"Sure."

Mike gave her a small salute and then closed the door. Kate made her way to the cockpit, wondering what was happening between her and Mike. She settled in her seat, tapped the pedals, pulled back on the throttle, and gave Mike a wave as she headed down the runway.

The next three days, Kate made stops at homesteads and villages. She was greeted by enthusiastic children and moms and dads. Some of the gifts had been donated while others were ordered by parents who'd anxiously been awaiting their arrival. Kate loved playing Santa.

As she headed up the coast and neared Kotzebue, the temperatures turned bitter and wind whipped across the frozen sea, sifting snow into the air and creating a ground blizzard. Once down, she might have to stay put for a few days.

Dusk closed over the tundra. Kate checked her compass and then gazed out over the empty white world below. The ground blend was bad, making it difficult to distinguish earth from sky. It was eerie. Native tales of ghostly visions and apparitions crowded her thoughts. She'd be glad to get on the ground and snuggle down in the Turchiks' warm little house.

An anemic-looking sun rested on the horizon, and Kate studied her position. She took another look at her map and stared at the terrain, trying to sear the image into her mind. She checked her compass again, then her elevation. Conditions like this had been the death of many a pilot. Unable to distinguish up from down, they'd been known to fly their planes into the ground or keep the nose up and climb into a stall.

The sun slipped away, casting the tundra into shadow. Momentarily, Kate felt disoriented and panic climbed up her insides. "Kotzebue—where are you?" She peered into the darkness and wondered where the moon had gotten to. Blackness pressed in. Kate realized she was holding her breath and gripping the stick with all her strength. *Relax. You can handle this.* Taking a couple of deep breaths and forcing herself to loosen her hold on the stick, she stayed on her heading and searched for the lights of Kotzebue. The town was out there. Kate knew she was close.

Rolling back tight shoulders, she remembered the enthusiasm she'd felt the morning she'd left Anchorage. She decided singing might lighten her mood, and faltering at first, she sang her version of *Jingle Bells*, her voice strengthening with each verse. The tension eased, so she kept singing while seeking signs of civilization in the dark wasteland.

Kate spotted something. Was it a light? Leaning forward, she stared hard, then hooted her relief. It was a light. "Thank you, God." She kept her focus on the tiny point of hope splintering the northern wilderness.

Soon more lights appeared and Kate sat deeper in her seat. "Kotzebue, you are a lovely sight."

She circled the town, looking for the airstrip. Firepots had been lit and set out to mark the runway. The Turchiks, no doubt.

When Kate came to a stop, someone carrying a lantern ran toward the plane. It was Joe. When she opened the door and stepped out, he smiled broadly.

"Kate! Good you are here!"

"I've never been so thankful to see a town in all my life." Kate hugged him.

He gave her a tight squeeze. "I have been praying for you."

"Thank you. And thanks for the firepots."

He nodded. "Nena has soup ready. She's been cooking and watching for you all day."

Kate felt buoyant. "Wonderful. I'm starved."

With Joe's help, she tied down the plane. After the oil was drained, the two of them draped a cover over the engine. She checked her watch. "I can hardly believe it's two o'clock in the afternoon. It's so dark."

"Yeah, that's how it is here in the winter."

The wind bit Kate's nose and her cheeks. She pulled her parka closed around her face.

Holding up a lantern, Joe grinned. "You cold?"

"I am. And don't tell me you're not."

He laughed. "This is nothing. It gets much worse."

Kate shrugged, not sure whether to believe him or not. "Better get the Christmas gifts unloaded and into your store. Tomorrow you'll be swamped by parents."

"Some came today, hoping you'd arrived."

While Kate reached into the plane, Joe held the lantern high, its flame flickering wildly. She grabbed two bags and handed them to him, then dragged out two more.

"There'll be some happy kids on Christmas," he said.

"I'm counting on it." Kate pushed the door closed and latched it, then huddling against the wind, she followed Joe toward town.

She barely stepped in the door when the boys came charging toward her. They wrapped their arms around her legs in an exuberant hug.

"Hello, Kate," said Peter.

"He . . .wo," said Nick.

Kate gave them both a squeeze, feeling as if she'd been welcomed home.

Nena sat on a chair, the baby in her arms. She smiled broadly. "I'm so happy to see you. I have been praying for your safety."

"I'm sure your prayers are what guided me. It was awfully dark out there." Kate gave the boys one more hug, then straightened and looked around the room. "I'm so glad to be here."

After a meal of fish soup with rice and roasted reindeer, Nena went into the back room and returned with a package wrapped in bright red paper. "I made this for you. For Christmas." She held out the gift.

Kate accepted it. She hadn't even thought about gifts for the Turchiks. She looked at it, not certain whether she ought to open it or wait until Christmas.

"Open it!" Peter said.

Kate shot a questioning look at Nena.

"Yes. Open."

She carefully unwrapped the bulky package, feeling like a kid on Christmas morning. The paper fell away, revealing a grass basket with a lid. There were images of tiny red and blue swans woven into the pattern. "It's wonderful. You made this?"

Nena nodded, her dark eyes turning into upside-down crescents when she smiled.

Kate examined the basket, marveling at the artwork and wondering just how anyone could weave such intricate designs. "I love it. Thank you."

Peter climbed into Kate's lap. "Look inside."

Kate lifted the lid. Lying in the bottom was something wrapped in the same red paper that had concealed the basket. She picked it up and removed the wrapping. A piece of yellow-white ivory fell into her hand. It had been carved to look like a whale and had a silver chain attached to it. Kate stroked the polished figure, then ran a finger over carved etchings.

"Joe made it," Nena said, pride in her voice.

"It's amazing. Thank you." Kate immediately undid the clasp and draped the necklace around her neck. "Every time I wear it, I'll think of you." She closed the hook and let the necklace fall against her chest. "It's perfect." Resting her hand over it, she said, "I wish I had brought something for you."

"You have—something of great value," said Nena. "You come when it is dark and cold. It is dangerous for you, but still you bring Christmas to Kotzebue." She smiled, her teeth looking white against her dark skin.

For the first time since arriving in Alaska, Kate saw her profession as more than a job. It was a mission. She hugged Nena and then each member of the family. At that moment she couldn't imagine a better life.

They ate Eskimo ice cream, called *akutaq*, a treat Kate had yet to develop a taste for. Her palate wasn't used to seal oil mixed with berries. However, unwilling to offend the Turchiks, she ate every bite.

During the night, the wind quieted and ground fog crept over the coastline. Before daylight Kate walked to the airfield to check the plane. Ice had formed on the wings and windows, but the engine had fared well. She'd have to wait for the fog to dissipate before taking off. She'd not be flying today.

Kate stayed one extra day at the Turchiks'. Her time with the native family was fun. Nearly everyone in town showed up to claim mail and Christmas packages. There were lots of smiles and giggling children. Every visitor thanked Kate for bringing the precious shipment to the village.

Peter and Nick included Kate in a game of bear hunting. Each of the boys pretended to be mighty hunters while she was the revered and much feared bear. When they caught her, they'd pounce on her back, then everyone would fall into a giggling pile. They also played tag, but it was a little different than the game Kate remembered from her childhood. When you tagged another player, you had to touch them in exactly the same spot each time or they weren't eliminated. It made for a lot of leaping and wriggling to stay out of reach.

The next day, the fog had lifted, and although Kate wished she could stay longer, she needed to be on her way. As she readied to leave, Joe approached her. "Are you going to Candle on your way to Fairbanks?"

"Yes. It's my first stop."

"Nena's sister lives in Candle. She's having a baby and asked Nena to come."

"I can take her."

"Nena, do you want to go?" Joe asked.

She nodded hesitantly. "She needs me."

"How much will it cost?" Joe asked Kate.

"For you? Nothing." Turning to Nena, Kate asked, "Will you need a flight back?"

"No. My sister's husband will bring me. He has a good sled and strong dogs."

"Okay. I'll have to get the plane ready. And we'll take off at first light."

"I'll be there." Nena's voice sounded small and wobbled a bit.

It was still dark when Kate made her way to the airstrip. Joe walked beside her, carrying a firepot to heat the engine. Kate had a lantern in one hand and a can of heated oil in the other. The lantern light flickered over glistening snow.

Joe pulled the tarp off the Bellanca, lit the firepot, and set it beneath the engine. Kate poured oil in and then went to work clearing ice from the plane.

Once the engine was warm enough, she cranked it and then started it. While the Bellanca ran, she did her usual check of the gauges and consulted her maps.

A light bobbed through the darkness. It was Nena with the baby in a pack, tucked in the front of her parka.

Kate stepped out of the plane. "Ready?"

Nena nodded. Her eyes looked wider than usual as she stared at the plane. "It's loud," she shouted.

"That's normal. Climb in. It's warmer inside than out."

Nena faced Joe, her hands on his arms. "I will be back soon."

He hugged her, then lifted the baby's hood and kissed the top of her head. "Send a message when you're coming home."

"I will." She kissed him, then turned and stared at the plane.

Joe put an arm around her and walked her to the door. He whispered something in her ear, and she leaned against him for a few more seconds. With a nod, she turned and climbed in.

"See you, Joe," Kate hollered, stepping in behind Nena. "I'll take good care of her."

Joe nodded and closed the door. Kate latched it from the inside. "You can sit up front with me," she told Nena as she headed for the cockpit.

Looking stiff and apprehensive, the native woman made

her way to the front and gently lowered herself into the passenger seat beside Kate. She gazed at the dimly lit sky.

"I'm glad I get to be the one to take you up."

Nena didn't respond. She looked downright scared.

"There's nothing to worry about. This is a good solid plane, and I'm a first-rate pilot. The weather's calm. We'll be fine."

"You think so?"

"I do. And it's not far to Candle." She smiled, hoping to instill confidence.

Kate revved the engine and throttled up. Nena grabbed hold of the side of her seat.

"It'll be all right. I promise," Kate reassured her friend.

"Thank you, but you cannot promise. Only God knows."

Kate wasn't sure how to respond. Over the years, she'd had lots of nervous passengers, and usually there was little that could be said to make them feel better, but Nena was a woman of faith.

Kate gave it another try. "God does know. So we'll be fine."

"What if he knows I'm going to die today?" Her eyes looked almost round.

Kate nearly laughed, but managed to remain serious. "I'm sure he wants you to live. You're too precious a human being, and you've got your children to look after."

"If I'm precious, he might want me in heaven with him." Nena smiled.

"I guess we'll just have to see then."

Kate turned the plane so it was lined up for takeoff and headed down the runway. When they lifted off a small "Oh" escaped Nena's lips. She clung to her little girl. Once in the air, she stared at the snowy world below. "How wonderful! I am seeing as God sees." She glanced at Kate. "It's beautiful. I think I like flying."

Kate laughed, thinking back to her first time in the air and the wonder of it. "I'll take you whenever you want—when I'm in Kotzebue."

"I'd like that." Nena took in a loud breath. "Oh, see there—the mountains. They look so different from here—even more beautiful." She turned dark eyes on Kate. "Thank you. Even if I were to die today, I would be happy."

"Your happiness is all good and well, Nena, but I'm more inclined to keep on living."

"Yes. I agree. It is a good day to live."

— 13 —

Kate pulled on her coat. It was nearly time to leave for Albert and Helen's place. Her eyes wandered to the end table where she'd left Richard's letter. She dropped onto the sofa, picked up the envelope, and opened it. She skimmed over his greeting—*"My dearest Kate."* She wished he wouldn't say that. She wasn't his Kate anymore. The words blurred and she blinked back tears, remembering how things had once been between them—a lifetime ago.

"I've been waiting, hoping and praying you'd come home. I've written and heard nothing back from you. I don't think a letter is asking too much."

Guilt clenched Kate's insides. She'd meant to write. She'd even started a letter, more than once, but didn't know how to tell him what she felt. She tried to focus on the words.

"Do you think you'll be coming home soon? I found a little place down by the river. It would be perfect for us. There's good fishing along that stretch."

Kate crumpled up the letter, tossed it in the wastebasket, and strode to her desk. She grabbed a sheet of paper, dipped a pen in ink, and fought for the right words. It was over. She had to tell him.

"*Dear Richard.*" The salutation glared back at her. She dipped her pen into the ink, then wrote, "*I'm sorry for not writing sooner. I meant to.*"

She stopped. The letter had to be honest and firm but not cruel.

Kate continued, "*I'll never forget what we had.*" She swiped at a tear. "*But everything's different now. I have a new life. I'm happy and doing what I've always dreamed of.*" She gripped the pen more tightly. "*I can't give it up, not even for you, not for anyone.*"

Kate studied her words. Did she mean it—was flying more important than everything else? She couldn't imagine life without it.

"*I tried to explain before I left, but I guess I didn't do a very good job of it. I'm sorry things have turned out as they have, but we're not meant to be together. You will always be a sweet memory, but it's time to go on with your life as I have with mine.*" Her pen hovered over the paper. "*I know there is someone for you who will be the kind of wife you need. I will always cherish what we had and I pray you'll find peace and love.*"

She reread the letter and signed it, "*Sincerely, Kate.*"

Kate gently blew on the paper to dry the ink, slipped it into an envelope, and put a stamp on it. Before she left the apartment, she fished Richard's crumpled letter out of the wastebasket, pressed out some of the wrinkles, and set it in the desk drawer.

On her way out of the store, she dropped the envelope in the mail slot, then pulled on her gloves and headed for the car. It was New Year's Eve—a time for new beginnings. She didn't want to think about Richard anymore.

When Kate pulled up in front of Albert and Helen's home, she wondered why there were no other cars out front. She'd expected a group of partiers. Shutting off the engine, she stepped into the cold and gazed at a clear night sky with patches of sparkling frozen fog. She walked up a path cut through the snow, ice crunching beneath her boots. Although Albert had spread gravel on the walkway, there were still slick spots so she put her feet down with care. She stepped onto a small porch where a Christmas wreath decorated with red ribbon and pine cones still hung at eye level.

Before she could knock, Albert swung open the door. "Evening, Kate. Come on in."

She walked indoors and looked around the front room. There were no other guests. "Am I early?"

Closing the door, Albert glanced at the clock. "No. Didn't Helen say eight?"

"Well then, I guess everyone else is late."

"The only one who'll be here besides you is Mike." He helped her with her coat. "It'll just be the four of us. Figure the other pilots didn't want to hang out with a couple of old codgers like me and Helen on New Year's Eve."

"Speak for yourself," Helen called from the back of the house.

Albert glanced toward the kitchen, then hung Kate's heavy parka in a closet adjacent to the entryway. Resting a hand on her back, he ushered her into a small living room.

Helen kept a tidy home. Colorful afghans hugged overstuffed furniture and a fire crackled in a Franklin stove. The occasional table and piano had become collection centers for family photos. Most of the pictures were of their two children, taken at varying ages. They both lived outside Alaska now, a heartache for Helen.

"My sweetheart's been baking all day. I almost think she likes New Year's more than Christmas." Albert grinned.

"Is there something I can do to help?"

"I think she's got things under control, but I'm sure she'd enjoy your company. Go on in."

Kate walked to the back of the house where Helen was taking a pan out of the oven. "What is that wonderful smell?"

"Apple strudel." Helen set the steaming dessert in the warming closet of her Windsor range. Closing the door and still wearing her mitts, she turned and hugged Kate. "So good you could come." She held her at arm's length. "This is going to be fun."

"Albert said it's just Mike and me."

"I'm glad. We'll have a chance to get to know Mike better. He only comes into the store once in a while, mostly to see you, I think." Helen tugged off her cooking mitts and set them on the counter beside the stove. "He seems like such a nice young man. I'd guess you two have a lot in common."

Kate lifted her brows. "If I didn't know better, I'd say you're matchmaking."

Helen chuckled. "Oh no. I'll leave that up to God." She smiled. "But you did attend Christmas services with him, didn't you?"

"Yes, but that's all. He got an emergency call and had to leave." Kate had been disappointed but wasn't about to let on. "We're friends—nothing more. There's no room in my life for romance, anyway. I have my career to think about."

"There's always room for romance." Helen's eyes sparkled with amusement.

"Mike and I have never even had a date." *Not a real one anyway.*

Helen offered a knowing smile. "If he has any brains, that'll change soon. Would you like some coffee?"

"That sounds good."

Helen filled two cups with dark brew and handed one to Kate. "There's cream and sugar."

"That would only ruin it." Kate took a sip. "You make the best coffee."

Helen poured cream into her cup, then added a spoonful of sugar. "To tell you the truth, it's a little strong for me. But that's the way Albert likes it." She sat at the kitchen table.

Kate settled into a chair across from her and took another drink of coffee. "I like it strong. But not like Sidney's. His is too much like mud."

"It is dreadful." Helen chuckled, then set her cup on the table in front of her, her expression turning serious. "You know, Kate, one day a career won't be enough. There's more to life than flying."

"I know that. But I've got to work hard while I can. The rest will come . . . later."

"And what if the right man comes along now?" Helen picked up a dish of chocolate drop cookies sitting on the table. "Cookie?"

Kate took one, wondering about Helen's statement. What would she do if she fell in love? Mike was a good man. She liked him, but could she love him?

"I have peanut butter and oatmeal raisin if you'd like."

"Thanks, but I better stick to one at a time." Kate took a bite of her cookie. "Even if the 'right' man came along, I'm not ready to see anyone, not like that. It hasn't been that long since I broke my engagement."

"Of course, that's right. I'm sorry. I'm being thoughtless."

"No. It's just that I got a letter from Richard. Sometimes it feels like he's still with me. He doesn't want to let go."

"Really? How so?"

"He keeps telling me that we belong together, that he loves me. And in his most recent letter, he told me about a house he'd found for us." Kate shook her head. "It's not like him. He almost sounds a little cracked, like he's not living in the real world. I thought he understood about my flying. I wrote back explaining that everything is over between us. I hope he gets it this time. It was a difficult letter to write."

"It's hard to let go of someone you love." Helen smiled softly. "I remember a young man I dated, back before I met Albert. When he ended our relationship, I thought my heart would break. I mooned over him for weeks and weeks. I even wrote him love letters that I never sent. I remember a few times going to the café where we used to meet, hoping he'd come in and realize how much he missed me."

Helen sipped her coffee. "It was so silly, but at the time I remember it felt as if my life had come to an end."

"So, what do you think I should do?"

"Just allow time, dear. He'll get over you eventually."

"I'm not even sure I ever loved him. Sometimes I think I told him I'd marry him because it was expected. Our families had been friends for years and we'd dated all through high school. Marriage seemed the reasonable next step."

"Usually being reasonable is good, but when it comes to love . . . well, there's just nothing reasonable about it." Helen dipped a cookie into her coffee and took a bite. The room turned quiet, except for the ticking of a porcelain plate clock that hung on the wall. Finally, Helen rested her arms on the table and leaned toward Kate. "I'm worried about you."

"Me? Why?"

"You're such a lovely woman, but you're single-minded— fly, fly, fly. That's all you think about."

"That's not true."

"No?" Helen leaned back, her eyes holding Kate's.

"I have other interests."

Helen didn't respond.

Kate rummaged through her mind to come up with something she enjoyed besides flying. "I . . . I like to read." It was true, but these days Kate rarely had time for books. "And I get to meet lots of interesting people in the bush. Once the weather warms up, I'll have someone show me the good fishing spots. I love to fish."

Helen smiled kindly. "It's all right, dear. I understand passions. I have my own. Just make sure to include time for friends and diversions other than flying, at least once in a while."

"You don't need to worry. I'm not bored, not at all. There's so much to learn about being a good pilot. Here everything's new and challenging." She propped her elbows on the table and rested her chin in her hands. "I still can hardly believe my job is doing what I love most."

"Why did you choose Alaska? It's so far from home. Your family must miss you."

"They do. But Mom and Dad plan to make a trip up next summer. I can't wait to show them Alaska."

"But . . . why Alaska, dear?"

"I wanted a challenge, a place where I could test myself."

"You've mentioned that before. Why do you feel a need to . . . prove yourself? You're a fine pilot. Everyone knows that."

Kate had never told Helen about Alison and what had happened at Rimrock Lake—that Alison was dead because of her—that if she'd been a better pilot, her dearest friend would still be alive. "I don't see anything wrong with challenging myself."

"No. Of course not. But you seem compelled to push too hard."

"I guess it's just the perfectionist in me," Kate quipped, trying to make light of the subject. She picked up her cup and took a drink. She knew what pushed her, why she took risks. There was no shutting out the voices in her head that accused her of being a failure, a lark-about, a murderer. Painful memories dragged her back to Rimrock Lake. Why couldn't she forget? It was part of the past and yet it still tormented her.

She had so many questions. If anyone could answer them, it was Helen. Kate set down her cup, her fingertips barely touching the smooth china. Her voice quiet, she asked, "Do you know why God allows good people to die?"

"We all die sometime, the good and the bad."

"But why would he take a young person, someone who deserves to live?"

"We can't know God's ways, dear. But he has his reasons. We just have to trust him." Helen's eyes turned more gentle. "What's troubling you?"

"I was just wondering."

Helen waited, as if she knew Kate needed to talk.

Kate sat back in her chair, draped one leg over the other, and folded her arms across her chest. She might as well tell her. Looking straight at Helen, she blurted, "A friend of mine died, and it was my fault."

Helen's expression looked grieved. "I'm so sorry." She reached across the table and rested a hand on Kate's arm. "I'm sure it wasn't your fault."

"It was." Kate closed her eyes, the terrible day rushing back at her. "I was nineteen. Alison was my best friend."

While Kate told her story, Helen kept ahold of her hands, gently squeezing from time to time. Kate told Helen everything, making no effort to hold back her tears. Sometimes it seemed there was no end to them.

Helen took a hankie out of the top drawer of a buffet and handed it to Kate. "It was an accident, dear. We can't be in control of everything."

"If I hadn't convinced her to go and if I'd turned back when I saw the fog . . ."

"You didn't know."

Kate wiped her eyes and blew her nose. "I knew better."

"You were just a girl." Helen moved to Kate and put an arm around her. "It's an awfully heavy burden you're carrying. Don't you think God could have saved your friend if that had been his will?"

"I suppose." Kate dabbed at her eyes. "Why do you think he didn't? Alison loved God. She was the kindest person I've ever known."

"I don't know why God does what he does. But I do know all things work out just the way he has planned. All we see of this world is what's right in front of us. But there's so much more, and God sees it all. Alison's life didn't end that day in the lake. She's still living, only in a place we can't see. She's with God." Helen took Kate's face in her hands and pressed a gentle kiss to her forehead. "I'm certain she's not angry with you."

Kate took in a shaky breath, envisioning Alison in heaven. It made her feel better.

"Is that why you left Washington, why you refused Richard?"

A knock sounded at the door, and Albert's greeting to Mike carried in from the front room.

Kate quickly wiped away her tears.

"Something sure smells good," Mike said as he walked into the kitchen, rubbing his hands together. "Thanks for the invite, Albert. Figure the best food in town is here."

With a light touch to Kate's hand, Helen stood and moved to Mike, giving him a hug. "We're so glad you could join us."

Kate glanced at him. "Hi."

"Hey, Kate." He looked more closely. "You all right?"

"I'm fine." She glanced away and dabbed at her nose with the handkerchief.

Helen rested a hand on her shoulder. "She's just a bit emotional—girl talk. You know how it can be."

Mike nodded, but obviously didn't understand.

Albert peered into the oven warmer. The smell of apples and cinnamon wafted into the room. He looked at Helen. "How about some strudel and a game of Parcheesi?"

"Sounds good to me. You men set up the game while Kate and I get the dessert and coffee."

"I'll pour the coffee," Kate offered, her mind still on Helen's words. Was it true—had it just been a freak accident? There were those who didn't think so, people who hated her—who would never forgive her.

— 14 —

Paul took a bottle of Jack Daniels down from an upper cabinet, uncorked it, and poured the liquor into a glass. He stared at the amber liquid. He was about to break his own rule to drink for medicinal purposes only. It was New Year's Eve and he was alone just as he had been for the last four years. After pushing the cork back into the bottle, he returned to his chair and the book *Call of the Wild*.

He sipped the drink, then set the glass on a table beside him and turned to the familiar story. But his mind wandered to previous New Year's celebrations. His family had always gathered for fireworks displays or an evening of game playing at his parents' home. One year, when he wasn't quite a man, he and his brothers raided their father's liquor cabinet. When their mother discovered them pickled, she'd given them a tongue lashing and then, grabbing the two closest to her, she dragged them by the earlobes to their rooms. The other boys followed, thankful they'd been out of their mother's reach.

Paul smiled at the memory. It had made a lasting impression.

Like a malevolent shadow, loneliness crept about inside of him. He tried to concentrate on the story, but couldn't block out his surroundings. The house felt too isolated, too empty, too quiet. He set the book in his lap, picked up the glass, and took a gulp. It burned as it went down, and heated his belly before gradually traveling to his limbs.

Eyes closed, he laid his head against the back of the chair. The indifference of the wilderness closed in, and a black hole of misery called to him. What lay ahead? Would he spend his life alone?

He returned to his book, but after reading the same paragraph five times, he set it aside. Taking the whiskey with him, he left his chair, went to the front door, and stepped onto the porch. It was quiet except for the sound of tree boughs in the wind and the clank of chains as the dogs roused. Clouds scuttled across a half moon.

He looked toward the Warrens' place. They'd invited him for dinner and game playing, but the idea of Sassa's match-making had kept him away. Jasper, the raven, cawed at him from his perch on the porch.

"You feeling lonely too?" Paul went to touch him, but Jasper flitted to a post out of reach. "What a friend you turned out to be. Go on, then," he said, feeling betrayed and flagging him away. The bird took flight.

Paul's thoughts wandered to San Francisco. What was his family doing? He allowed his mind to roam back to the last New Year's he'd shared with Susan. If he'd known their time together would be so short, he'd have made sure to do something special—perhaps a night on the bay, sailing under the radiance of a bright moon with the city lights glistening off the water. She'd always loved sailing.

Instead their last celebration had been spent at his mother's. That year everyone had gathered at the piano. They'd started with fun songs like "In the Shade of the Old Apple Tree," "Let Me Call You Sweetheart," and "The Red River Valley." His mother had suggested some of the sacred tunes—she always did. Her favorite was "Beautiful Home Somewhere." Susan had insisted they sing "When the Roll Is Called Up Yonder." His heart squeezed at the memory. It still didn't seem possible that she was gone.

He tried not to think about her, but loneliness yawned at him from the night. Paul downed his drink, then returned to the kitchen for another. He filled his glass, pulled on a coat, and headed back outdoors. This time the dogs whined, hoping for a romp.

A braid of green light rippled across the sky. There was another, and then one that blazed red and pink reached toward heaven. Paul never tired of watching the Northern Lights. They were startling and mysterious. *I wish* . . . He stopped the thought. Wishing did no good. Some things weren't meant to be.

He leaned on the porch rail and sipped his drink. The wind gusted, sifting frozen snow across the top of the railing. He stared at the sky where the winter spectacle of lights had quieted. Clouds shielded all but a few winking stars.

"Why did you take her from me? Why? She was so beautiful, so good. She deserved to live." The acrid taste of bitterness tracked a familiar path inside him.

His glass empty, Paul returned to the kitchen for a refill and downed another drink. Grabbing the bottle of whiskey, he dropped onto a chair at the table. The world was tilted and out of focus. He replenished his glass, slopping whiskey over the edges of the tumbler. He gulped down the fiery liquid. The lantern blurred and the room spun slowly. He'd had too much. Fresh air would help. He grabbed his coat, taking several tries to get his arms through the sleeves.

Paul stumbled onto the porch and down the steps. Slipping on the frozen boards, he barely caught hold of the rail before landing on his backside. He hauled himself upright, then strode to the dogs. He gave each a pat. "Sooo," he slurred. "You wanna romp?"

He nearly fell over when Buck leaned against him. "Watch it, buddy." His tongue felt thick and his words came out mangled. Giving the dog a good scrubbing around the neck, he unhooked his chain. Buck bounded around him, then took off up the trail. The other two dogs whined and lunged on their leads. When Paul freed them, they chased after Buck.

Walking a wavering path, Paul set off after them. They were soon out of sight and sound. Strong winds gusted, scattering ice and snow that lay on frozen birch and alder branches. Paul held out his arms, enjoying the shower. The world tipped, and he fumbled his way to the snow-covered ground where he lay on his back gazing up through tree limbs. Clouds had moved in and blocked out the stars.

Paul felt warm and mentally numb. He lay there a long while. Snow started to fall. He closed his eyes, enjoying the feel of the lacy crystals on his face. The sound of the dogs crashing through underbrush roused him from his stupor. He sat up and stumbled to his feet.

"Hey, Buck, where are you?" His words were slurred and indistinct. He peered into the forest, then hollered, "Jackpot. Nita." They didn't appear. Paul called again. Still nothing. "Where've you gone off to? Nita, you need to take care—you've got pups to think about."

Dizzy, he leaned against a birch, wondering if he had enough wherewithal to make it home. The wind howled now, and the snow no longer drifted but came down in a heavy white curtain. Paul glanced about. Even in his drunken state, he knew he needed to get back to the cabin.

After one more unsuccessful call for the dogs, he staggered up the trail. A strong blast of wind stripped snow and ice from trees, and Paul heard a loud pop. He looked up just as a limb whacked him across the skull. Pain and bright colors exploded in his head. Then the world went black.

The next thing Paul felt was something warm and wet on his face. He struggled toward consciousness and tried to pry open his eyelids. He blinked and peered through spruce boughs and snow. He could make out dusky light. Buck stood over him. Paul pushed a tree branch off his head, and Buck enthusiastically washed his master's face. Trying to avoid the unwanted bath, Paul turned his head, but the movement sent piercing pain through his skull, down his neck, and into his right shoulder. He tried to sit up, but the world spun and nausea rolled through him. He lay back down, closing his eyes tightly. Buck continued to lick him.

"Cut it out." His eyes still closed, Paul pushed the dog back.

Buck whined and nudged him.

"Okay. Okay." Paul looked up at the big dog's face, only inches from his own. He could feel the warmth of his breath.

Moving slowly this time, he looked around, but didn't see the other two dogs. "Thanks for staying with me, boy."

His head throbbing, Paul pressed a hand to his brow. How long had he been out here? Buck lay beside him and rested his big head on his master's chest. Paul buried a hand in the dog's thick coat.

Knowing he needed to get back to the cabin, Paul forced himself up on one arm. Immediately the dizziness and nausea returned. He waited and gradually the spinning slowed. He brushed snow off his coat and pants and tried to make sense of the revolving world as he managed to get to his feet. Standing amplified the throbbing in his skull. He leaned against a tree, thinking back to the previous evening. He remembered the whiskey and the snowstorm. He was lucky to be alive.

Home seemed a long way off, but he managed one step and then another. How far had he come? With Buck at his side, Paul moved forward, his stomach churning and his head thumping. He probably had a concussion. *Keep going. Don't stop.*

"Paul?" A voice echoed through the trees.

He looked up the trail. It was Patrick. Relief seemed to take the strength out of his legs, and Paul dropped to his knees.

Patrick ran to him, his narrow face lined with worry. "Thank the Lord I found you."

"How'd you know I was out here?" Paul's voice sounded raspy.

"Your dogs. Jackpot and Nita showed up at my place this morning."

Paul pressed a hand to his head. "I got hit by a tree limb. Knocked me out."

Patrick leaned down and examined Paul's face. "No frost-bite, that's good."

"Buck stayed with me. When I came to, he was licking my face."

"Good dog. And the other two showing up at my place was smart. I think they wanted me to find you." He eyed Buck. "Figure when Nita has her pups I'll be wanting one."

Paul placed a hand on Buck's broad head. "You can have your pick. That is, after Kate chooses."

"Kate?" Patrick lifted an eyebrow.

"She needs a companion, especially when she flies."

"Sure." Patrick grinned. "Not a bad idea." He put a hand on Paul's shoulder. "Do you think you can make it or should I get the sled?"

"I can walk. My head feels like a bomb went off inside, though."

Patrick gently pulled back Paul's hood. "Ooh wee, you've

got a mess back here. A bad cut, blood everywhere, and a mountain-sized lump."

"Figured. I could feel something sticky back there," Paul said, knowing he was lucky to have regained consciousness.

"Sassa will stitch up that cut. She's good at that kind of thing." Patrick grimaced and leaned away from Paul. "Smells like you had a one-man party last night. Figure you'd have a headache even if a tree didn't hit you." He shook his head. "There are better ways to greet the New Year."

"Yeah. I know."

"Didn't think you drank."

"I don't—not usually and not again."

Patrick leaned down and got a shoulder under Paul's arm and hefted him to his feet. The two hobbled down the trail.

Sassa stepped into the bedroom, carrying a bowl of soup. "This will warm your insides."

"You don't need to do that. I'm all right." Paul lay on his bed, propped up on pillows.

"After what you've been through, you better stay put for a few days." She handed the bowl to Lily, who sat on a chair beside the bed. "Make sure he eats."

She nodded.

"Lily doesn't have to stay. I'll be fine."

"You've been walloped on the head. Never know what might happen. She'll take good care of you."

Paul didn't respond, too weak to battle.

"She'll stay with you today, and I'll be back tonight." The bossy, though kindhearted, native walked toward the bedroom door. "Praise the Lord you're all right." Her expression turned stern. "That was a stupid thing you did. I thought you had more sense."

"So did I."

Sassa stepped out of the room. Lily scooted a chair closer to the bed. "Mama makes good soup." She ladled a spoonful.

"Thanks, Lily, but I can feed myself." He reached for the bowl, and Lily handed it and the spoon to him.

"While you eat, I'll clean up the place," she said and quickly exited the room, acting as if she were embarrassed to be there.

"One thing you can do for me," Paul called, squeezing his eyes shut at the pain screeching through his head when he'd raised his voice.

Lily appeared at the door.

"How about slicing off a piece of moose meat for each of the dogs? They did a good thing last night."

Lily smiled. "They did. You could have died."

Paul tasted the soup. He didn't want to talk about his poor judgment.

Lily started to leave when Paul said, "Wait."

She turned to look at him.

"Thanks . . . for staying."

Her cheeks flushed and her brown eyes turned warm. "You're welcome."

Two days later, another storm swept up Cook Inlet and moved inland. Recovering from his concussion, Paul was confined to the cabin. He'd convinced Lily she didn't need to stay, so he was on his own with a head that still throbbed and a sore, stiff neck.

Wind pelted the little house and snow drifted into piles, transforming the landscape into mounds of white. Paul watched, thinking about all the work the storm was creating. He'd have to clear the snow from the outbuilding doorways, shovel off the porch and steps, and clear drifted snow from beneath the cache and around the wood stack. The dogs had managed to burrow holes so they could climb in and out of their houses, but Paul would have to shovel away enough snow to give them room to move about.

For now, all he could do was tend the fire, sleep, and keep himself and his dogs fed. In spite of his frustration, he knew rest was the best thing for him. However, he couldn't keep from thinking about his trapline and the animals that might be suffering. He usually checked the traps every other day.

He stepped onto the porch. The thermometer read twenty-five degrees—up ten degrees in the last couple of hours. Still, the storm gave no sign of abating. He wouldn't be going anywhere, not yet.

The wind increased and snow came down heavily as the temperature continued to rise. It was almost thirty-two degrees, nearly warm enough to rain. Paul had never seen rain in January, not since moving to the creek.

The storm pummeled southwest Alaska for three days. By the time the weather cleared, so had Paul's headache. The cut on his skull was healing well but still felt tender to the touch. He could move his neck with only little discomfort. He was ready to get outdoors.

The trapline would have to wait one more day while he cleared snow. The porch, woodshed, and outhouse were highest priority, so he tackled them first. By the time he'd completed that, he was sweating and exhausted, and the pounding in his head had returned. He pushed past his discomfort and, after a short break for lunch, went back to work, clearing snow from around the dogs' leads, the shed door, and the cache, and stomping down trails between buildings. At the end of the day, he was too exhausted to bother eating and fell into bed half dressed.

He rose early the next morning, hungry and eager to get to his trapline. After a breakfast of pancakes and bacon, he made a lunch to take along, then pulled on his parka. With his pack draped over one shoulder and his snowshoes over the other, he headed outdoors.

It was warm. Snow melt dripped from the roof. Wet snow would make for difficult travel. He looked at an overcast sky and noted the winds, which were light and coming from the north. Likely the temperature would drop. He tramped to the sled and placed his pack and snowshoes on it, then headed for the cache for bait. With everything ready to go, he strapped Buck into the harness.

They set off, the big dog lunging through chest-deep piles of white. It was slow going, and Paul soon realized he should have used two dogs. But he'd come too far to go back so they pushed on. When they left the trail, traveling became more difficult, but Buck charged forward. To lighten the load, Paul walked behind the sled. Although Buck and the sled helped pack the snow, soon his muscles ached and his boots felt heavy, as if they'd been filled with buckshot.

By the time he reached the first trap, his headache roared. The leghold was buried and the bait was gone. He cleared away snow, reset the trap, and rebaited it.

At the second leghold, his spirits lifted when he found a marten. It was only partially frozen. He'd have to skin him out as soon as he got back to the cabin.

By midday, Paul had made it through half the line. The takings had been scant—one marten and a fox. His stomach rumbling, he pulled the sled to a stop, fed and watered Buck, then sat on a stump to eat his lunch.

The forest was silent, except for the drip, drip, dripping of melting snow and the occasional *whoomph* as a mound fell from tree boughs. Buck lay with his head on his front paws, eyes closed.

Paul took a long drink from his canteen and fished out one

of two sandwiches. He ate both, then three oatmeal cookies Lily had made. They were good.

Finished, he returned to the sled where Buck was up and ready to go. As soon as Paul gave him the okay, he lunged in the harness and plowed forward.

Paul ran most of the way except when Buck headed down a hill, then he rode the footboards. They headed into a gully. When they reached a stream at the bottom, Paul ran behind while Buck trotted across without difficulty.

When Paul stepped onto the ice, it cracked and popped. The next thing he knew, his left foot broke through to the icy water and he lunged forward to gain a foothold. He moved on, the ice breaking with each step.

Freezing water seeped into Paul's boots and soaked his pants up to his thighs. Afraid the sled would break through, he yelled, "Hike up!"

Buck moved faster, pulling the sled onto the bank and up the hill on the other side.

Paul sloshed to shore, then ran to catch up. "Buck! Whoa, Buck!"

The dog kept moving.

"Buck!"

Paul forced his tired legs to keep moving. When he caught the sled, he pushed down the brake, which planted claws into the snow. The big dog stopped and looked back at Paul, a questioning look on his face.

Paul checked his boots and pants. They were soaked, but he decided the temperatures weren't cold enough to cause frostbite, so he pushed on.

By the time he made it back to the trail, his feet felt numb. They ached and burned. He needed to get home and warm up. To make better time, he forced himself to run behind the sled instead of riding. Each step sent shocks of pain through his feet and into his lower legs.

Buck moved along steadily. When the cabin came into view, he picked up his pace, stopping only when he reached the yard. After taking Buck out of the harness, Paul left him free while he put the sled away. It hadn't been a good day—two pelts and two frozen feet.

In spite of his need to get inside to warm up, Paul took care of the dogs first, giving them fresh water and food. Not until he skinned out the marten and fox and stretched them on a board did he finally limp to the house.

Closing the door behind him, he hobbled to the stove and checked for live embers. Some still glowed red, so he added kindling. He filled a pan with water and set it on the cast iron range. After limping to his chair, he dropped onto its soft cushion and pulled off his boots. He could barely wiggle his toes. The kindling crackled to life, so Paul added wood, then shuffled back to the chair and removed his wet pants and socks.

Lifting one leg, he rested the ankle over his knee so he could examine his foot. It was red and mottled. Paul pressed his thumbnail into the skin. He could feel the jab. *Just cold is all*. He massaged the foot, then checked the other one. It was the same. When they heated up, they'd hurt, but there wasn't any frostbite.

I should have known better, he thought. He added more wood to the fire, made a pot of coffee, then put on clean clothes. Feeling slightly better, he dropped into his chair, and rubbed his feet.

About the time the coffee was ready, so was the water. Paul finally settled in his chair and placed his cold, naked feet in warm water. He could barely feel the heat, but knew that would soon change.

He rested his head against the back of the chair and closed his eyes, wondering what he was doing in Alaska. Nothing had changed. He was as incompetent here as he had been in

San Francisco. Two stupid decisions in one week—maybe he didn't belong here. But if not here, where?

When his feet felt mostly normal, Paul put on socks and slippers. Drowsy, he pulled a blanket around his shoulders and rested his feet on a homemade ottoman. He closed his eyes and thought of home. He could almost feel the touch of a cool breeze and hear the sounds of the city, the clack of trolley cars.

A picture of old Klaus, who lived upriver, imposed on his memories. Would he end up like Klaus, alone and cranky? What would have happened if he'd stayed in San Francisco? He'd run without thought.

Paul dozed, thankful to leave behind his doubts. When he woke, his feet felt nearly as good as new, so he tidied up the cabin and mixed a batch of sourdough bread. After a light meal, he stepped outside to check the temperature. The thermometer registered twelve degrees. The north winds had brought frigid weather just as he'd expected.

He gazed at stars shimmering against a dark sky, then looked at the Warrens' place. The windows were alight. It was still early; maybe he should stop in and say hello. They'd welcome him; he was sure of that. But remembering Lily, he decided it would be better to keep to himself.

In the distance the howl of a wolf sliced through the emptiness. Paul gazed into the dark forest, wondering where the call had come from. Another cry echoed, this one slightly different from the first. *Even wolves have families.*

Wanting somehow to connect, Paul let out a soft howl. It sounded pathetic. He tried again, only this time he cupped his hands around his mouth and called more loudly. He waited, hoping for a response. There was nothing but the quiet wilderness with its sigh of tree boughs sounding like a lonely whisper.

— 15 —

The shop was quiet, except for the pop of wood in the stove and an occasional sniffle from Jack, who had a cold. The smell of overcooked coffee hung in the air, and Sidney and Jack sat across from each other, playing a game of checkers.

Kate leaned back in her chair, bored and wishing the fog would lift. The heat and inactivity made her sleepy. Through half-closed lids, she watched a smirk appear on Jack's lips.

"Who taught you to play checkers, your sister?" he asked.

Sidney remained focused. "Nope. The best player in Kenai—my grandpa."

"There's tough competition down there—grannies and girlies." Jack snickered. He picked up a black checker and jumped one of Sidney's red ones. He snatched up the game piece and stacked it on two others he already possessed. "Got you now."

Sidney continued to study the red and black squares. Kate wished he'd make a play. He always took forever to make a move.

Maybe I should go home. Nothing happening here. She looked out the window. Ice fog draped itself over the world, coating everything with a heavy shimmering frost.

Sidney jumped two of Jack's pieces, then set them down casually on his side of the board. A look of surprise hit Jack's face. "You can't do that."

"The heck I can't. That's a—" the phone rang—"perfectly good move." The phone jangled again. "Give me a second and I'll explain it to you." His voice was laced with sarcasm. Sidney rolled his chair to a phone hanging on the wall and picked up.

"Hello." His *h* sounded like a *y*. Kate could barely make out the sound of someone's voice on the other end of the line. Their tone was sharp. "Yep, that's me," Sidney's brows creased. "How bad is he?"

Kate sat up, dropping the front legs of her chair to the floor.

"Doesn't sound good. Thought they had a doc up there." He glanced at Kate. "Yeah." His eyes went to Jack. "Fog's bad here. I'll see what we can do." He was quiet while he listened. "Give me a few minutes. I'll get back to you."

He hung up the phone. "That was the hospital. We got a mercy flight. Independence Mine up in Hatcher Pass said one of their men took a fall. He's in a bad way. Has a back injury, probably broken ribs. Said if they don't get him to a hospital, he'll likely die."

"What do they expect us to do? It's freezing and thick as pea soup out there." Jack pushed away from the table. "Can't they just truss him up for a day or two?"

"He's having trouble breathing. And they don't know how long he can hold out."

Jack glanced at the window and shook his head. "I'm not going out in this. Especially not for some rummy who probably fell 'cause he'd been at the hooch." He folded his arms across his chest.

Sidney turned to Kate.

She wasn't sure what she ought to do. The idea of flying in the fog made her stomach churn. She knew what could happen. She glanced at the window. "How bad you think it is out there?"

"Well, let's have a look." Sidney pushed to his feet and walked to the door. Opening it, he stepped into the freezing mist. "You probably have a few hundred yards' visibility . . . at most." He shook his head. "It's risky. But the fella said there wasn't any fog at the mine."

Kate stared into the icy vapor, turning her gaze skyward. "What do you think the ceiling is?"

"No way to tell, not until you get up there." Sidney's breath hung in the air. "You don't have to go."

"If I don't, that man could die."

Jack stepped into the doorway. "He could die just by getting in a plane with you." He chuckled.

Kate lifted a lip in contempt. She took in a deep breath. "I'll go."

"You're a bigger fool than I thought," Jack said. "Why risk your neck for someone you don't even know?"

For once Jack made sense. Yet, she couldn't put the suffering man out of her mind. She walked back inside the shop. "I've been up there before. The landing strip's not great, but it'll do. Shouldn't be a problem, especially since they don't have fog."

Sidney followed her. "It's colder than the dickens, though, and the winds can get bad through there." He closed the door, leaving Jack standing outside. "I'll make sure they stomp down the runway and set out signal fires."

"Thanks." Kate grabbed her oil pot and set it on the stove to heat. "I'll be fine," she said, but her mind whirled with memories of the last flight she'd made in the fog. She shook off her fear. Everything was different now. She was a better pilot with a lot more experience.

"The hospital's sending over a nurse to fly up with you."

Kate headed for the door. "I'll get the plane ready."

Sidney followed her. "You're sure? Your job description doesn't include offering up your life for someone else's."

Kate stopped and faced him. "It doesn't? I thought it did." She smiled and her tone teased. More seriously she asked, "Do you think I can do this?"

Sidney's eyes shifted away from Kate's. "It's a tough run even for the best pilot."

Kate had hoped for more enthusiasm. "Keep the lights on. I'll be back." She marched across the field.

"I'll bring out the oil as soon as it's warm."

"You're a fool," Jack said just loud enough so Kate could hear.

She ignored him, her mind already calculating what she needed to do to take off and find her way to Hatcher Pass.

Kate sat in the cockpit, letting the engine warm up while Sidney inspected the outside of the plane and cleared it of ice. Lights cut through the fog and a car stopped in front of the office. A woman bundled in an oversized parka stepped out and hurried across the field.

Kate moved to the door.

Sidney greeted the woman. "You from the hospital?"

"Yes."

The nurse didn't look exceptional in any way. She was small with short brown hair and blue eyes. Kate figured she couldn't be more than thirty. She climbed out of the plane and walked toward her. "Hi. I'm Kate."

"Doris Henson."

"Good to meet you." Kate reached out to shake her hand.

"You're the woman pilot I've been hearing about."

"That's me all right." Kate smiled, hoping to infuse the reticent woman with confidence.

Sidney was all business. "Time to go. Make sure to watch your altimeter. Don't want you flying into any mountains." He grinned, but the warning was serious. "And keep an eye on your inclinometer. It'll help make sure you're flying flat."

Kate nodded. She appreciated Sidney's concern, but she'd already been giving herself the same instructions.

"Fog's like a grafter," he continued. "It can con you, makes you think you're gaining altitude when you're losing it. And you can list heavy to one side, even get yourself upside down without knowing it." He pulled his coat closed. "I knew a guy who thought he was climbing, when all the while he was heading straight for the ground." Shaking his head, he continued, "Good thing he figured it out in time."

"Yeah, I know. I've heard that story before." She couldn't keep the dry tone out of her voice. Kate turned toward the plane. She knew this run was dangerous.

Sidney grabbed her and swung her around so she faced him. "I know you know, but . . . well, just keep an eye on your instruments."

"I will." Kate gave him a smile, unwilling to let him know she had her own doubts. She turned to Doris. "You sure you want to go along?"

Doris looked at the plane, compressed her lips, and then said, "There's a patient who needs me." She offered a tremulous smile.

"All right, then. We're on our way." Kate stood beside the door. "You can sit up front with me."

With a nod, Doris climbed in and headed toward the cockpit.

Kate took her place, nerves tight.

Doris held out Kate's Bible. "It was on the seat."

"Thanks." She took the book and stared at it. A piece of Scripture reverberated through her mind. *"In your unfailing love you will lead the people you have redeemed; in your strength you will guide them."* Lord, guide me now. She tucked the book into her pack. "All set?"

"I'm ready," Doris called over the noise of the engine.

Moving down the airstrip, Kate barreled through the fog. She had the sensation of moving through a milky tunnel. Picking up speed, she stared into the disorienting white haze. When the wheels left the ground, she felt almost dizzy. She pulled back on the stick and prayed the fog would give way to clear skies.

It didn't. Kate finally leveled off, the icy cloud encasing the plane. Her inclinometer told her she was off level so she tapped the rudder, watching until the ball moved back to center. Kate reminded herself of the years she'd spent in a cockpit. She knew enough to feel her way. She just needed to keep her heading.

Kate looked for any sign of clearing skies. There was nothing but a thick mist. Inclined to let off her speed, she watched closely so as not to cut back too much and stall out. She looked at the gauges repeatedly. Any mistake could prove fatal.

Her fingers tingled from gripping the stick. Her father's voice came to her. How many times had he said she was the best natural pilot he'd ever known?

He's right. Trust your instincts.

She checked the compass, which assured her she was on the right heading. With mountains to the north and the east, it was imperative she stay on course. She'd have to navigate the Matanuska Valley to get to Hatcher Pass. She kept waiting and praying for the fog to dissipate. *It'll probably be clear by the time I reach the valley.*

When a hole opened up, Kate got a peek at the ground. Instead of alder and birch forests there was water! Panic spiked through her. How could she have gotten so far off course? She rechecked the gauges. Everything looked fine. Tapping the compass, the needle dipped toward the south, then sprang north. The compass was off!

Kate had no idea where she was. She could be heading out to sea or flying directly into a mountain. There was no way to know. Her heart sped up, and her breaths came short and quick. She had to find a way out of the fog.

Her mind flashed back to that day at Rimrock Lake. She'd been confused, unable to tell which way was up or down. She'd made a bad choice then. Alison's sweet face swirled through her memories. *I killed her.* Glancing at Doris, who trusted her, she refocused on getting herself and Doris down safely.

Occasionally the fog thinned, giving her glimpses of what lay below. There was too much water for it to be anything other than Cook Inlet. She spotted a portion of coastline and then the fog closed in again. *I've got to find a place to land.*

"Doris." Kate tried to keep her voice calm. "The fog's too dense. I'm going to set us down."

The nurse gazed out the window. "Where?"

"I'll wait for an opening. There'll be a piece of beach. You'll see."

Doris nodded slightly, staring into the fog.

"We'll be fine. I'm a good pilot," Kate said, although she didn't think it would make an awful lot of difference who was flying just now. She needed something more powerful than herself. A Bible verse she'd heard as a child popped into her mind. *The Lord will never leave you nor forsake you.* "I need you now," she whispered.

Gripping the stick, Kate prayed for a break in the fog.

Staring into the mist, she tried to imagine a day in the future when she'd be telling the story about how she managed to get out of this jam.

She checked her altimeter. Should she climb or stay low? Either way it was a risk. If there were hills or mountains in front of her, she'd need more altitude, but to find a place to land she'd have to remain close to the ground.

I shouldn't have come. Jack was right. I am a fool. Her mind went to the man at the mining camp who was counting on her to rescue him. She felt sick. He'd probably die.

Like a shroud, the fog cloaked escape. Holding her breath, Kate pushed forward on the stick, dropping closer to the sea. She wondered what it felt like to die. A picture of her mother and father flashed through her mind. *I'm so sorry.*

Stop it. You'll find a way.

She kept flying, searching for a hole and hoping for a miracle.

Nita lay on the bed Paul had made for her in the house. She was edgy. Panting, she'd pace, then return to her bed and lie down only to get up again and pace some more.

Paul knelt beside her. "How you doing, girl?" He patted her head. She looked at him, her eyes sorrowful and questioning as if she didn't know what was happening to her.

He rested his hand on her side and felt the muscles tighten. "It won't be long."

Moving to the kitchen, he broke off a chunk of pound cake and stepped onto the porch. Jasper sat on his perch. Paul offered the bird a piece of cake, which the raven gulped down. "One of these days, you'll fly off and never come back." Paul felt a twinge of sadness at the idea. The bird had been interesting company.

He poured himself a cup of coffee, then cut a slice of pound cake for himself and turned on the radio. It was almost time for the Mukluk News, his daily connection with the rest of the territory and its happenings.

He moved to the window and stared out. Fog hovered and ice encrusted the trees and bushes. It was pretty to look at, but Paul preferred the warmer fog they'd had in San Francisco. Rather than holding the city in an icy grip, it had seemed to embrace it.

The radio crackled to life and a man's voice erupted from the small wooden cabinet. "Good afternoon. Welcome to the Mukluk News."

Nita stood and whined, searching for the source of the voice.

Paul sat at the table.

"Temperatures are dropping across the territory," the man said. "Those of you up around Barrow can expect temps to drop to fifty below tonight. You're going to need your long-johns for this one. No snow in the interior. And in South Central Alaska, expect more ice fog, and there will be heavy snowfall in the southeast.

"There's a message for Tom and Jenna Barkley. Your package is on its way. You can expect delivery Wednesday of next week, so be looking for it." He chuckled. "'Course from what I hear, your kids won't be too happy about it—think it has something to do with school."

Paul took a bite of cake and watched Nita for a few moments. She stood and turned around and then settled back down. The sound of crackling paper came across the airwaves. The broadcaster continued, "Congratulations are in order for Wilbur and June Harris. They had their first baby last Saturday—Robert James. Word is the little fella's robust and thriving."

There was a break for music. Paul checked on Nita and offered her fresh water. When the music ended, the announcer returned. "Word just in. There was an incident at the Independence Mine today. A man was injured in a fall. No news on his condition. A pilot who set out on a mercy flight didn't show up. Her plane is missing."

"Her?" Paul moved closer to the radio. The only female pilot in the area was Kate.

"Kate Evans flies for Sidney Schaefer who has a small outfit in Anchorage. The only passenger was a nurse, Doris Henson. A search is pending until weather conditions improve." There was a pause and then the man continued, "Our prayers go out to you tonight, Kate and Doris."

Paul sank into a chair, questions pounding his mind. What had happened to Kate? Was she down someplace? Was she safe? Or had she crashed? His elbows on the table, he put his face in his hands and tried to pray. It had been a long time and he felt guilty asking now—he'd ignored God for so long. "Lord . . . you know where Kate is. Help her."

His mind reeled back to San Francisco. He'd prayed then too, but God hadn't answered him. Paul pushed away from the table and walked outside. Staring in the direction of the creek, he wished there was something he could do. He was powerless. He gazed into drifting fog. Why would Kate go out in weather like this? Why did she have to push so hard?

The dogs set to barking and he turned to see a light bobbing through the fog. It was Patrick. "Did you hear?" he asked.

"Yeah."

Patrick clapped a hand on Paul's shoulder. "They'll find her. I'm sure she's all right."

Paul nodded. "You want to come in? I've got coffee on and there's cake."

"Sure."

Patrick followed Paul inside. His eyes went to Nita. "She having her pups?"

"Probably by morning."

Paul had planned to give one to Kate. Now . . .

Trying to block out morbid thoughts, he moved to the kitchen counter and cut a slice of cake for Patrick and then poured him a cup of coffee. He sat across the table from his neighbor.

Patrick took a bite and chewed. "Almost as good as Sassa's. Don't tell her I said that." He cut into the cake with his fork. "Kate's a good pilot. She most likely set down somewhere to wait out the weather."

"Yeah. You're probably right."

Patrick took a drink of coffee. "I'll radio Sidney if you want."

"The man on the news said they couldn't search right now because of the fog. Doubt Sidney knows anything."

Heaviness of heart pressed down on Paul. If something happened to Kate, the world would seem a little less bright. He'd miss her. *We barely know each other*, he thought, realizing he wanted time to know her better.

Paul kept the radio on while assisting with the delivery of five male and four female puppies. Unfortunately, the station signed off without additional news.

Unable to dismiss thoughts of Kate, he couldn't quiet his anxiety. His body vibrated with tension. He checked on Nita. The puppies were nursing while their mother gave them another bath.

"You're a good mom," Paul said, resting his hand on her head.

She pushed against his palm, then went back to cleaning her babies.

Imagining all sorts of horrific scenarios, Paul couldn't sleep. He tried to pray but couldn't believe anyone was listening.

Sometime in the middle of the night, he climbed out of bed. After stoking the fire, he made a quick check of Nita and her new family, then dropped into his chair. He picked up his Bible and stared at it for a long while. Finally he opened to Psalm 50 and read the fifteenth verse. *Call upon me in the day of trouble; I will deliver you, and you will honor me.*

Once he'd believed those words. But when he'd needed God the most, he hadn't been there. Paul closed the book, set it back on the table, and returned to bed.

— 16 —

Huddled beneath a blanket, Kate sat with her knees bent and pulled close to her chest. She stared at a fire made from driftwood and frozen grass. Cold air sucked the heat from the flames and carried it into the darkness.

She and Doris had cleared a small area at the edge of the beach out of reach of the inlet's extreme tide changes. She looked at Doris. "I'm sorry. This is my fault."

"It's your fault that we're alive." Hands trembling, Doris pulled her hood closer around her face.

Kate added more wood to the fire. It flared, sending a spray of burning embers into the air. "I shouldn't have taken the run."

"I chose to go with you. We were both thinking about that poor man." Doris's tone was persuasive. "And you couldn't control the compass."

Kate wanted to accept the heartening words, but the armor she'd worn for so long deflected them. "You want anything more to eat or drink?"

"I'm fine. And we better save some for tomorrow. If the weather doesn't change, we could be here awhile."

Kate gazed into the blackness, feeling dismal at the thought of spending days trapped on this frigid beach. There were enough provisions for a few days, but beyond that . . . she'd have to get creative. She rested her chin on her knees and closed her eyes. *Lord, please get us out of here soon.*

Kate envisioned what was happening at the airfield. Sidney and the pilots were there, ready to search the first moment weather allowed. Albert and Helen would probably be there too. Someone would have notified her parents. She felt a pang of sadness at what they were going through—wondering what had become of her. If only she could tell them she was all right.

Doris bunched up a travel bag, then lay down and rested her head on it. She bundled deeper into her coat and burrowed beneath two wool blankets. She gazed at the fire for a long while, then in a small and timorous voice, she said, "I thought we were done for. It was a miracle you spotted this beach. And then your ability to get us down—well, I'm thankful for my life."

"God was looking out for us." Kate lay as close to the fire as she dared and pulled blankets over her. "If it's clear in the morning, we'll head on up to the mine and see if we can help that miner. We can call Sidney from there and let him know we're all right." She studied the flicker of blue, yellow, and orange flames. "Do you think he's still alive?"

"It's hard to know. But it sounded like he was seriously injured."

"Yeah," said Kate, her heart heavy. "Well, we better get some sleep."

———

Paul lay on his back and stared at the ceiling and thought about Kate. She reminded him of a spring day. Her smile was warm and genuine, and her hazel eyes flashed with spirit. He imagined trailing a finger down her cheek, smoothing the smattering of freckles.

No one in their right mind was a bush pilot. Why Kate?

He rolled onto his side and finally slept, though fitfully. Each time he woke his thoughts turned to Kate. At five o'clock he was wide awake. Unable to stay in bed any longer, he got up and put on a pot of coffee.

He forced himself to do the mundane, scrambling eggs and making toast. He ate, barely tasting the food. He was wiping out a cast iron skillet when Patrick showed up. He knocked and, before Paul could answer, stepped inside.

"Morning."

"Hi." Paul set the fry pan in the cupboard. "I was wondering if you could contact Sidney. Maybe he knows something."

"Sorry. No news. I already radioed him. That's why I came by." He patted Nita's head and looked at the pups. "How many she have?"

"Nine—five males and four females."

"They look good. Might want one of those males."

"Sure," Paul said, not thinking about pups. Where was Kate? "Just let me know which one and he's yours."

"I will." Patrick headed for the door. "I'll let you know if I hear anything."

Paul did his best to stay busy the rest of the day. He put on a pot of beans, skinned out two marten and a fox he'd brought home late the previous day, and chopped kindling. He kept a close eye on Nita and the puppies. They all looked healthy. Nita was a little thin, but that was to be expected.

Daylight faded and still no word. Paul was antsy for the Mukluk News to begin. He fed and watered Nita, then turned on his battery-operated radio and rotated the dial. There was nothing except a buzz, but he left it on.

Paul lifted the lid off the pot and steam whooshed into the air, carrying the aroma of beans and pork. The radio crackled to life, and a man's baritone voice said, "Good evening to all you listeners across Alaska. We have news to report. Missing pilot, Kate Evans, showed up this afternoon in Anchorage. She and her passenger, Doris Henley, were both in good condition. It seems the Alaskan women are tough and fared well after a night in the bush. Sadly, the injured miner died. His name has not been released."

Relief erupted inside Paul. He set the lid back on the pot and moved to Nita's bed, where he knelt and gave her a massage. "Did you hear that? Kate's all right."

He picked up the smallest pup in the litter, a female with just the beginnings of silver markings on her face. "You're the one for Kate."

Holding her against his chest, he stroked the puppy's soft hair. She made a mewling sound and nuzzled him. Nita watched attentively and finally stood, as if to tell Paul she wanted her baby back.

"Okay. Okay. Just a minute." He turned the puppy on its back and rubbed its round tummy.

His thoughts returned to Kate. She'd fly until it killed her. No matter how pretty she was or how much he admired her, he couldn't allow himself to care too much. If he did, he'd be like this pup, exposing its underbelly.

And he couldn't do that.

After her ordeal, Sidney ordered Kate to take a couple of days off. When she returned to work, she hated to admit that she was nervous. Her thoughts kept circling back to her battle with the fog. She'd done everything she knew to do and still nearly died. Being reminded how quickly things could go bad was unnerving.

Walking to her plane, she tried to act nonchalant, hoping no one sensed her nervousness. She checked out the Bellanca, double-checking the new compass, and after cranking the flywheel, started the engine. When she left the ground, her muscles felt tight, her stomach uneasy. It was a good flying day, but she was unable to reel in her apprehension.

Kate felt like she'd failed . . . again. More than that, she'd been foolish . . . again, and nearly gotten herself and Doris killed. She was more like Jack than she wanted to admit—too confident in her own skills.

Kate dragged her mind to the present. She had mail to deliver.

When she set the plane down on the sandbar at Bear Creek, Patrick and Sassa waited to greet her.

Sassa pulled her into plump arms and held onto her as if she'd never give her up. "When I heard the news, I started praying. I was so scared. I thought your plane had cracked up." She stepped back and smiled. "But here you are."

"The Mukluk News said you were headed to Independence Mine. The ice fog was bad. Why'd you go out?" Patrick asked.

"The people up at the camp said they had a man injured so badly he'd die if he didn't get to a hospital. I thought I could do it, and would have too, but my compass went haywire. I ended up off course." She glanced at her feet, then back at Patrick. "God was looking out for me. The fog opened up enough for me to land."

Patrick gently grasped her upper arms in his large hands. Moisture in his eyes revealed his affection for Kate. "You gave us a scare, girl."

"Well, I'm fine now." She glanced toward Paul's cabin. "And I've got mail for you." She handed Patrick an envelope, unable to keep her eyes from wandering back to Paul's house.

"He's not coming," Sassa said.

"Who's not coming?"

"Paul." She smiled kindly.

"Is he sick?"

"I don't think so. He asked us to get his mail . . . from now on."

Disappointment touched Kate. "Is something wrong?"

Sassa shrugged. "Sure. But we don't know what exactly. He carries a big hurt inside."

"Now, Sassa, you don't know that." Patrick's voice was stern.

She lifted one eyebrow. "I do know."

"He's never told us." Patrick's tone held a warning.

"If you see him, say hello for me," Kate said, unable to conceal her dejection. She headed for the plane.

When she took off, she glanced down at Paul's cabin. Smoke trailed from the chimney. The sight of it made her feel lonely. She thought he was lonely too. *Lord, whatever it is that torments him, please mend it.*

In the weeks to follow when Kate stopped at Bear Creek, the Warrens and Klaus were the only ones to meet the plane. Kate liked the crusty old German.

One afternoon when she touched down on the Susitna, no one came to meet her. She had a letter for Paul so decided to deliver it in person. She stepped into the frigid February air and trudged across snow-covered ice, her boots crunching through a frozen crust. A path leading from a dock to Paul's house was clearly marked. Someone had kept it packed down.

As she neared the house, a sharp pop echoed from somewhere behind the cabin, then a rending sound like splintering wood followed. She moved along the path and to the back of the cabin.

His back to Kate, Paul picked up a chunk of spruce and set it on a chopping block. Hefting a double-headed axe, he brought it down, easily splitting the wood. He chopped each half into two smaller pieces and threw them into a pile. He picked up another round and set it on the block. Kate had the uncomfortable sensation that she was spying on him so she cleared her throat, hoping to get his attention. He swung around and looked at her.

"Hi," she said, holding up the envelope. "There's mail for you. No one came down to meet the plane so I brought it up." She took a step toward him. "I figured you'd want it."

"Sure." He closed the space between them and took the envelope. "Thanks."

The dogs started barking as if they only now realized someone had come to visit. Nita, who was indoors, planted her big feet against the front window and woofed at Kate.

"That's enough," Paul said. When the dogs didn't stop, he hollered, "Quiet." This time they obeyed.

"They're beautiful. Are they friendly?"

"If they know you." Paul rested his axe against the stump. "I'll introduce you." He moved toward them. "The big one is Buck."

Kate smiled. "Like the one in *Call of the Wild*?"

"Yeah." Paul gave Buck a pat. "You've read it?"

"At least a half dozen times. It's a wonderful story."

"One of my favorites." Paul reached for Buck and got hold of his lead. The dog wagged his tail and pulled on the leash, trying to reach Kate. "Hold out your hand, palm down, and let him sniff you."

Feeling a little nervous, Kate did as he said. "He's the biggest dog I've ever seen. What kind is he?"

"Malamute. Anyway, that's what the guy said who sold him to me."

Buck sniffed Kate's hand, then pushed his nose under her palm. Kate stroked his broad head. He moved close and leaned against her.

"He likes you." Paul moved to the black dog. "This is Jackpot. He's a mix."

Kate stepped up to Jackpot, who greeted her with exuberance. "He has an interesting name."

"I won him in a poker game."

Kate nodded. "I guess the name makes sense, then." She patted the dog. "So, these are sled dogs?"

"Uh-huh. I have one more. She's in the house."

"Oh." Kate looked at the window where she could see a dog that resembled Buck, staring out. "Can I meet her?"

"I . . . guess."

Paul's tone sounded as if he'd rather she not go inside, but Kate didn't know how to graciously change her mind without embarrassing herself or Paul. He walked toward the porch and she followed.

"She had pups six weeks ago. I've been keeping her and the litter indoors, but the puppies are getting too rambunctious, so it's about time for them to move outdoors." He walked up steps cleared of snow and opened the door. Nita bounded out, giving a warning growl to Kate. "Nita! No!" The dog sat, but kept a wary eye on Kate. "This is a friend of ours," Paul said, holding the dog by her collar. "She's extra protective because of the pups."

"I don't blame her." Kate wasn't sure if it was safe to move. "Maybe she doesn't want me to see them."

"She'll be fine."

"She's a good-looking dog. Is she malamute too?"

"No. Husky."

"She looks like Buck."

"Huskies and malamutes are similar. The malamutes are usually bigger and built broad and heavy. They're all good sled dogs. Buck's the strongest, but this one's the smartest." Holding Nita firmly, he took a step toward Kate and allowed the dog to sniff her. "She's okay now."

Tentatively, Kate put out her hand and stroked Nita's head.

"You want to see the puppies?"

Warily, Kate stepped inside. Her first look at Paul's cabin surprised her. It was neat and clean with touches that made it feel homey. She hadn't expected that from a bachelor living in the bush.

A quilt made of squares cut from red, gold, and blue fabric was draped over the back of a small sofa and crocheted doilies protected both arms. A cabinet packed with books stood next to the sofa. An overstuffed chair rested against the wall opposite the front window, and a table with a lamp sat beside it. The room was crowded but comfortable. The kitchen had more than ample shelving, and a rustic table with four chairs divided it from the living area.

"This is nice. Did you build it yourself?"

"Yeah, with Patrick's help."

She moved toward the bookcase and picked out a book, *Moby Dick*. "So, you like to read."

"I do. That one was a little dry for me, though. Have you read it?"

"No." Kate put it back on the shelf.

"Out here, especially during the winter, there's lots of time for reading."

A door Kate guessed led to a bedroom was at the far end of the living area. She noticed a sewing machine in the front corner of the room and remembered her meeting with Paul at the store and her surprise when she discovered that he sewed. The memory made her smile.

Whimpering and yipping sounds drew her attention to a wooden crate in the corner of the kitchen. With a glance at Nita, she walked slowly toward the box. Nita was attentive, but didn't seem hostile.

"She had nine pups in all." Paul moved to the crate. "They're getting fat. I've already got homes for most of them."

"How did you do that?"

"Last time I went into Susitna Station I asked around. People are always looking for good dogs. I'll be making another trip next week and plan to take the pups with me."

Enraptured, Kate watched the plump puppies walk over one another; some growled and tussled, while others tried to climb the sides of the box. "May I hold one?"

"Sure."

Kate studied them a moment, and then her eyes landed on the smallest of the litter. She picked it up. With its tail acting like a propeller, it wiggled and whimpered. Kate held her up in front of her to have a better look. She had a sweet, masked face. Kate's heart warmed.

"She's the runt, but she's smart. And brave. She can scrap with the best of them." He smiled. "She'd be just right for you."

"Me?" Kate looked at the puppy. "She's sweet, but I can't . . . I'm gone too much."

"Take her along with you. It'd be good to have a dog . . . for protection and company."

The idea appealed to Kate. She pressed her cheek against the pup's downy fur. "She's adorable." Kate captured it against her chest. "I wonder how the Towns would feel about me having a dog? It's a small apartment."

"I doubt they'd mind. In fact, they'd probably feel better,

knowing she's with you. When she's full grown, she ought to be a good watchdog." He paused. "I know I'd feel better." His tone sounded almost tender.

Kate looked at him. A question had been pestering her and she needed to ask it. She took a breath. "Paul, are you mad at me?"

"Mad? Why would you think that?"

"You haven't met the plane for the last six weeks."

"You've been counting?" His smile teased.

Kate compressed her lips, embarrassed. She had been counting. "I . . . always keep track of my runs." She forced her eyes to remain on his. "So, are you mad?"

"No." He moved to the kitchen. "You want a cup of coffee?"

"I need to get back to work. I've got a couple more stops to make." The puppy tried to scramble up her neck and licked her chin. "If you're not mad, why haven't you been down to get your mail?"

"Been busy."

"Not that busy."

Paul turned and faced her. "Okay. I . . . was mad, kind of. When your plane disappeared, I got scared."

"For me?" The idea warmed Kate's insides.

"Yeah." He filled the coffeepot with water. "I don't understand why you've got to fly in the bush. There are lots of other jobs, safer ones."

Kate was surprised at the intensity of his tone. She didn't know how to answer.

He turned and looked at her. "Why do you fly?"

She looked at the pup and scratched behind its ears. Paul's stare was intense. "I have to. I don't think I could be me without it."

"Can't you fly somewhere else, someplace safe?"

200

"Life can't always be about staying safe." Kate suddenly felt angry. She was tired of people telling her how to live. "Is that why you hide out here in this cabin? Are you staying safe?" The words were out and Kate wished she could take them back.

Paul's expression turned stony. "Why I live here is none of your business."

Kate felt her face warm from embarrassment. Her anger had gotten the better of her again. "You're right. It isn't." She put the puppy back in the box. "I'm sorry. I shouldn't get so defensive about what I do."

Silence pervaded the room. Paul set the percolator on the stove. "So, you want the puppy?"

Kate looked at the little girl. "Yes. I do."

"Okay. I'll get a box."

"You mean, take her today?"

"She's old enough." Paul didn't wait for an answer, but strode out of the house.

Kate picked up the pup and followed Paul to the shed.

Inside it smelled musty and damp. Kate held up the puppy. "So, what shall I call you?" She studied her. "You look like a little angel. I'll call you Angel."

Paul grinned. "She might not be such an angel. Huskies tend to have a mind of their own." He picked up a box. "This ought to do." He dumped out wood chips and then grabbed a rag and laid it inside.

A raven flew into the shed and perched on a shelf where it cawed and stared at Kate. She stared back. "What in the world?"

"That's Jasper. Found him in one of my traps. He broke his leg and I helped patch him up. He decided to stay."

Kate wondered what other things she didn't know about Paul. She hadn't met a man from the bush who gave a whit about a bird. "You have a regular menagerie here."

"Guess I do." He took Angel from Kate and settled her inside the box.

Kate felt a sudden tenderness for this quiet man she barely knew. "Thanks, Paul. I'll take good care of her."

"You will or answer to me." He grinned.

Holding the box in front of her, Kate started down the trail, then stopped and looked back. "Now you'll have to meet the plane once in a while . . . you'll want to see how she's doing."

"Guess I will at that."

— 17 —

With a grimace, Kate finished off a cup of Sidney's overly sturdy coffee and then refilled her mug. She glanced at Mike.

"You must be desperate," he said.

"Can't seem to wake up. And I've got a couple of long days ahead of me. After my mail run, I'm heading to Kotzebue." Leaning against the wall, she sipped the stout brew, trying to keep the heat of the liquid away from a sore tooth.

"Maybe you should take a thermos of that with you."

"Don't think my stomach could tolerate that much of it." She took one more swig, then set the cup on the counter and grabbed two mail bags, slinging one over each shoulder. "My plane ought to be warmed up by now." Flashlight in hand, she headed for the door. "I'll see you in a few days."

"See ya," Sidney said, without looking up from the workbench where he sorted through tools.

She nodded at Mike, then stepped into snow flurries and strode toward her plane. She heard the shop door open and close behind her and glanced over her shoulder to see Mike following.

He caught up to her and took one of the canvas sacks.

Kate kept walking, trying to ignore an ache in a right lower molar.

When Mike opened the door, Angel greeted him by planting her big feet on his chest and licking his face. He chuckled and pushed her aside. "Yeah, I love you too. But I already took a bath today." He gave her a pat and then hefted the mail inside the plane. "She's getting big."

"Yeah, growing fast and she loves to fly." Angel liked him. That was a good sign. Dogs knew who they could trust.

"She's ready to go, all right," Mike hollered over the engine.

Kate handed the second bag to him. "I think she likes flying as much as I do."

"Not much mail going out today." Mike kept Angel under control with one hand.

"That means fewer stops, which gives me more daylight to make McGrath."

Angel tried to squeeze past Mike and out the door. He shoved her back. "Settle down." He turned to Kate. "Aren't you pushing yourself a little hard?"

"Yeah, maybe. But don't we all?"

"Yeah, I suppose so." His expression turned tender and he rested a hand on her arm.

"I'll be fine." Kate stepped up on the ladder and Angel licked her face. "All right, that's enough or you're going back to Paul's." She grabbed the dog's collar and wondered if Paul would meet the plane today. She hoped so.

Keeping a hold of Angel, she climbed inside. "You know Paul Anderson? He lives out on Bear Creek."

"The guy you got Angel from?"

"Uh-huh."

Mike rested a hand on the door frame and looked up at Kate, his expression slightly annoyed. "Why?"

"Just wondering. He's kind of mysterious."

"Mysterious? I'd say more like secretive." Mike frowned. "There are a lot of fellas like him up here." He stared at Kate. "You interested in him?"

She could see hurt in Mike's eyes. She knew he cared for her, though he'd made no declarations. "No," she said, wishing she'd kept quiet. She didn't want Mike to think she wasn't interested in him. She wasn't sure what she felt yet. "I'm just curious is all."

He furrowed his brows. "My guess is he'll tell us about his past when he's ready. Best to leave him be."

Angel jumped out of the plane, putting an end to the discussion. Tail wagging, she pressed against Mike. Giving her thick fur a good rub, he glanced at Kate. "She cause you any trouble when you're in the air?"

"No. She's great. Once we're flying she settles right down and sleeps mostly." She eyed Angel's crate. "Her favorite place, though, is the front passenger seat, which means I'm constantly cleaning up dog hair so my passengers don't have to wear it."

Angel trotted across the field and disappeared into the darkness. Kate wasn't worried. She'd be back. She never missed a chance to fly.

Kate glanced at the eastern sky, which hinted at sunrise. "Summer will be here soon—more daylight and more flying hours. I've got to make hay while the sun shines." She looked up at drifting snowflakes. "That is, if the sun were shining." She grinned. "Anyway, I want to buy a place of my own so I've got to work while I can. Over the winter my bank account has dwindled."

"Always does that. I'll be happy for more hours myself."

Kate turned her attention to the Chugach Mountains. They looked like hulking gray shadows in the dawn light. She took in a breath and cold air found its way to her inflamed tooth. She winced and put a hand to her cheek.

"You all right?"

"Yeah. Just a bad tooth."

"I know a good dentist."

"I'm hoping it'll just go away."

"Tooth pain rarely just goes away." Mike shook his head slightly. "Sorry."

"When I get back I'll go in and see the dentist," Kate conceded. "I better go." She whistled for Angel and the pup came running, jumped into the plane, and burrowed into her bed. "See you tomorrow or the next," Kate said, climbing in.

Before she could pull the door closed, Mike leaned in and asked, "Dinner together when you get back? My place? I'll cook."

"Okay. I'd like that."

He grinned and closed the door. Feeling lighthearted, Kate moved to the front of the plane. An evening with Mike would be fun. He was a nice guy . . . and handsome. And he understood how she felt about being a pilot. They were a good match. *Don't get ahead of yourself. You don't know him well enough to be thinking about a long-term relationship.* Not to mention that Kate couldn't keep her thoughts from straying to Paul. There was something appealing about him.

Once in the air, Angel trotted to the front and settled into the passenger seat. Kate rested a hand on her head. Paul had been right about her having a dog. Even in the remotest areas, she never felt alone.

Not far out of Anchorage, the snow flurries stopped and morning sunlight splintered scattered clouds. The world almost looked warm. When Kate made her stops, there was a different feel in the air, a promise of spring. People walked with a lighter step and their smiles seemed brighter than usual.

Her last delivery completed, Kate headed north. It had been a good day, all except for the throbbing in her tooth. Mike was right—toothaches never just went away.

Before setting out she'd taken medicine for the pain. Now the molar ached mercilessly. She reached into her pack and grabbed a bottle of pain reliever. Twisting off the lid, she tapped a tablet into her palm, replaced the lid, and tossed the container back into her bag. Pressing the aspirin on the sore tooth, she gently bit down, swallowing away the bitter taste.

Gradually the pain abated some and Kate found herself feeling drowsy. What little time she'd had for sleep the previous night had been interrupted by the miserable tooth. Her eyelids drooped and she wished she'd taken Sidney up on his offer of a thermos of coffee. Even that would be better than falling asleep.

Trying to distract herself, she checked her map, then drank some water, which sent jolts of pain through her tooth. She considered the cookies Helen had packed, but didn't dare eat anything sweet.

Sunlight warmed the cabin, the engine droned, and Kate fought sleep. All of a sudden she woke with a start. The engine sounded peculiar and Angel whined. The nose of the plane was slanted down. She was in a dive!

The forest hurtled at her. Fighting panic, she pulled back on the stick, wrestling the Bellanca. She had only seconds to get the nose up or she'd die. The ground rushed at her.

"God, help me!" Using both hands, she hauled on the stick and the plane finally responded. Kate brought it back to level.

Her body thrummed. Her heart banged inside her chest and her hands shook. She'd nearly done herself in.

She glanced at Angel. "Sorry, girl." Angel nosed her hand, and Kate dug her fingers into the dog's thick coat.

Taking a heartening breath, she looked out over the terrain. Nothing looked familiar; then she spotted the Alaskan Range behind and the Kuskokwim Mountains ahead. She had her bearings.

I've been pushing too hard.

She wished it weren't so far to McGrath. Following the Kuskokwim River, her eyes roamed the landscape to the point where the sun's light shimmered pink in the sky as it settled behind the mountains.

With another hour left until she reached McGrath, Kate was grateful for a full, butter-colored moon that cast its light across a dark sky and illuminated soft, rounded, snow-covered mountains. She felt God's presence so strongly she almost expected to hear his voice declaring pleasure at his creation.

By the time she reached McGrath, the throbbing in her tooth was almost more than she could bear. Kate paid for a night at a roadhouse, thankful for a bed. Fevered and chilled, she placed another aspirin on the troublesome tooth, then climbed beneath wool blankets and managed to disappear within sleep for a few hours.

The following morning, she set off at first light. Her tooth still throbbed, and she knew she had a fever, but there was nothing for her to do but to continue.

Along the coast, heavy mist hugged the ground. She moved northward, praying Kotzebue would be free of it. She'd already had two bad experiences with severe fog—they'd been enough for a lifetime.

With each passing mile, the pain in her tooth and jaw grew more intense. She shivered from chills. After swallowing two aspirin, she put another on the defiant molar.

I hope Nena knows what to do for this. She pressed a hand to her cheek, feeling heat and swelling beneath her palm.

By the time she approached Kotzebue, darkness reached a hand across the tundra. The ground fog had thinned. Kate watched for landmarks, expecting the little town to appear at any moment.

When she spotted the village at the edge of the Bering Sea, she relaxed tight muscles. Thankfully there was very little fog. Firepots had been set up along the landing strip. She'd have to thank Joe. He was always looking out for her.

He greeted Kate and Angel, then helped her tie down the plane and put it to bed for the night.

As they walked toward town, he asked, "You feeling all right? You're not looking so good."

"I've got a bad tooth."

He nodded. "Know how that can be."

When she stepped into the Turchik house, Nena greeted her with a hug, then stepped back. "You are very warm." She studied Kate. "You are sick?"

"Bad tooth," Joe said.

Nena placed a cool hand on Kate's brow. "You have a fever. And your cheek is swollen."

"It's just my tooth."

"How long since it started hurting?"

"A few days ago. Do you have something that will help?"

Nena shook her head. "No. It is very bad. I don't have medicine for that. It will probably have to be pulled."

Kate's stomach dropped. "There must be some kind of native medicine, something that . . ."

Nena shook her head no.

Kate needed to face up to the truth. She'd have to see a dentist, but couldn't imagine how she'd manage until she got back to Anchorage. "Is there a doctor here in Kotzebue?"

"No white man's doctor, but there's Alex Toognak. He will fix you up. He learned from sages before him."

Kate suppressed a groan. She didn't want some shaman messing with her mouth. She needed a dentist or a real doctor.

"I will take you to him," Nena said kindly.

With no other options, Kate followed Nena to Alex Toognak's house. From the outside, his place looked like most of the others in town, small and in need of paint. Nena knocked.

An elderly man opened the door. He was bent at the waist, and a wild mane of white hair surrounded a small brown face. Dark eyes settled on the two of them. "Hello."

"Alex, you are looking good." Nena smiled and placed a hand on Kate's arm. "This is my friend, Kate. She has a bad tooth and needs your help."

Alex turned to Kate. "Come in." He stepped back, holding the door.

Kate followed Nena inside. The room seemed saturated with the odor of fish and herbs. Bottles containing plants and other mixtures crowded shelves, and a pestle sat on a counter.

"You sit." Alex gave a nod toward a wooden chair. "I will look."

Fighting an urge to bolt for the door, Kate lowered herself to the chair.

Alex gently placed his hands on the sides of her face. He looked into her eyes, then pressed his palm against her forehead. He ran a finger along the cheek that hurt. "Very swollen. Can you open your mouth?"

Kate did as he asked, but she hadn't forgotten her last encounter with a dentist and a bad tooth. It had been extremely unpleasant. Her heart pounded so hard it felt as if it would fly out of her chest. At first he simply looked inside her mouth, and using one finger, he probed. Kate caught the scent of whale oil and fish. He gently touched the gum tissue, then put pressure on the tooth itself.

"Ouch!" Kate pulled away.

Alex straightened. "It must come out." He moved to a shelf.

"There's no other way? Some kind of medicine?"

"No." He filled a glass with water, spooned powder from a bottle, and sifted it into the glass and stirred. "This will help the pain. Drink."

Kate felt doomed. She sniffed the concoction. Its sharp odor burned her nose, but she drank the bitter elixir anyway.

Alex went to a drawer and took out what looked like small pliers. Kate made an effort to slow her breathing and told herself that pulling a tooth was no big deal.

He washed the tongs and filled a large glass with water, then set a piece of gauze beside the glass. Kate gripped the arms of the chair.

Nena sat quietly. When her eyes met Kate's, she smiled kindly.

The throbbing in her jaw lessened and Kate felt mildly sleepy. She figured it must be whatever Alex had given her. Maybe this wouldn't be so bad after all.

Alex placed the pliers, gauze, and water on the table next to Kate. "So, we are ready?"

Kate nodded and opened her mouth, relinquishing control to Alex.

When he grabbed hold of the tooth, pain shot through Kate's jaw and into her neck and skull. For a moment she thought she might pass out. She willed herself to remain still, but as Alex worked she couldn't suppress a moan.

Seemingly unaffected by Kate's distress, Alex worked

swiftly. He wrenched the tooth to one side, then pushed it in, and then pulled. Agony exploded in Kate's mouth.

When the roots of the tooth held fast, Alex repeated the process. This time it came free. Wearing a satisfied smile, he gripped the devilish tooth in the tongs and dropped it into a tin.

A deep ache burned through Kate's jaw and into her skull. She leaned forward, pressing a hand to her cheek. How could a tooth create so much havoc?

"You will get better now." Alex gave Kate the water and told her to rinse her mouth, offering a bowl for her to spit in. There was a lot of blood in the water.

He made a paste that smelled of cloves and pressed it into the empty socket, then put gauze over the top. "Bite on that until there is no more bleeding."

He measured out two packets of medicine. "For pain. You take it tonight before you sleep. And then in the morning. After that, you will be better."

"Thank you," Kate mumbled through clenched teeth. Her face and head pulsed, and whatever he'd packed in her gum tasted vile. "How much do I owe you?"

He smiled. "Nothing. You keep flying to Kotzebue, that is enough."

Nena escorted Kate back to the house, resting a hand tenderly on her arm. "You sleep now. You can use our bed."

Kate didn't argue. Gratefully she lay on the lumpy mattress and pulled blankets up around her. The pain had eased. Closing her eyes, she quickly fell asleep.

The next thing she knew was Joe's voice. He was upset.

"Kate, there's a man. He's very sick. You must fly him to the hospital."

Groggy, Kate sat up. The throbbing resumed. "What's wrong with him?"

"He has very bad pain in his chest." Joe pressed a hand in the middle of his chest. "He can't breathe. Alex Toognak cannot fix him. He says if the man doesn't go to the hospital, he will die."

Weariness and pain vanished. Kate sat up, pulled on her boots and coat, then headed for the airfield. Angel trotted ahead.

Nena was already there with the oil warmed. A firepot heated the engine.

Three men arrived, carrying a man on a litter. A woman, whom Kate guessed must be the man's wife, stayed at his side, holding his hands and reassuring him. Kate checked him briefly. He was obviously gravely ill. *If only there were a doctor.*

"Lay him on the floor inside the plane," she said.

Angel had already leaped aboard. She watched the men lift the litter and carry the man inside. The patient groaned, clutching his chest.

Nena handed Kate the pot of oil. Hands trembling, Kate poured it into the oil tank, then capped it off and climbed inside. Her passenger wasn't improving. His breathing was still labored. His skin looked pallid and he was sweating profusely. "Who's going to take care of him while I'm flying?"

"I can do it," a young man said. "He's my uncle."

"I'm going," the woman said, looking down at the man, fear etched into her face. "We have been together for thirty years. I will not leave him today."

"Okay. Let's go." There was a doctor in Nome, but Kate knew in her gut that Nome was too far away to be of help to this man.

With Angel on the seat beside her, she fired up the plane. Waiting for it to warm up felt like an eternity, but finally they were in the air. She checked her maps and glanced back.

The sick man was quiet except for an occasional moan. He looked bad.

"Ma'am! Ma'am!" The young man's voice sounded strident. "He's not breathing!"

The woman held her husband's hands in hers. "No. John. Please."

John's lips were tinged blue.

"Turn him on his side," Kate ordered. "Give him a hard slap on the back between the shoulder blades."

The nephew smacked him again and again, but there was no response. The young man finally stopped his efforts. His voice flat, he said, "He's dead. He's gone."

Arms wrapped about her upper body, the woman rocked back and forth. She didn't make a sound, but tears trailed down her cheeks.

Kate turned the plane around and headed back to Kotzebue. The sick feeling in her stomach wasn't from yesterday's fever but from the brutal reality of life in this wilderness. Sometimes she hated being a bush pilot.

— 18 —

Although she was uncertain it was a good idea to have dinner at Mike's place, Kate pulled her Plymouth up in front of his house. She pushed in the clutch and dropped the gear into park. Was she getting into something she'd regret? He seemed like a lot of fun, and she wanted to get to know him, but would he assume too much?

The door opened and he stepped onto a small front porch and waved. Kate turned off the engine. It was too late to change her mind. She was here.

Mike hurried down the steps and out to the car, managing to open the door before Kate did. Wearing his usual friendly smile, he said, "Just on time."

His blue eyes danced with pleasure, and Kate couldn't resist his natural charm. She instantly warmed to him.

"Didn't want the 'best' spaghetti in all the territory to go to waste," she said with a grin.

"You jest, but you'll see. It's my mother's recipe." Mike placed a hand on Kate's back as the two walked up a gravel pathway leading to the house. The outside of the home screamed for attention—it needed paint, and weeds had

215

sprouted in the flower beds. There was no sign of spring flowers.

"Come on in." Mike opened the door and held it for Kate and followed her inside.

Although it was sparsely furnished, the house was tidy with a large floral area rug in the living room. "This is nice," she said, noticing fringed curtains on the windows. She breathed in deeply. "And something smells good."

Mike grinned. "That would be my spaghetti. I also baked a fresh loaf of sourdough bread and an apple pie."

"Where did you get the apples?"

"I held some over through the winter, just for special occasions."

Kate felt herself relax. This would be fun.

"How's that tooth of yours?"

"Better." Kate put a hand to her cheek, which was still tender to the touch. "I had it pulled in Kotzebue."

"They have a dentist in Kotzebue?"

"No . . . not exactly." Kate chuckled. "Alex Toognak, the local sage, pulled it. He did a good job, but it hurt like crazy."

"Glad it was you and not me." He grinned. "Here, let me hang up your coat."

Kate slipped off her jacket and handed it to Mike. He hung it in a small closet.

"It's such a nice day, I almost decided not to wear a coat. It's colder than it looks, though."

"April's a little early for shirtsleeves—have to wait 'til June." He walked into the kitchen. "Hope you're hungry. I made plenty."

———

Kate and Mike sat across from each other at a small table in the kitchen. He'd managed to find a set of plates, but the glasses and flatware didn't match. Mike dished spaghetti straight from the pot onto Kate's plate and handed it to her.

"Looks good," she said, setting the dish on the table in front of her. She took a slice of bread and buttered it.

"Not fancy, but I figured you wouldn't mind."

"I like things simple." Kate stuck her fork into the spaghetti and twirled it until she had more than a mouthful. She'd never mastered the art of getting the proper amount of spaghetti on a utensil. She managed to get it into her mouth without slopping too much sauce on her chin. Using a napkin, she dabbed up the spill and chewed. The mingling flavors of spices, meat, and tomato sauce delighted her palate. "This is delicious. If I ever have a real kitchen, I'll have to get the recipe."

"I thought you hated cooking."

"No. I just said I'm not very good at it. When I have my own place, I might give it a try." She took a bite of bread. "Didn't know you were such a good cook."

Mike leaned his arms on the table, fork in hand. "Truth is, this is the only thing I know how to make." He grinned. "Good thing you like spaghetti."

Kate laughed.

Mike and Kate talked flying mostly, but they also discussed life in Alaska versus that in the states. The conversation turned to their families, and Mike told her a little about growing up in Chicago. Although he seemed somewhat reluctant to talk about his family, Kate did learn that his father had been a drunk, and his mother raised him, his brothers, and a sister on her own. Kate figured it must be Mike's determination to be nothing like his father that made him so principled and loyal. Her admiration grew for her flying comrade.

After dinner, Mike served coffee and apple pie. He made

good coffee, but the pie left something to be desired. The crust was tough and overcooked, but the apples tasted good.

They sat in the living room—Mike on a well-worn sofa and Kate in an easy chair. Mike looked around the room. "Figure one day I'll fix things up."

"I like it. I think too much stuff makes a room feel cluttered."

"Maybe, but it could use a woman's touch."

Kate wondered if he was hinting about a relationship between them, but she chose to ignore the implication.

"The outside needs a lot of work, but I've already bought paint, so when I get a few days off this summer I'll spruce it up." He leaned forward, placing his arms on his thighs. "It's not much, but I own it, free and clear. And the lot's big enough so I can add on . . . one day . . . when I have a family." His expression warmed.

An alarm went off inside Kate. She hoped he wasn't leading up to something.

"I was wondering how you'd feel about us dating . . . more seriously." He hurried on before Kate could answer. "We've got a lot in common, you and I. And with both of us being pilots, we understand the job with its long hours and everything else . . . and . . . well . . . I'm crazy about you. Never knew anyone like you, Kate."

She didn't know how to respond. "I-I . . . like you . . . too," she stammered. "But I'm not sure about—"

"I don't mean we have to get married or anything, but maybe just think about a future."

Kate studied Mike. She did like him . . . a lot. And he was good looking. But she wasn't sure she could ever love him. "It's kind of soon. You know I was supposed to marry Richard last summer . . . and I'm new here and still learning so much. I don't know if I ought to get serious about anyone."

Kate knew she was rambling. "But maybe. We'll see. You're a fine man and I do think a lot of you." She clamped her lips together. She'd already said too much.

"Okay. That's good enough for me." He smiled. "There's a new movie at the cinema. Maybe we can go later this week?"

"Sure." Kate stood. She needed some space and time to think. "I'd better be going. I've got mail to deliver tomorrow."

Mike walked her to the car. The two stood for a moment in the growing dusk. Kate couldn't get the door open because Mike had his hand on the handle. He leaned close and pressed his lips to hers, gently, demanding nothing. It was a sweet kiss, and despite her reluctance, Kate liked it. She opened her eyes and found Mike staring at her.

"You're really something, Kate," he said softly.

"You too," she managed to say. "But, I have to go."

"Right." Mike opened the door and held it for her while she slid onto the seat. "See you," he said, then closed the door and stepped back.

Her heart pounding, Kate pushed in the clutch, turned the key, and put the car into drive. With a small wave, she moved off, leaving Mike standing in the road, staring after her. *Me and Mike?* She pressed her fingers to her lips. She'd liked the kiss. *Maybe.* She smiled.

Kate dropped down over the Susitna, and set up to land on the sandbar at Bear Creek. Paul and Patrick were already waiting. With breakup over, she knew using pontoons and landing on the creek made more sense, but she wasn't ready for the switch. The thought made her stomach roil. She hadn't attempted a water landing since the accident on Rimrock Lake. Deciding not to think about it, she made a wide turn over the trees and headed upriver for her approach.

As usual, Angel was in the front seat. She stood panting and gazing out the window. The dog was well acquainted with the mail run and knew this stop included Paul, who almost always took time to play with her. Kate brought the plane down with one little hop and then cruised to a stop.

Angel leaped off the seat and hurried to the door. When Kate opened it, the dog bounded out and headed straight for Paul.

Wearing a broad smile, Paul knelt and captured the large pup in his arms. He gathered the bundle of black and silver fur against his chest and tried to avoid her wet kisses. "She's looking good. Getting big." He laughed. "A little wet, though."

"I almost think she likes you better than me." Kate breathed deeply. The cool air was scented with new vegetation and the fragrance of spruce. "It smells like spring. I love it."

Before she finished speaking, mosquitoes descended. Kate waved them off, but the pests persisted. Slapping one, she said, "These are the only thing I don't like about this time of year. Are they always this bad?"

"Worse." Patrick's mouth lifted in a sideways grin. "Wait another month. You won't want to get out of your plane."

With another swipe at the buzzing mosquitoes, she said, "Only mail I have today is for Klaus."

Angel tore across the sandbar, chasing after a seagull.

"I'll take it to him," Patrick said. "He was going to come today, but wanted to plant one more row of carrots."

Kate handed him the letter. "Tell him hello for me. Is he doing all right?"

Patrick glanced at the envelope. "Since the weather warmed up, he's doing pretty good."

Patrick slapped a mosquito that had landed on his neck. "If someone came up with a repellent for these little beasts, he'd be rich." He scratched a large welt on his arm.

"Heard the natives use cow parsnip," Paul said. "They rub the flowers on their skin. You ever try it?"

"Yeah. Only trouble is, they don't bloom for another couple of months." He scratched his arm.

"I'll pick up a tonic for the itching when I'm in Anchorage."

"When are you going in?" Kate asked.

"Figured I'd get my boat set up today and head out in the morning." He glanced at the cloudless sky. "As long as the weather holds."

"I could give you a ride."

Paul considered the invitation. "Sounds good, but how do I get back?"

"If you don't mind staying a few days, I'll bring you out next week. Or one of the other pilots might have a trip this way."

Paul lifted his hat and resettled it on his head. "Guess that would work." He turned to Patrick "You think one of your boys could look after the dogs?"

"Douglas'll do it. He's still hoping you'll let that one pup go."

Paul scrubbed his cheek. "You tell him if he takes care of the dogs and keeps the weeds out of the garden, the pup is his."

Patrick raised an eyebrow. "You sure about that? He'll be a fine sled dog."

"I don't need four dogs, just hated to part with him. He'll be happier with Douglas anyway."

"It'll make his day."

From the safety of the cockpit, Kate watched Patrick row his dory across the creek toward her. Paul sat up front in the boat. She wondered if she'd get answers to some of the questions she had about him.

221

When the boat reached the sandbar, Paul leaped out, then gave Patrick a push off to free the boat from the rocks.

Patrick waved and headed for home.

With a pack slung over one shoulder, Paul trudged toward the plane and Kate moved to the door. When she opened it, Angel bounded out again, ready to romp. She grabbed a stick and trotted toward Paul. When he tried to grab the branch, she darted out of reach.

"I'm not playing that game." With a glance at Kate, he straightened and folded his arms over his chest.

"She loves to play keepaway," Kate said.

"She'll bring it to me. Just wait." Paul acted as if he didn't care about the dog or her prize. A few moments later, Angel returned and dropped her stick in front of him.

He picked it up and sent it flying. Angel chased after it. This time she brought it back.

Kate warmed at the sight of the two playing and would have loved to stay awhile, but work waited. "We've got to go," she said reluctantly. "I've got a couple more stops to make. Hope you don't mind."

"Not at all. It'll be a nice break, something new." Paul moved to the side of the plane. "I'll crank it."

Kate started the engine, and Angel settled in her usual spot beside her. "Not today, girl." Kate gently tugged the dog's collar, dragging her off the seat. Angel found a place in back and laid down to gnaw on her stick. Kate knew there'd be a mess to clean up, but she didn't have the heart to take the dog's prize.

With the engine roaring, Paul dropped into the seat beside Kate. He lifted a basket off the floor in front of him, which held Kate's Bible. "Didn't know you were religious," he said, picking up the book.

"Guess there's always something new to learn about a person." She looked straight at him. "How about you?"

A flicker of discomfort touched Paul's eyes. "You mean, am I religious?" He returned the Bible to the basket and set it behind his seat. "I'm not."

Paul's tone made it clear he didn't want to discuss religion, so Kate said simply, "The Bible belonged to my grandmother. She was one of the finest people I ever knew."

"Was?"

"She died a few years ago." An image of her grandmother's small hands with their translucent skin came to mind. "I miss her."

Paul leaned back in his seat and folded his arms over his chest. "Sorry to hear that."

"Do you have family still living in California?"

"Some." He didn't look at her.

Kate figured she'd probed enough for now and concentrated on taking off. Once in the air, she didn't know what to talk about.

Paul was the first to speak. "So, how've things been going for you?"

"Good. I've been flying a lot—thanks to the longer days. Had a little trouble in Kotzebue—had a tooth pulled by a medicine man, for one thing."

Paul chuckled. "Really? Sounds interesting."

"It was, believe me. But the worst thing was what happened after that."

Paul studied her with interest.

"I had a passenger die right in my plane."

"What happened?"

"I don't know for sure. By the time we got in the air, he was in bad shape—pain in his chest and sweating profusely."

"Trouble breathing?"

"Yeah. He was really struggling." Remembering the ordeal

brought back the panic and sense of helplessness. "I was trying to get him to Nome. They have a doctor there."

"Sounds like he had a heart attack."

"It was horrible. A nephew and the man's wife stayed with him during the flight. They tried to help, but no one knew what to do. If there'd been a doctor, the man might have lived."

"Not likely," Paul said, tight-lipped.

Kate's mind recaptured the emotions and dreadful events of the flight. She gazed down at the river, then glanced at Paul. "There'll be more emergencies . . . like that one. I'm just a pilot, but people expect me to know how to handle every kind of crisis."

"That's pretty unreasonable."

"Yeah. I guess. But I wish I knew more. And if there'd been a doctor in Kotzebue—"

"You can't worry about that. The people choose to live there." He paused, then added, "And dying is part of living. None of us will escape it." His tone was somber. He gazed out the window. Neither spoke.

After Kate's last stop and they were on their way again, Paul asked, "Do you have a favorite place in Anchorage to eat?"

"There's a café not far from where I live. The food's okay. They have good pie."

"Would you like to have dinner with me?"

The invitation took Kate by surprise. Paul didn't seem like the social type. He'd barely spoken the entire flight. "Sure. I guess that would be okay." She felt a twinge of guilt. What would Mike think?

"I wouldn't want to twist your arm," Paul said with a grin.

"No. I'd like to go." Again guilt about Mike prodded her. *We're not serious,* she told herself and glanced at Paul. *And besides, Paul's intriguing. I'd like to know more about him.*

Kate dropped Paul at his hotel, then hurried home to clean up and change. She couldn't decide what to wear and wondered why it mattered. Finally, she chose a simple gingham dress. She brushed her short mahogany hair and fluffed out the flatness from wearing her flying helmet. After applying fresh lipstick, she dabbed on Evening in Paris perfume. She was ready.

Kate pulled on a sweater and fastened the top button. Tossing a compact and lipstick into a handbag, she headed toward the front of the store.

Helen worked at the cash register. "You look nice. Where you going?"

"Just out to dinner." Kate didn't want to tell her with whom.

"With Mike?"

"No."

"Oh. I thought you two were—"

"We're dating. That doesn't mean I can't go out with a friend."

"Of course. Who are you going with?"

"Paul. The man from out at Bear Creek." To her surprise, her heart did a little flip at the thought of him.

"Oh yes. He's a nice young fellow."

"I flew him into town today, so in return he's taking me to dinner." That wasn't exactly what happened, but Kate figured that's probably the reason he'd asked her.

"That's wonderful." Helen wore her "I'm delighted" face.

"Don't make too much of it. We barely know each other."

"I'm just happy to see you having some fun. You work too hard." She reached out and caressed Kate's cheek. "You look very pretty. Have a good time."

Kate hurried out of the store. The May air was cold and she wondered if she ought to go back for a coat. Deciding against it, she got into her car and pulled onto the street.

When she stopped at Paul's hotel, he already stood out front. She'd never seen him in anything other than work-clothes. Wearing slacks and a white shirt made him look even more handsome. Kate's heart did that little flip again.

Paul stepped away from the hotel, opened the car door, and slid onto the front seat. "Nice car. Used to own a Plymouth—it was a good ride."

"Mike found it for me." She tried to ignore his dark good looks and the tantalizing smell of his cologne.

He glanced at her. "You look nice."

"Thanks. So do you."

"You smell good too." He smiled gently, almost regretfully. "My guess is you're wearing Evening in Paris?"

"That's right. How'd you know?"

He looked out the car window. "I knew someone once who used to wear it."

Kate wondered who, but decided against asking.

The café was closed, so they headed downtown. The first restaurant they came to, Paul said, "I've been here before. It's nice and they have good food."

Kate pulled to the side of the street and got out before Paul could come around and open the door. She didn't want him thinking this was a "real" date. They stepped into the restaurant and Kate realized immediately it was a place for upper-crust types.

"This is probably very expensive," she whispered.

"Don't worry. I'll get the tab."

Who is this man? He dresses and lives like a sourdough, but talks like a gentleman and money is no problem?

Paul walked up to the maitre d' and gave him his name. A few moments later, a waiter escorted them to a table set with white linen, crystal goblets, and silver flatware. Kate felt out of place and underdressed.

Paul ordered a bottle of wine. He was very unlike the man she knew who lived in a cabin in the bush. The question about why he was out there burned inside her. Placing her hands in her lap, she tried to come up with a way to ask.

He leaned back in his chair. "How do you feel about Alaska now that you've been through a winter?"

"I love it, mostly. During the winter, the long nights are hard to tolerate. It's tough to find enough flying hours." She picked up her spoon and then set it back down. "It's beautiful, though. I feel like I belong here."

A native couple stepped in and approached the maitre d'. The man said something, but was ignored. He tried again. Finally, the maitre d' turned a condescending look on the man and said, "No Indians allowed. You'll have to leave."

Kate straightened her spine. "Did you hear that?"

"What?" Paul looked over his shoulder toward the lobby.

"That man told those people they aren't allowed because they're native."

"My money is as good as anyone else's," the small man told the maitre d'.

"We don't want your money."

By this time, everyone in the restaurant watched the exchange.

Kate felt her ire boil. "Can you believe that?"

She stood, and before she realized what she was doing, she'd crossed the room and stepped between the native couple

227

and the maitre d'. "Did I hear correctly? You're refusing to serve these people because they're natives?"

"That's right. No Indians. It's posted."

Kate hadn't seen a sign. She felt Paul's presence beside her and felt stronger. "That's un-American."

"Alaska's not a state, miss. And this is none of your concern."

"It certainly is. These people have every right to eat in this restaurant. In fact, they have more right than you or me. The Indians lived here long before the rest of us."

The maitre d' looked down at her and sniffed. "No Indians is our policy." His voice was tight and controlled. "They're unruly, especially when they're drinking."

She glanced at the couple. "They look sober to me."

He compressed his lips, then sputtered, "I must ask you to leave the premises."

Defiance blazing, Kate folded her arms over her chest. "I'm not leaving."

"I'll call the sheriff. You're being a public nuisance."

Kate wondered if he'd really call the sheriff. And was she up for that kind of trouble? "Fine. I didn't want to eat here anyway. In fact, I wouldn't eat here if you paid me to." She spun on her heels, grabbed her handbag from their table, turned, and walked out. Paul had to hurry to keep up.

The native couple followed Kate and Paul out the door. When the man approached Kate, his expression was not one of gratitude. "I do not need you to fight for me."

Flabbergasted, Kate didn't know how to respond. "I'm sorry. I was just trying to help."

The woman smiled an apology, then hurried to catch her husband who was already headed up the street. The couple walked away, shoulders back, spines straight.

Paul wore a smirk.

"What's so funny?"

"You." He leaned against the building. "Remind me to never get you mad at me."

"Sorry if I embarrassed you. I was so angry." She turned and looked at the restaurant. "I didn't even know I felt that way. It just came out. When I think about the Turchiks and Patrick and Sassa . . ."

"I know." Paul took her arm and steered her toward the car. "Where do you want to go now? All this excitement has made me hungry."

Kate elbowed him. "It's not funny," she said, but she couldn't keep from smiling.

"No, but it is exciting to watch a redheaded female with blazing hazel eyes go after the establishment." He grinned.

Kate felt a flush of pleasure. Unable to conceal her smile, she asked, "How about the store? There's a table and chairs and I'm pretty good at making sandwiches."

"Sounds perfect."

19

Paul rolled over, fluffed his pillow, then peered at the hotel window through half-closed lids. Light slanted into the room. He turned onto his back and laid an arm over his eyes to block out the light, hoping for more sleep. It didn't help. His mind was already occupied with Kate.

He thought back to the previous evening and the way she'd squared off against the maitre d'. *She's got guts.* He liked that about her. He also liked that she'd made no apologies for the cheese sandwiches and Orange Crush she'd served for dinner.

They'd decided to spend the day together. It was up to him to come up with an adventure. Paul kicked off the blankets and sat up, his mind still occupied by the tall, striking adventurer. He was drawn to Kate, even though he knew a woman was the last thing he needed in his life.

He moved to the window and gazed at the road below. It was early and the street was empty except for a man walking at a fast clip along the sidewalk. He stopped in front of a shop, unlocked the door, and disappeared inside. Paul turned his gaze to the Chugach Mountains that stood east of town. Powerful and rugged, they compelled admiration.

They were Alaska, which demanded respect like no place he'd ever known.

His mind wandered back to Kate and the plans for the day. What should they do? It ought to be something special, something Kate had never done before. Combing his fingers through his hair, an idea materialized. Yakima, her hometown, lay far inland from the ocean. He doubted she'd ever been clamming.

Down around Ninilchik there was an abundance of razor clams and the tide table in the store had said there was supposed to be a minus tide today. He could envision Kate chasing after clams—soaking wet and muddy. She'd love it.

Paul and Kate set off for the bay. When Paul suggested clam digging, Kate hadn't been taken with the idea, but Paul stubbornly stuck to his plan, certain she'd change her mind.

On the Cook Inlet side of the Kenai Peninsula, Kate followed the coastline. When she neared Ninilchik, she dropped to a lower elevation. "I know a good landing site along this stretch of beach."

She kept her eyes on the rocky shore. "I've never dug clams before. I've never even eaten one." She looked at Paul, her brows knit. "And I'm not sure I want to." She wrinkled up her nose.

Cute nose, Paul thought, then forced his mind back to clamming. "It's fun, you'll see."

"Okay. I'm trusting you," she said, sounding less than enthusiastic.

Maybe he should have come up with a better idea. "We can do something else if you want." The scent of Evening in Paris wafted through the cockpit. He wished she hadn't worn it.

"No. You've got my curiosity up. Now I've got to find out what it's all about."

"I think you'll love it."

She offered him a crooked smile.

"Razor clams aren't like other clams. They know when someone's after them and they don't want to be caught. There's no easy shoveling and then dropping them into a bucket. You've got to chase them."

"You're pulling my leg. Chase a clam?"

Paul grinned. "It's the truth."

Kate's hazel eyes widened slightly. "Okay."

She turned her attention to the ground. "This is the spot." She flew low over a stretch of pebbled beach, made one pass to check for debris and mud, then a second sweep, and finally turned for her approach. They touched down smoothly.

"Good, the tide's out," Paul said. He waited for Kate to remove her hat and fought the impulse to tousle her short auburn hair. "You brought extra clothes, right?"

"They're in my pack."

He moved to the back of the plane where the gear was stashed. Angel already waited at the door. The moment Kate opened it, the dog leaped out and tore down the beach, chasing after gulls.

Kate clambered out, and Paul handed her a couple of buckets and two shovels.

He stepped down and a sharp wind caught hold of his jacket. "Breezy." He pulled his coat closed and zipped it.

"And cold," Kate said.

"Once we start digging, you'll warm up."

They headed toward the water, each carrying a shovel and a bucket.

"The clams are beneath the surface," Paul explained. "But they have to stick their necks up to breathe, which makes a little dimple in the sand. That's how you find them."

He stopped. "Here's one." Kneeling, he pointed at a small

hollow spot. "Once you put the shovel in the ground they start burrowing to get away, so you have to dig fast." He looked at Kate. "Ready?"

"Just dig," she said with feigned irritation.

Gently putting the tip of the shovel against the surface, Paul rested his foot on it, and in a blast of energy, he pushed the shovel into the earth, rapidly scooping out sand and tossing it to the side. When he'd dug a foot or more, he dropped to his knees and using his hands like miniature shovels, he scooped away more sand. Sweat beaded on his forehead and dripped into his eyes. Ignoring gouging rocks and the bite of broken shells, he kept working.

Angel trotted back and intently watched Paul's activity.

When he was nearly up to his shoulders in the hole he'd dug, Paul's fingertips touched the edge of the clam shell, but it managed to dig out of reach. Paul kept after it and finally grabbed hold of the creature and held on.

"He's fast," he called, exhilarated by the chase. Holding the shell with one hand, he scooped sand from around it and pulled it free. "Got him!"

He lifted the long slender clam from the hole, now filling with water, and held it up. "It's a good-sized one." He wiped away sand to reveal a shell that glistened with swirls of brown and gold. Angel tried to grab it. "Oh no you don't." Paul held it out of her reach.

Kate leaned close to get a good look. She touched the long, oval shell. "It's pretty, all except for this." She pointed at its fleshy neck.

Paul dropped it into his bucket, then presented a bleeding finger. "The shells are sharp."

"I suppose that's why they call them *razor* clams?" Kate grinned.

"Guess so."

She looked at the sizable hole, now half full of sea water. "It seems like a lot of work for one little clam."

"By the time we're done, both buckets will be full." Paul smiled. It had been a long while since he'd felt this light-hearted.

He moved down the beach. "Let's find one for you." Moments later, he stopped. "Here's one."

Kate studied the dimpled sand doubtfully.

"You have to try sooner or later," Paul said.

Just as he had done, Kate rested the tip of her shovel against the sand and then pushed it in and started digging. When she didn't unearth the clam, she chased after it with her hands. "I can feel it!" she shouted. "I've got it! I've got it!"

Angel jumped in and started digging. Kate shouldered her away. "Angel. No!"

She kept after the clam. Her head was down in the hole when a wave washed in and splashed her.

Paul laughed. "Keep going!"

Finally she sat back on her heels. "He got away." The wind caught her burnished hair and tossed it into her eyes. She wiped her hands on her trousers. "I thought I had it."

"You'll get the next one." The sight of Kate looking disheveled and unpretentious caught Paul off guard. She was beautiful. "Try again," he barely managed to say, his voice feeling as if it were caught in his throat.

Kate pushed to her feet and wiped sand off her pants. "I don't think I'm cut out for this." She looked at him, eyes wide and innocent.

Needing distance, Paul moved away. "You'll get the hang of it." As Angel took off after another seagull, Paul headed down the beach. The dog splashed into the surf and the bird rose above the waves, lifted by the wind.

When Paul spotted another likely spot, he was glad for the

distraction and immediately took up the chase. He caught the clam and held it up. "Got another one," he shouted, holding up the ill-fated mollusk.

"I'm not giving up," Kate said, catching sight of another likely spot. She started digging. Water washed in, but undaunted she kept after the clam. This time she captured the creature and dragged it out of its gritty home. "Got it!"

"Good for you." Paul laughed. Unexpectedly, a longing welled up inside, a wish that the day would never end.

By early afternoon, Paul and Kate had nearly filled both buckets. Hard work had produced ravenous appetites, so they stepped into the surf to wash filthy hands and arms, then toweled off and returned to the plane to get the lunch basket.

They sat beside a large chunk of pallid driftwood. It would shield them from the wind. Shivering, Kate pulled on her coat and sat down, leaning against the log. Panting, Angel dropped down beside her.

"That was fun," Kate said, opening the basket. "What do we do with them now?"

"We've still got more to dig, but we'll have to work fast. Tide's turning." Paul sat across from her. "When we get back to Anchorage, we clean them and then cook 'em."

She handed him a sandwich. "Hope you like salmon."

"Love it." Paul took off the waxed paper, wadded it up, and tossed it into the basket. Taking a bite, he gazed out over the inlet. In the distance mountains stood misty blue and white. "It's pretty here."

"I love it. Maybe we can come back."

"Sure." Paul heard the hesitancy in his voice. He wanted to spend more time with Kate, but he was afraid. He liked her . . . too much.

She glanced at the sun. "It almost feels warm."

A gull dove over their heads. Angel sat up and stared at it, but she'd done enough chasing for one morning and lay back down, resting her head on her paws. Kate threw a piece of her sandwich into the air and the bird caught it. "That's amazing. How do they learn that? There can't be many people out on these beaches."

"Must be an old seagull, one with lots of life experience." Paul's mouth tipped into a sideways grin.

Kate took a bite of her sandwich, then tore off a piece for Angel. Talking around a mouthful, she asked, "Most of your mail comes from San Francisco—is that your home?"

Without looking at her, he said, "Uh-huh."

"Never been there. But I'd like to go some day."

"It's nice."

"You have family there?"

"Yeah." Paul knew where the questions would lead, so he diverted the conversation. "How about you? Did you say you're from Washington?"

"Yakima. My parents own a farm there. They grow apples mostly."

"You miss it?"

"Sometimes."

"And flying, where does that come from?"

"My dad. He was flying way back when all the planes had open cockpits."

"That'd be a thrill."

"There's nothing like it."

Paul took another bite of his sandwich, enjoying the heady flavor of the fish. He finished it off. "You don't happen to have another one of those sandwiches, do you?"

Looking smug, Kate reached into the basket and held one up. "I came prepared."

"They're good. Who said you can't cook?"

"It's pretty simple, just some mayonnaise, salt and pepper, and canned salmon." She took out a container of brownies. "These are thanks to Helen."

After finishing off their lunch, Kate and Paul went back to work. When the second bucket was full, they loaded the clams and gear into the plane, then took turns changing into dry clothes. Paul cranked the plane, then climbed in and closed the door. He dragged Angel off the front seat while Kate turned the plane into the wind for takeoff.

Paul dropped down beside Kate. "So, still think you're not cut out for clam digging?"

"Guess I'm not too bad at it, after all." She flashed him a smile and headed the plane down the beach. "That was fun. Can we go again?"

"Sure. Next time I'm in Anchorage."

"My parents are going to be here in a few weeks. I'd love to take them."

"Let me know if you need my help."

"I think they'd like it." She glanced at the buckets. "We've still got to clean them. Don't figure that's going to be much fun."

"It's not bad. I'll show you."

As they lifted into the air, Paul sat back contentedly, folded his arms over his chest, and allowed his mind to replay the day. It had been one of the best he'd had in years.

When Paul and Kate carried their trophies into the store, Helen was working at the front counter, tallying the day's receipts. Kate proudly held out one of the buckets.

"Look what we got." She smiled broadly.

Helen peered into the bucket. "Oh my. You did well."

She looked from Paul to Kate. "Where do you plan to clean them?"

"We were hoping you'd let us use your place. Paul said he'd make some chowder."

"Albert loves clam chowder. And I've got fresh-baked bread."

"There are plenty of clams," Paul said. "Probably enough for canning too, if you want them."

"I certainly would." Helen closed the till. "Go on over to the house. Albert's there. I've got about another hour's worth of work to do."

"Okay," Kate said. "But I'd like to shower and change first. I feel like I've got grit everywhere."

"I can wait," Paul said, although acutely aware of the salt and sand in his hair, on his skin, and beneath his fingernails.

Helen seemed to read his mind. "Feel free to clean up at the house."

"Thanks."

When Kate and Paul arrived at the Towns's place Albert was on his knees weeding a flower garden. He pushed his slender frame up from the ground.

"Hi, you two. Helen called and told me you were coming." Brushing dirt from his hands, he moved toward the front porch. "I can already taste the chowder. Come on in."

After a shower, Paul felt more like himself. He and Kate stood side by side at the sink. He showed her how to pry open the clam shells, scoop out the insides, then cut away the guts and rinse off the sand. It wasn't unpleasant. The clams had a fresh, tangy smell.

"They feel slimy." Kate cut the guts away from the meat. "I'm not sure I'm going to like chowder."

Albert chuckled. "It's delicious, you'll see."

Helen arrived just as Paul and Kate were finishing the last couple of clams. "What do you need me to do?" she asked, tying on an apron.

"We need you to sit and watch while we cook," Paul said. "I've got my grandmother's recipe imprinted in my mind. It's the best I've ever tasted." He looked around the kitchen. "You have onions?"

"I do." Helen took one out of a basket hanging inside her pantry door and handed it to him. "The least I can do is make coffee." She moved to the percolator and dumped out the morning's leftovers.

While the chowder simmered, everyone moved to the living room. Coffee in hand, Paul settled into a chair. He felt at ease. Glancing at Kate, he wondered how much of his good mood was because of her. The idea of spending more time with the spirited woman was appealing. He wished he hadn't already arranged a flight home with Mike for the following morning. A few more days in Anchorage would be nice.

He caught Helen's eye and lifted his cup as if offering a toast. "Good coffee. Just the way I like it."

"Thank you. Hope you'll come back and visit."

"I'd like that, but it's quite a trip from the creek to Anchorage." He glanced at Kate and caught her studying him.

Her cheeks pinked slightly. "It's not so far by plane," she said innocently.

"No, I guess not." He smiled. "Next time I come, you cook the chowder?"

"You have a deal."

20

K ate's coupe bounced through a pothole, and she let off the gas, then floored it again as she hurried toward the airfield. Her parents were due, and she was late.

Searching the skies, she pulled up at the shop. No sign of her father's bright yellow Stinson. With Angel trotting at her side, she walked into the office.

"Morning," she told Sidney who sat behind his desk.

He took a cigar out of his mouth. "Today's the big day, huh?"

"Yeah, they ought to be here any time." She stepped to the door, opened it, and looked out. "Didn't realize how much I missed them." She peered south, hoping to catch a glimpse of her father's plane. "Can't wait to show them Alaska. They'll love it."

Leaving the door open, she stepped halfway back inside and glanced around the shop. "You the only one here today?"

"Yep." Angel rested her head on his lap. He gave her a pat, then stuck his cigar back in his mouth.

Kate searched the skies again.

"Don't blow your wig. They'll be here."

With a shrug, she finally committed to staying inside and

closed the door. Angel padded over to a braided rug that sat in front of the woodstove and lay down.

Sydney leaned on the desk. "We're behind the grind, you know—too much business." He furrowed his brow. "Parents or not, I'm going to need you."

"I know. I'm available. I told Mom and Dad I'd have to work, at least part of the time. Wish they were staying longer."

"How long they going to be here?"

"Three weeks. Dad's got to get back to his orchards." She glanced out the window. "Albert and Helen promised to show them around while I'm working. It was nice of them to let my parents stay at their house."

She heard the drone of a plane and hurried to the door. Angel perked up. "That's got to be them." Looking skyward, her eyes found her father's Stinson and felt the unexpected sting of tears as a rush of homesickness and memories swept through her.

The plane touched down and Kate ran onto the field, Angel loping alongside her. Kate's father was the first to appear at the door. He jumped to the ground and then turned to help Joan.

Kate ran full out. "Mom! Dad!"

Bill opened his arms just in time to pull Kate into them. He held her against his chest, and Kate hugged him back as hard as she could. When he released her, Kate stepped into her mother's embrace. She breathed in the familiar fresh-scrubbed scent of her mom. Oh, how she'd missed her.

Finally, Kate forced herself to step back, and gazed into her mother's loving eyes. "I can hardly believe you're here."

"Me too. The trip seemed to take forever." Joan pulled Kate close again and smoothed her daughter's bobbed hair. "It's so wonderful to be here." Holding Kate away from her, she said, "Now, let me have a look at you." She placed her hands on Kate's cheeks. "I declare, you're more beautiful than when you left home." She let her eyes take in the rest of her daughter. "You're a little skinny though."

"I've lost some weight, but that comes with the job. I'm fine." Kate couldn't stop smiling. With one arm tucked into her mother's, she leaned against her father. "How was the trip?"

"Couldn't have had better weather. And we saw some of the most beautiful country God ever created." He turned and faced the Chugach Mountains. "You've got some incredible mountains up here."

"You haven't seen anything yet. I can't wait to show you around. There's so much I want you to see."

Angel barked a greeting.

"Well, who's this?" Bill asked.

"That's Angel, my dog. She's friendly."

"I can see that." Bill bent down and smoothed the dog's heavy coat. "Beautiful animal."

Kate spotted Sidney standing in the shop doorway. "I'd like to introduce you to my boss," she said, and the three headed across the field with Angel romping alongside.

Kate drove along Lake Spenard, her thoughts with her parents. She'd had so much fun showing them Alaska, and they'd been properly impressed. Albert had taken her father fishing while she and her mother had done some shopping. Kate had never really liked to shop, but helping her mother find souvenirs to take home had been fun.

They had only a few days left of their vacation, and sadly Kate had to work today. However, tomorrow they planned a day of clam digging. They'd love it.

Their time together had been even better than she'd hoped. In spite of her job, Kate had managed to show them a good deal of the territory. She almost thought she had her father convinced to move up, but he wasn't yet ready to let go of the farm. Maybe one day.

Her parents both admitted to understanding why she'd stayed in Alaska. Still, Joan confessed to hoping Kate might return to Washington, eventually. Kate was startled to hear that Richard was still waiting and hoping she'd come back to him. There'd been no more letters, and she'd assumed he'd gone on with his life. There was nothing more she could do—he'd accept the truth sooner or later.

She spotted Jack's plane floating free, several yards from shore with one pontoon mostly submerged. Kate stopped the car and got out for a better look. How had the plane come free of its moorings? One pontoon looked badly damaged. Jack would be furious.

Wondering if he knew about the plane's condition, she climbed back into the sporty little Plymouth and pulled up in front of the office. Surprisingly, all the pilots' planes were on the field, and Kate wondered why everyone was grounded. She'd expected to be working today.

Angel trotted into the shop ahead of Kate. Pilots didn't like it when they weren't flying, and the atmosphere inside was subdued. Jack leaned back in a chair, arms folded over his chest and a toothpick bouncing between his lips as he chewed on it. Obviously he didn't know about his plane. Kate needed to tell him, but could already hear his outrage and recoiled at the idea of being the one to share the news.

Angel sauntered over to Mike who gave her a good rub-down.

"No work today?" Kate asked, trying to figure out how to tell Jack. She glanced at him, then walked to the schedule tacked on the wall and flipped through the next couple of days—nothing for her.

Sidney leaned on his desk. "Kate, since things are so quiet today, it'd be a good time for you to practice taking off and landing on the lake."

Her stomach clenched. She'd been dreading this day.

"You said it'd been a long while since you'd done any water landings."

"Yeah," Kate said, quaking inside. "But first we'd better check out Jack's plane."

"My plane? Why?"

"When I drove by, it was . . . in the lake, floating freely. It's off its moorings and looks like one of the pontoons is damaged."

"What?" Jack exploded, leaping out of his chair and striding to the door.

Kate's eyes met Mike's. Everyone followed Jack outdoors. He strode toward the lake, cussing all the way.

Mike hung back with Kate. "What happened?"

"I don't know. I just noticed it when I drove in." Kate hurried to catch up with the guys.

At the dock, Jack gaped at his plane, then turned accusing eyes on the group. "Who in blazes did this?"

No one spoke.

Sidney was the first to offer an explanation. "I'm sure it was an accident. No one here would set your plane afloat."

"So you're saying the plane did it all by itself?" The veins in Jack's forehead bulged and his face was crimson. Cursing, he waded into the water. By the time he reached the plane, he was neck deep. He checked it over, then examined the pontoon. Looking angrier than ever, he grabbed the line and headed back toward the dock.

Mike and Frank splashed in to help. Mike stood on the side with the good pontoon and Frank moved around behind the plane. The three worked together to steer the Stinson back to the dock where Jack tied it off.

Once secured, he examined the pontoon. He straightened, and looking ferocious, he bellowed, "Someone gouged a hole in it!" He glared at the pilots. "I know you're jealous. I've got two good birds. And you're lucky just to have one pathetic piece of junk." His eyes stopped at Kate. "Fess up."

"No one did anything to your plane," Sidney said. He walked to the end of the dock. "We wouldn't do that, not even to you." He looked at the plane. "All it needs is a new pontoon and it'll be good as new. I don't know why you've got your shorts all up in a wad."

"Replacing it will take more than pocket change."

"Yeah, well, you've got plenty of that." Sidney shook his head.

"No one's jealous of you," Kenny said, puffing out his chest and shoving his hands into his pockets, seemingly proud to be standing up to Jack.

"Is that right? You don't care that I get more business than every last one of you, or that I've got two planes, or that I'm the best pilot?"

He sloshed out of the water, wrung out the front of his shirt while still wearing it, then directed a derisive look at Kate. "That albatross of yours can barely get off the ground."

Just then, Kate's parents walked up. She could see by her mother's expression that what she'd just seen and heard distressed her.

"I thought you went sightseeing," Kate said.

"We thought we'd stop by here first." Joan looked over the bunch of men, her gaze stopping on Jack, unable to hide her revulsion. She moved close to her daughter and softly asked, "Are you sure you're safe . . . working here among these ruffians?"

"They're not ruffians," Kate said under her breath. "Jack just lost his temper because his plane got damaged."

Frank squeezed water from his pants legs, then followed the rest of the men to the shop.

Joan pressed her palms together. "Maybe moving up here wasn't such a good idea."

"She's fine," Bill said. "I'd be upset too if something happened to my plane."

"You get upset, but you never behave the way that man just did." Joan stared at Jack.

"Maybe so, but Kate will be fine. She can hold her own against anyone." Bill gave Kate a squeeze.

She leaned against her father. "Thanks, Dad."

"We're heading for Palmer today. See you later?"

"Sure." Kate considered asking if she could go along. It would mean she didn't have to practice water landings and takeoffs, at least not today. But she knew it was time to face her fears.

Mike stepped out of the shop and headed toward Kate. "You ready? We need to get the pontoons on your plane."

Anxiety set Kate's pulse racing. "Sure." She hugged her mother. "I'll see you later. Have fun." Kate watched them go, then turned toward the shop, her stomach roiling.

Every nerve on edge, Kate eased into her seat. Mike remained on the pontoon and cranked the flywheel. She pulled the starter and the engine lit off.

"We're all set," Mike said with a wink and dropped into the seat beside her.

Kate nodded, keeping her eyes on the water. *I can do this.* She gripped the stick.

"Kate?" Mike looked at her more closely. "Something wrong?"

"No. I'm fine." She tried to keep her voice from quaking.

"You have done this before, right?"

"Sure. No problem."

"You look kind of tight."

Kate ignored the comment and moved out across the lake. Memories pummeled her—Alison's scream, the icy water . . . *I* CAN'T *do this.* She stopped, then, without looking at Mike, turned back toward the dock, and shut down the engine.

"Kate, this isn't going to work," Mike teased. "You've got to be out in the water with the engine running if you want to take off."

She didn't respond.

"Kate."

She looked at him. "I . . . I can't do it."

"What do you mean, you can't?"

"I just can't." She didn't want to tell him. She didn't want him to know what she'd done.

"Hold on. You flew, on your own, from the states to Alaska. You've been all over the territory—landing on all kinds of airstrips, places without runways with nothing more than a cleared place in a field or a sandy beach—in fog, wind, snow, and rain. And you're telling me you can't take off from a lake on a clear day?"

She swallowed hard and nodded, fighting back tears.

His voice gentle, he asked, "Why? Tell me."

She looked at him, swallowing hard and blinking back tears. "The last time I landed on a lake, I crashed."

Mike seemed to relax. "Those kinds of things happen. You've just got to get back on the horse."

"You don't understand."

"Maybe you should tell me about it." His eyes were kind.

Kate looked down, weighing his comment. He was a good friend, one that she could confide in. "I wasn't supposed to be in the air that day. I convinced my friend Alison to leave work early and we went flying." She glanced at him. "She died. I killed her." Tears spilled over. "It was my fault. I just had to go larking about." Her voice had a hard, blaming edge to it.

Mike rested a hand on her arm. "I'm sure it wasn't your fault. What happened?"

"When we took off, it was clear, but by the time we reached the lake, fog had set in. I'd done plenty of pontoon landings before and figured I could make it . . . I was wrong."

"You said Alison was your friend. Do you think she'd want you to punish yourself?"

"No. But I just can't do this." Kate looked out over the lake. "All I can see and hear is the fog and the water—it was like ice. I heard her scream, and then we hit. I got out, but I couldn't help her." Kate gulped down a sob.

Mike took her hand. "I'm so sorry. How long's it been?"

"Seven years."

"That's a long time ago. You were a kid. And I don't know about your skills then, but you're a good pilot now. And you can do this. You need to do this."

Kate swiped away tears. Mike was right. She had to try. Pulling together all the determination she possessed, she turned over the engine and slowly headed back onto the lake.

"When you reach your takeoff speed, don't forget to retract the water rudders and pull back on the stick."

Kate nodded and cranked up the power. Soon she was skimming over the surface of the lake. Her muscles were tight, her hands trembled.

"Okay, just a little back pressure," Mike said.

Kate felt the plane ease out of the water. They were free and headed skyward, leaving the lake behind. Gulping in air, she gripped the stick and looked at the blue pool below. Now, how was she going to get down?

"Perfect!" Mike whooped, then leaned over and kissed her cheek. He smiled broadly. "Now make a few passes over the lake and we'll head back. It's just like landing on any other airstrip—keep your nose up but don't set your tail down in the water."

Kate wet dry lips. She made another pass over the lake, checking for debris. She was a little heavy on the pedals and the Bellanca rocked back and forth.

"Calm down, now. You'll be all right."

She took in a shaky breath. The crash tried to push its way into her mind. *Focus.* She gently pushed the stick forward and soon cruised just above the lake. Careful to keep the nose up slightly, she was also conscious not to let her tail drag in the water. She felt the pontoons touch and the Bellanca gently settled on the lake. She was down.

"You did it! Good job."

Kate's hands shook, her heart pounded, but she managed a smile. She'd done it. "Thank you, Mike. Thank you." She wanted to kiss him, but instead gave him a hug. Now there was so much open to her. She'd be able to use the lakes and rivers to make landings instead of having to trust unpredictable and rough landing strips.

He held her tightly for a moment, then looked into her eyes. "I knew you had it in you."

"I couldn't have done it without you."

"Okay. You owe me one, then. How 'bout dinner tonight?"

"I'd love to, but my parents will be expecting me. Maybe next week?"

"It's a long ways off, but I guess I can stand it." He grinned.

21

K ate walked across the airfield, her parents on either side of her. Angel padded along in front. Keeping her eyes on the dog, Kate fought tears. Her parents were heading home. She looped her arms with theirs.

Joan smiled at her daughter. "Thank you for showing us Alaska. It's a remarkable place." She gave Kate's arm a squeeze. "I could almost imagine living here myself."

"Maybe you should think about it." Kate leaned against her mother.

"We will," Bill said. "When I'm done farming."

"You'll never leave your orchards."

"Gotta retire some day." He grinned.

"The Matanuska Valley has good fertile land."

"Yeah, but it's not right for apple trees. I checked." He released her arm and rested his hand on her back. "We can't come right away, but one day."

"I'm going to miss you," Kate said, struggling to keep the tremor out of her voice.

Bill stopped and gazed down at his daughter. "We'll be back."

When they reached her father's plane, Kate walked around,

giving it a thorough inspection. "You have your maps and charts?"

"Sure do. Figure we'll do a little sightseeing on our way home."

"Be careful. The coastal weather can change in a flash. "

"I'm not worried." He glanced at Joan. "My copilot here will keep me in line."

"Don't believe a word he says." Joan shot him a teasing look. "He does as he likes, always has." She turned to Kate, her expression more serious. "I always knew you were special, Kate. I'm proud of you." She glanced at the Chugach Mountains. "This is a beautiful place, but it's awfully rough. You be careful."

"I will. I promise."

Bill nodded at Mike, who stood in the shop doorway, hands in his pockets. "Figure he'll watch over you." He smiled. "Nice fella. Wouldn't mind seeing more of him."

Kate glanced at Mike, not sure what she felt for him. He was a good friend. Could he be more than that? "Well, you just might."

Bill raised an eyebrow. "Really?"

"We're dating, that's all for now." Kate shrugged.

"He's a fine person, I can tell." Joan hugged her daughter. "Time we were on our way. You have a mail run to get to."

Bill pulled his daughter into his arms and held her tight. "See you next spring or sooner if you can make it down before winter." He gave Angel a pat. "I'll miss you too, girl."

Her tail beat the air and she snuffled his hand.

"Maybe by next summer I'll have a house," Kate said. "That way when you come for a visit, you can stay with me."

Joan kissed Kate's cheek. "Love you, dear." She stepped up to the plane and Bill gave her a hand in.

Kate watched as they taxied down the runway. Her father waved and her mother blew her a kiss. Sadness soaked into Kate. It was unlikely she'd have a chance to fly down before winter, and next summer seemed a long way off.

Her father's Stinson lifted into the air. Kate watched until it disappeared into the haze of blue sky. She headed to the shop, Angel trotting alongside her.

Mike offered her a smile and draped an arm around her shoulders, giving her a squeeze. "You'll see them again soon."

"Sure."

"Did you have breakfast this morning?"

"Yeah. With my parents."

"Oh. Well, how about dinner with me tonight? We can go to the café."

Kate felt a bubble of delight, but thoughts of the day ahead tamped it down. "I've got my mail run and I'm getting a late start, so I probably won't be back in time for dinner."

"We can eat anytime we want. The café stays open late. And I've got a couple of short runs, so I won't be back before six o'clock anyway. How about seven?"

"Probably ought to make it eight."

"Eight it is."

When Kate stepped into the shop, Sidney was in his usual position—leaning back in his chair, feet propped on the desk. "So, they've headed home, huh?"

"Yeah." Kate sighed.

"Nice folks."

"They are. I wish they'd move up."

She walked into the back room and started sorting envelopes and packages. Angel lay just inside the door, head resting on her paws. Kate came across a letter for Paul from Robert Anderson in San Francisco. He wrote to Paul often.

She wondered which Anderson he was—brother, cousin, father? She hoped Paul would meet the plane.

"You need help?" Mike asked.

Kate shoved the letter into the delivery bag and glanced at him, feeling guilty and wondering why. She and Mike weren't exclusive, and there really wasn't anything between her and Paul. "No, I'm just finishing up," she said, feeling her face flush. She felt as if she'd been caught daydreaming about Paul.

"At least I can help you carry these out to the plane." He picked up two mailbags.

Kate slung another one over her shoulder and headed for the door. "See you later, Sidney," she called stepping outside.

Mike closed the door behind them.

Angel galloped ahead, beating Kate and Mike to the dock where her plane was moored. She was still a little nervous about water landings, but with each run she gained confidence.

Mike opened the door and Angel leaped in. He set the mailbags inside, then took the one Kate carried and placed it with the others. He moved to the front of the plane and grabbed the flywheel lever. As he made his way to the back toward the door, he and Kate met. He placed a hand on her arm, pulling her closer.

Kate could smell his spicy aftershave. When he kissed her, she made sure it was brief. Apprehension niggled at her thoughts. She liked Mike, but he was moving too quickly.

"Figured I'd crank her for you," he said, holding up the lever. His blue eyes held a mix of mischief and tenderness.

Kate squeezed past him. "I better get moving."

"I'll see you later."

"Yeah. Later." Still feeling the touch of his lips, Kate made her way to the front of the plane.

Thoughts of Mike popped into Kate's mind throughout the day. She couldn't decide how she felt about him. One moment she thought he could be the one for her and the next he felt more like a pal. And there was Paul. She'd felt something between them, but just what, she didn't know. In any case, he'd made it clear he wasn't interested in a relationship.

Most people she met along her route were busy with their gardens or hauling in the early run of salmon. She tried to imagine Mike and herself sharing that kind of life but couldn't see either of them being content living mundane lives. She replaced Mike's image with Paul's. He didn't seem right either, maybe because he acted as if there was no room for anyone in his life.

There were no answers right now, so Kate tried to focus on work.

At one stop, she had a good view of the Ninilchik River, which was inundated with spawning salmon. There were so many, it looked as if someone could just reach in and grab one.

With fishing season under way, drying racks were full, and the tantalizing aroma of smoldering wood chips wafted from smokehouses. Gulls flocked riverbanks, feeding on leftovers from fishermen and bears. From the safety of her plane, Kate thought the bears were fascinating and beautiful.

When she put down on Bear Creek, she expected to see the Warrens and Paul on the bar. It was empty. She motored to Paul's dock and waited, but no one showed up. She had mail for Paul so decided to leave it at his place. With Angel at her side, she followed the trail up from the creek that led to his cabin. Willow branches caught at her hair and clothing. The air was heavy with the scent of damp vegetation.

Paul's dogs barked, greeting Kate before she could see them. Angel charged up the trail ahead of her. When Kate reached the cabin, the dogs were busy getting reacquainted and barely noticed her.

She walked up the steps to the back porch and knocked on the door. Jasper flew from a tree near the house and settled on his perch on the porch. He cawed, sounding as if he were trying to shoo away an intruder. Kate tried to touch him, but he pecked at her hand and then hopped to a woodpile.

"Fine, be that way," she teased and turned back to the door and knocked again. Still no answer.

Wondering if Paul might be working in the garden, Kate walked around to the side of the house. His large plot was crowded with young vegetables, but Paul wasn't there. Kate strolled along a row of carrots, stopped, and pulled one. Wiping away dirt, she took a bite of the crisp young tuber. She took another bite and thought about how one day she'd have her own garden. Would she share it with Mike? Glancing at Paul's house, the idea gave her a sense of discontent. She shrugged off the feeling.

After having a look around, Kate returned to the cabin, figuring she'd leave the mail inside. She knocked once more just to make sure he wasn't there, and when he didn't come to the door, she stepped inside and set the envelope on the table.

The room was in disarray, which was unusual. Paul usually kept the house tidy and scrubbed. A cup half filled with coffee sat on the table and dishes were piled in the sink. Something was wrong.

A raspy cough carried from the back room. "Paul?" Kate hurried to the bedroom door. "Paul?" Another cough answered her.

She stepped into the room. He lay on the bed, wearing only the bottom half of his long johns. He quickly pulled a sheet up over himself. He looked fevered and pallid.

Kate crossed to him. "Are you all right?"

"I will be," he croaked. "In a few days."

"You sound and look awful."

"I feel awful."

"What's wrong?"

"Septic sore throat," he whispered, pushing up on one elbow and picking up a cup of water from the bedstead. He grimaced as he sipped. "Feels like swallowing glass." He set the water back on the table.

"Is there anything I can do?"

"No. I'll be fine," he rasped.

"I can't leave you here alone. Are the Warrens home?"

He shrugged.

"You need help. I can stay."

"No. You'll end up sick too."

"I'm healthy as a horse. I'll see if Patrick can send word to Sidney." *And to Mike,* she thought, sorry she'd miss their date.

Kate looked around the room and wrinkled her nose. "This place is a mess." She walked to the door. "After I get you something to eat and drink, I'll tidy things up."

"Can't eat."

"If you can swallow water, you can get down some broth. I'll make you some." She headed for the door, picking up dirty clothes as she went.

Paul tried to sit up, but sank back into his pillows. "I'm warning you, this is contagious."

"I'll be fine." She dropped the clothes into a basket.

He stared at her with an amused expression. "Stubborn. You're pure stubborn."

"I've been told that." She picked up the basket. "What else can I do?"

"I need some aspirin. It's on the bureau."

Kate picked up the bottle of aspirin. A photo caught her attention. It was a younger version of Paul with a man and woman she guessed were his parents. Three young men and three women were also in the photo. "Is this your family?" She picked up the photograph.

Paul's expression closed. He nodded.

Kate returned it to the bureau, wondering why it troubled him.

"Can you bring me a cloth and a bowl of cool water?" he whispered.

"Sure." Kate took his glass, filled it with water, and returned to his bedside. "How many tablets do you need?"

"Four."

She looked at the label. "It says one or two."

"Four," he croaked.

"You're sure?"

He nodded.

Kate unscrewed the lid and dumped the pills into her palm, then gave them to him along with the water. She watched while he swallowed one at a time, closing his eyes and grimacing each time. "Are you sure you don't need a doctor?"

"Nothing they can do." He handed her the glass and sank back on his pillows. "Fever's high. Can you get the pan of water?"

"Sure." Kate studied him. His eyes were only partially open and his breathing seemed rapid and shallow. Her mind flashed to the man who had died on her plane and panic coursed through her. *I don't know what to do. What if Paul dies?*

Wearing a pretense of confidence, she filled a bowl with

water and found a washcloth, which she dropped into the basin. She returned to his bedside, setting the bowl on the bedstead.

"I'll take care of this."

"You're too sick. I can do it."

Paul didn't argue. He pushed himself upright and pulled the sheet down to his waist.

Kate tried to ignore his well-muscled chest and arms.

He rolled onto his stomach. "Wipe my arms and back with the moistened towel. It'll cool my skin."

Acting as nonchalant as she could manage, Kate dipped the towel in the water, wrung it out, and then sponged his heated skin. "You're awfully hot. You should see a doctor."

"There aren't any."

When the water turned lukewarm, Kate replaced it with fresh. Paul rolled onto his back, exposing his broad chest and handsome face. Kate tried to focus on his well-being and not his looks. Still, she was glad his eyes were closed so she could study his face.

She gently ran the cloth across his broad brow, allowing her index finger to smooth furrowed skin. She brought the cloth down along his cheekbone and across his strong jaw, then down to his neck. He looked like he was sleeping. She wondered what it would be like to kiss him. Her skin prickled at the unexpected thought.

After she'd cooled his face, she moved to his chest, then lifted one arm and bathed it and did the same with the other. She didn't wash his abdomen. That was too intimate. When she finished, she set the bowl and cloth on the bedstead and pulled up the bed covers.

"Leave them off."

"But you'll get chilled."

"It's better for the fever."

"For a homesteader, you know an awful lot about doctoring."

He didn't respond.

Kate returned to the kitchen and set the bowl and cloth in the sink, then filled a pan with water and set it on the stove. She found canned meat in the shed and added it to the simmering water. In the garden, she pulled fresh carrots and green onions and added them to the meat and broth.

Paul slept while Kate cleaned the cabin and washed his clothing. She heated a kettle of water and dumped it into a tub. Using a washboard and a bar of soap, she scrubbed Paul's shirts. Soon her arms and back ached, and she was more thankful than ever for Helen's Windsor washing machine.

Once she had his clothes clean, she hung them on a line strung between the shop and a birch tree. She'd never been the domestic type, but doing all this for Paul felt good.

When she checked on him, he was still asleep, so she walked to the Warrens' place. She needed to let Sydney know she wouldn't be back today. Angel loped ahead of her. She was less familiar with Patrick's dogs, so when Kate caught up, the dogs were going through the ritual of raised hackles and sniffing.

Patrick met her on the porch. "I heard the plane a while ago. Figured you'd be long gone by now."

"Paul's sick so I stayed."

"Bad sick?"

"Yeah. He'll probably be all right, but he needs someone to help him."

"What's he got?"

"A throat infection with a fever and a cough. I'll stay the rest of the day and tonight, but I've got to get back to work. I was wondering if Sassa would mind helping out tomorrow."

"She and the kids are at her sister's. Won't be back for two more days." He scratched his head. "I can come over."

Kate knew Patrick meant well, but she wasn't sure she trusted a man to properly care for Paul. "That's all right. I can stay until she returns."

"Let me know if you need anything."

"Could you radio Sidney to let him know I'm safe and that I'll be here a couple of days?"

"Sure thing. Anything else?"

"I was supposed to meet Mike Conlin. Could you make sure Sidney tells him where I am?"

Patrick raised an eyebrow. "You have a date tonight?"

"No. Nothing like that," Kate lied, not certain why she felt the need to cover up.

She headed back to the cabin. Paul was awake and his fever was up. She gave him more aspirin and another sponge bath.

That night while he spooned small amounts of broth into his mouth, Kate sat on the chair beside his bed. "How come you know what to do for fevers and all that?"

He swallowed a spoonful of broth and winced, then whispered, "Had a mother who knew everything. And, I've had this before."

It took a while, but Paul managed to get down most of the broth. He looked at her and swallowed with a grimace, then asked, "Can you feed the dogs for me?"

"Sure."

"There's dried fish in the cache." He closed his eyes.

Kate left him to sleep, made sure the dogs were fed, and checked on him periodically to make sure he was all right.

Exhausted, she took a quilt from a shelf and lay on the small sofa in the front room. Angel curled up on the floor beside her. Resting a hand on her companion's head, she quickly fell asleep. She wondered how Mike felt about her missing their date. It would have been fun, but she didn't mind lying here on Paul's sofa.

The following morning, Paul showed no signs of improvement. Kate gave him broth and made sure he drank water and took his aspirin. She cooled his body with another sponge bath. While he slept, she went to work pulling weeds in the garden. That afternoon, he managed to eat a more substantial soup and then slept some more.

Kate woke the next morning to sunlight and warbling birds. She let Angel out, made a trip to the outhouse, and then checked on Paul. He was awake. She rested a hand on his brow. "Fever's down. How are you feeling?"

"Better."

"Do you need anything?"

"I need to get out of this bed." He sat up and dropped his feet to the floor. He remained like that for a few moments, tottering slightly. "I'd like to change into clean clothes."

"Oh, sure." Kate grabbed clean underclothes, a shirt, and pants and set them on the bed beside him. Then she got his slippers and set them on the floor beside the bed.

Kate hovered, wondering just how to help the big man.

"I can dress myself," he said gruffly.

"Okay. I'll be right out here." Kate hurried from the room and stood just outside the door.

Several minutes later, Paul called weakly, "I could use a hand."

When Kate stepped into the room, Paul had managed to dress himself, but he sat on the edge of the bed, looking weak. He glanced at her, humiliation on his face. He pushed to his feet but was so unsteady Kate rushed to his side and offered him a shoulder to lean on. They shuffled to the front of the house. He stood at the door, resting against the frame.

"You all right?"

"Just a little dizzy."

"Maybe you should sit down?"

"No. I'll be fine."

Kate watched him, staying close just in case she was needed.

Finally he straightened and stepped onto the porch. "Gotta use the outhouse."

Thank goodness no more bed pan, Kate thought, feeling the embarrassment.

Jasper, the raven, cawed at him from his perch. Paul shook his head. "Never taught him to say a single word."

"Ravens can speak?"

"Heard some can if you teach them. But he never got it." Paul headed toward the steps. "Can you get me that stick over there?" He nodded at a stripped branch leaning against the house.

Kate handed it to him, but couldn't keep from remaining close in case he needed her to steady himself.

"I can get there on my own," he said dryly.

She stepped back and watched him slowly make his way down the steps. *He'll be all right*, she decided. *I wonder if he's hungry.* She returned indoors to start breakfast.

When Paul stepped back inside, he was accompanied by Patrick. The tall, gangly man smiled. "Morning. How you holding up?"

"Just fine."

Sassa walked in behind the men. "Kate, I'm sorry I wasn't here to help."

Paul shuffled to the table and sat. He wiped sweat from his face.

"Good to see you up and about," Patrick said. "When I stopped in yesterday, you looked pretty bad."

"Still a little rough, but I'm on the mend." He glanced at Kate. "Thanks to my nurse."

"Do you think you could eat some eggs?" Kate asked.

"I'll try."

"I can stay and help," Sassa said. "And so will Lily."

Paul rested his arms on the table. "I think I can make it on my own now."

Sassa eyed him in a way that said she wasn't sure whether to believe him or not. Finally she said, "Okay. But we'll stop in to check on you."

———

Kate shared breakfast with Paul, then cleared away the dishes and washed them. "That's it," she said, drying the last plate and setting it in the cupboard. "I'd better get moving."

"Thanks for the help." Paul pushed out of his chair.

"You stay put. I'll get my bag."

"Appreciate what you did." His voice sounded raspy.

"Glad I could help." Kate headed for the door and stopped. "I'll see you next week."

"Next week," Paul said with a nod.

As she walked down the trail, Kate realized she still knew almost nothing about him. She'd been tempted to snoop, but her conscience wouldn't allow it. After spending nearly three days with Paul, he was still a mystery.

I'll probably never know. Doesn't really matter. I like him no matter what he's hiding.

22

When Kate stepped into the shop, Sidney glanced at her from beneath the rim of his cowboy hat. A mass of paperwork sprawled across his desk in front of him. "Morning." He didn't smile.

"Why you so grumpy?"

He leaned back and stared at her. Using the tip of his pencil, he pushed up the brim of his hat. "What? I look cranky?" His tone was sarcastic. He flung the pencil onto the desk where it rolled across the chaos of papers. "Government interference—that's what's got a burr under my saddle."

"What's up?"

"There was a day when pilots could do what they wanted, where they wanted, and how they wanted. No one nosed in. People might have thought we were crazy, but they were grateful. Now the American government is butting in. They want a list of all my pilots. They want to know what you fly and where you fly." He pressed his elbows on his desktop. "What do they care? They know nothing about our business, nothing about Alaska and what life's like up here. Bush piloting isn't a pretty package that you can tie up with a bow. We do what we have to." He shook his head. "If they have their way, we'll end up with our hands tied and we'll be a useless bunch of has-beens."

Kate rested a hip against Sidney's desk, took a piece of peppermint out of his candy dish, and popped it into her mouth. "If they knew how many hours we log in during the summer, they wouldn't believe it."

"Turn their hair gray." Sidney picked up a dead cigar from the ashtray and clenched it between his teeth while he tried to light a match.

"Speaking of work . . ." Kate stood. "Any runs for me?"

"Had a call a while ago, a fellow from Idaho. Said he and his wife are staying with friends here in Anchorage, but need to get to Fairbanks. Sounded kind of desperate, but I haven't seen hide nor hair of them."

Disappointment filtered through Kate. "At this rate, I'll never have enough money to buy a place of my own."

Sidney pressed his back against the chair and gave her a hard stare. "You think you're the only one hurting? Compared to the rest of the country we're in the money. At least we have work."

He picked up a newspaper lying amidst the muddle on his desk. "*Seattle Times* has a story about folks living in shanty-towns. Call 'em Hoovervilles." He opened to the article. "Says they got 'em all over the country. Got a picture of one right here." He turned to the page so Kate could see.

She looked at the photograph. "When I flew over Seattle, I saw it. It's terrible—whole families just trying to survive."

"Hard to believe people are living in cardboard boxes and abandoned crates. Never thought I'd see the day."

Kate felt a flush of guilt. "Sometimes the Depression seems far away."

"Yeah, I'd say we're not doing too bad up here. When

you're flying, you get paid good money and so do I." Instead of sounding thankful, though, Sidney's tone was angry.

Kate wondered what was up. She looked at her hands, studying her short nails. "I do have a lot to be thankful for."

"You betcha. We all do." He closed the paper, folded it, and glowered at the paperwork on his desk.

Sidney wasn't acting like himself. "Is something going on?" Kate asked tentatively. "Has something happened?"

He didn't answer right away. Finally, he took the cigar out of his mouth and studied it. "My brother lost his job and his house. All our growing-up years, he was the one the family figured would be a success. He's the studious type, hardworking. Now, he's hitting the pavement looking for a job, any job." Sidney picked up the pencil and, holding it between two fingers, tapped the eraser on the desk. "Told him he could come here, but he says Alaska's not for him."

"He'll find something."

"Yeah. Something'll come up." Sidney didn't sound convinced.

Kate moved to the woodstove. "Won't be long and you'll have to light this. Nights are getting cold."

"We've still got a few good weeks left."

A car pulled up in front of the office. "Hope that's the rider to Fairbanks." Kate moved to the window.

A tall man wearing a suit hurried around to the passenger side of the car and opened the door. A woman dressed in a stylish pink skirt and a tailored maternity blouse stepped out. Although she was very pregnant, she managed to look elegant. She wore a smart hat with a broad brim that matched her pink skirt. It mostly concealed a chic short hairdo.

The man held the woman's arm as they walked toward the door. When they stepped inside, Sidney unsuccessfully tried not to stare at the woman's abdomen.

The man removed his hat. "Morning. I'm Fred Dorsey. I called earlier about a flight to Fairbanks."

"Right." Sidney stood and crossed to the man to shake his hand. "We've been waiting for you."

"This is my wife, Jean."

Sidney gave the woman a friendly nod.

"We have family in Fairbanks waiting for us," Jean said. "We've got to get there right away."

Sidney took the stogie out of his mouth. "I don't mean to be indelicate, ma'am, but you look like you're just about ready to have a baby. It's probably not a good idea for you to fly."

She smiled and rested a hand on her protruding stomach. "I'm fine, really. I'm not due for another week." She tipped her head slightly, peering at Sidney from beneath the brim of her hat.

"A week's not so far off. Babies come pretty much when they want, don't they?" He put the cigar back in his mouth and puffed. "You'd better stay put. Anchorage has a good hospital."

Jean tucked a blonde curl in place beneath her hat. "Please. I promised my sister I'd be there. She's having a baby also, and we've always done everything together. Our due dates are the same, and if I don't make it, she'll be hugely disappointed."

Sidney wasn't convinced. "I'd like to help you out, but you should have done your traveling sooner."

"I'll pay extra." She dug into her handbag.

Sidney shook his head. "It's not the money. I don't want you to have your baby on one of my planes."

"I'm not having it right now. And if I understand correctly, the flight's not that long."

Fred stepped forward, his expression earnest. "This means a lot to my wife. I assure you the doctor says she's fine."

Sidney gave Kate a sidelong glance.

Kate thought about the money. "I don't mind, Sidney. I'll take them."

Fred looked at Kate, as if seeing her for the first time. "She your only pilot?"

"Right now she is." Sidney leveled a serious look at Kate. "It's not a good idea."

"You heard her. She's fine. And the doctor gave permission."

"And if she decides to have that baby between here and Fairbanks?"

"What are the chances?"

Sidney thought a moment, then with a shrug said, "Okay by me, but if something goes wrong, it's not on my head."

Fred grinned. "Thanks." He shook Sidney's hand. "I'll get our bags out of the car." He headed outside, Jean following slowly.

Kate grabbed her pack. "See you later."

"You don't need the money that bad."

"You worry too much."

"That's my job. Someone's got to keep the business afloat." Sidney watched them out the window. "I don't know. She had that look."

"What look?"

"Can't explain it exactly, but I've seen it before—right before . . . well, you know."

Kate laughed. "If you could predict births, you'd be a rich man." She opened the door. "See you later."

Mike pulled up just as Kate stepped onto the field. He waved at her, then disappeared inside the shop. A few moments later, he reappeared and loped across the airstrip. "Hey, Kate. Can I catch a ride with you? I've got business in Fairbanks."

He glanced at the man and woman slowly making their way across the airfield. "You have passengers—will that be a problem?"

"Not at all." She smiled. "It'll be nice to have your company."

"Okay, then." Wearing a smile, he hurried toward the man lugging two bags and took one from him.

Mike reached out and gently touched Kate's arm. "Glad we get some time together. Seems all we do is work."

"That's how summers are."

Kate glanced at Fred and Jean. They sat side by side, holding hands. They looked comfortable and content. Kate felt reassured.

"So, you fly much?" Fred asked.

"All the time," Kate called back. "I've been to Fairbanks more times than I can count. The weather's clear so we ought to make good time—three hours or so."

"We appreciate you taking us," Jean said. "It's extremely important to my sister. Her baby was due five days ago, so I've got to get there. She could have it any time."

"I thought you said you were due the same day?"

Silence answered Kate's question. She swung around and stared at the couple. "You lied to me."

"You wouldn't have taken us otherwise," Fred said.

Kate turned an accusing look on Jean. "So, you're past due?"

"We don't know that. Due dates are mostly conjecture," Fred said.

Kate thought she saw Jean wince. "I ought to turn this plane around right now." She was furious.

Mike leaned close and said into her ear, "Simmer down. It'll be all right."

"Please, don't go back. I'm fine, really," Jean begged.

She sounded fine and Kate wanted the fare, so she stayed on her heading.

"What's your dog's name?" Fred asked.

Kate wasn't over being mad, so she didn't answer.

"She's beautiful. What kind is she?"

Rudeness didn't come naturally to Kate. She heaved a resigned sigh and said, "Her name's Angel, and she's part Siberian Husky and part Malamute."

Angel heard her name and trotted up to the seats and rested her head in the woman's lap, or what was left of it. Jean rested a hand on her head. "She's so sweet."

"She's a great dog," Mike said.

"So, what do you do?" Fred asked Mike.

"I'm a pilot."

"But I thought . . ." Fred stopped, then nodding said, "Oh . . . yeah. I remember you came in just before we left."

"No reason for me to fly. Kate's a great pilot."

"I can see that."

Kate glanced at Jean. "You doing all right?"

"Yes, but I am thirsty. Do you have any water?"

"Under your seat."

Fred reached beneath the seat and pulled out a thermos. "This?"

"No. That's coffee. You can have some if you like, but it's Sidney's and it's pretty awful." She grinned, feeling less angry. "The water's in a jar."

Fred reached under again and came up with the jar. He handed it to his wife.

Kate thought she saw perspiration on Jean's upper lip. What would she do if Jean were to go into labor? She tried to calm her fears by reminding herself babies take hours to be born.

Then she heard it—a moan.

She glanced at her passenger. Jean was bent over and clutched her stomach. "What's wrong? I thought you said you were fine?"

"I am." Her answer came out through clenched teeth. "I've been having pains for a few days. It's nothing. It'll pass."

Nothing? What do you mean, nothing? She glanced at Mike, and his look of alarm only fueled her own.

Jean moaned again. Kate tried to ignore it. But no more than two minutes later, the woman cried out. Kate swung around. "You sure you're all right?"

Jean gave Kate an apologetic expression. "I don't know." Tears mixed with perspiration on her face. "I'm sorry. I didn't know this would happen."

"*What* would happen?" Panic rode through Kate.

Fred gently placed an arm around his wife. "What do you mean? Are you having the baby?"

"I . . . I don't know."

He tried to stand but was too tall for the cabin, so he stood bent over. "What do we do?"

"How should I know? I've never had a baby before," Jean said.

Kate tried to focus on flying. She was a pilot, not a doctor. Panting now accompanied the whimpers and moans. *Babies take a long time to get born. Don't they?*

Jean yelled.

Kate jumped, then hollered, "What's going on?"

"I . . . I think she's having the baby." Fred sounded terrified. "We need a doctor!"

"Well, there's no doctor up here!"

"It hurts. Oh, it hurts." Jean grabbed the front of Fred's shirt. "Help me. Please help me."

"Everything's going to be all right, sugar." He moved up front and got close to Kate's ear. "You've got to get us to a hospital!"

Kate couldn't believe what she was hearing. "Look out the window. Do you see any hospitals down there?"

Fred gazed at endless tundra. "What's the closest place?"

"Fairbanks. And if your wife is getting ready to have a baby, that's too far."

Fred went back to Jean. "Can you wait, honey?"

"No! It's coming! I can feel it!"

Fred moved back to the cockpit. "You've got to help us. I don't know what to do. She's never had a baby before . . . Do you know what to do?"

"No." Kate looked at Mike. "Have you ever delivered a baby?"

"Are you kidding?"

Kate glanced at Fred. "You'll have to handle it."

Sweating and pale, he stared at her, his eyes wide.

Kate knew he would be absolutely no help. "All right. I'll look for a place to put down." Her eyes scanned the wilderness below them. "Outsiders. They've got no business being here," she muttered.

"I can keep flying while you help with the baby," Mike said.

Kate looked at Fred, then back at Mike. "No. That's not going to work. I need your help."

Mike went pale. "I don't know—"

"I need you. And I'm putting down. Help me find a place." Kate could hear the alarm in her voice and tried to quiet it. "Please . . . look for a place to set down."

Kate scoured the Nenana River, hoping for a quiet spot to land. "Jean, hang on just a little longer. And whatever you do, don't push."

272

"That looks like a good spot," Mike said, pointing at a quiet stretch of water.

Kate dropped down to get a better look. She didn't see any debris.

Mike moved to the back and sat with Fred, who was clearly distraught.

"All right. Just hang on." Kate turned the plane and came back around. As gently as possible, she skimmed the surface and dropped onto the water.

Jean screamed.

Her blood pumping, Kate steered toward the bank.

Mike opened the door. "I'll tie us off," he said and leapt out.

Kate scrambled out of the pilot's seat and went to check on Jean. "Let's get you in the back where you can lie down. Fred, get those bags out of here. We need room."

He handed one out to Mike, then disappeared with the other one. Kate didn't know what she'd do now. She'd seen dogs and kittens born, even a calf. Was this much different?

Holding her abdomen, Jean stood and made her way to the back. "It hurts. Ohh, it hurts."

Fred returned, soaked from the thighs down. He helped Jean lie down. She rolled onto her side and pulled her legs up to her stomach.

Mike climbed in and crouched beside Kate. "What do you want me to do?"

Angel tried to nose in. "Angel, not now. Get back." The dog retreated.

Kate nodded at one of the bags she always kept with her that held incidentals. "Grab that pack. We'll put it under her head."

Kate's mind clicked through what needed to be done. She'd taken one class in emergency training, but the teacher had spent only a few minutes on births. "In my survival pack there are scissors. And I'll need antiseptic and some blankets."

She knelt beside Jean. "How you doing?"

Jean didn't seem to hear. She squeezed her eyes closed and groaned.

"I'll need some water," Kate hollered.

Fred smoothed damp hair off her face.

"I'll get it." Mike grabbed a can and disappeared out the door.

Still pale and sweating, Fred asked, "Is she going to be all right?"

"I'll do the best I can." Kate unfolded two blankets and pushed one up next to Jean's back. "Jean, I need you to lie on your back. And then lift your bottom so I can get this blanket under you."

"Do you know how to deliver a baby?" she asked, rolling onto her back and raising her hips.

"There can't be that much to it. It's a natural thing, right?" Kate hoped she sounded composed. Her insides quivered.

Mike stood in the doorway, watching and looking helpless.

Jean shrieked as another contraction hit her.

Kate wasn't angry anymore. Instead she was afraid—for Jean and the baby. She didn't know what to do. What if something went wrong? *Lord, show me how to do this. Help me.* She held Jean's hand. "Everything will be fine. Soon you'll have your baby in your arms."

I've got to find out how close she is to delivering. "I need to look . . . to see if the baby's coming out."

Jean nodded.

Gently Kate lifted the woman's skirt and removed her undergarments. "Sorry. I know this is embarrassing."

Jean didn't hear. She was in the midst of another contraction.

"Bend your legs." Groaning, Jean managed to pull her legs up. Kate gently parted her knees just enough to get a look. "Oh!" she exclaimed. "It's almost here. I can see the head."

"I've got to push!" Jean screamed and bore down.

"Go ahead."

Two pushes later, the head was completely out and resting in Kate's hands. One more push delivered the shoulders and the baby slid free. Kate caught her, then holding her in one hand, she wiped the infant's mouth and face with a cloth. The baby let out a squall.

"It's a girl! You have a little girl." Kate felt like laughing and crying all at the same time. She held up the infant so the parents could see.

"Mike, get me some string out of my bag. I need to tie off the cord. Fred, I need you to hold the baby."

He nodded and took the child, staring at her with adoration and wonder. He held her so his wife could see. "She's beautiful."

Mike moved in closer, amazement on his face.

Kate wasn't sure where to tie the cord but took a guess and then cut the child free of its mother. She shook antiseptic powder on the cord. She glanced over her shoulder at Mike. His eyes were flooded with tears.

"I had no idea," he whispered, then looked at Kate with adoration and pride. "You were wonderful."

"I mostly just caught her. Jean did all the work."

While Jean and Fred admired their daughter, Kate cleaned up the blood and water with a towel, then disposed of the bloodied blanket and afterbirth.

She and Mike sat on the bank, giving the parents a few

moments alone. Kate felt surprisingly peaceful. She pulled her knees close to her chest. "I've never been part of anything like that before."

"I had no idea," Mike said, his voice still filled with wonder. His blue eyes found Kate. "One day I'd like to have a family. With the right woman."

Kate knew he was talking about her. "I'd like to have children . . . some day." She rested her chin on her knees. "But I have a lot I still want to do before I settle down."

23

P aul shoved a spade beneath a potato plant, then lifted it and shook out the dirt. Tender vegetables clung to the roots. He'd had a good season. There would be plenty for eating and for trading.

Wiping sweat off his face with his shirtsleeve, he looked at the August sky. Ribbons of translucent clouds reached across the pale blue canopy. Fall was fast approaching.

He laid the shovel across the top of the wheelbarrow mounded with potatoes and pushed the cart to the root cellar. By the time he finished transferring the potatoes to wooden boxes, it was time to clean up. He was due at Patrick and Sassa's by six o'clock for dinner.

Standing in an outdoor shower, Paul shivered while icy water splashed over his head and cascaded down his body. He quickly soaped down, then pulled a cord that released more water to rinse off most of the soap. He grabbed a towel and rubbed down to dry off. With the towel wrapped around his waist, he hurried indoors.

Freshly shaven and wearing clean clothes, Paul followed the trail to the Warrens' place. Seeing movement in a thicket near the creek, he stopped. A massive set of antlers rose up from the bushes and seemed to rotate all by themselves. They rested on the head of an enormous moose. Using his tongue, the beast pulled greenery into his mouth. He'd been grazing on tender shoots that grew along the creek bank.

Paul never tired of watching the wildlife and now stood enthralled, gazing at the animal. The huge beast lowered his head with its heavy load and plucked more grass from the pool, capturing vegetation between bulbous lips. Seeming at peace with the world, he chewed contentedly.

At the shoulders, the animal must have been at least seven feet. He'd provide enough meat for an entire winter. *Hope you'll still be around come hunting season.*

Reluctantly, Paul moved on.

When he arrived at the Warrens', he was met by the two oldest boys, their arms loaded with firewood.

"Hello, Mr. Anderson," Douglas said politely.

"Evening."

"Hi," Ethan said, flashing a smile over his pile of wood.

Paul hurried ahead of them and opened the cabin door. "Looks like your dad's put you to work."

"Mom," Douglas said.

"I'm sure she appreciates the help."

"She does," Ethan said. "At least that's what she always tells us." He followed Douglas inside, and Paul followed.

When Paul stepped into the kitchen, Sassa looked over her shoulder at him. "Welcome!" she said, continuing to knead a mound of dough. "Hope you like biscuits."

"If they're yours, I do." He looked around the room. "Where's Patrick?"

"He's getting turnips out of the garden." She glanced out the kitchen window. "He'll be back any minute. Sit." She patted out the dough until it was about a half-inch thick.

278

Paul walked to the counter and stood beside her, watching. "I can taste them already."

Lily came in, tying an apron around her waist. Her steps faltered when she saw Paul. She smiled, but the expression in her eyes was gloomy. "Hi." She walked to the table where carrots were piled on a cutting board.

"Hello," Paul replied.

Lily didn't look up. He wondered what was wrong, but figured it wasn't his business.

The door opened and Patrick stepped in, holding a handful of turnips by the stalks. "Howdy, neighbor." He held up the vegetables. "Just getting the last of our supper." He laid the vegetables in the sink, then strolled into the living room. "Come and sit."

Paul settled into a threadbare armchair. "Looks like your garden's doing well."

"It is." Patrick picked up a pipe and a packet of tobacco from an end table. He sifted the tobacco into the pipe and tapped it down. Striking a match, he held it over the bowl and took several small puffs until smoke curled into the air. He shook out the match and set it in an ashtray. Settling back in the chair, he said, "I've got more than enough vegetables for trading. Figure on making a trip to Susitna Station before the month's out."

"It's been a good year." Paul clasped his hands over his stomach. "I miss tomatoes and corn, though. Wish we could grow them up here." He closed his eyes for a moment. "And fruit. Have you ever eaten an orange or apple fresh off the tree?"

"Can't say that I have."

"Used to have them all the time when I lived in California. Makes my mouth water just thinking about them. Nothing's as good as fresh picked. What we get up here only resembles the real thing. Being picked half ripe and then shipped ruins the flavor."

"We got wild berries. Ever see those down in California?"

"Sure. All kinds." Paul felt as if he were defending his old home.

"Oh." Patrick took several puffs off his pipe. "Do you know anyone who could ship you some fruit?"

"Yeah, but getting it up here fast enough is the challenge. Even if you pick it and ship the same day, it takes too long by steamer. It'd have to be flown in." Paul could almost taste the crisp sweetness of a ripe apple.

"Someone could go down, get it, and then fly it back. How about Kate? Her family owns an apple farm."

"That's a long trip just for fruit. Course if she was already going down . . ."

"Didn't she say she wanted to make a trip this summer?" Patrick asked.

"Don't think it's going to happen. She's busy, and she hates losing flying time." Paul wished she would make a trip. They could go together. He might even stop to see his family.

A dinner of caribou stew and biscuits was set on the table. Sassa called everyone to dinner. The boys dominated most of the table talk. They couldn't wait to share the day's adventures. They'd gone fishing and had spotted bear tracks along the creek. They'd also wandered over to Klaus's place and helped him with his garden. Afterward he'd shown them how to whittle and promised to teach them more next time they came.

"Klaus is good with a knife and a chunk of wood. He's carved some amazing figures of Alaskan birds and animals," Patrick told Paul. "Ever see them?"

"Yeah. In fact, he gave me a real nice figurine of a moose. Real quality work."

Lily was quieter than usual. She barely looked up the entire meal. Paul wondered what was troubling her.

"I did it again," Paul said, setting down his fork. "Sassa, that was so good I made a pig out of myself." He pushed away from the table.

Sassa smiled and cast a glance at her daughter. "Lily did a lot of the work."

He looked at the young woman. "Thank you, Lily. Wonderful meal."

An almost imperceptible smile touched her lips.

Patrick patted his stomach. "How 'bout you and I take a walk?" he asked Paul.

"Good idea."

The men followed a trail along the creek. The sound of buzzing insects and the smell of highbush cranberries were in the air. Paul told Patrick about the moose he'd seen.

"I saw him too, couple of days ago. What a brute."

They ended up at a place where the trail sloped down to the creek. In the cool of evening, flies and mosquitoes danced across the top of calm waters. Occasionally a fish broke the surface to feed, leaving a circle of ripples.

"Nice here," Patrick said, sitting on a log. He swatted at a mosquito. "Except for the blamed bugs."

Paul sat beside him. The two stared at the water, listening to the sounds of approaching evening. The world quieted. Birds' evening songs were joined by the chirp of squirrels. A splash announced the presence of an otter family across the creek.

Patrick pointed them out. "The two new kits made it through the summer."

Silence settled between the two men again. Patrick ended the quiet and asked, "So, what do you figure you'll be doing in the next year or two?"

"Don't know for sure," Paul said, thinking it an unusual question. "Probably what I'm doing right now."

"You ever think about heading back to California?"

"No. Nothing there for me anymore."

"What about your family?"

Paul wondered what was up. Patrick had always respected his privacy. "My life's here now."

"This is a fine place to put down roots." Patrick picked up a stone and tossed it into the water where it plopped and sent out widening ripples. "Me and Sassa came out from Anchorage nearly twelve years ago. Built the place ourselves. We've had a good life."

Paul rested his arms on his thighs, still staring at the water and wondering where Patrick was heading.

"We kept each other going. Couldn't have done it alone." He picked up another stone. "And the children have been a blessing." He chucked the rock into the creek. "Man's got to have children."

Paul suddenly felt defensive. "Not everyone's meant to have a family."

Patrick continued, as if Paul hadn't spoken. "Those boys are hard workers. Don't know what I'd do without them. And Lily . . . well, she's a treasure. Couldn't have asked for a better daughter." He glanced at Paul. "She's a fine cook and a help to Sassa and me."

Paul's stomach tightened.

"Did you know that once she stood her ground against a grizzly? Brought it down with one shot, then skinned it out and put up the meat." He rocked his whole upper body in a nod. "Not many women in the world can do that."

"No, don't imagine there are."

Patrick took a deep breath and blew it out. "She'd make a fine wife."

"She would." Paul was used to Sassa playing matchmaker, but never Patrick. He wondered if Sassa had put him up to it.

Patrick turned serious eyes on Paul. "It would please me and Sassa if Lily were to marry a man . . . like you, Paul."

"Me? I'm still green, a cheechako." Trying to make light of the conversation, he grinned, but inside he felt sick and wished he could change the subject.

"All the more reason for the two of you to match up. You need her. She could teach you a lot."

Paul pushed to his feet and shoved his hands into his pockets. "Are you asking me to marry your daughter?"

"You'd be a good match. And I'd be proud to have you as part of the family."

Paul stared at the creek. It flowed quietly, barely moving, a picture of serenity. Inside Paul felt a drone of misery. Measuring his words carefully, he said, "I'm honored you feel that way. You and your family are like my own." He turned and looked at Patrick. How could he explain? "Lily's a fine person, but I don't plan to marry."

Patrick stood. "A man needs a woman, someone to share his life."

"I had a wife once." A tomb of silence fell between the men. "I'm better off alone."

Patrick furrowed his brow. "I didn't know you'd been married before."

"It was a long time ago." Paul took a step toward the stream and steered the conversation back to Patrick's proposal. "And Lily's still a girl."

"Seventeen's not that young. If you two get married, you can live on the crick. You both love it here. And she'd be close to her family, to Sassa." He studied the otters. "And being married before doesn't mean you can't get married again."

This was going to be more difficult than Paul had anticipated. Would it take the truth to stop Patrick? "What about love?" Paul broke off the top of a reed. "Lily doesn't love me."

"How do you know that? Have you ever asked her?"

Paul thought back over their exchanges. She had, at times, seemed interested in him. It didn't matter. He wasn't fit to be a husband.

"She's pretty, smart, and hardworking. She'll give you children."

"Patrick. Stop." Paul's gut tightened. He knew what he needed to say. "You don't want me for a son-in-law. I wouldn't be a good husband."

"What do you mean—"

"I killed my first wife."

Patrick stared at him. "What do you mean? I don't believe it."

"Believe it. It's true. She'd be alive today if not for me." Memories pummeled Paul. "I thought I knew everything— me, the young and gifted doctor." His voice dripped with derision. "I knew she wasn't feeling well. She was nearly due to deliver our son and she wasn't feeling well. She was retaining water and she'd had a seizure. I decided that bed rest would be enough."

"What more could you do?" Patrick's voice was filled with compassion.

"I should have put her in the hospital, delivered the baby . . . something." Memories ripped through Paul. He'd found her in the hallway, facedown. She'd died of heart failure three days later.

Patrick put a hand on Paul's shoulder. "It wasn't your fault."

"I was supposed to know. I was a doctor." The strength

284

seeped from Paul's legs. He sat on the log and put his face in his hands. "She trusted me. I should have known."

Patrick sat beside him and placed an arm over his shoulder. "I didn't know you were a doctor. Go easy on yourself. Even doctors make mistakes."

Paul gazed at Patrick through a blur of tears. "She was my wife." He sucked in a ragged breath. "She and my son counted on me." He swiped away tears and tried to focus on Patrick. "So, you see I can't marry Lily or anyone else."

"All I see is a man carrying a load of guilt . . . unnecessarily. God doesn't hold you accountable for a mistake. You did your best. And your wife wouldn't want you to throw away your life."

"My best wasn't good enough." Paul shook his head. "And I don't even know if I believe in God anymore. Where was he for Susan and our little boy?" He pressed the heels of his hands against his eyes, holding back tears.

"Some questions in this life have no answers. But God knows."

"I'm done with him and with marriage," Paul nearly shouted and then stalked up the trail toward his cabin. Fresh anger and anguish swelled inside. He felt as if he'd been skinned. Would it never get better?

As he approached the cabin, he spotted Lily sitting on his porch steps. Before he could turn around, she saw him. Why was she there? Was she going to plead her case for marriage? He hoped not. He forced down his emotions, slowed his stride, and walked up to the porch.

She stood as he approached, but only glanced at him.

"Hello, Lily. Nice to see you." He tried to keep his tone light. "I didn't expect to find you here."

"Didn't figure you would." She gripped the railing. "We should talk."

"Sure." Paul sat on the bottom step and motioned for her to sit.

She settled on the top step. "I know my dad talked to you tonight . . . about us getting married."

"He did."

"I can't be silent."

Paul steeled himself against what she had to say. He didn't want to break her heart.

"I admire you, Paul, and I think you would make a fine husband."

He groaned inwardly.

Lily looked out into the forest, then back at him. "I love my father and mother, and I want to make them happy, but . . . I can't marry you."

It took a moment for her words to penetrate his mind. They weren't what he'd expected to hear.

"You're a good man, but I want to get away from here. I want to see other places and meet new people. I've never been anywhere."

Paul let out a relieved breath. "I don't think your parents know how you feel."

"They know. But they think I'm too young to make my own decisions." She clasped her hands. "If I stay here and marry you, I could be happy—we would have a fine life, but I want more than fine. I want adventure. I want to be like Kate."

"You want to be a pilot?"

"No. I want to be *like* her. She had a dream and she went after it. She's so brave." Lily looked at Paul, her brown eyes gentle. "I don't think you want to marry me, either."

"It's not you, Lily. It's just that I don't want to marry any-one." Jasper flew in and landed on his perch. "If you want to see the world, then I think you should."

"There's so much out there I want to experience." Her

voice trembled with excitement. "All I've seen are pictures of places. I want to see them for myself."

"There's lots of beauty in the world, but there's evil out there too. And greedy people who could hurt you. You've got to be careful."

"I know. But people like that live right here in the territory."

"True." He studied Jasper who was preening. "Going away won't necessarily make you happy. Happiness is something you possess, no matter where you live."

Lily was quiet for a long moment, then asked, "But isn't that why you came here? To find happiness?"

What could he say? Is that why he'd come? Finally he said, "I wasn't looking for happiness exactly."

"So, have you found what you came for?"

"Not yet."

— 24 —

Humming "I'm in the Mood for Love," Kate headed down Third Street. She'd heard the song on the radio that morning and it stuck. She pulled her coupe to the side of the road in front of Paul's hotel. He was already waiting on the sidewalk and ambled toward the car.

"Good morning," Kate said as he slid onto the front seat.

"Morning."

"Great day for a fair." She put the car in gear.

"Perfect." He rolled down his window. "Lucky for me that I stopped by the store yesterday."

"Yeah. I'm glad you could join us. It should be fun—the more the merrier." Kate pulled onto the street. "Is it true, Lily left for the states?"

"Yep. That's why I was in town. I came in with the Warrens. Lily's ship sailed yesterday."

"Where's she heading?"

"Seattle first. After that, I don't know. She's pretty excited, though."

"How do Patrick and Sassa feel about her leaving?"

"Sassa was in tears. They're both worried, but that's normal. Lily's never been out of Alaska."

Kate nodded. "I'm happy for her." She rolled down the car window. "Warm for September."

"Enjoy it while you can." Paul settled back into his seat.

"I've got to go by Mike's to pick him up. Frank and Sidney are at the airfield. Frank had a run to Fairbanks last night, but he's supposed to be back."

When Kate pulled up at Mike's, he was sitting on the porch steps. He strolled toward the car, his arms swinging freely at his sides. Opening the back door, he climbed in behind Kate. "You're late," he said, leaning forward and dropping a kiss on her cheek.

Kate glanced at Paul. She wasn't certain he knew about her and Mike. "I'm not late."

Mike clapped a hand on Paul's shoulder. "Good to see you."

"It's been a while," Paul said, his tone brittle.

Mike sat back, a smile on his face. "This should be a doozey of a fair. Heard there's going to be speeches, a rodeo—all kinds of excitement. Folks are wound up over this being the colonists' first crop."

Kate caught a wink from him in her rearview mirror. "When we get there, what do you want to do first?" she asked.

"I'd kind of like to see the giant cabbages. The paper said there's one that weighs twenty-five pounds." Mike shook his head. "Can't imagine a twenty-five-pound cabbage."

Paul glanced over his shoulder at Mike. "Wouldn't mind seeing that myself."

"Who cares about cabbages?" The wind blew Kate's hair into her eyes. "I want to ride the Ferris wheel. One was brought in just for the fair."

When they pulled into the airfield, Mike leaned out the

window, giving the field a good look. "I thought Frank was coming with us. Don't see his plane."

"Probably got held up somewhere." Kate shut off the engine. "Sidney'll know. Hope he can come. He was really excited about going."

Mike hurried out of the car and opened Kate's door for her. "He's been having trouble with his plane. Wonder if he was forced to put down somewhere."

"He might be stuck in Fairbanks making repairs," Kate said, trying to quiet the alarm going off inside.

The three headed for the shop. Mike opened the door and held it for Kate and Paul before following them inside. Sidney was at his desk, going over a map.

"Where's Frank?" Mike asked. "Thought he was going with us to the fair."

"He never made it back." Sidney's tone was grave.

"Did he leave Fairbanks?" Kate asked.

"Yeah. He called in and told me he was on his way. Should have gotten in hours ago."

"What time did he call?" Mike's voice was sharp.

"'Bout five o'clock." Sidney looked at a map in front of him. "Figure he set down somewhere's around here." He ran a finger along the map. "He always follows the Nenana River." Sidney glanced out the window. "Kenny and Jack are already out looking for him." He lifted his hat and scratched his head. "Wish he'd put a radio in that plane of his. Every one of you ought to have one." Sidney sounded angry.

"If they didn't cost an arm and a leg, we would." Mike's voice prickled with irritation.

Sidney stared at him. "I'll bet right about now Frank's kicking himself for not spending that arm and a leg."

Mike ignored the comment and headed for the door. "I'll get up in the air and have a look."

Sidney resettled his hat on his head. "A couple of pilots from Merrill Field are searching too. One more pilot wouldn't hurt, though. Most likely someone's already found him, and they'll be back in time to join you at the fair." His tone was cheerful, but worry lay behind his eyes.

Mike turned to Kate. "You and Paul go ahead. We'll join you later."

"I'm not going while Frank's missing." Kate folded her arms over her chest. "I want to help."

Mike pulled a pack of gum out of his shirt pocket. "Frank really wanted to go to the fair." He unwrapped a piece and stuck it in his mouth. "He wouldn't want all of us to miss out. It's the biggest fair in Alaska, for crying out loud." He chewed. "He'd want you to go. We'll meet you there. I promise."

Kate wasn't convinced. "Another searcher will help."

"What, you going to follow me?" Mike chewed furiously. "We know his flight path. Shouldn't be too tough to locate him." He threw the gum wrapper in the trash. "You know him, steady, dependable. He always takes the same route."

Kate was torn. Mike was probably right. "Okay, but if you guys don't show up soon, I'm joining the search."

"You got a deal." Mike smiled. "Don't worry. We'll find him."

He headed for his plane. Sidney walked Kate and Paul to the car. Kate stood beside the coupe and watched while Mike readied his Fairchild. *I ought to be helping.*

As if reading her thoughts, Sidney said, "Go and have a good time. I'll let you know if I need you."

"Okay, but I won't have a good time, not until I know Frank's safe." She opened the door and slid behind the wheel.

Paul climbed in the other side and closed the door. "So, Frank's a good pilot?"

"Yeah. He's one of the best." Kate turned the key, pushed in the clutch, and put the car in reverse. "He's probably fine." Her mind envisioned Frank, calmly sitting on a stump somewhere beside his plane, drinking a Coke while waiting to be rescued. She couldn't imagine anything terrible happening to him.

The fairgrounds parking area was jammed with cars and trucks. Kate ended up sandwiched between an old sedan and a farm truck with manure piled in the bed.

She wrinkled her nose at the smell. "Looks like whoever owns that rig decided to come at the last minute."

Paul and Kate walked side by side across pastureland. Shouts from barkers, excited squeals, and laughter carried over the open field.

Kate watched a Ferris wheel rise above the exhibits and booths and tried to put Frank out of her mind. "That's where I'm headed." She picked up her pace.

Once in the midst of the activities, excitement caught hold of Kate. There were vendors selling hot dogs and candy. Carneys called to people, luring them to spend money on games. Kate had to admit she loved the games and planned to drop a little cash in some of the booths before heading home.

Paul had his eye on the Ferris wheel, which rose high above the fairgrounds. "You ready?"

"You bet."

Paul and Kate stepped into line with several others waiting their turn on the main attraction. A little girl in front of them gripped the hand of a boy who looked only slightly older than her. Kate figured it must be her brother. The girl's eyes were wide as she watched the wheel go round and round. She looked frightened.

Kate knelt beside her. "No reason to be afraid. It's great fun."

"Really? How do you know?"

"I've ridden lots of times. It's almost like flying."

The girl didn't look reassured, but moved forward with her brother. She climbed onto a seat and clung to the boy's arm as the bar was locked in place in front of them.

Kate glanced toward the parking lot, hoping to see Frank and Mike walking across the field. There was no sign of them.

When it was their turn, Paul gave Kate a hand onto the rocking bench and climbed in beside her. They were pressed together, his broad shoulders taking up a good deal of space. Kate didn't mind. Paul's eyes were bright with anticipation, and she realized she'd rarely seen him look excited or happy. She wondered, again, what kind of sorrow he carried.

When the Ferris wheel started turning, enthusiastic shouts resonated from other riders. When they crested the top, Kate couldn't hold in a laugh. "This is my favorite part." She gazed across the grounds to the fields and forests at the feet of nearby mountains.

Paul smiled broadly. "It's impressive."

Kate looked down at the people below. "Everyone seems so small."

"Guess you could say we have a bird's-eye view." He chuckled.

Kate studied the carnival activity. Remembering Frank, she searched for him and Mike. Still no sign of them.

Paul rested an arm across the back of the bench. It was almost like having his arm around her. Kate liked how it felt being close to him. Her mind went to Mike. He wouldn't like it. Kate leaned slightly away from Paul.

"Have a look at that," he said, pointing at a corral with people crowding the fence. A chute opened and a calf broke free. It leaped and twisted, doing its best to unseat a boy clinging to its back.

"Boys . . . they always love a challenge."

"And girls don't?" Paul smiled. "Especially ones like you?"

"Okay. Some do." Kate smiled, enjoying the camaraderie between her and Paul. "I almost forgot how much fun carnivals can be. It's been a long time since I've been to one."

"Me too." Paul's expression turned pensive. He stared out over the concession stands to the mountains bordering the valley. The joy seemed to drain from him.

"Have you been to many fairs?" Kate asked, hoping to recapture his good mood.

He looked at her as if he'd forgotten she was there. "What? I'm sorry. Did you say something?"

"Just wondering what kind of fairs you used to go to."

"Bigger. But they're all pretty much the same."

When the ride ended, they walked toward a row of booths where men called out to passersby, tempting them to put down money to play for trinkets.

"You thirsty?" Paul asked.

Kate nodded.

"How about a Coke?"

"I wonder if they have root beer."

"Well, we'll find out." Paul took her arm and steered her toward a stand advertising popcorn, candy, and drinks. "You want something to eat?"

"No, not yet." She scanned the crowd, hoping to see Mike or Frank, and feeling disappointment when she didn't spot them.

Paul bought them each a pop and they strolled down a row of vendors. "What do you want to do next?"

"Your turn to pick." Kate smiled, thinking this was beginning to feel like a date. It wasn't meant to be. She wondered how Paul felt about it. He seemed to be having a good time.

"Let's have a look at those giant cabbages," he said.

"Okay." They headed toward the produce barn. "You think they've found Frank yet?" Kate asked.

"We can go back to the airport if you want."

"If they don't show up soon, we'll go."

After looking at some of the biggest vegetables Kate had ever seen, she and Paul wandered toward the animal barns. They stopped to watch a pie-eating contest. Kate couldn't imagine eating so much pie so quickly. Just the thought made her stomach ache.

Frank's friendly face flashed into her mind. "I wish Mike and Frank would show up."

"You want to go?"

"Yeah. Do you mind?"

"'Course not."

"I just can't stop thinking about him."

They set off for the car. "Have you had any interesting runs lately?" Paul asked.

Kate remembered the birth that happened on her plane. "If you call delivering a baby interesting, then yes." She grinned.

"You did what?"

"About a month ago I had a passenger, a woman who was very pregnant. She needed a flight to Fairbanks and neglected to tell me or Sidney that she'd been having birth pains. After we got into the air, the baby decided it was time to meet the world. Things got serious so fast I had to put down. Her husband was no help."

Paul smiled, admiration in his eyes. "You delivered the baby?"

TOUCHING THE CLOUDS

"Mostly I caught it. The mother did all the work. Still, I wish I'd had a doctor with me or Doris Henley, the nurse from Anchorage hospital."

Kate started across the field outside the fairgrounds. "Alaska needs doctors. For the most part, people in the villages don't have any medical care. But the trouble is, most doctors don't want to spend their lives flying from one Alaskan village to another."

"I can understand that." Paul sounded defensive.

Kate wondered why he'd be defensive and was just about to ask him about it when Mike's car pulled into the parking area. He was alone. The set of his jaw and the angle of his shoulders gave Kate a chill. Something was wrong. She ran to meet him.

When he stepped out of the car, she knew the truth but still had to ask. "What is it? What happened to Frank?"

"Kenny found his plane. He cracked up just north of Talkeetna."

Kate waited, sick to her stomach and hoping her gut was wrong.

"He's dead, Kate. The plane came apart when it hit."

Kate felt her legs weaken. It couldn't be true. Not Frank. He was the sensible one. He wasn't supposed to die.

Eyes shimmering, Mike pulled Kate into his arms. Holding her against his chest, he smoothed her hair. She clung to him. "Why Frank? He was a good man." She felt Paul's hand on her back. She glanced at him and, again, saw the wound he kept hidden inside.

Mike didn't answer, but held her more closely.

Stepping back, Kate asked, "Do they know what happened?"

"A couple of us'll go and have a look. Maybe we can figure it out. But planes are just unreliable."

296

Without a word, Paul walked away, cutting across the field. He walked in a hurry, as if he were angry.

Using the back of his hand, Mike brushed away tears. "Frank said the carburetor had been giving him trouble. That might have been it. I should have helped him fix it. He wasn't a very good mechanic. We've got to look out for each other."

The following day, Kate flew Paul back to his cabin. They didn't talk much. Kate's mind was with Frank and his accident. A lot of pilots died. Would her life end that way too?

By the time they reached the creek, a sharp wind kicked up small breakers on the water and sinister-looking clouds drooped above the forest.

Paul climbed out of his seat. "You want a cup of coffee and something to eat before you head back?"

Kate knew she ought to hurry on to get ahead of the storm, but Angel whined from the back of the plane and she enjoyed Paul's company even though he'd been quieter than usual since learning about Frank. "I guess. Angel needs a run."

They moored the plane, then walked up the trail to the cabin. Paul's dogs greeted them with exuberant barking.

Once inside, Kate sat at the table, elbows propped, chin in her hands. She watched while Paul started a fire. With a deep sigh, she said, "I still can't believe Frank's gone."

"Yeah. It's a shame." Paul's voice sounded tight. "He seemed like a nice guy." He added larger chunks to briskly burning kindling. Wood popped and sizzled. He slid the stove plate back in place, filled the percolator with water, and added coffee to the basket.

"How does bread and cheese sound? Or I could make soup."

"Bread and cheese is fine." Kate moved to the window. Wind slapped the bushes and grabbed tree boughs. It didn't look good. She turned to Paul. "Do you see the Warrens much?"

"Yeah, quite a bit. They're good neighbors." He cut a slice of cheese, then glanced out the window at the storm. Wind whistled under the eves.

"The storm's picking up. I better go."

"Okay, but take some bread and cheese with you." A gust blasted the side of the house. "You sure you ought to fly? It's looking fierce out there."

"I'll be fine."

"Like Frank was fine?"

Shocked at the statement, Kate stared at Paul, wondering why he'd say something like that. "I'm not Frank. And I'm sure he was being careful. It was just an accident."

"Yeah, I know. But . . . well, for crying out loud, Kate, bush piloting is dangerous work. Have you ever thought about not flying?"

"That would be like not breathing."

"You could work somewhere else. Fly safer routes."

"To do that I'd have to leave Alaska."

Paul wrapped the cheese and bread in waxed paper. "You have family and friends down south." He handed her the small meal.

Kate thought about her friends in Alaska that she'd miss. Paul was one of them. Interestingly his face came to her mind before Mike's. "There are people here who matter to me too." She forced a smile. "I'm a good pilot."

"Frank was too." Paul stared at her solemnly. "Working somewhere else is better than dying."

"I'm not going to die. And I thought we were friends. You don't seem to care where I live as long as it isn't here."

"That's not true. But sometimes being a bush pilot is just plain foolish."

"You think I'm foolish?" Angry and not sure why she felt rejected, Kate headed for the door. Before Paul could say anything, she stepped onto the porch and into the storm.

— 25 —

Wind buffeted Paul as he stepped onto the porch. He shielded his eyes from blowing dust and debris. *It's idiotic to fly in this weather.* He headed for the trail.

When he reached the path, he spotted her immediately. "Kate!" he hollered.

She glanced back just as a small branch, carried by the wind, smacked her face. She pressed a hand to her cheek and hurried on.

"Stubborn woman," Paul muttered, running after her. Closing the distance, he called again, but she ignored him. Finally catching up to her, he grabbed her arm. "Stop! Listen to me!"

She whirled around and faced him. "What do you want? I've got to get to Anchorage."

"If you go, you're crazy."

"So, now I'm crazy *and* foolish?"

"I didn't mean it like that." He gazed up at the maelstrom of whipping tree limbs and flying leaves. "You can't fly in a storm like this."

"I can do whatever I choose."

Still gripping her arms, he said more gently. "Kate, stop it." He didn't want anger to push her into doing something deadly. He purposely spoke in a steady tone. "I'm sorry for what I said, but this is a bad storm. You can't go up."

The fight seemed to go out of Kate. She glanced at the sky, shielding her eyes from heavy rain. "I know." She looked around. "The storm blew in so fast."

He looked at the plane, bobbing in choppy waters. "Come back to the house. You can stay until it passes."

"I've got to secure the plane."

Together they covered the engine, pulled a tarp across the front window and around the sides, adding more rope to hold it firmly. Kate stepped back and studied the Bellanca bobbing wildly in the chop. "I hope it'll be all right."

"Can't see what else we can do."

Kate nodded and headed back up the trail, Angel trotting ahead of her.

Once inside the cabin, Paul moved to a shelf and took down a pot and filled it with water. "I'll make soup." He set the pan on the stove. "Be right back. I need to get some meat and vegetables." He headed for the door, but stopped and looked at her. "You have a change of clothes? You're soaked through."

"Yeah. In my bag on the plane."

"I'll get it." He pulled on a rain slicker, stepped outside, and headed for the plane. *Most bullheaded woman I've ever met.*

The Bellanca pitched in the stormy waters. Hanging onto the seats as he searched, Paul found the bag stashed behind the pilot's seat.

He hurried back to the cabin. Thankful to close the storm outside, Paul stepped into the house and handed the bag to Kate. "Here you go. You can change in my room."

"Thanks." Her voice quiet, she added, "I wasn't gonna go."

"You weren't? Why were you so set on getting to your plane?"

Kate shrugged. "I was mad and didn't know what else to do."

"I'm glad you stayed," Paul said, feeling more thankful than he understood. He headed for the door.

"Thanks for coming after me."

He looked at her, wearing a half smile. "Couldn't let you go. What would I do without my mail lady?"

"So, it's the mail you care about."

"No. You weren't listening. I said, the mail *lady*." Paul's tone was tender.

"Oh." Kate smiled.

Paul's stomach did a little flip as he gazed into Kate's warm eyes. He cleared his throat. "Well, I better get the meat and vegetables." He stepped outside. The storm had intensified, howling through the trees. Inside the shed, the sound of rain and debris pummeling the tin roof was deafening.

Paul selected an onion from a sack hanging from the ceiling, then headed for boxes of vegetables where he grabbed a handful of carrots. He stuck a bunch under one arm and picked out some potatoes. Next, he took a jar of moose meat off a shelf and then headed back to the house, his mind on the meal. *Biscuits would be good.* When he reached the door, he knocked on it with his foot.

Kate opened it and unloaded some of the vegetables. "I could have helped." She set the produce on the counter next to the sink.

He closed the door. "Storm's brutal." He noticed her Bible on the table. He used to read his, but couldn't see any reason

302

for it now. He set the vegetables in the sink. Glancing at her, he said, "You look better."

"Dry clothes and a hairbrush can do wonders." She grinned. "So, what can I do to help?"

"Vegetables need washing. After that, you can chop them if you want."

"I think I can do that."

He twisted the ring off the jar of meat, popped the lid, and dumped chunks of meat into simmering water. Kate worked on the vegetables while he started on the biscuits.

Working alongside Kate reminded Paul of the day they'd gone clam digging. It had been a good day. He smiled at the memory of her digging for her first clam. She'd seemed almost childlike.

"What are you smiling about?"

Embarrassed at being caught daydreaming about her, Paul checked his emotions. "Am I smiling?"

"Yes, you are."

He shrugged. "Just thinking about the biscuits. I can already taste them." He wasn't about to let himself care too much for Kate. Besides, she and Mike were a couple.

Kate held up a potato. "My mother peels potatoes. Not me."

"No problem." Paul's mind went back to the argument between him and Kate, before she'd slammed out of the cabin. "Earlier . . . why did you get so mad?"

Kate cut a potato in half and then into fourths. "I don't know." She shrugged. "I guess . . . it felt like you didn't care about me, as if you wanted me to leave Alaska."

A crash accompanied by the sound of splintering glass reverberated from the back room.

"What the . . ." Paul ran into the bedroom. Kate followed.

Cotton curtains flapped like flags in the wind. Rain pelted the broken windowpane and soaked the bedroom floor. A treetop rested on the windowsill.

In three strides Paul crossed the room. He examined the damage. "I'll have to cut it free from outside." Heading for the front of the house he called over his shoulder, "Stay put. I don't want you getting hurt."

Kate stepped into the doorway. "I can take care of myself, thank you."

Paul stopped and looked at her. "I've no doubt you can." He couldn't conceal a smile and shook his head slightly from side to side. "Is it ever all right for someone to protect you?"

"Sometimes." Her voice sounded guarded.

"You know, it's good for people to watch out for each other."

"True, but . . ." Her eyes held his. "I'll bet if it were Patrick here with you instead of me, you wouldn't have told him to stay put."

Paul exhaled through his nose. "Okay, you can help me. But I'll need you to do that from inside."

Her pursed lips softened into a smile. "Sure."

After the tree had been removed, the glass swept up, and a tarp stretched over the broken window, Kate and Paul returned to dinner preparations.

"Most of the water's boiled away. I'll have to add some more. It'll take a while to heat up," Paul said. "And I barely got started on the biscuits. Dinner could take a while."

"I can wait. My stomach's not growling too loudly. And I've never made biscuits before. I'd like to learn."

"Okay. If you can wait, I can. The recipe is my grandmother's—best biscuits you'll ever eat." He glanced at the window. "Hope Jasper found a place to weather the storm."

"He's still hanging around?"

"Yeah, but less these days. He comes in once in a while, looking for a free meal." He rested his hands on either side of the mixing bowl. "Now to the biscuits."

Paul put the biscuit dough together, explaining each step to Kate. When he finished, he smeared lard into the bottom of a Dutch oven. "Just put spoonfuls in a pot like this and cook." He dropped dollops of dough into the pan, closed the lid, and set the pot on the stove. "Won't take long."

"I might actually be able to make them." Kate rested a hip against the counter. "Now what?"

The beef and broth was boiling and Kate added sliced vegetables.

His mind flashed to a rainy day when he and Susan had prepared a meal together. It felt peculiar doing something so similar and domestic with Kate. He needed a distraction.

"Most of the coffee boiled away. I'll make some fresh," he said.

With dinner cooking, Paul glanced out the window. "Getting dark. Time to light the lanterns." He lit two lamps in the living room and one hanging on the kitchen wall.

Kate moved to the window and gazed out. "I don't think I've seen a summer squall this bad since I moved here."

"It's pretty wild out there." Paul checked the coffee.

"Hope my plane rides out the storm all right. Can't afford to replace it." She paused. "You have a big family?"

Paul looked at her. She was leaning against the windowsill, studying him. "What?"

"There are a lot of people in that picture on your bureau."

"Oh. Yeah. There are a lot of us—me, my three brothers and two sisters, six kids in all." He lifted the lid of the pot to check the biscuits. "I pretty much had a charmed life growing up."

"Aren't there three women in the picture, not including your mother?"

"Oh. Right." Paul didn't want to talk about Susan, but figured Kate might as well know about her. "The other gal . . . she was my wife. She died."

"Oh. I'm sorry. I didn't know."

"It was a long time ago."

The room turned quiet, the pop and sizzle of burning wood the only sound.

Kate sat at the table. "It was just me and my parents. I never had any brothers or sisters."

"Were you lonely?"

"I always wished I had a sister, but I wasn't lonely. Mom and Dad are the best."

"You miss them?"

"Yeah. I wish they'd move up. I think Mom's ready, but Dad's not about to leave his apple ranch. He loves farming."

Paul stirred the soup. He took down two bowls from the cupboard and set them on the table along with cups and silverware.

"What about your family?" Kate asked.

"My dad's gone now. He died several years ago. My mother lives in San Francisco. She's getting frail, but my brothers and sisters live nearby so they help out."

"Do you ever visit them?"

"It's been a while." Searching for a way to turn the conversation in another direction, Paul poked a carrot to see if it was done.

"How long?"

"Actually, I haven't been back since I settled here, four years ago. It's a long way to California." He replaced the lid on the soup and moved to his chair in the front room and sat down.

"Do they come to see you?"

"No." Paul threw one leg over the other. Wind howled under the eaves. "Boy, that storm's really kicking up. Hope our repair holds."

Kate looked out the window. "Even the dogs have gone into hiding, they're all inside their houses." She glanced at Angel lying on the floor in the front room. "I'm afraid I've spoiled her."

"That's okay." Paul reached over and scratched Angel behind the ears. She got up and moved closer, resting her head on his lap. "She's a beauty."

"She looks like Buck."

Paul stood and returned to the stove to look at the biscuits. "These are done." He carried the Dutch oven to the table, stirred the soup one more time, and then placed it next to the biscuits.

"Smells wonderful. My stomach's roaring now." Kate grinned.

"We'll see how it tastes." Paul spooned soup into the bowls. "Help yourself to a biscuit."

Kate scooped a biscuit out of the pan. She broke it in half and steam escaped.

"They're best with jam. I've got some elderberry." He walked to the cupboard, took down a jar of preserves, and set it on the table.

Kate dipped her spoon into the jar. "Where did you get the jam?"

"Picked the berries and made it."

Kate glanced at the sewing machine in the corner. "Oh, that's right. You sew, cook, can—you do just about everything."

"Out here a person's got to."

Kate smeared jam on her biscuit and took a bite of the flaky roll. "Delicious."

A gust of wind rattled the house. Paul and Kate both looked at the ceiling.

"Hope I got those shingles down good and tight."

Dusk settled over the cabin as Paul and Kate finished their meal. "Sidney's probably worrying about me," Kate said.

"I'll have Patrick get a message to him on his radio." Paul pulled on his coat and stepped to the door. "I'll be back in two shakes."

Huddled against the storm, Paul headed for Patrick's, but his mind remained with Kate. Having her in the house made the place feel like a home. It would be nice to have a woman around. He remembered the way Mike had held Kate and how she'd clung to him after Frank's death. Envy squeezed his heart, but he knew it was better that she wasn't available—entanglements only made life more complicated.

By the time Paul returned, Kate had the kitchen tidy. "You didn't have to clean up. You're a guest."

"I wanted to. I might not be a good cook, but I'm a whiz at cleaning." Kate grinned.

"Do you play cards?"

"Now and again."

"You want to play? I've got a deck."

"Sure."

Paul and Kate settled across the table from each other. At first they talked little and focused on the game. Kate won the first two hands. Gradually stories about hunting and fishing trips bounced between them.

"I swear hunting and fishing is all Alaskans talk about," Kate said.

"Suppose that's because we do a lot of it. Would you rather talk politics?" he teased.

"No thanks."

Silence pervaded the room. Kate stared at her cards. Paul

could feel tension between them and knew Kate had something to say. He doubted he wanted to hear it.

Finally she looked up. "Paul . . . why are you here? Is it because your wife died?"

Paul put down his cards. He stared at them for a long moment, then said, "There are some things in life better left alone." He stood and moved to the kitchen and refilled his cup with coffee. "You want more?"

"No thanks. I'm sorry for prying."

"It's all right. I understand. I'm just not ready to talk about it." He returned to his seat and took a drink of coffee. "You want to play out your hand?"

"Sure."

She picked up her cards and studied them. Paul studied her. The copper in her hair glistened in the lantern light. He longed to reach out and touch it, to make Kate feel safe and loved. The thought sent a shock through him. *You can't love her. You can't love anyone.*

26

K ate rolled onto her side, rested her back against the divan, and stretched her arms over her head. The outside world sounded hushed. She sat up and looked out the window. Sunlight winked from behind clouds left from the storm.

She'd fallen asleep to the shrill cry of the wind, feeling awkward in Paul's cabin. It hadn't felt that way when he was sick. But last night they'd talked and laughed, said good night, and gone to their respective beds. She'd lain awake a long while thinking about him and wondering if he was thinking about her.

"I've got to get up and back to work," she said, throwing off her covers and placing her feet on the chilled floor. She shuffled to the kitchen sink, took a glass from the cupboard, and filled it with water from the hand pump. *Paul must still be sleeping*, she thought, until she heard footfalls on the porch.

The door opened and he stepped inside. "Wondered if you were going to sleep the morning away." He grinned.

"What time is it?"

"After eight."

"I didn't know you were up."

"Long enough to feed the dogs—"

"Oh, Angel. Where is she?" Kate glanced around the house.

"She's having the time of her life." He held up four eggs, two in each hand. "Thought you might like some breakfast."

"Sure." Kate suddenly remembered how she must look and tried to tame her hair. "Just need to make a trip outside and clean up, and I'll give you a hand."

While Paul cooked eggs and slabs of bacon, Kate sliced bread and toasted it in the oven. When they were done, she spread fresh butter on them. Paul managed to have the coffee, eggs, and bacon ready by the time Kate had finished the toast.

She scooted a chair up to the table. "You seem to be good at everything."

"Not everything. But I can cook. When I was a kid, we all had to help with the household chores, including cooking. And out here if I don't cook I don't eat."

"So, what's my excuse?" Kate asked, a curious sense of contentment coursing through her.

"I bet you're better in the kitchen than you think. Probably just need a little more practice."

"Never did like domestic work. Growing up, I kept busy climbing trees, building forts, fishing, or flying with my dad." She took a bite of egg. "Mom and I were always at loggerheads. She tried to tame me, and I was always fighting to not be what I was expected to be."

Paul chuckled. "That doesn't surprise me."

Kate set her fork on her plate. "I love my mom and dad. I had a great childhood, but so much of my life I've felt out of step . . . with the rest of the world."

Paul picked up his coffee and rested his elbows on the table. "I think we're supposed to welcome who we are."

311

Kate warmed inside. "I like that. But most of the time it feels like no one else understands or agrees with it."

"Yeah, well, that's all right. No need to worry about what other people think."

Kate knew she was overly concerned with what others thought about her. But how did she change it? She scooped eggs onto her toast and took a bite. Talking around the food in her mouth, she said, "I've got to get back to Anchorage. Sidney's expecting me."

"I'll have Patrick let him know."

"I'm trying to save up for a radio in my plane. But they're expensive." Angel whined at the door and Kate let her in. "Did those dogs wear you out?" She gave her a quick rubdown, then returned to the table.

Angel sat beside Kate, watching and waiting for a taste of breakfast.

"Don't think she was tired, just hungry." Paul gave her a piece of bacon.

"It's my fault. I spoil her." Kate slipped her a bite of toast.

Conversation waned. Kate wasn't sure what to talk about. The previous night everything had been so congenial between them. Now the comfortable friendliness seemed to have evaporated. When she finished eating, she put her plate and cup in the sink. "I gotta go. Thanks for breakfast."

"Oh sure." Paul sounded disappointed.

Kate wondered if he was. Paul was a mystery she couldn't figure out. There were moments when she thought he might be keen on her and other times when he acted as if she was the last person he wanted to see.

She pulled on her jacket and grabbed her pack. "Hope my plane's all right. Don't know what I'd do if something happened to it."

"I'll walk down with you. It was a doozy of a storm—the trail's liable to be a mess. Good thing you weren't in the air."

Kate felt the heat of embarrassment at the thought of how she'd stormed out of the cabin the previous day. She'd acted like a child.

A cool breeze greeted her when she stepped onto the porch. It stirred the treetops, filling the air with the sound of rustling boughs. Everything was soaked and smelled of rain and damp vegetation. Kate took the steps two at a time and headed for the trail, littered with leaves and branches. Paul walked ahead, clearing away limbs.

As Kate approached the creek, the trail turned steep. She slipped in the mud, but Paul grabbed her arm, keeping her from ending up flat out and muddy.

"Thanks," Kate said, getting her feet under her.

"Gotta watch your footing along here. It's always slippery after a rain."

Anxious to check out her plane, Kate couldn't keep from hurrying. As soon as the Bellanca came into sight, she could see the storm had bombarded it with branches and other debris. She ran the last several yards, praying it was only superficial damage.

"I hope she's all right." Kate pulled a branch off a wing, and with Paul's help they cleared the rest of the plane. It was in good shape—no broken windows or tears in the fuselage or wings.

Kate stepped back. "Thank the Lord it's all right."

"She looks good."

Kate made one last inspection of the flaps, then hurried around to the door. Her feet hit a slick spot on the wet boards and she lost her footing. Knowing she couldn't stop her fall, she stuck out one arm to catch herself. When her hand hit the dock, she felt her shoulder wrench, and pain shot across her chest.

With a moan, she rolled onto her side and grabbed hold of the injured arm. The shoulder throbbed so intensely she thought she might be sick.

"Kate. You all right?"

She shook her head no. "My shoulder. I did something to it." She could barely talk. She tried to move the arm, but it wouldn't budge. "I think I broke it." With Paul's help, she managed to sit up. "How am I going to fly like this?"

"I better have a look at it." Paul helped her stand.

He kept a hold on her good arm and guided her up the slick trail to the house where he sat her down at the table. "We'll have to get your jacket off."

Kate nodded, and blew out a breath, knowing that any movement would be excruciating.

"Hang on, I'll do it." He slid off the sleeve on the uninjured shoulder and helped Kate extend the bad arm just enough to slide off the left sleeve.

Sweat beaded up on Kate's face. She wanted to holler but managed to hold it in. "It's like my shoulder's on fire."

"Almost got it."

Kate clenched her teeth and sucked in air.

Finally the jacket was off. "Got it." He draped it over the back of a chair, then examined both arms, comparing the two. "Your left arm is sitting at an abnormal angle and it's longer than your other one."

"What's wrong with it?"

"Could be a broken collarbone or shoulder . . ." He scrutinized the injury. "I think it's a dislocation."

Kate looked at him, wondering how he would know. He moved the arm and pain burst through her shoulder and arm.

"Do you have to do that?" she snapped.

Ignoring her, Paul probed, feeling the joint through her blouse. "I'm pretty sure it's dislocated." He straightened. "I'll need to get a better look at it."

"And how will you do that?"

"You'll have to remove your shirt."

"I . . . I can't do that."

"There's no other way . . . if you want me to help you."

She studied him. "Do you know what you're doing?"

"Yeah, I do. On those hunting trips I used to take, inevitably somebody got hurt. I had a brother who dislocated his shoulder more than once. And I was the least squeamish of the bunch, so I'd always help."

"But—"

"Kate, I'm not interested in looking at your body, I just want to help you."

Embarrassed, Kate started to explain, "I didn't think that, but . . ." Realizing further explanation would only cause more awkwardness, she gave in. "All right. I'll get it off."

"Let me get a towel and we'll keep you covered as best we can. Okay?"

While Paul held the towel, Kate undid her buttons. After removing her blouse from her good arm, Paul draped the towel over her. Still partially bare, Kate felt more embarrassed than she could remember—this was Paul.

He slipped off the shirt. Feeling utterly exposed, Kate decided not to look at him, but for just a moment their eyes met, and she could see embarrassment in his too.

He turned his attention to her shoulder. Hanging on to her arm with one hand, he placed the other on her shoulder and gently manipulated the arm.

Kate trapped her groans inside, but couldn't stop the tears.

"You're lucky," he said.

"Lucky?"

"You've got a dislocation. It could be a lot worse." His expression serious, he said, "I'm going to have to put it back in place. It's going to hurt."

Kate thought he seemed too much an expert at all this, but decided to just be grateful for now. She took a breath and gave a nod. "Okay."

"I'll do this as fast as I can. Hold still." Paul held the lower part of the arm and kept one hand on the shoulder. "If we're lucky, it'll go in the first time."

He pulled her arm toward him. Pain flared through Kate's shoulder and across her chest. She yelled when he manipulated it, and then blessedly, she felt it slide back into place.

The room spun and turned dark. Kate thought she might faint. Gradually the pain retreated. "Thank you. It's better."

Wanting to cover up, she reached for her shirt, and Paul helped her put it on.

He made a sling from a piece of cloth. "That ought to help."

Studying him, she asked, "Tell me again how you knew what was wrong? And why do you know how to fix a dislocated shoulder?"

Paul didn't answer right away. "Like I said there were accidents—my dad was a doctor and—"

"Don't give me another story about your father or your grandfather. Tell me the truth. Regular people don't know what you know." She stared at him.

Paul held her gaze. "The truth?"

The door opened and Patrick stepped in. "Kate, thank God you haven't left yet. I got a call from Sidney. He needs you right away in Homer. A girl fell from a tree. She's hurt real bad. They need to get her to a hospital."

"There isn't anyone at the airfield?"

"Sidney said the two planes left on the field were damaged by the storm and the other fellas are too far away."

Patrick seemed to actually see her for the first time, and he asked, "You all right?"

"Yeah. I took a fall and hurt my shoulder. Paul helped me, though." She stood and reached for her coat. "Okay. I've got to go." Her injured shoulder throbbed.

"You probably shouldn't use that arm," Paul said. "Can you fly without it?"

"No. But I'll manage." She headed for the door. "Can someone crank the plane for me?"

"Sure, I'll do it," Patrick said.

Kate stopped Paul at the door and looked at him squarely. "Are you a doctor?"

He didn't answer.

"Tell me. Right now. There's a little girl who needs one." Her mouth set, Kate held Paul's eyes.

"Yes. Yes, I'm a doctor."

Patrick's eyes widened. "It's about time the truth was told."

"I used to be. I'm not anymore."

"Well, you are today," Kate said.

"Just today." Paul grabbed his coat and followed her out.

Neither of them spoke until they were well on their way.

"Why didn't you say anything?" Kate asked. "All this time . . . I told you we need doctors up here and you said nothing."

"I *used* to be a doctor." Paul kept his eyes on the sky in front of them. "But no more."

"Why not?"

He didn't answer.

"Fine. Don't tell me."

Frustrated and in pain, Kate did her best to manage the plane.

"Is there something I can do to help?" Paul asked.

"Do you know how to use the stick?"

"Not enough."

Kate shook her head. "Then I'll manage," she said, trying to ignore the throbbing in her shoulder and doing only what was necessary to maneuver the plane.

They flew in silence. When they touched down at Homer, a small group of people were huddled at the side of the landing strip. A little girl lay silent and pale on a makeshift gurney.

Taking long strides, Paul crossed the field and knelt beside the child. He quickly examined her. "Has she been conscious at all?" he asked a woman who lingered close to the child.

"No," she said, sniffling into a handkerchief.

"Are you her mother?"

The woman nodded.

"What happened?"

"She fell from that tree." She pointed at a nearby alder. Turning to Paul, she asked, "Is she going to be all right?"

"We'll get her to the hospital," Paul said. "They'll take good care of her."

"Ma'am, he's a doctor, so try not to worry," Kate said. Then turning all business, she ordered, "Let's get her in the plane." She looked at the child's mother. "You can come with us."

"Thank you." She followed as men carried the little girl inside, then sat on the seat closest to her while Paul monitored the child's condition.

He glanced at the mother. "What's her name?"

"Charlotte." The woman started to cry. "I should have been watching her more closely."

"Kids are kids," Paul said. "Accidents happen." He looked at her more closely and said kindly, "I'm Paul. What's your name?"

"Irene."

He turned back to Charlotte and checked her pulse. He lifted an eye and looked at it closely. He did the same with the other eye, then listened to her heart. "Well, Irene, she may have a concussion, but I think she's going to be fine."

Charlotte let out a low moan and opened her eyes. She looked at Paul and started to cry. "Mama. I want my mama."

"She's right here." Paul motioned for Irene to move closer.

"I'm here, honey." She took her daughter's hand and smiled down at her.

"My head hurts." Charlotte's crying increased.

"It'll be all right." Irene gathered her daughter into her arms and rocked her gently.

A doctor and nurse met the plane at the airfield. Kate watched while Paul consulted briefly with the doctor. The little girl was loaded into an ambulance and whisked off to the hospital.

Kate and Paul stood side by side. Kate didn't know what to say to him. She was angry, but she was also thankful he'd been there to help. She turned to him. "You're a good doctor. The people in this territory need you."

"Take me home." He headed toward the plane.

Confused and furious, Kate watched him go. How could he just walk away from this? Didn't he care?

27

I t would be a long day, but Kate didn't mind—Nena was
with her. She glanced at her native friend. "I'm glad you
came to Anchorage."

"I loved it. I had very much fun." Nena smiled broadly.

Flying beneath gray clouds, Kate left Cook Inlet and followed the Susitna River inland. "I wish you could have stayed
longer."

"It's time for me to go. I miss my Joe and the children."
She glanced toward the back of the plane. "I hope they like
their gifts." She shook her head slightly. "I never seen so
many stores."

Kate laughed. "Too many."

As she approached Bear Creek, her thoughts went to Paul.
She hadn't spoken to him in three weeks, not since the day
she'd hurt her shoulder. She rotated it—almost no pain. It
had healed nicely.

After the emergency run they'd taken, Paul had stopped
meeting the plane. Kate missed him, and it hurt that she'd
driven him away. In time, she hoped the rift between them
would heal. She couldn't imagine life without him being in

it. Her emotions were so strong she wondered what her true feelings were—certainly more than friendship.

"It has been so nice to meet the people on your route," Nena said.

"My friends Sassa and Patrick live at the next stop. They usually meet the plane. Sassa's native—Aleut, I think."

She set the plane down on the creek and steered toward the Warrens' place. Patrick and Sassa stood on their dock and offered a wave of greeting. Kate powered back and glided alongside the platform. Her tail wagging, Angel waited at the door and rushed past Kate the moment it was opened.

Kate grabbed the mail, climbed onto a pontoon, and stepped to the dock. "Hello. How are you two?"

"Good." Sassa's eyes went to a package in Kate's hands. "Is that for me?"

"It is." Kate handed her the small box.

"I've been waiting for this." The pitch in her voice rose.

"Makeup." Patrick rolled his eyes. "She's been waiting for weeks. Don't see why she needs it."

Sassa held the box against her chest. "There's nothing wrong with using a little bit of lipstick and rouge."

"And that stuff you put on your eyes. I know you ordered it." Patrick tried to keep a stern expression, but his lips lifted in a slight smile. "As if makeup could make you more beautiful than you already are." He winked.

Sassa smiled and leaned against him. "You're teasing, but I like it."

Nena stepped out of the plane and onto the dock.

"I'd like you to meet my friend from Kotzebue," Kate said. "This is Nena Turchick. Nena, this is Patrick and Sassa Warren."

"Good to meet you," Nena said, offering a quiet smile.

"So glad to finally meet you," Sassa said. "Kate has told us about you."

Patrick gave her a friendly nod. "I suppose this is very different from Kotzebue."

"Yes. There are trees and it is much greener."

"Nena's been visiting. I'm taking her home today."

"Did you like Anchorage?" Sassa asked.

"Yes, very much, but it will be good to be home again."

Kate handed Patrick an envelope. "Can you give this to Paul?" She glanced down the creek toward his house.

"Sure. Don't see much of him these days. Keeps to himself mostly."

"Is he all right?"

"Down in the dumps. Figure he's wrestling with himself." Patrick lifted his hat and used it to swat at a mosquito buzzing his arm.

"Can you stay a little while?" Sassa asked.

"I wish we could, but I've got one more stop to make before we head for Kotzebue. And with the days getting shorter, I'll be hard-pressed to make McGrath." She glanced up the river. "Clouds are thinning, that will help."

"Nena, maybe you can come again some day," Sassa said.

"I'd like that." Nena smiled. "Next summer, maybe?" She looked at Kate for affirmation.

"You just tell me when."

"Okay. We'll count on it," Sassa said with a nod.

Nena stepped back to the plane. Before disappearing inside, she waved farewell.

With one more glance at Paul's place, Kate said, "Gotta go. Come on, Angel." The dog came running and leaped inside.

"See you next week." Patrick took Sassa's hand and stepped back while Kate returned to the cockpit.

Patrick gave the plane a shove, and the Bellanca floated free of the dock. Kate turned the plane so it faced upstream and increased speed until she glided over the quiet water, and then lifted off, soaring over the trees. Glancing down at Paul's cabin, she prayed for him. *Lord, I don't know what's hurting him or why he's hiding, but you do. Help him with whatever it is.*

"The sun makes everything even more beautiful," Nena said.

"You want to see something special?"

"Yes. Of course."

Kate headed back toward the inlet. "Mount Susitna was hidden by clouds when we flew in, but she's clear now." When Kate was at the mouth of the river, she turned back so the plane faced the mountain. "Look. Can you see her?"

Nena studied Mount Susitna. "What am I supposed to see?"

"The Sleeping Lady." Kate chuckled. "Look more closely. If you use your imagination, you can see a woman lying on her back, her face looking at the sky, and her hair flowing down around her shoulders."

"Yes. I see her."

"Some people see her lying on her side, but I like to think of her gazing at the sky." Kate smiled. "Let's have a closer look." Kate headed toward the mountain. "This is one of my favorite places. It's beautiful here, not as rugged as a lot of the territory. This is a gentle mountain."

Lakes below sparkled like blue gems resting among the forest. "I drop off a lot of fishermen out this way."

Nena wrinkled up her nose. "What is that smell?"

Kate sniffed. It was oil. Had she left an oily rag up front? She didn't see anything.

Something splattered the windshield. Kate leaned forward to get a better look at it. Her pulse picked up. Oil!

She looked at the oil pressure. It was low. *I better get us on the ground.* More black splashed the windshield and smoke rolled out from beneath the engine.

The temperature gauge read hot and the oil pressure had dropped even more. She was losing the precious fluid quickly. If she lost too much, the engine would seize. There wasn't much time. The plane bucked and trembled.

"What's wrong?" Nena asked, her voice tight. She gripped the edge of her seat.

"Oil's leaking."

"Is that bad?"

"It's not good, but we'll be all right. I'll find a place to set down."

Oil continued to spew. Panic reached for Kate, but she forced her mind on flying and doing all she could to keep them in the air until she could find a place to land. Angel paced and whined.

Kate turned back, searching for the lake she'd just passed over. She couldn't see it. Where was it? *Why did I decide to go sightseeing today? No one knows where we are. And I don't have a radio.*

Smoke billowed out of the engine. The oil pressure no longer registered. She was out of time. The engine sputtered. *Where's that lake?* The Bellanca shuddered.

"Nena, I'm going to have to put her down now."

Gripping her seat, Nena nodded.

Panic rising, Kate searched for an open field. The pontoons would probably come apart, but open ground was far better than trees. *Stay calm. You can do this. Lord, show me where to land.*

She'd always felt like her Bellanca was a friend that would never let her down. But the engine sputtered and the plane vibrated violently. They were losing altitude fast.

"Come on. Come on." Kate urged the bird to fly.

All of a sudden it was there—the lake, looking like a blue point of hope. She turned toward it and prayed the engine would hold up long enough to get her there.

It's not far now. Come on, girl.

As she dropped down barely above the trees, Kate felt as if she were wrestling with the plane. Nearing the lake, she pulled back on the stick, trying to keep the nose up. The trees were close. Gripping the stick, she feared the belly would skim the treetops. The plane trembled. The engine seemed to gasp and then stopped altogether. Everything was eerily quiet. They were going down. Kate tried to keep the bird in the air. The lake was so close.

"Nena, grab hold of something!"

The nose dropped and they clipped a tree. The plane dove toward the lake. The day at Rimrock Lake flashed through Kate's mind. *Dear God, not again.*

When they hit, the Pacemaker slammed into the water. Kate was thrown out of her seat and into the windshield. Pain exploded in her head. Her arm hit something and it felt like a hot knife had been shoved through it.

Nena screamed. Angel yelped.

The plane stopped.

It stood on its nose, and then toppled onto its back, dropping Kate and Nena to the ceiling.

When Kate fell, she landed on the side of her neck and felt a painful wrenching. She couldn't distinguish up from down.

The plane floated for a moment, then shifted and started to sink. Disoriented and in pain, Kate called to Nena. There was no response.

"Dear Lord, no! Please no!" She grabbed her friend. "Nena!"

Blood coursed down the side of Nena's face. Her eyes were closed. *I've got to get us out!*

Thankful Nena was tiny, Kate grabbed her beneath the arms and dragged her out of the cockpit toward the back of the plane. Water seemed to pour in from everywhere.

Still holding onto her friend, Kate scrambled through the upside-down cabin, ducking under the tops of the seats.

"Angel!" she hollered. She could hear the dog whining. "Angel!"

Seconds later the dog was beside her.

When Kate reached the door, she tugged the latch, but it wouldn't budge. She yanked it and finally realized she was turning it the wrong way. She tried again. This time the bolt came free. She pushed against the door, but it barely moved. Water pressure from the outside held it shut.

She rammed her shoulder against it and pain flared inside her joint. The door moved only a couple inches. Icy water gushed in. As the depth increased, Kate continued to push, all the while struggling to keep ahold of Nena. She couldn't let her die. As the water deepened inside, the door finally gave way enough to allow escape.

"Come on, Angel."

The dog lunged past her and into the freezing water. Kate climbed out and dragged Nena free. Already below the surface, the plane was going down quickly. Hanging onto Nena's shirt, she pushed off against the door frame with her feet and swam toward the light.

Feeling as if her lungs would burst, Kate broke through the surface and sucked in oxygen. She looked at Nena. Blood still flowed from a cut on the side of her head. Her skin looked pallid. Was she breathing?

"Nena!" Kate shook her. *No. God, please not again. Please.*

Kate fought to stay afloat while turning Nena onto her back. She looked at the plane. The bottom of the fuselage and the pontoons were just barely above water. One pontoon looked like it was smashed in front and the other was angled away from the cabin. With an ugly slurping sound, the Bellanca sank amid swirling water and bubbles.

A moment later, there was no sign it had been there at all.

Whining, Angel paddled in circles around Kate.

"It's all right, girl. Come on."

Thankful for the swimming lessons her mother had forced her to take, she headed toward shore, careful to keep Nena's face out of the water. "You're not going to die," she said vehemently. "Not this time."

Inch by inch, the shore came closer. Kate's shoulder ached and the arm she had around Nena felt numb. Finally her toes touched the bottom of the lake. *Just a couple more feet.* She kept pulling, and at last she was able to get her footing.

For a few moments she didn't move while she caught her breath. With her arm still around Nena, she waded through muck and slippery rocks toward the beach. As the water grew shallow, it was difficult to handle Nena. Finally Kate hefted her into her arms and stumbled onto a grassy shore. Shivering and exhausted, she laid Nena on her back and dropped to her knees beside her friend.

Pressing her ear against her chest, she listened for a heartbeat. It was faint, but she was still alive. She didn't look like she was breathing. Kate rolled Nena onto her side and pounded her back. Water dribbled out of her mouth and then Kate heard a strangled breath. She continued to slap her between the shoulder blades until Nena's breathing evened out.

She rolled her friend onto her back. "Nena?"

There was no response, not even the flutter of an eyelid.

Kate dropped back, sitting on her heels. All of a sudden,

deep gulping sobs rose up from inside. She pressed her head against her friend's chest. "Please, don't die."

Angel pushed a cold nose against Kate's face. She wrapped an arm around the dog and hugged her, then pressed her face into the dog's ruff.

Her sobs subsided and she turned to look down at Nena, hoping for some sort of movement. Angel walked a few paces away and shook out her coat, then set off to explore. Kate sat and pulled her knees against her chest and stared at the place she'd last seen her plane. She'd done it again. Tears trailed down her cheeks.

I'm still nothing but a lark about. She pressed her forehead against her knees. "What was I thinking?"

She looked at Nena. She needed medical attention, now. And everything Kate had that might help was at the bottom of the lake.

She shivered and took in her surroundings. Heavy forests pressed in on all sides. There was no sign that any man had ever been in this place.

No one knew they were here.

— 28 —

Kate pressed her fingertips to Nena's wrist. The pulse was steady. *Thank you, Lord.* She pulled off her jacket and draped it over her friend. It was wet, but might help hold in a little warmth.

Kate's head throbbed. She put a hand to her forehead and discovered a large bump. It was tender. She figured it couldn't be too serious—she was conscious. Gingerly she turned her head to the left and then the right. Her neck was sore. A cut on her right arm bled, but didn't look serious. She had a lot to be grateful for—no broken bones, and she and Nena were alive.

Taking a deep breath, Kate brushed strands of wet hair off her face. She gazed at the quiet lake, which reflected the surrounding wilderness. The accident rolled through her mind. She'd become too casual about flying.

"I'm sorry, Nena. I'll get us out of this mess. I promise." Guilt and hopelessness swept through Kate. What could she do to save them?

She pushed to her feet and studied the place where the plane had gone down. There'd been no time to salvage anything. Her pack, her survival gear, her grandmother's Bible were all at the bottom of the lake. Her hand rested on the sheath attached to her belt. At least she had a knife.

Angel loped up to Kate, who knelt and pulled the soaking wet dog into her arms.

"Good girl." She smoothed Angel's hair. "Someone will find us."

She said the words with conviction, but wasn't convinced. Fear mounded up inside and like a wet leather strap wrapped itself around her heart, growing tighter with every negative thought.

"At least we have plenty of water to drink," she joked, but didn't laugh. Looking down at Nena, covered in her jacket, she knew she needed to dry it out. The sun might warm her enough for now.

Kate removed the coat and hung it over a tree limb. She also hung up Nena's jacket and dress, hoping they'd dry before the sun set. After dark, the temperatures would plummet. She needed a fire, but had no matches. They were in her pack.

An idea worked at the fringes of her mind. Kate pulled off her shoes and socks. She did the same for Nena. She set the shoes on a downed log and hung the socks on a tree limb.

Walking along the beach, she studied the place her plane went in. It wasn't that far out. Maybe the water wasn't very deep. She might be able to get some of the things she needed like blankets, an axe and a shovel, and the matches she kept in a watertight container. And she'd feel safer with her pistol. She had to try.

Although dreading returning to the icy water, she sat down and stripped off her pants and shirt and laid them on the log beside her shoes. Shivering, she waded into the lake.

Angel splashed in.

"No, Angel. You stay."

The dog looked at her with a question in her eyes. Kate moved farther out. The dog followed.

"No! Stay!"

Angel stood in the shallow water and watched Kate.

Her shivering intensified, but Kate kept swimming, stopping only when she thought she'd reached the place where the plane had disappeared. Putting her face in the water, she searched for it, but couldn't see anything. She swam a little farther and looked again. Still nothing. She moved on and this time she spotted her plane, lying quietly on the bottom. How far down was it? She couldn't even make an approximation.

Only one way to find out. Kate dove, heading straight for the submerged Bellanca. She'd almost reached it, when her craving for oxygen forced her back to the surface. Unwilling to give up, she treaded water for a few minutes, then took several deep breaths and went down again, pulling hard with her arms and kicking furiously. Her shoulder hurt, but not enough to stop her. She managed to reach the plane this time, but didn't have enough air in her lungs to get inside. She barely made it back to the surface before taking a breath.

She spotted Angel swimming out. "No! Go back!"

The dog kept on, intent upon reaching her. Deciding more attempts to retrieve anything from the plane were useless, Kate swam to shore.

Chilled through, her body rattled from the cold as she stepped out of the water. Dressed in only her underclothes, she sat in the sun beside Nena, pulling her legs close to her body and wrapping her arms around bent knees. What was she going to do?

She looked around at the woodlands, feeling small and alone. Fear closed in again, threatening to cut off her breath. Looking at Nena, Kate dug for resolve. Her friend needed her. She couldn't give up.

Kate had often thought about what she'd do in an emergency. But in all her imaginings, she'd had her survival gear to rely on. *I wish I were more prepared. I should have taken a course or at least read up on how to survive.*

She tried to come up with a way to signal anyone flying overhead, but she had nothing to use and the trees pushed in almost to the ridge of the lake. All she could do was wait.

We'll need shelter. I can do that.

Kate checked on Nena again. There was no change. Did she have a concussion, or something more serious? Was her brain damaged? *If only I knew how to help her.*

Kate set off, searching for a place that would offer them protection. The best she could come up with was a large tree that had fallen. If she braced branches against the trunk, she could create a lean-to.

She cut evergreen limbs from trees and broke off ferns. The activity seemed to stir up flies and mosquitoes, which feasted on her exposed skin. No amount of swatting discouraged them. After gathering the evergreens, she placed them against the roots of the tree. Standing back, she studied the shelter. It wasn't fancy, but it would do for a night or two. She took some additional boughs and placed them over Nena, hoping they would offer some protection from insects and the cold.

If only she could start a fire.

She thought back to every survival story she'd ever heard or read that included fire building. She had a vague memory of someone using a wooden rod and a block of wood. Maybe she could do that.

Keeping an eye on Nena, Kate scoured the area for the wood she'd need. She found some she thought might work and took them to the shelter. After coming up with some dry grass and bits of timber, she sat down and pressed a chunk of soft wood on the ground in front of her. Using a small branch, she cut the end into a dull point and placed it on the wood chunk, then rolled the branch between her palms, back and forth. Several times it flew out of her hands. She dropped it again and again. This was impossible. In the end, all she had to show for her efforts were raw, red palms.

Fighting tears, she berated herself for not being prepared. "I should know how to do this."

Unwilling to give up, she decided to try something else she'd read about. She might be able to create a spark by striking rocks against each other. She just wasn't sure what kind to use.

With the last of the day's sun fading, she scoured the shoreline for stones that might work. No luck.

Kate took Nena's damp clothing off the tree and dressed her. She'd figured by now Nena would have shown signs of consciousness, but there'd been no change.

"Nena, please wake up."

Kate pulled on her own half-dried clothes. At first they made her feel colder, and she shivered so hard her teeth chattered. Gradually her body warmed the clothing and she felt slightly better.

As darkness descended, Kate carried Nena to the tiny shelter and pulled her inside, then lay down and held her close. Angel snuggled against Kate's back. The air turned chill and it seemed like the mosquitoes were hungrier than ever. She pulled Nena's hood over her face, hoping it would help protect against biting insects. Pressing her own face into her bent elbow, she tried to sleep. Her empty stomach rumbled, and she decided that with first light she'd search for berries. Maybe Nena would be awake by then.

Sleep eluded Kate. Her neck and arm ached and the bump on her head throbbed. The cold and biting insects brought more misery. She couldn't imagine another night like this one. *God, please help us. Don't let Nena suffer. Please forgive me for my foolishness.*

Kate felt God's presence. It was as if he was right beside her, quieting her fears.

She imagined what was going on at the airfield. Sidney would be keyed up and nervous, spouting orders. Dear Mike, he would be in the air, searching. Kate's heart warmed at the thought of him. He'd do everything he could to find her. He was a good man. Albert and Helen would be at the field, helping in any way they could. And they'd be praying.

Kate closed her eyes and thought about Frank. Had he suffered?

Cold and bug-bitten, Kate finally slept, though fitfully. Sometime during the night, she heard movement in the forest. Angel let off a low growl. Kate shushed her, not wanting to attract a predator.

She stared into the inky blackness. The crackling of brush and an occasional woofing noise cut through the night. *It's probably just a moose*, she told herself and hoped she was right. She moved deeper into her shelter, pulling Nena with her. She took her knife out of its sheath and held absolutely still, breathing as quietly as possible.

Finally, whatever was out there moved away. Angel settled down. Shivering, Kate huddled against the dog as exhaustion pulled her back into a restless sleep.

In the morning, her first thoughts were of Nena. Had she awakened?

Kate pushed up on an elbow and looked at her friend. "Nena? Nena."

Not even a stir of an eyelid. Fearfully, Kate pressed two fingers against Nena's throat and was thankful to feel the beating of her heart.

Driven by thirst, Kate climbed out of the shelter and headed for the lake. Her clothes were still damp and felt scratchy and stiff.

Early morning sunlight cast a glow on the trees and hillsides but hadn't yet reached the lake, where a mist hung above the water. The lonely sound of a loon echoed from an inlet. Kate walked to the edge, removed her shoes and socks, and waded in just deep enough to scoop water into her hands and drink. She hoped the liquid would quiet the ache in her empty stomach.

When her thirst was satiated, she straightened and searched the skies, willing a plane into sight. None came. Would they even think to look here? First they'd explore the areas that were part of her route. When they didn't find her, they'd widen the search.

A frightening thought exploded in her mind. *What if they think I went down in the inlet or the river? They'll give up.* Fear vibrated through her. They'd assume she was dead.

She turned and stared at the forest. Could she walk out? Everything she'd been taught said stay with the plane. But it was at the bottom of the lake. She decided to wait. Besides, how would she get Nena out? She couldn't leave her.

Kate's rumbling stomach drove her to search for food. Looking for berries, she headed to the edge of the forest. She stayed close enough to the lake so if she heard the sound of a plane, she could run out into the open and wave it down.

Some of the bushes had half-shriveled fruit. Kate snatched them up and shoved them in her mouth, then offered some to Angel, who quickly caught on to how to pick her own. Happily, Kate found patches of plump, juicy berries. As she foraged, she kept an ear and eye out for bears. They'd be eating the last of the summer crop too.

With her hunger pangs quieted, Kate returned to the lake.

Not sure what she was looking for, she walked along the shore. She picked up several rocks and tried to produce a spark, but none of them worked.

When she saw the flash of a fish in the water, her pulse picked up. Maybe she could catch one. Removing her shoes and rolling up her pants, she waded in. Standing absolutely still with her hands just above the water, she waited and watched, her feet aching from the cold. When one swam by her, she grabbed for it, but he darted away. She tried again and again, but she was never fast enough. Finally, she got her hands on one. Squeezing tightly so it couldn't wriggle free, she ran toward shore, but before she could get out of the water, it twisted away and fell back into the lake. Kate hollered her frustration, hit the water with her fist, and then kicked at it. Finally, she sat on a rock and ruminated over her situation.

She needed a spear. If she could find a suitable branch, she could make one. She set out to find one. It didn't take long. Using her knife, she whittled a point on the end, then waded back into the water. Standing perfectly still, she waited and finally a fish swam near. She flung the homemade lance, but missed.

She tried again and again with no luck. Finally, she sat on a log and stared at the lake. What was she going to do? She tossed a rock into the water. *If I'd gotten a radio, I could have told Sidney where I was before I ditched.*

Kate saw something move in the shadows on the far side of the lake. Every nerve in her body sprang to life. She straightened, trying to get a better look. It was an animal of some sort. A wolf? Fear prickled through her. Squinting, she tried to make out what it was. A lynx emerged from the shadows and cautiously moved to the water's edge to drink.

She'd never thought to be afraid of a lynx. Did they attack

people? She remained still, hoping it wouldn't see her. Finally it returned to the forest, leaving Kate feeling defenseless. A spear and a knife would be of little help against anything like a wolf or bear.

At the end of the day, Nena still hadn't regained consciousness even when Kate tried to rouse her. She began to worry that if Nena didn't drink, she'd die. Using her knife, Kate cut a section off the bottom of her shirt. She walked to the edge of the lake and dipped the fabric into the water, then returned with the soaking material. Opening Nena's mouth, she squeezed water from the fabric. Most of it dribbled down her friend's chin, but Kate thought some had been swallowed.

She tried several more times and hoped the moisture would be sufficient. With darkness stealing over the lake, Kate pulled on her coat and hunkered down between Nena and Angel. The air felt colder than the previous night. Peering out of the shelter, Kate looked at the sky with its stars glittering in a black universe.

"God, do you see us? We need you." Kate hated crying, but she couldn't hold back her tears. "Please, help us. Don't let us die."

That night the mosquitoes seemed more ruthless than the night before. By morning Kate's arms and legs were covered with red, itching bumps. They'd even bitten through her clothing. She could feel welts on her face and neck. Nena looked as bad as Kate felt. She remembered Patrick telling her that cow parsnips soothed the itching, so she searched for some, but didn't find any.

The day passed, and Kate busied herself foraging for and eating berries. Angel had pounced on a rabbit, but it escaped. The loss of food left Kate's stomach feeling emptier than before.

She continued giving Nena water, hoping it was enough. She also tried fishing again, but by the time the sun went down, she returned to the shelter, hungry and weak.

The night sounds were less frightening. The rustle of a small creature in the grass and a screech owl's call cut through the blackness. They made her feel less alone. Later she heard a distinctive stomping sound and figured it must be a caribou or moose. In spite of hunger, bugs, and the cold, she slept.

The next morning, she woke to cramps from an empty stomach or maybe too many berries. She wasn't sure which. A light drizzle fell and a heavy mist obscured the lake. Everything was soaked. The earth gave off a musty scent and the air smelled of evergreens and overripe berries.

She climbed out of the shelter and headed to the lake for a drink, then returned with water for Nena. She huddled inside the small haven to wait out the rain. When the sun broke through the clouds, she moved outside to warm herself and search the skies, listening for the sound of a plane.

No one came.

No one was going to come.

Scanning her surroundings and the distant hills and mountains, Kate knew the direction civilization lay. She might be able to hike to Susitna Station or get lucky and stumble across a homesteader's cabin. She'd follow the sun and keep her bearings by the mountain peaks. She recognized most of them. But how would she carry Nena?

Kate decided to make a litter. That way she could pull Nena along behind her. She gathered sturdy branches, then ripped her shirt into strips, which she used to lash the limbs together. It wasn't fancy, but it ought to work.

Before setting out, Kate gathered stones from along the shore. She placed them beside her camp in the shape of an arrow, pointing the way she'd planned to head.

"At least if someone comes, they'll know which way we went," she told Nena. She wished there were some way to carry water, but she'd have to rely on streams and morning dew.

After hefting her friend onto the litter, she gave Angel's head a pat. "You ready for a hike?"

The dog whined and leaned against her, wagging her tail. Kate got her bearings, said a prayer, and set off.

In no time, the trees closed in behind, blocking the lake and the mountains from view. Using her knife, Kate scored the trees every ten or fifteen feet. That way she wouldn't get lost and if someone came looking for her, hopefully they'd see the markings. She kept moving, using the sun as a guide and hoping for openings in the woodland that would help her stay on course.

Pulling the litter meant slow going. And Kate wasn't even sure it would hold together. She had to stop several times to tighten the cloth strips.

With no trail, Kate fought her way through brush and downed trees. When clouds moved in, blocking out the sun, it became more difficult to maintain a constant heading. Still, she continued, trusting in her sense of direction.

Kate could only guess at how long they'd been traveling, but it must have been several hours. She was tired and thirsty and now wondered if she'd made a terrible mistake. She considered going back, but to what? Their only hope was to push ahead.

When a soft rain started, she stopped and tipped her face up, catching drops in her mouth. She moved on. She'd find her way . . . somehow. That night they slept beneath a tree huddled together—vulnerable.

The next morning, she stopped at the top of a ravine and

studied a creek winding its way through the bottom. She needed water and remembered hearing that, when lost, a person should follow moving water downstream. It would inevitably lead to a larger stream or a river, and with any luck, people.

Making sure the litter was secure, she started down the steep bank, pushing the heels of her boots into soft earth. Without warning, the ground gave way. Kate started to slide. She leaned backward, planting her feet into the loose soil, but she was moving too quickly and the litter came apart behind her. She pushed her feet deeper, but the toe of her boot caught on a branch, and she tumbled forward and somersaulted down the side of the ravine, leaving Nena behind.

Her head struck something. Pain and colors exploded behind her eyes. After that, there was nothing, only the oblivion of unconsciousness.

— 29 —

Paul brought his axe down on a chunk of spruce, splitting it in half. He picked up one wedge, cut it again, and tossed the two sections into a pile. He did the same with the other half. He kept at it, splitting chunk after chunk and wishing he could empty his mind. But no matter how hard he worked or how much his muscles ached, Kate's disappearance stayed with him. What had happened to her? Where was she? Was she even alive? The same ache he'd known when Susan died mushroomed in his chest.

Grabbing another piece of wood, he set it on the stump. The dogs started barking and he looked to see what had set them off. Patrick walked the trail between the two homesteads. His expression was grim. Paul prepared for the worst.

Hands in his pockets, Patrick stepped into the clearing. "Heard from Sidney."

Paul steeled himself against bad news.

"No sign of her."

Taking a breath, Paul turned back to the wood, raised his axe, and brought it down, splintering the spruce into three pieces. "She might still be alive." He chucked the firewood aside and turned to Patrick. "I've got to do something. I can't just wait around, wondering."

"There's not much you can do. People are searching, the best pilots are out."

Paul straightened and looked squarely at Patrick. "I've gotta help."

"The best thing you can do is pray."

Paul pressed the head of his axe against the ground and leaned on it. "I've been praying. It's not enough."

Patrick glanced up the creek toward the Susitna River. "They'll find her."

"And what if they don't? It's been three days. She could be suffering, maybe even dying. Do you know what it's like to wait for rescue and have it not show up?" Paul felt the heat of disappointment in his belly. He knew, all too well, what it felt like to wait, only to discover there would be no help.

"They'll find them," Patrick said with certainty, placing a hand on Paul's shoulder.

Paul shrugged it away. "You can't know that."

"Every time she went up she knew the danger. She chose to live with risk."

"That doesn't mean she should be left to die out in the bush somewhere."

"'Course it doesn't. No one's saying that. But she lived the way she wanted."

The word *lived* reverberated through Paul's mind. *Patrick thinks she's dead.* Paul lifted the axe and swung it, burying the blade in the stump. "Can you get Sidney on the radio?"

"Probably."

"I want to talk to him." Paul headed toward the trail.

While Patrick cranked the radio, Paul paced. He stopped when Patrick finally connected.

"Sidney, Paul's here. Says he wants to talk to you." Patrick removed the headset and handed it to Paul. "Speak into this." He pointed at a microphone.

Paul put on the headphones and leaned close to the radio set. "Sidney, this is Paul Anderson from Bear Creek."

"Sorry about Kate," Sidney said. "We're doing everything we can." A buzz rolled high and low across the lines.

"I want to help."

"There are a lot of pilots out looking for her. We'll find her, believe me."

Sidney's positive tone did nothing to allay Paul's anxiety. "Can you get me on a search team?"

"Like I said, I've got a lot of guys on it already. You might as well stay put and stay safe."

"Get me on a plane. I can be an extra pair of eyes."

There were a few moments of silence, then Sidney said, "Guess it can't hurt."

A weary sigh crackled across the airways. "Mike's going out again in a few minutes. He planned on flying up the Susitna. I'll have him swing by and pick you up."

"Thanks. I'll be on the dock."

"Paul . . ."

"Yeah."

"She's a good pilot, one of the best. If anyone can make it, she can. She's probably just waiting for us to find her."

"That's what I figured."

The line went dead and Paul removed the headset. "I better get some gear."

Toweling her hands on her apron, Sassa moved into the front room. "Don't give up hope."

"I'm not." He headed for the door.

———

Paul stood on the dock for what seemed like hours before he heard the drone of a plane. He watched Mike set down, and as soon as he was close enough to the dock, Paul leaped onto a pontoon and climbed in, squeezing his tall frame into the front seat of the Fairchild.

"Morning," Mike said, turning toward the middle of the stream. He looked worn out.

"What's the word?"

"Nothing new." Mike scratched several days' growth of beard. "She stopped here and no one's seen or heard from her since." He sounded weary and discouraged.

"With two of us, we might be able to cover more territory."

Mike revved the engine, moved up the creek to set up for takeoff. He glided over the water and lifted into the air. "I'm going to have one more look along the run we know she made, and then . . .well, then we pray God shows us where she is."

"Have you searched the Mount Susitna area? It's one of her favorite places."

"I know that." Mike's voice sounded testy. "I've been over it a dozen times."

"Sorry. I know you've been at it for days." Guilt sliced through Paul's middle. He wished Kate was his, but Mike was the one who deserved her.

Mike flew at a low altitude while Paul watched the river, its banks, the forest, and the wetlands. He gripped the edge of the window. What if they didn't find her? Then what?

When they passed over Susitna Station, Mike asked, "You think she might have flown over Mount Susitna?"

"She loved it. But she liked the Chugach too."

"I doubt she'd go east. She had Nena with her and was headed up to Kotzebue."

"Yeah, that's what Patrick said." Paul wished he'd met the plane that day. Why hadn't he? "What about some of the peaks to the west?"

344

"Pilots are looking at those now."

Paul's eyes turned to the Sleeping Lady. "Let's make another search around Mount Susitna. Kate was fascinated with it."

Mike smiled. "She told me once if she were a mountain, that's the one she'd like to be 'cause she never got enough sleep."

The knot of jealousy returned. Paul hated that Mike knew things about Kate he didn't.

Mike turned the plane toward the mountain. Pockets of fog drifted between earth and sky.

Paul hadn't done much praying in recent years, but he did now. There was nothing else he could do.

With the engine droning and Paul's hopes waning, they flew patterns over the mountain forests and lakes. There was no sign of Kate or her plane. Paul kneaded his neck. The muscles ached from craning to see out the window.

"Not much light left, ought to head back." Mike sounded miserable.

Paul didn't reply, but stared below, unwilling to give up. Then he saw something in one of the lakes that just didn't look right.

"Hey, swing back over there." Paul pointed at the lake.

"What? Did you see the plane?" Mike did as he was told, dropping just above the trees. "What'd you see?"

"I don't know. Maybe it's nothing. Might just be a shadow."

Mike flew low, his eyes scanning the water. "Something's there." He pulled up and looped back. "Can you see it? What is it?" He came around for another look. "Is that a plane in the water?"

Paul's hopes of finding Kate alive faded. There was a plane, but it sat on the bottom of the lake. He searched the shore, hoping to see her jumping and waving to signal them. There was nothing but an empty beach.

"Could it be Kate's Bellanca?"

"Maybe." Mike's voice was morose.

"Well, put down. Put the plane down!"

"Hang on to your suspenders." Mike made a wide turn and came back around, landing on the crystalline waters. He moved toward the place they'd spotted the plane.

Both men climbed onto the pontoons and stared down into the lake.

"Can't see anything from here, too much reflection," Mike said.

Paul lay flat on his belly and put his face in the water, searching. When he came up, he sputtered and pushed back wet hair. "There's a plane down there, all right. It might be Kate's."

He pushed to his feet and stared at the beach again, hoping for some sign of her. She wasn't there. Where was she? Paul climbed back inside and stripped off everything but his long johns.

Mike stuck his head inside. "Whattaya doing?"

"Someone's got to look. We have to know." Paul moved back onto the pontoon. "She . . . might still be in there."

Unable to discuss the possibility further, he dove in, the cold water sending shock waves through him. He kicked hard and pulled with his arms, propelling himself downward. By the time he reached the plane there wasn't enough air left in his lungs for time to get a look inside, but he did see her name written on the fuselage. Sickened, he headed for the surface. When he broke free of the water, he gulped in oxygen.

"Did you see anything?"

"It's Kate's plane, but I didn't get a look inside." Breathing hard, he said, "I'll try again."

He took in several more breaths and dove. He headed for the front of the plane, hoping to see through one of the windows. He managed a quick look. There was no sign of anyone inside. Pulling for the surface, he struggled not to take a breath.

When his face broke free of the water, he gulped in a lungful of air. "Didn't see anyone." He could barely get enough air. "I think she got out."

"Let's have a look around then." Mike sounded hopeful. He climbed into the cockpit and cruised toward shore while Paul balanced on a pontoon. When they reached shallow water, Paul jumped in, taking a line with him to secure the plane.

Holding Paul's clothes and boots out of the water, Mike waded ashore. "You might want these." He handed the clothing to Paul.

"Thanks." Shivering, Paul dressed while Mike did a quick search of the beach.

Just as Paul was tying his last lacing, Mike called, " Hey! I found something!"

Paul jogged up the shore where Mike stood near the tree line.

"Looks like a shelter. They must still be alive!"

Paul's eyes followed the rocks Kate had set out that pointed in the direction she'd headed. "Looks like she hiked out." He stared into the trees, trying to penetrate the darkness.

Mike moved toward the forest. "She's a determined woman," he said, his voice filled with pride.

"She might still be close." Paul put his hands to his mouth and hollered, "Kate! Kate!" He waited for an answer. There was none. He called again. Nothing.

"We should be able to track them." Mike studied the prints leading away from the camp. "Looks like someone's pulling a litter. There's only one set of footprints, plus the dog's. And these scuffed tracks. One of them must be hurt."

Mike headed for the plane. "We'll need my pack and some gear, plus a stretcher . . . just in case."

With the sun fading, Mike and Paul set off into the woods. It wasn't long before they discovered the blazed trees.

"That Kate's a smart cookie. We'll find them in no time." Mike hurried his steps.

As the lake disappeared behind them and the canopy overhead thickened, Paul imagined Kate and Nena . . . lost in the wilderness. Which one of them was injured? He couldn't imagine Nena pulling a litter with Kate on it. She was a tiny woman. Kate must be pulling Nena.

"This must be really hard on Kate," Mike said. "After what happened."

"What do you mean?"

"I figured she'd told you." Mike turned quiet.

"Told me what?"

"Maybe she didn't mean for anyone else to know."

"Know what?" Paul hated that he'd been left out of something important in Kate's life.

Mike didn't answer right away, then sounding reluctant, he said, "She had a crack-up once . . . in a lake. A friend of hers died in the accident."

"I didn't know." Paul kept walking, wishing he had known, wishing Kate had trusted him with her secret. But why should she? He'd never told her about his past.

As the men moved through the forest, flies and mosquitoes descended, finding their way beneath their hats and inside their coat collars. It only reminded them of how miserable the women must be.

Occasionally they'd stop and call Kate's name. Then Nena's. The only answer was an occasional chirp of a bird and the buzz of insects.

Several times they lost the trail and had to backtrack to pick it up again. When darkness enveloped the woods, they were forced to stop. Paul built a fire, his mind on Kate. Did she have anything to hold back the darkness or to keep her warm? He looked into the forest. It was black as ink. *Lord, I know I haven't talked to you much these past years, but that's not Kate's fault. She loves you. Please help us find her. I know she's praying—please don't let her down.*

The following morning the men set out at daybreak.

"They've come a long way," Paul said. "Must have set out a full day ahead of us."

"Even though it's Kate, I wouldn't figure she'd come so far so fast."

Midmorning they crested a hill and Mike stopped suddenly. Kate's footprints disappeared amongst fallen leaves. The ground was disturbed and torn up.

"Looks like something happened here. She might have fallen," said Mike.

Paul hollered. "Kate!"

"Here. I'm here," she called back.

Shocked to hear her voice, he gazed down the steep incline. He couldn't believe what he saw—Kate waving her arms and smiling. "I'm here."

Angel stood up, tail wagging.

Paul hustled down the hill, planting his feet in the soft soil. He could hear Mike close behind him.

Angel sprinted toward Paul. He gave her a pat and headed for Kate.

Mike rushed past him. "Kate! Thank God, girl, it's good to see you." Mike pulled her into an embrace and held her. She clung to him.

Paul held back, feeling awkward and wishing it were his arms that held her.

Finally Mike took a step back from Kate. "You all right?"

"Yeah. I took a tumble down the hill and got a good bump on my head, but I'm all right. I brought Nena down here next to the stream. We've had to stay put for a day." She looked at Paul. "I can't believe you guys found us. I was beginning to give up hope."

"You left a good trail," Mike said, wearing a grin.

Paul's attention turned to Nena. He pulled off his gloves and knelt beside her. He felt her pulse, lifted one eyelid and then the other. He rested a hand on her chest to feel her respirations. "How long has she been like this?"

"Since the accident."

"We need to get her to a hospital. She's badly dehydrated and at the very least has a severe concussion—could be a brain injury."

Mike opened up the stretcher. He glanced at the one lying beside Nena. "Pretty creative of you, Kate. But I figure this one will be easier to use."

"You did a good job taking care of her," Paul said, removing his coat. "Put this on. How you feeling?"

"I'm worn out and hungry, but I'm all right."

He nodded and put his hands on her cheeks, looking closely at her eyes, then traced the bloodstain on her forehead. "Looks like you've got a good knot there. Any trouble with your vision? Headache?"

"My vision's fine, but I do have a headache."

He examined the cut on her head. "Pretty good gash. Probably too late for stitches, though. You'll have a scar."

Her hands shaking, Kate buttoned up the coat.

"I've got something for you." Mike pulled a container out of his pack. "Helen sent these along . . ." His voice caught. "They're for when we found you." He lifted the lid and the smell of cinnamon wafted into the air.

"Oatmeal raisin?" Tears filled Kate's eyes and she took a cookie, biting into it. Stuffing the rest of it into her mouth, she said, "I've never tasted anything so good in all my life." She grabbed another one and took a bite.

"Slow down. You don't want it to come back up," Paul said. "How about something more substantial?" He offered her half a peanut butter sandwich.

"This is the best meal in my entire life." Kate laughed. "I'll never look at peanut butter the same way."

Kate gave Angel half of her sandwich, then sat while Mike and Paul transferred Nena to the stretcher. After tucking blankets tightly around her, Paul asked, "You think you're strong enough to make it back to the plane?"

Kate nodded. She rested a hand on Nena's shoulder. "She looks so sick. Will she be all right?"

"The sooner we get her to a hospital, the better."

"Well, let's go then," Kate said.

Mike picked up one end of the gurney and Paul the other, and they headed toward the lake with Kate and Angel following.

— 30 —

Kate stood at the door of Nena's hospital room. It had been five days since their rescue. Nena was still unconscious. Kate studied Joe who had remained at his wife's side since she'd been brought in to the Anchorage hospital. Kate's heart squeezed. *Lord, please let her wake up.*

She felt a hand on her shoulder. Startled, she turned to see Mike. "You scared me."

He smiled. "Sorry." His eyes went to Nena. "She any better?"

"No change." Kate's gaze returned to Joe and she let out a heavy sigh. "He never leaves her."

"If you were the one lying there, I wouldn't leave either." Gentle eyes rested on her. "I'm thankful it's not you."

"I wish it was. I wouldn't feel so guilty."

"There's nothing to feel guilty about." He dropped a kiss on her cheek. "Come on. You've been here almost nonstop." He took her hand. "You need rest."

"I can't, not until I know she's all right."

"How about a walk? Maybe a change of scenery will help you relax a little." He started down the hall, Kate in tow.

Mike opened the hospital door for Kate and followed her out. He caught her arm. "Kate, can we talk?"

"Sure. What is it?"

"I want to ask you something." He faced her and took hold of her hands.

Instinctively Kate knew what he was about to ask. She stepped back. "Mike . . . I . . ."

"Please hear me out." He glanced at the sky, his eyes tearing. "When you were out there . . . I thought I'd die if we didn't find you. I promised myself if you were okay that I wouldn't wait any longer to ask you . . . to . . . marry me." His eyes implored.

Kate gazed at him, warming toward this fine man. He was the best friend she'd had since Alison. But she didn't love him . . . not the way he needed her to.

"You know how much I care for you, Mike. You're a true friend. I don't want that to change." She squeezed his hands. "And I love you . . . like I would a brother." She stared at her feet. She didn't want to hurt him. Looking at him squarely, she said, "I can't marry you. It wouldn't be right. You deserve someone who's crazy for you."

Mike couldn't disguise his grief when he finally spoke. "Sure . . . I understand . . . Friends. I figured." He glanced at the road. With a shrug, he released her hands. "Well, I gotta go. Have a lot to do. See ya." He walked away, hands in his pockets.

Kate watched him go, wishing she loved him enough. Maybe they were right for each other, but she couldn't make herself feel something that wasn't there.

Paul stood in the shadow of a doorway. His heart wrenched at the sight of Mike and Kate, their clasped hands. They were a perfect couple, the way he and Susan had once been.

They talked for a few minutes, then Mike walked away. He seemed upset. Kate looked bereaved. Something was wrong. Paul wondered what it could be.

Although he hadn't heard a word of what had been said, Paul felt like an eavesdropper. He forced his mind back to Nena, the reason he was there, and walked down the hallway to her room.

He put on a smile as he stepped inside. "Joe. How are you?"

"Okay. I guess."

"Any change?"

He shrugged. "She's the same."

Tempted to examine her, Paul studied the native woman.

"Do you think she'll wake up?" Joe asked.

Paul knew that each day she remained unconscious, her chances of coming back were less likely. "We can't know exactly what's going on inside her head—she obviously has some sort of injury, possibly bleeding in the brain. Sometimes all a person needs is rest. Have you talked to her doctor?"

"He has no answers." Joe sounded angry. He stood and walked to the window where he stared out at the city street.

"Try to be patient. I'm sure he's doing all he can. In situations like this, all we can do is wait." Paul hated these kinds of cases. He'd seen too many that didn't have happy endings.

"She never wanted to fly." Tears brimmed in Joe's eyes. "I convinced her it was safe. If I'd just left things as they were." He returned to the chair beside her bed, picked up Nena's hand, and pressed his lips to the back of her fingers. He rested her palm against his cheek and closed his eyes.

"Joe, you need some rest."

His eyes full of sorrow, he looked at Paul. "I'm afraid if I leave . . . she'll be gone when I get back."

354

Paul nodded and moved to the door. He stood watching and willed Nena to wake up. Without warning the past sprang at him, like a stalking lion leaping on its prey. He'd lived this. And Susan had never come back to him.

"Paul," Kate said.

He turned. "I was just leaving."

"Please don't go. I wanted to ask you some questions. Could you stay for a few minutes?"

"Sure."

Joe glanced at Kate.

She approached him. "Joe, how long has it been since you had a break?"

He shrugged.

"Why don't you get something to eat, maybe take a walk or a nap. I'll stay with her."

Joe stared at Nena, uncertainty on his face.

"You won't be any good to her if you collapse," Paul said.

"I won't be long," he told Nena, then pushed to his feet. He shuffled out of the room, stopping at the door for one last glance before stepping into the corridor.

Kate took Joe's place. She gazed at Nena. "I just want her to wake up."

Paul crossed to the window.

"Do you believe God does miracles?" Kate asked.

"He never answered one for me."

"Never?"

"Not when it counted."

He stared down at a streetlight blazing in the darkness and wondered why life was so unjust. A couple, clutching one another, walked across the parking lot. The woman looked like she was crying. He wondered what kind of tragedy they were experiencing—hospitals were full of all kinds.

"It's my fault she's here, like this," Kate said.

"It was an accident."

"Like before—an accident." Kate's insides churned.

"Before?"

"That's right. I never told you about my past."

"Mike did. What happened doesn't have anything to do with now."

"My best friend died because of me."

"Nena's not dead. And you couldn't have known about the engine. That wasn't your fault."

"I shouldn't have been sightseeing."

"It was an oil leak. And it would have happened no matter where you were." He faced her. "Nena's alive *because* of you. You risked your life to save hers. You could have abandoned her in that plane. Some would have."

Kate heard the conviction in his voice. His words chipped away a piece of the armor she'd worn all these years.

"I'd fly with you any day."

Deep affection and gratitude bloomed inside Kate. Paul always seemed to know what she needed. "Thank you. But . . . first Alison, now Nena. I don't know how to forgive myself."

A sigh or was it a moan escaped Nena's lips. Had she imagined it? Kate stepped closer. "Did you hear that?"

"I heard something." Paul moved to the bed. "Nena. Nena. Wake up."

She remained unresponsive.

Kate picked up her hand. "Nena. I'm here. Everything's all right. Please, wake up."

Her fingers closed and then opened. "She moved!" Kate laughed. "That's right. Come on. Now open your eyes." She squeezed Nena's hand. "It's time to wake up."

Nena weakly gripped Kate's hand. Her eyelids fluttered.

"That-a-girl. You can do it," Paul said, standing over her.

"I know you can hear me," said Kate. "Just open your eyes and look at me."

Nena lifted heavy lids and settled dark brown eyes on Kate. She stared at her as if trying to figure out who she was looking at. Then understanding dawned. "Kate?" Her voice was barely more than a whisper.

"Yes! It's me!" Kate laughed. "You're back!"

"Have I . . . been somewhere?"

"Have you been somewhere?" Kate giggled.

Nena put a hand to her forehead. "My head hurts."

"You had an accident."

Nena closed her eyes, then opened them again and glanced around the room. "Where am I?"

"You're in the hospital. The plane went into the lake. Do you remember?"

Nena's eyes widened. "Yes. I remember."

"I'll get a nurse," Paul said. "And Joe." Wearing a smile, he crossed to the door, but stopped before stepping into the hallway. "I guess maybe I do believe in miracles."

Two days later, Paul met Kate as she walked out of the hospital. "Good morning. How's Nena?"

"She had some breakfast and sat up in a chair for a little while. The doctors think she'll be able to go home in a week or so. She seems fine, just weak. She doesn't remember any of our ordeal except right before we went into the water. But it's incredible. I was so afraid—I thought she was going to die."

"If it weren't for you, she would have." Admiration for Kate swelled inside Paul. And love. He loved her. He couldn't deny it. But he had no right. She belonged to Mike. And love meant risk—he wasn't ready for that.

Kate looked at him with adoration, which only made Paul's battle for reason more difficult. "Have you had breakfast?" she asked.

"Helen offered, but I wanted to get down here and see how Nena's doing."

"It must be nice staying with Albert and Helen."

"It is. Helen's spoiling me." Paul patted his stomach.

"I'm starved. There's a café down the street."

"Sounds good."

After a waitress had taken their orders and made sure they both had cups of coffee, Kate said, "This is on me."

"No. I'll pay."

"Consider it a thank-you for rescuing me and Nena."

Paul thought he saw more than affection in Kate's eyes. No. *She's just grateful. That's all.* He took a drink of coffee. "It was mostly Mike's doing. He's crazy about you."

"I'm grateful to both of you."

"I'll be heading back to the creek this afternoon. Mike said he'd take me."

"It'll be good to get back, I suppose." Kate's tone had gone flat. "I'll miss seeing you every day."

"Me too. But now that Nena's recovering I've got to get back to work. There's a lot to do before winter sets in."

Kate glanced out the window. "Can't believe another summer's already gone."

The waitress returned with two plates, one piled with bacon, pancakes, and eggs and the other a simpler fare of eggs and toast. She set the larger meal in front of Paul.

"Breakfast never seems like breakfast without bacon." Paul picked up a piece and took a bite.

Kate smiled at the waitress as she slid the other plate in front of her. "Thank you."

Paul wondered what the sadness in her eyes was all about. When the waitress left, he asked, "What's wrong, Kate? Something's troubling you."

She picked up her fork, then set it back down. "I don't know what I'm going to do about a plane."

"You plan to continue flying?"

She poked at her scrambled eggs and then took a bite. "Sure. But I have to find another bird. It'll take every dime I've got. I guess my house will have to wait."

"Wish you'd stop flying." Paul had lost his appetite.

Kate stared at him, a troubled expression on her face. "I thought about it. Sometimes I think I should stop. But I'm not reckless—I understand that better now. Alison's death and this crack-up were accidents, nothing more. But I admit I'm afraid. But I was afraid once before—after Alison. And I walked away from flying. I won't this time."

"I worry about you."

"Thanks. It's nice to know you care." Kate took a bite of toast.

Paul finished off a pancake, then pushed his plate aside.

"I thought you were hungry."

"Guess my eyes were bigger than my stomach." He smiled, but inside he had a throng of emotions swirling around. "Have you ever thought of doing something besides being a pilot?" he asked as nonchalantly as he could.

"For about two seconds."

He nodded. "You almost died out there."

"True, but it doesn't change anything."

"I don't know if I could have stood it." Paul hadn't meant to tell her, but now it was out.

Kate stared hard at him, then in a soft voice said, "I can't quit."

"I know."

"God gave me my love of flying. I can't let fear keep me from what he meant for me. None of us can."

The comment hung, suspended in the air.

Kate set her gaze on him. "What keeps you from doing what you want, Paul?"

"What do you mean?"

"You're a doctor who doesn't practice medicine. You live in the Alaskan bush and you never see your family. You barely leave the creek. It doesn't make sense."

"I'm not meant to be a doctor. And I like my life just as it is."

"I don't believe you." Kate gently added, "I think you're afraid."

"Of what?"

"I don't know. Do you?"

Paul didn't answer. He knew. But how could he tell Kate he was afraid someone depending on him to save their life would die, and then he'd have to live with it? Or that he was afraid to love anyone ever again?

Kate glanced at a couple who moved out of a booth and headed toward the register. "Whatever it is that holds you back, you can't avoid it forever. Eventually you'll have to face it." She brushed a stray hair off her face. "You're a talented doctor."

"It's not for me. I told you."

"I've watched you. You're good. You care about people." She reached across the table and took his hand in hers. "I'd trust you with my life."

Paul's hand shivered beneath her touch.

"Don't you think it's time you did what you were meant to do—either here in Alaska or in San Francisco?"

"It's been too long." Paul removed his hand and picked up his cup.

"Do you really believe that? The people here need you."

"There are better doctors than me."

"That may be true, but they aren't here and you are." Kate kept her eyes fixed on him.

He stared down into his nearly empty cup. "I suppose I could help out once in a while. But I'm not committing to anything . . . not permanently."

Kate smiled broadly. "Some of your time is better than none." She held out her hand. "So, we have a deal? I fly and you doctor?"

Paul accepted her handshake. "Okay. But on a trial basis only." What was he getting into? Still, he couldn't quell the sense of excitement—working as a doctor again, spending time with Kate—it sounded like a dream.

Kate stood. "I better get back to the hospital."

"I'll walk with you."

Paul and Kate strolled down the road toward the hospital.

Kate took in a deep breath. "It smells like fall."

She looked up at Paul, her hazel eyes brimming with joy and her auburn hair ruffling in the breeze. Paul stopped. He loved her. He didn't want to—it would only mean more heartache, but he couldn't extinguish his feelings.

"What? What is it?"

"Kate . . ." The words stuck in his throat. "I . . . I love you. I know it's wrong—you belong to Mike, but I can't help it. I'm in love with you."

"I don't belong to anyone." Kate met his gaze. "And Mike's a wonderful friend, nothing more."

"But I thought—"

"He asked me to marry him. But I said no."

Overwhelmed by the merging of hope and passion, Paul pulled Kate close and kissed her tenderly.

"I love you too," she whispered, then circled her arms around his neck and pressed her lips to his.

Paul deepened the kiss.

When they parted, Kate smiled up at him. "So, partners? I fly, you doctor, and we'll see about the rest?"

Paul chuckled. "Okay. Partners." He pressed his cheek against her hair, breathing in the fragrance of it. "And, yes, we'll see about the rest."

Acknowledgments

Like all books, this one required the minds and hearts of many. When I set off to create the story of Paul and Kate, my journey began with a visit to the Tillamook Air Museum in Tillamook, Oregon. There I met Christian Gurling, who shared some of his knowledge about planes with me and connected me with others who could help, such as Pat Benning and Silver Hanrahan. I owe you, Christian. Thanks so much.

Silver Hanrahan, an aviation expert, is a man I knew only as Silver through online communications. I could count on him to answer any technical question about aircraft. If he didn't know, he'd find out. I'm very grateful for his help. It was a pleasure to know him. Sadly he died before the book was completed.

Gayle Ranney moved to Alaska as a young mother and teacher. She began flying in 1966, only six years after Alaska became a state. As a bush pilot, she's done it all and seen it all. It is her experience and expertise that brought the flying sequences in this book to life. Thank you, Gayle, for answering my many questions and for all the extra hours of research you did to find out what we didn't know. Your skill put me in the pilot's seat. You made this book possible.

Several family members helped me with this story. My mother, Elsa Trover, a native of Alaska; Susan Hightower; Billy Hightower; and my brother, Bruce Campbell, could all be counted on for real-life input when I needed it. Your knowledge and love of Alaska made it possible for me to write about your extraordinary state. And I offer special thanks to Bruce. I sometimes think you were born 100 years too late. Your real-life adventures provided depth and authenticity to many of the scenes in this book.

My critique group came through as always. Thanks to Bunny Bassett, Billy Cook, Julia Ewert, Diane Gardner, Sarah Schartz, and Ann Shorey. Thank you for sticking with me.

Thanks also to Cheryl VanAndel and her creative, hard-working team for the wonderful cover. You guys are great.

Barb Barnes, I'm grateful for your attention to detail and your soft touch in editing, which allows my work to remain mine. It is a pleasure to work with you.

Huge thanks go to Lonnie Hull DuPont, executive editor for Revell. We sweated through this story. You cared enough to push for my best. I'm grateful for your tenacity and your great eye for a good story.

Last but never least, I want to thank my agent, Wendy Lawton. You are my favorite cheerleader. Your belief in me helps me to press forward even through the tough days when creativity seems out of reach. Thanks for helping me believe in myself.

Bonnie Leon dabbled in writing for many years but never set it in a place of priority until an accident in 1991 left her unable to work at her job. She is now the author of several historical fiction series, including the Sydney Cove series, Queensland Chronicles, the Matanuska series, the Sowers Trilogy, and the Northern Lights series. She also stays busy teaching women's Bible studies, speaking, and teaching at writing seminars and women's gatherings. Bonnie and her husband, Greg, live in Southern Oregon. They have three grown children and four grandchildren.

Visit Bonnie's website at **www.bonnieleon.com**.

Discover the
SIDNEY COVE SERIES!

Get lost in these heart-gripping stories of two people journeying toward forgiveness and love.